2

THE OTHER MARGARET BEAUFORT

MARGARET COUNTESS OF STAFFORD

BY J.P. REEDMAN

Copyright June 13 2022 by J.P. Reedman/Herne's Cave

Cover-J.P. Reedman/Pixabay

PROLOGUE: 1473, Littlecote Manor, Wiltshire

Rain pours outside the manor of Littlecote. Night has fallen and leaves patter on the roof like tiny feet. My husband, Richard Dayrell, is away; business in the shire often keeps him occupied elsewhere, and I must admit that I am glad of his absence, even though that makes me a wicked, unloving wife who does not honour her husband. Richard is frugal with his money to the point of miserliness—that has not changed in some ten years of marriage—and keeps as few servants as possible in the sprawling manor, so comforts are sparse.

Our daughter Margaret, nicknamed Pearl, as there are so many Margarets within the family, sleeps in a chamber below, with sound walls where the wind does not whistle through the cracks. Except for my maid, Lucie, the household staff eye me with cold indifference, but out of the corner of my eye, I see them cross themselves after I walk by. My behaviour at certain times has become quite legendary; I swear they think I bay at the moon and dance in toadstool rings.

Still, for all the deficiency of house and household, far better at Littlecote than in the 'care' of my husband's mother, Elizabeth Calston, which I endured when I carried Pearl in my womb. The woman had no love for me. She is dead for some years now and although I have forgiven her sins against me, I cannot forget. Often, she was even more miserly than her son, her purse as pinched as her lips, and she harangued Richard all the time for money towards my keep, which he was reluctant to pay despite many promises. She told all and sundry what a wondrous martyr she was looking after Richard's wife, the moonstruck woman, the embarrassing 'imbecile'.

I am no imbecile. Grief have I suffered, almost beyond enduring, and for a while, something frail within my mind, my heart, broke, like glass shattered, and darkness wrapped itself around my thoughts and dictated my actions.

That blight seems to have gone now, leaving just a lingering mournfulness in my soul, but the rumours of my 'lunacy' remain. Richard Dayrell's moonstruck wife.

I had stayed with Elizabeth because my sudden collapse threatened the life of the baby and my husband feared he might lose his potential heir. Richard had no idea how to handle my distress, so he let his mother take me to her house to see that I was cared for—and unable to harm myself or the child. After a long and dangerous travail that almost killed me, Elizabeth was happy enough to coo over Pearl's cradle, but within weeks she spoke of me as a burden and a drain on her precious coffers. Sometimes in my worst moments of despair, I swore she would have preferred I had died in childbirth so that Richard could be free to wed a more stable, fruitful woman.

And from whence sprang her hatred?—one reason, I suspect, is because of my heritage. The prestige of marrying a widow of royal lineage was the motivation for Richard to wed me, but he and his grasping mother soon found themselves disappointed—I did not bring the expected riches (my father had a fine bloodline but little money, and my dower lands from my first marriage were few and poor) and the men of my family all either fell fighting battles for the losing side or faced the executioner's axe for treason. Bearing but a single female child instead of the much-wanted son was also a strike against me. Disappointment often brings resentment, and resentment breeds hatred, no matter how unwarranted.

Elizabeth Calston also implied I had too many 'airs and graces', but it is the Dayrells, ruling a little patch of Wiltshire as if they were feudal lords from the Conqueror's time, who put on such pretensions. Many locals fear the Dayrells rather than treat them with respect; the men are notorious for brawling and wild tempers, the women for haughtiness and avarice.

So what Elizabeth Calston claimed is a lie and sadly, repeated often enough, lies take on a strange, warped life of their own. I was a mistake, and so I am worthy of scorn—the bride who should have tied the Dayrell family into the highest nobility by producing a son but who brought nothing but embarrassment. Although Elizabeth is in her grave, resentment still flows from Richard, when the mood is upon him, although our paths cross less and less and he is less unpleasant than he once was. I am now as a piece of furniture in the hall, to be passed without a glance.

My name is Margaret Beaufort. No, not the daughter of John Beaufort, the second Duke of Somerset, who returned from war-torn France under a cloud and possibly committed, through shame, the despicable crime of self-murder.

That Margaret, six years my junior, is my cousin. John Beaufort was my uncle; my father his younger brother, Edmund who became Duke after him. My life and Margaret's have run strangely parallel at times, however—both of us Beauforts on the paternal side and Beauchamps on the maternal, both wed to sons of the Duke of Buckingham and both mothers of sons called Henry…Such strange coincidences!

But whereas Margaret is learned, cool-headed and pious, her quick mind ever spurring her on through even the darkest days, I am quiet and weak, accepting the blows that fall upon me with little complaint. Perhaps my timidity is my true failing…and perhaps from it burst the seeds of my supposed 'madness.'

Sighing, I press my face against the bubbled amber glass of the window, its surface crisscrossed by fine cracks like embedded streaks of lightning; rain beads on the outer surface, making the outside world, when viewed through the bubbles, warp and bend to create a surreal, storm-tossed world beyond. Clouds twist down, grey as winding sheets; trees sweep and straggle, their bough pinching hands. Down in the meadow, where the gardeners often find strange old tiles, dirt-clogged bangles and rings, and bent coins bearing the heads of unknown monarchs, I fancy I can see figures, thin as mist…but who would walk abroad on such a foul night, save ghosts?

Ghosts of the past…

My temples feel tight and I rub them with the heels of my hands. As lightning flares over the lawns and the gale claws slate tiles slide from the roof, sparks appear at the periphery of my vision, spreading outward in a jagged ring. Another sign of 'madness', Elizabeth Calston had sneered, although the physician my father summoned when I was a young girl, bedridden and hurling up the contents of my belly, called it the 'megrim' or 'half-head' pain.

Nausea makes my legs tremble. It is always so with these megrims, that come more frequently these days, forcing me to lie in the dark for hours with a pounding skull. My affliction confirms my frailties to the servants, of course, who whisper in the town of 'Mad Margaret.'

I stumble to the bed and stretch out upon it, head reeling, the lights in my eyes streaking like shooting stars. I could call for my maid, Lucie, to bring wormwood or skullcap to ease the pain, but I am too dizzy and enfeebled to walk to the door.

Sinking into the slightly damp softness of the feather mattress, I stare at the overhanging canopy through the ring of lights covering half my vision, noting that several spiders dangle on skinny webs—the servants have not bothered to clean the room well with Richard away. I rub my throbbing forehead, willing the pain to depart and my head to clear. Tomorrow I must we well, as I am expecting a visitor, one who will bring me joy in a world where such happiness seems so scarce.

My son, Harry Stafford—Henry, Duke of Buckingham—is coming to visit, riding in from London. Several years have passed since last I saw him, and he is nearing eighteen summers old, no longer the little boy I once knew. He is married to one of the Queen's sisters, a match he abhors, for he thinks a knight's daughter is beneath him, even though her sister is a Queen.

I shake my head, thinking of his wounded pride in marrying that Woodville girl. He must learn, as I have learnt, that he cannot have all in life as he would wish it. If he does not learn, harsh disappointment will mar his life as it marred mine.

Lonely and needy in the dark, I sigh, recalling my long-gone youth, the years before I arrived at Littlecote, with its shadowed rooms, lonely green walks, and buried secrets…

As the night draws in and the rumble of thunder dissipates in the north, I remember all those I have loved…and lost.

CHAPTER ONE

My mother, Eleanor Beauchamp, bustled into my bedchamber in the manor of Milton Fawconbridge without so much as a knock or by-your-leave. The maids who attended me and my sisters dropped curtseys then filed from the room, heads bowed in modest respect but surreptitiously eyeing each other, eager for gossip.

"You, too." Mother gestured with a languid hand to my sisters Nell, Joan and Anne, who all shared the chamber. Nell pouted, fearing she would miss out, but Mother cast her a stern look and she scuttled out after Joan and Anne.

Mother was the daughter of a great magnate, the old Earl of Warwick, Richard Beauchamp, who had been a great warrior, capturing the banner of the Welsh prince, Owain Glyndwr and fighting for King Henry V in France. She wore the role of a great lady well, tall and beautiful, her skin lily-pale, her eyes a deep, rich sky-blue. She wore indigo brocade to set those eyes off, and sapphires around her throat embedded in a band of gold. She had borne nine children to my father Edmund but one would never have thought it to look at her with her narrow waist and endless grace and poise.

"Margaret—Meg—" She used my formal name first, which brought a shiver of alarm, for I was 'Meg' to my parents unless I was to be chastised for some error whether real or imagined. However, her expression was mild enough and I had been indoors for days owing to the rainy weather, so I had no opportunity to get up to any mischief.

"Your father has returned from court with happy news," she said, smiling, although there was always a hint of frost in her smile when she spoke of my sire, Edmund Beaufort. At first, her marriage to Father had been blissful, almost like a chapter from an Arthurian tale; they had fallen in love and married without license, which caused a scandal in the royal court. They were only pardoned for their transgression the year before my birth. But as time passed and many children arrived, both boys and girls, a gulf widened between my parents. Gossips whispered that Father was more than just a close advisor to the Queen, and that the child she carried, a miracle after eight years of barrenness, was not the King's but Father's. Rumours also flew that he had fornicated with the old Queen, Catherine of Valois, when he was a handsome and lusty young man of one-and-twenty and she a lonely widow—and thus were laws enacted that a Dowager Queen could not remarry without permission of the monarch...and King Henry being but six years old at the time was unlikely to do such a thing, as his Uncle Humphrey of Gloucester, who pushed for this new law, knew all too well. Distressed, Catherine fled the court...but she soon ignored the decree to secretly wed a humble Welshman called Owen Tudor, who served her at table and tasted her food for poison. Some wicked men insisted, though, that her eldest child was my sire's, not Tudor's, and that her clandestine marriage to Owen was to hide her earlier sin—why else would she name the child Edmund, a name neither French nor Welsh, the very name my father bore? But we did not speak of this matter at home.

Mother approached me, fixing me with a thoughtful gaze. She lifted a handful of my hair, dark brown burnished with red-gold from my Plantagenet ancestry. "Your hair is your best feature, Meg," she said. "Make sure your maid brushes it one hundred times a night and puts sweet oil on it." She then pinched my chin and looked me over even more closely as one might look over a horse, I thought. I dared not pull away. She sighed, "You have not the beauty of your sister Nell, but you will do."

'Do' for what? I frowned, and Mother waggled a finger before my nose. "Do not make such miserable faces—it will spoil what looks you have and it is important you look your best...since your father has, at last, found a husband for you, Meg."

My breath railed between clenched teeth. A husband! I had both longed for and feared this day. I wished to wed, for I had no calling for the church, but Duke's daughters seldom had a choice of husbands. If Father thought it might make a good alliance, bringing prestige and supporters, I might end up marrying a greybeard in his dotage or a babe in swaddling, who would not mature for many years, leaving me to wait for him for long, lonely years.

"I think you will be happy," said Mother, as if reading my frantic thoughts. "Your betrothed is young and has not been married before. His father is a Duke and he is his eldest son and heir."

"A Duke's son!" I breathed, startled. My mind whirled as I tried to remember all the available male children of the Dukes of England. York had a son or two, younger than myself, but he and Father had no love for each other, so an alliance there was unlikely. Could it be Suffolk's son? Exeter's heir was already wed...

Mother swiftly put me out of my misery. "You look like you are about to burst, Meg. You are holding your breath and have gone red. Most unseemly; stop it at once. Your intended is Humphrey, heir of the Duke of Buckingham. He has already been made the Earl of Stafford. It is an excellent match, Margaret. Just think of it—your eldest son shall be a duke in time and royal blood shall course through your children's veins, not just from your own descent from John of Gaunt, but on your husband's side from Thomas of Woodstock, the youngest son of Edward III. Your children will be in the line of succession—distantly, 'tis true, but the link remains, and hopefully King Henry will bestow many favours on them. Buckingham is quite close to his Grace and very loyal."

"I am most pleased to marry Earl Humphrey," I said, "but..."

"What do you mean 'but', Meg?" Mother cast me a glare, her pretty mouth pursed, making her look older. She would hate to know that. "You always seem to find a flaw, something to fear or fret about. What is it this time?"

Embarrassed, I licked my lips. They felt dry as paper. "N-nothing, Mother. Only that I would not expect too much from King Henry... Not now. Look at the condition he is in..."

"*Margaret!*" Mother's eyes crackled angrily; they were a stormy blue now, almost black. "It is highly impertinent to speak thus about our sovereign. Your sire would be appalled."

"F-forgive me," I stammered, my hands knotting together nervously. "I say only what others have said...that the King lies abed in a sleep more like death, and he has shown no response to any of the potions, syrups, confections, gargles, laxatives given by the royal physicians. They even scarified him and shaved his head, to no avail!"

"You need to indulge in more ladylike activities such as embroidery and dance," said Mother, icily disapproving, "and not in tittle-tattle that you have heard from some gossiping servants!"

I had heard the 'tittle-tattle' from Father on his last return from Westminster, but I dared not say so, for to contradict Mother would make her grow even more wroth. Demurely I cast my eyes down. "Yes, Mother, I will endeavour to do as you say. More embroidery. May I ask one more question, though?"

"That depends on what it is?"

"When do I marry the Earl?"

"Midsummer," she said, almost triumphantly. "Just after the Feast of St John. And I am going to make certain it is a grand occasion, fitting for the daughter of a Duke...even though, it should have been your sister Nell rather than you, since she is the elder. But Edmund, for some reason, chose you instead. I think he believes she is flighty and has little to commend her save her looks. I do not know why; every man likes a pretty woman, and she is much like me in that regard!"

I wed Humphrey Stafford at Pleshey, one of the castles of the Dukes of Buckingham. So many splendid had people gathered for the occasion that I felt quite dowdy and plain, although I was the bride. The Duke and Duchess of Buckingham strolled through the hall, he wearing a fire-red chaperon and a collar of jewelled Lancastrian 'esses', she in midnight-blue brocade and a vast headdress wreathed with veils.

It was, of course, the first time I met Humphrey, my husband-to-be. He was of middling height with a solid, almost stocky build, his face handsome enough, if a bit fleshy, his eyes dark blue and his curls a burnished deep gold, almost pale brown but fair in the sunlight. He hastened to greet me, speaking courteous words which sounded a little as if they were learned rather than heartfelt. I schooled myself from disappointment; how could it be any different? He, at least, did not look upon me with disgust, which sometimes happened—one old-time Queen of France, Ingeborg, was cast aside owing to her husband's revulsion—*'discarded like a dried and diseased branch'* she had told the Pope.

After the greetings were over, the wedding celebrants processed to the door of the castle chapel, where Humphrey and I began to recite our vows before a diminutive bald priest with a deep, booming voice that seemed preposterous coming from the mouth of a man so dwarfish. An urge to laugh rose up in me, but I stifled it, as such mirth would have been regarded as highly inappropriate. I saw Mother giving me a disapproving stare, which made the urge to laugh grow even stronger. The smell of incense wafting from the thuribles made my head spin, as did the excitement—and apprehension—of the day. My lips moved to make my vows, but it seemed they came out all a-jumble, as if my tongue was tied in knots. Mother frowned again, a thin line daggering between her eyes; I swear she was mouthing the words as if by sheer will alone she could force me to say them correctly.

At last, I managed to fumble my way through the rest of the marriage vows to the tiny priest's satisfaction. The terms of my dowry were read aloud, as was customary, and accepted by the Staffords, and Humphrey pressed a purse of gold coins into my hand, for later distribution to the poor. I fumbled with the purse-strings, almost dropping the bag to the floor; my fingers felt cold and numb, out of my control.

Mother's gaze went from stony to despairing as I snatched at the purse, catching it just before the contents spilt out onto the tiles. At my side, Humphrey shifted uncomfortably, pretending not to have noticed my clumsiness. However, his father, the Duke of Buckingham cast me a reassuring smile; he seemed a kindly man from what little I had seen. The wedding ring Humphrey had brought to the chapel slid, cold as ice, onto the finger of my right hand.

It was done. I was a wedded wife. The House of Beaufort was joined with that of Stafford.

The chapel doors screeched open and the wedding guests, aunts and uncles and cousins from Stafford and Beaufort and Beauchamp affinities flooded in, followed by other notables close to the Duke and his son. A canopy was erected, gleaming blue silk covered in finely embroidered Stafford Knots, and Humphrey and I stood beneath it while the nuptial Mass was said.

When Mass was done, the priest gave my new husband the Kiss of Peace, and Humphrey turned, bent, and gave the kiss to me in turn. His closeness filled me with wonder, but trepidation too. Was he pleased with me, despite the incident with the purse? Did he have any liking for my person? I could not tell; I was only sixteen and had no knowledge of such things, yet I was aware that his touch was gentle and respectful. I hoped that could only bode well for the future.

"Let us feast well, good friends and kinsmen," the Duke of Buckingham cried aloud, as Humphrey and I emerged from beneath the fringed tassels of the silken canopy. Minstrels wandered into the chapel, playing on flutes, rebecs and lyres, and then the gathered assembly, in high spirits, moved almost as one toward the Great Hall of Pleshey Castle.

I was carried along with them, the wives and daughters of Dukes and Earls, Lords and Barons surrounding me in a heady haze of sweet fragrance; smooth, flowing silks; spangled sleeves that swept the flagstones. All those around me were joyous, celebrating the happy occasion, but I felt as if caught in a dream, almost as if I were not truly there, as if it was another Margaret, a false Margaret, who smiled and bobbed her head and played the part of a demure bride. The torches became hazy blurs in my peripheral vision, and the scents from the kitchen overwhelmed. I prayed God would spare me a *megrim* on this day of all days!

As my knees wobbled, I began to fear I might faint. My cheeks were hot though my hands remained icy-cold—not a good sign. Mother would be so ashamed if I fell upon the floor, insensible. Her gaze was boring into my back even now as she watched my every move. I was a fish out of water, gasping, flailing through uncertainty…and then, merciful Jesu, the wedding party reached the Great Hall.

Inside, flambeaux flared and candelabras were a sea of hot stars. The long trestle tables were covered in starched white linen, glowing pale in the torchlight, and decorated with sprays of scented summer flowers, sun-gold, blood-red, azure-blue. The chief steward, a tall man in a black and red houppelande with the Buckingham's badge on his shoulder, escorted me to the top table where I took the seat of honour under a canopy. Humphrey emerged from a crowd of male relatives and sat down next to me, smiling out at the celebrants…but, to my dismay, he did not look at me. The Duke and Duchess of Buckingham took their seats beside their son and my parents, Duke and Duchess of Somerset, took their places upon my left.

Up in the galleries, the minstrels assembled and began to play, a welcome distraction. The 'warners' arrived on silver platters—sumptuous subtleties and wobbling jellies that heralded the first course. The jellies were shaped into the semblance of shields and swords; some were black from the addition of boiled animal blood, others vivid red from a heavy mixture of sandalwood spice. Sugared paste figures accompanied them, glittering in the candlelight—swans (an emblem used by Buckingham), saffron-tinted coronets and castles with silver foil turrets. Then the servers drifted in, keen youths dressed all alike, carrying baskets of bread rolls and fennel *salat* drenched in oil and bitter vinegar, along with mackerels sluiced in mustard sauce and woodcocks on long skewers made from their own beaks.

It was delicious fare but my nerves were so frayed I managed to eat little more than a mouthful and spent much time dabbing at my mouth with the supplied linen napkin. "Smile, for Jesu's sake, Meg," Mother whispered in my ear at one point. "It's a wedding, not a funeral."

I had to be happy. I *was* happy. Why should I not be so? My husband was young, wealthy and attractive enough—what more could I desire? I forced a smile and raised my goblet to be filled with Burgundian wine by a lad bearing a silver decanter with a swan's head for a spout.

The wedding banquet continued on, decadent in its array of food—stuffed partridge and goose, goat and venison, salmon and hake, cheese and mince pasties, followed by pears stewed in red wine, cherry pottage and rose pudding. Candied violets were set by every trencher to freshen the breath after the copious spices and wine.

As we finished the last course, an array of dancers and tumblers entered the hall, leaping in white painted masks around the old-fashioned central fire-pit. Wings made of real feathers strung together flapped on their backs; I supposed they represented either angels or swans; I could not tell.

At the end of their merry dance, they lined up before the high table and one of them scurried up proffering a wicker basket. As the dancer drew near, he leaned over and sprung a catch on the basket. Three rabbits sprang out and ran madly about the rushes on the floor. The Duke's hounds sprang up growling, and I gasped, as I thought the conies would be torn apart before my very eyes, but Buckingham spoke sternly to his dogs and instantly they lay down, looking rather glum.

Frightened by all the commotion, the rabbits raced around the Great Hall, white tails flashing, while the onlookers cheered and threw bones and bits of bread to make them move faster. The animals looked terrified, their flanks heaving, their eyes glassy, and my own heart pounded wildly, as if I were running with them, equally fearful. Before I knew what I was doing, I stood up, almost knocking over the platter before me. "Stop…"

Mother reached up and caught my sleeve. "Meg, what do you think you are doing? Sit down!"

"This…this is cruel sport," I gasped.

"Nonsense. It is all in good fun. The rabbits were brought in because they represent fertility. They breed. Hence, they symbolise *your* fertility and the future continuance of the Stafford line."

"I…am not an animal." Big-eyed, I stared at her. "Or maybe I am. Neither the coneys nor I am free…Do you not understand?"

Her lips thinned. "I understand you are in the throes of one of your silly turns." She leaned closer, appearing to onlookers like a loving mother giving advice, but loving she was not and her advice was harsh orders. "You will do your duty, to me and to

Humphrey Stafford and his family. You will smile, you will be gracious, you will do all that is asked of you. Do *you* understand?"

Tears stinging my eyes and threatening to run down my cheeks, I nodded. "Go from the room," muttered Mother, her voice low but commanding. "You cannot risk having his Grace, the Duke of Buckingham see you in such a state. I will tell the Staffords you have gone to the privy if they should ask. Return when you have composed yourself. Do not be overlong, Margaret."

Eyes averted, I made my excuses to Humphrey, my husband, and exited the Hall, hoping the wedding party would think my hanging head was caused by maidenly modesty. I sought the privy, found it with the aid of a servant, sat in silence upon the cold wooden seat a while. Then when sadness and anger stopped churning in my breast, I crept back out into the corridor. A cool breeze whistled down it, making the bracketed torches dip and ruffling my skirts; in the distance, uproarious laughter emanated from the direction of the Great Hall. I supposed the feasters must be watching tumblers or jugglers or dancing bears—or perhaps they'd let the Duke's hounds devour the rabbits in the end. I wondered if anyone had even noticed my absence at all.

At that moment, my legs seemed to gain a will of their own, and I found myself rapidly striding down the passageway. Before long, I stumbled down a poorly-lit spiral staircase to the lower level, found a fortuitously unbarred door, and entered the night-swathed castle gardens. Luckily, it was not full-dark—the stars were out, ringing a large round moon that bore a reddish tint.

I wondered if Mother would come searching for me. If she did, she would be full of wrath…but I could not go back to the heat, the raucous laughter, not yet. I needed a few minutes alone, to breathe the fresh air of the night. To gather my thoughts. To gather courage to face my new life.

I wandered beneath a trellis covered in blossoming vines, the moonlight leaching the colour from the petals and making the flowers look eerie and ethereal. In the distance, over the castle walls, a solitary owl hooted as it sought for prey. Careful not to trip in the gloom, I began inching towards an arbour where, earlier in the day, I had spotted a stone seat.

But…there was someone else in the arbour. I gaped. It seemed a little child was sitting there, or a statue of a child, so still was she. Her raiment was dark so that only her long, thin face showed, glowing in the moonbeams. She was glancing down intently, and as I took one further step, I realised she was running a string of rosary beads through her fingers. Closer I came, and heard the beads clack against each other, the sound a clear, bell-like tinkle—they must be wrought of glass, so expensive.

Suddenly the girl on the seat became aware of my presence and glanced up sharply. Her face was rather foxy, not pretty, and not smiling or winsome either. Her eyes, however, they entranced—set deep in her face, they were extraordinarily dark and intense.

"Who are you?" I asked. Being some years her elder, I assumed an almost parental demeanour. "You should not be out here alone, not at your age."

"God will protect me; I have no fear." The girl's voice was strange, its timbre almost more adult than child, rather as I imagined a mystic's voice might sound. "As for my identity, do you truly not know?"

I shook my head. "I fear I do not. But I take it you know mine?"

She grinned. It was not a natural expression on that bony little face and now she almost looked like an imp instead of a saint, a gnome stepped out of some ancient tale. Many of my sire's holdings were in the far west of England and the ordinary people there often believed in such beings, piskies that led men astray in bogs, rock-throwing spriggans, and knockers who haunted old mines.

"Yes, I do know you. You are Meg Beaufort, daughter of Edmund, Duke of Somerset, and today you have become Countess of Stafford. I, Margaret, am also called Margaret Beaufort, and I am your cousin, for our sires were brothers."

Surprised, I stared at the girl—my cousin. I had not expected she would attend my nuptials. Perhaps I should have paid more attention to who was invited, but I had let others wiser in such matters deal with the guests and had not become too involved. "Well, greetings, Margaret," I said, remembering my manners. "Are you here with…" I frowned, searching my mind. "With your husband, John de la Pole?"

A shadow flickered over Margaret's face. "No, *that* marriage was annulled this year. It was never a true marriage anyway. John's father was slain and that changed *everything*…"

Well I remembered the dreadful story. William de la Pole, the Duke of Suffolk, had been blamed for the loss of French lands, and for other misdemeanours, some perhaps true, many not. The King had banished him for his own protection, but as he fled the country for Calais, the great ship Nicholas of the Tower intercepted his cog and took him prisoner. He was given a sham trial on the deck and then beheaded with a rusty sword. His body was tossed upon the beach at Dover.

Margaret must have seen my horrified expression. "Do not worry," she said. "It was God's will. Duke William was not a good man anyway; he had the nickname 'Jackanapes', you know. Now that I am free, my wardship has now been granted to the King's brothers, Jasper and Edmund Tudor. It was they who permitted me to come to Pleshey as a companion to my mother, Lady Welles by her most recent marriage. They had no stomach for weddings themselves, they said—but that was Jasper. He can be a tease. In any case, they must attend a wedding ere long, like it or not, for I am to marry Edmund…soon."

"You…you are rather young," I said, "to be married so often."

My words were meant as a jest but Margaret did not take it as so. "My first marriage was annulled because I was not yet the age of consent."

"You are still not," I said pointedly.

"No, but I feel…I *know* my marriage to Edmund Tudor will be the right one. God himself told me through his messenger, Saint Nicholas. I fasted vigorously, then prayed for guidance on my knees every night in the chapel…till one morn, around cock's crow, the Saint materialised in a nimbus of light, a brown-faced man with a long grey beard and a bishop's robe and mitre. He raised a hand to bless me and told me that it was my duty to marry Edmund, and that all the glories of the world would come to me through that union." She sat back on the bench, her expression grown strangely smug and satisfied. "What do you do think of that, cousin?"

"I—I think…perhaps I should be heading back to the Hall." I had no idea what to make of young Margaret's supposed vision of St Nicholas. A childish fantasy, maybe—but she spoke like an adult with all the seriousness of an old abbess in a convent. "You should come with me, Margaret. I am surprised your mother is not out searching for you."

She hopped off the seat. The rosary beads glinted like ice-chips around her spindly white fingers. "You may well be right. As for your new husband…he will think you have upped and gone over the wall rather than marry him."

Her jest, for such it was, caused a twinge of fear to knot my belly. What if the Duke or Humphrey or my parents started searching the castle? I had been gone much longer than was normal for a simple garderobe trip. "Oh, I hope that he does not deem me so faithless," I said with a nervous laugh.

"I will go to the hall with you," said Margaret. "Although I admit I find such affairs nearly as tedious as Edmund and Jasper do. Mother wished me here, though, and one must honour one's parent's wishes, especially since I am the only child of her first marriage and we see each other all too seldom."

Together Cousin Margaret and I returned to the castle through the garden door, passing swift and wraithlike through the winding passageways. As we approached the Great Hall I felt a stab of trepidation—and it would seem I was right to do so, for Mother suddenly stormed around a corner like an Amazon leading an army, her women, pale-faced and frightened clustered around her, holding tapers.

A search party! As they saw me, the women began to laugh in nervous relief and blew out the candles.

Mother cast them a withering glare and lunged in my direction. "Margaret, where in God's name have you been? I was becoming increasingly worried that you had done something foolish."

"Foolish? Like what?"

"Like...like hurl yourself into a pond or such...just to spite your family."

"I do not understand your anger, Mama." I bit my lip. "I have told you—I am happy to have married Humphrey Stafford. Have I ever said otherwise or that I would fight against your will?"

"No, but your actions speak louder than any words." She grasped my arm, her fingers biting. "I never know what you might do. You...you are so unpredictable! You always have been. Ever...ever since..." Her face darkened, and she shook her head as if dispelling evil demons from her mind. I said nought, dared not...for I knew of what she spoke, and how it had affected her too.

"My Lady Duchess." Little Margaret stepped from the shadows into the light. "I beg you not be too hard on Cousin Meg. She was not avoiding her duties. She went into the garden...to see me. She saw me outside and feared for my safety, as I am only of tender years."

"And you are?" Mother's gaze scored Margaret's white, calm face. "You look familiar."

"Margaret Beaufort. We met long ago when I was much smaller. You are my Aunt, wife to my Uncle Edmund."

"Is this true?" Mother whirled back in my direction. "You went to check on your cousin's wellbeing?"

I nodded dumbly. It was not exactly a lie...once I had spotted her, hidden and strange, secreted in that flower garth.

Mother's anger seemed to wash away; she now looked merely weary. "Come along then—God knows what the Buckinghams are thinking. Poor Humphrey, last I saw him, he looked distraught, although he has attempted to make the best of the situation. And as for you, young Margaret..." She peered closely at the little girl whose face remained immobile and unmoved. "Go to your mother, Lady Welles at once and beg her forgiveness. I have no idea why she let you out of her sight."

Margaret respectfully curtseyed to Mother then turned her to me. "Good luck in your marriage, Cousin Meg, from this day until whenever God decrees. I pray you will wish me the same when my time comes, and that we both have glorious futures with many sons to do our Beaufort ancestors proud."

Then she was gone, a slight will o' the wisp running into the crowd of servants, revellers, and acrobats within the Great Hall.

Gathering my skirts, I returned to the high table, attempting to look serene. Mother followed, smiling falsely and pretending nothing had been amiss. Old Duke Humphrey looked relieved as I sat beneath the canopy and; the Duchess of Buckingham, more perceptive, looked faintly peeved and called sharply for her wine goblet to be re-filled. My husband, Humphrey, just looked happy I had returned. Under the table, he reached over and clasped my hand.

"Margaret, I was afraid…"

"You need not be, husband," I said, emphasising the word 'husband'. "All is well and will be well. I will be a good wife to you, Humphrey, I swear it! And please, call me Meg. You are family now; we must not be over-formal with each other. Not if we…we are to…" Blushing, I cast down my gaze, not quite able to express what I felt.

He smiled over at me, caressing my hand with his, which was warm and strangely gentle. Most brides would have been charmed and so I was. But at the same time, deep within my being, I felt a dolorous chill, a sense of doom like a dread hand reaching out to still the beating of my heart. Or Humphrey's.

Maybe I *was* moon-touched, as Mother had implied.

"More wine!" I cried, gesturing to the nearest page and holding up my cup.

There were ways to quell the fear…

CHAPTER TWO

After the wedding celebrations were done, the bedding completed, my dowry firmly settled and most of the guests dispersed, Humphrey and I said our farewells to the Duke and Duchess of Buckingham and to my parents, and rode towards Wales, making for the Stafford stronghold at Brecknock. I had never fared further west than Bristol, so it was a strange learning experience crossing into that rugged and wild country.

The land was fierce and verdant, full of bald hills, little brooklets and craggy stones that oft looked as if they were not deposited there after God's Flood, but had instead been carried hither and raised on high by some primitive race of men. Hawks curled in the sky and the trees on the roadside seemed to whisper deep dark songs in the tongue of the Welsh, which, of course, I could not understand.

"Some of the servants at Brecknock are Welsh," Humphrey told me, turning around in his saddle. "Do not be alarmed if you hear them talk in their own tongue."

"Welsh! But…but," I cried, alarmed, "how shall I understand what they say?"

"If you, their mistress, should deign to speak to them, they will respond in English. They know they must; it is a condition of their employment at my castle."

A cold wind blowing off those barren, cloud-dappled hills scored my cheek. "They…they might turn about and say horrid things about me, things I cannot understand."

A mocking little smile crossed his lips. "Most probably they will, my dearest. I shouldn't let it worry you. It is something we get used to, in our position. The Welsh do not love us—and truth be told, why should they? Those Vaughans down the valley at Tretower, however…"

"They won't attack us, will they?" I said nervously.

"No, the Vaughans are not fools…but they are no friends of ours, even if they smile to our faces. Trust them to aid us? I would not even trust them with a sheep. Indeed, I *especially* would not trust old Vaughan with a sheep." Merriment crinkled the edges of his eyes; I did not fathom what he meant until his squires began to titter, and then I realised he had made a ribald joke. Blushing, I hung my head.

"I am teasing you," said Humphrey, noting my crimson cheeks. "I beg your pardon; my jests are not fit for lady's ears. But they do come from fierce stock, Black Vaughan and his wife being the fiercest of them all."

"His wife, too?"

"Oh yes, Ellen the Terrible they call her. In her youth, she dressed as a lad, took up a bow and shot dead the man who had killed her brother at an archery competition."

"Revenge, then. Does that seem so terrible? Men seek revenge all the time."

"Well, aye, they do…but it was unusual, her being a…" He cast me a silly smile that charmed me. I was beginning to fall in love with my new husband. "Oh, never mind, Meg. Just remind me to watch my back if ever I should perturb you, lest you treat me in the manner of Ellen."

"If you promise not to kill my brothers, I can assure you that you will be safe from my wrath," I teased back. Humphrey reined back his mount and rode closer to my tame, well-trained palfrey. Reaching over, he clasped my gloved hand in his own and gave it a little squeeze. "Soon we will be home, Meg."

Home. In this strange, foreign land….

We entered Brecknock through one of the stone gates that bored through the grey walls surrounding the town. Smoke coiled in sheets over the rooftops of the little houses, some made of timber, others of slatey stone, and over a tall-towered church with damp, weather-greened crenels poking like a row of teeth at the pendulous clouds.

"Is that the church we will attend?" I nodded in its direction.

"No, no." Humphrey shook his head in a disbelieving manner, as if I had suggested that we worship in a barn. "That is St Mary's, built for the denizens of the town. We have our own private chapel in the castle, of course, but a short walk away stands the Priory of St John the Evangelist. The prior is on friendly terms with my family and I often attend Mass there when in residence in Brecon. The abbey has a famous Rood fashioned from gold that attracts pilgrims from miles around."

"I look forward to seeing it," I said, as our entourage crossed through the town in front of a gathering crowd.

Humphrey leaned over his horse's mane, gesturing to the left with a hand. "And there, my Lady wife, is the castle, our home."

My gaze followed his pointing finger. Across the deep, swift-flowing river, reached by a wide stone bridge, stood ancient Brecknock Castle. Built from weathered dark red stones, its keep thrust up like a clenched fist into the clouds. The Stafford banner, flapped from its uppermost turret, stretched taught by the sharp wind, the cross of St George flaming in the joist before a swan bearing a crown upon its body, with the words *Humble and Loyal* barely discernible below. The castle had a watch-tower overlooking the river, swathed in rustling ivy and with antiquated arrow-slit windows, running up the stonework like a series of lightless little eyes. Brecknock's appearance was martial, rather than friendly; I had grown up in fortified manor houses and castles in England's southwest that had lost their war-like aspect over the years. Breckon had not.

Humphrey was gazing up at the fortress with an expression akin to adoration, however. "It was built by a lord called Bernard Neufmarche. A Norman from near Rouen. He was involved with the founding of the priory too."

"How did the Stafford family come to own it?" I asked, suppressing a sigh, wishing I was domiciled at another of the Stafford properties such as Penshurst or Thornbury manor…comfortable modern houses on the safe far side of the border.

"Through the Bohuns, my ancestors," Humphrey replied, ignoring my wistful sigh. "They were granted it after the de Braose family, a troublesome lot. My forebear, the great Prince Thomas of Woodstock, youngest son of Edward III was wed to Eleanor de Bohun, so their descendants had a rightful claim on it, although the Welsh Prince Llewellyn held it awhile, and it was only in the reign of our present gracious King that it was officially given to the Staffords."

We had now left the streets of Brecknock and started to cross the bridge that spanned the deep blue churn of the River Honddu, which, I was informed, joined a second river, the Usk, at the town's Watergate. The middle section of the bridge was covered by a strong wooden drawbridge, already lowered into position to facilitate our arrival. Soldiers lined the route through the twin-towered gatehouse, wearing the red and black livery of the Dukes of Buckingham and with silvered badges of Flaming Cartwheels on their cloaks.

I attempted to look every inch the Lady, regal and cool-headed, but my heart quailed as I passed beneath the gatehouse with its leaking, moss-furred stones. However, I schooled my expression to impassiveness so as not to offend my new husband.

The entourage had entered the bailey. It was livelier here, with a bakehouse and a brewery, and servants busy at work building and fetching and carrying. The Constable emerged from the hall-block, wearing a polished chain of office, followed by the Steward in a sweeping robe trimmed with fur. They came before us, bowing as we dismounted, and grooms took our steeds away to the stables under the direction of the Marshal.

"We are home at last!" said Humphrey, offering me his arm as we crossed the inner courtyard. "Brecknock is a little old-fashioned, I'll admit, but you will come to love it, of that I am certain. I was dubious when first I saw it, truth be told…but since then Wales in all its wildness and strangeness has filtered into my blood and bones. The hunting is wonderful in the nearby forests, deer and boar are rife—do you hunt, Margaret?"

I shook my head. "I have flown a few hawks but never hunted with dogs. Father did not think it appropriate for girls and I am not a very skilled rider."

"Hawks? I will purchase one especially for you, a fine lady's hawk, a goshawk or a sparrowhawk. I'll also teach you to ride so that you can accompany me on a full hunt with the hounds. Your father, His Grace of Somerset, must be rather old-fashioned to keep his daughters from enjoying the chase; women of rank are usually expected to enjoy hunting with their husbands."

I smiled wanly. "He could be unyielding and so could Mother."

"You will come to *love* the hunt...and this castle," Humphrey repeated with vehemence, almost as if reinforcing his assertion and daring me to say it would never be so.

But as I gazed upon the damp-stained, storm-battered red towers and walls that rose in a ring around me, cutting off the outside world, I felt that I never truly would.

Humphrey was soon called back to England by his father, for there was much afoot at court. "Trouble is brewing, I fear, Meg," he said grimly as he prepared to leave, gesturing to servants and pointing out what raiment he would take within him in his baggage. His squires were running about madly, bringing more personal things—including daggers and his sword.

"It's not another rebellion, like that of Jack Cade?" I asked, recalling the rebellion that took place four years ago. Peasants and disaffected men from Kent had marched on London, demanding an end to taxation they deemed punitive—and a return from Ireland of Richard, Duke of York.

I feared York and loathed him, although we had never met. He and Father were bitter enemies, and I was sure York's faction were the ones who spread rumours that Father had cuckolded the King and fathered the young Prince Edward. York had also humiliated Father when he came to London, declaring that he was the King's truest subject—but then demanded the removal of my sire from his offices. Demanded that he be cast into prison.

The King, never steady in his wits, had almost acquiesced to York's wishes, but Margaret the Queen luckily intervened. Englishmen despise her, both for being a woman and for being French...but she saved my family that day, and for that, I can find nought but admiration for her. Father hung on grimly to his position from there on, but York's star was still ascendant, and all men knew his claim to the throne was a strong one, some even said better than the King's, for Henry's grandsire, Henry Bolingbroke, had usurped the throne. Richard II had made his Mortimer kinsman, young Edmund, the heir presumptive, but Edmund had been displaced by Bolingbroke and imprisoned for the entirety of his youth. Richard of York was the son of Edmund's sister, Anne Mortimer, who Henry IV had treated poorly too, leaving her destitute when her mother died. Anne descended in the female line from Lionel of Antwerp, son of Edward III, who was the elder brother of John of Gaunt, Henry IV's sire, and my own Father's grandfather.

"No, it's not another of Cade's ilk," said Humphrey darkly, "the trouble is from one of higher standing." I grimaced, knowing my worst fears were realised. It was the Duke of York stirring trouble again.

"How is the King?" I asked in a tiny, tremulous voice. We who served the Lancastrian faction loyally had been praying for the King's wellbeing ever since he fell into a stupor in the summer of 1453. He had been enjoying a restful stay at the Palace of Clarendon when he had received the terrible news of the loss of Bordeaux to the French. He had fallen into a stupor and would not be roused, not even responding to the birth of his long-awaited son and heir.

"Archbishop Kempe has died." Humphrey's voice was flat as he directed a squire to carry his armour out to the wains. "Even that news did not waken his Grace. Not that I expected it to, considering that he has not even acknowledged his own heir. My father brought the infant to the King's side, hoping against hope that God might perform a miracle…but Henry did not stir. His physicians, Gilbert Kymer and John Marchall, are at their wit's end, not knowing what to do next."

"So the land is essentially kingless," I murmured.

"York does not think so," said Humphrey. "I swear he means to see that crown upon his brow one day…No, I *know* it, Meg. Here…" He took my hand and led me towards a bench leaning against the wall of our solar. "I want you to sit down a moment…"

"You have come to impart bad news, is that not so?" A cold wave rushed over me. "Your journey to London…You expect trouble. Real trouble, not just rumblings from the disaffected in York's party."

"Yes," he nodded, "when I am in London, Parliament is set to meet and discuss the problem of the King's illness and his inability to govern in any meaningful way. My father says there is every likelihood…" he swallowed, and the pressure of his fingers on mine grew firmer "that Richard of York will be made Lord Protector of England."

"Oh, God help us!" I had feared this, or something like it, for months, but Humphrey speaking those fears aloud made them sharper, more real, near enough a certainty. "My Father…he…he hates York and York despises him in equal measure, stemming back to their time in France. If York should take high position, I fear what he might…"

"Hush, Meg." Humphrey released my sweating hand and set both hands on my shoulders, holding me down, calming me. "The worst has not happened as yet. I swear that my sire and I will do everything we can to aid your Father, Somerset, and keep York from power. My father is firmly on the side of the King and knows that his Grace loves his Beaufort kin dearly, so there is one important voice to speak for Duke Edmund, even though Henry, in his present state, cannot."

"But will it be enough?" I whispered. "There have been accusations…that my sire did not do all he could while in France. That he mismanaged finances and failed to hold English ground, and hence lost the King's lands to the enemy."

"Well, many men feel that is true," said Humphrey honestly, making me wince, "but primarily York. However, your father needs to make recompense to the King in some way. Loyalty alone and shared blood is not enough."

Humphrey's words scored me like a whip; it was hard to hear what men thought of my family—even those who were on the same political side. Unable to control myself, I burst into noisy sobs. Face mortified, my husband flung himself away from me as if my tears might burn his flesh. Like many men, he could not abide womanish tears. "You are distraught, Meg. I will send your ladies to you at once. I ride from Breckon before the Vespers bell."

The old Marcher castle of Brecknock seemed full of ghosts. With Humphrey gone, I wandered its lonely halls, disconsolate. The household staff were deferential and well-trained but disinterested; my tiring women, young girls from good local families, were efficient but slow to speak, guarded, their lips pressed shut and their eyes shuttered lest I see what was in them. They were never rude but showed no signs of liking, let alone friendship. I was an outsider.

Around me, the castle stones vibrated, buffeted by the winds howling down off the Beacons. I thought of one of the tenants of yesteryear, a knight named William de Braose. He had fallen afoul of King John centuries ago, over his wife Maude's unguarded tongue—she had accused the King outright of murdering his nephew, Arthur, who had a better claim to the English crown. William had fled to France to avoid the King's wrath, but Maude de Braose had been flung into Corfe Castle's oubliette with her eldest son. When the gate over the pit was finally lifted after many days, she lay dead of starvation, and her son with her, sprawled between her knees. She had, it was whispered, eaten the flesh of his cheeks in her final moments of desperation.

Shivers stippling my spine, I imagined Maude de Braose's haggard revenant gliding down the castle corridors, weeping…or perhaps cursing King John. At night, in my bed, fearful without Humphrey to hold me close and console me, I would sit up suddenly, breath ragged in my lungs, the gale howling around the look-out tower, and imagine Maude was there, white-clad, mourning her brutal death…but when she turned to face me, her mouth was a mad, crimson grin full of long, bloodied teeth. Maude had not been a popular mistress, my women told me when I dared to ask about the de Braose tenure at Brecknock—throughout the Marches, she had become a legendary figure of evil, an ogress or giantess who built castles in the night from stones she carried in a huge apron.

All foolish Welsh whimsy...but not so whimsical or laughable in the dead of night at lonely Brecknock Castle.

I tried to assuage my fears, my loneliness, in prayer, hurrying in my heavy cowl to the nearby priory for solace and comfort. Yet even within its austere walls, bleak imaginings haunted my thoughts. The Holy Rood, an object of pilgrimage, gleamed dully in the shadows behind the rood screen, but its beauty was muted, dulled by the tenebrous roof-beams into which it soared. My gaze was drawn instead to the nearby wall-painting of a raven, a carrion-eater, that overlooked the wooden walkway where the faithful clustered to venerate the Rood. The raven appeared to dance on its spindly clawed legs, its wings showering darkness as the cresset lights flickered below it. Incense smoke belched, drifting in curlicues from censers and thuribles, its sickly-sweet scent making my stomach churn. No, there was no peace for me, even in God's House, with that raven stamped on the wall, its beak as cruel as a sword. Even the font, seeming as old as time, bore a sinister carving of wild-eyed woodwose with vines sprouting from his distended mouth. An old religion seemed to clash with the new here in Brecknock.

Once I dared ask the prior why such a primitive figure decorated the font—a font where, perhaps, my own children might even be baptised in the future. His expression had shown unease, even displeasure, perhaps because a woman dared ask such questions about an ancient relic of his priory. Clearing his throat, he answered me in clipped tones, "Rabanus Maurus, a theologian of old, thought that such figures represented the sins of the flesh...earthy things, one might say."

A gasp of embarrassment escaped my lips and I flushed. The prior smiled wanly at me, a little friendlier, perhaps amused or approving of my modesty. "I am not sure if I believe it, though, my Lady. Others say the Tree from which the Cross that bore our Lord was hewn, grew originally from seeds placed beneath the tongue of the deceased Adam in his grave—and so, in stone carving, depictions are often made of men with foliage spurting from their mouths. Some scholars in the Divinity Colleges of Oxford and Cambridge have even surmised that Jesu himself is

Lord of the Vine, born of divine union, bringing eternal life and hope to the unhappy, sinful world."

I could see nothing Christ-like or holy in the wild creature on the stone bowl—but who was I to argue with scholars of Divinity, a mere woman and not greatly educated? Dread and confusion rose in me, as they did when I thought overmuch on unhappy events and of my own inadequacies.

"Are you hale, my Lady?" asked the prior, his eyes locked on my face, questioning and concerned. "You have grown suddenly wan…"

"I am fine." I rasped, as I gathered my heavy woollen cloak around my body. The priory was cold—it was always cold in Brecknock, with the winds skirling down off the hills—and my breath hung a white mist in the air. "However, I am not yet used to the climate of Wales. I must return to the castle. Thank you for your time and for your helpful teachings, prior."

The man nodding, looked expectant…as did that contorted head graven upon the font. Hastily, I scraped in my belt-purse for coins to offer. "For the maintenance of the Holy Rood of Brecknock," I said.

The prior smiled. The coins glinted like gold in the candlelight. The head on the font grinned its ancient Bacchic grin and the painted raven danced on into the gloom.

Shivering, I turned away, seeking the daylight outside the large west door, no matter that it was a grey, cold light, the sky a flat ashen expanse marked by the wings of fleeting birds. Nearby the river rushed, its voice low and gravelly, singing ancient and mournful songs in an unknown tongue.

Howling through the trees, the wind pushed me and my bored tiring women back to the rust-hued fang that was Brecknock Castle.

The ghosts inside awaited me in sullen hall and dripping wall...

Night had descended and I was tucked up under a pile of sheepskins in my canopied bed when the clip of hooves rang on the cobbles of the courtyard many feet below. I never slept well even at the best of times, and the sound dragged me from my bed to the shuttered window. The maids on their truckle beds made unhappy groaning noises, wakened despite my light footfall and not liking it one bit.

"Lady, I can make you a posset if you cannot sleep," offered Anchoret, the most pleasant of the three girls. She clambered up, bare feet slapping on the cold floor, her toes nearly purple with cold as she threw a heavy robe over her kirtle.

"No, there is no need, thank you, Anchoret. Did you not hear the noise? A rider has arrived. At this time of the night, it may well be news from Humph…from the Earl."

I unclasped the latch on the thick oak shutters covering the antiquated window slits of my bedchamber. Freezing night air slid into the chamber, bringing more moans from the sleepy-eyed women behind me. I thrust my head outside, turning out the sound of their displeasure. Over the castle wall, the crescent moon slashed at a low ridge of bubbled cloud that fringed the edge of heaven like a monk's tonsure circles his head. On the pinnacle of the look-out tower, the Buckingham Swan, swimming on a blue pennant, seemed to flap its wings as if about the fly away into the shadows, toward that sickle moon.

Below, torches blazed, casting orange light over the courtyard; the cobbles shone slick with night dew. Servants milled about, I saw the steward striding across the glassy stones in his great pointed shoes, and then knights burst into the ring of torchlight and I saw the Stafford Knot badge. Humphrey was home; his grey stallion, Tencendur, named after Charlemagne's steed, was being led towards the stables by a groom.

My heart jerked to know my husband was home safe, but fear roiled in my belly at the same time, tempering my joy. What news would he bring of the sick king? Or ambitious York and his enemy, my father Edmund, no doubt accused of many calumnies?

"Jennet, Eva, Anchoret, attend me," I said, my voice sharper than was my usual wont. "My Lord the Earl has returned. Ready me at once."

Anchoret was at my side in a flash. The other two women leapt from their beds, their complaints silenced. They frowned, trembling in the chill, but with the master of the castle back, they dared not play the part of sluggards. Hastily they threw open a large wooden chest and drew out a tawny gown of fluted silk that imitated samite, its sleeves and hem trimmed with golden threads. Having laced me into the dress, tying the laces so tight I thought I might faint, Jennet then brought over a demure headdress seeded with pearls as pale as the moon outside and all three ladies toyed with it, tucking in my braided hair until not one strand was visible. I rubbed rose-scent on my neck, pinched my wan cheeks to give them a hint of colour, and then hastened from behind the bedchamber screens with their paintings of the life of the Virgin to await Humphrey's arrival in the solar.

I longed to rush out into the castle grounds to find my husband, but restrained my enthusiasm, for such an action would be considered undignified and would embarrass him. I had to wait, steeling my features to calmness, even as perspiration coiled at the nape of my neck and ran between my shoulder blades. "Damp down the fire, will you, Anchoret?" I said, nodding towards the lit brazier, which Eva had only just lit. Once again, I sounded more cross than was my usual wont. "I cannot bear the heat."

"Heat! Madam, it is freezing!" said Jennet, hugging herself.

I saw Anchoret's brows draw together in perplexity but unlike Jennet, she made no complaint and threw a handful of dirt from an earthenware container beside the brazier onto the struggling flames. A cloud of rank smoke belched up, making everyone flap their hands and fan their faces.

"Are you sure you are well, madam?" asked my waiting-woman, Eva, with artificial politeness. "It is certainly not warm, the fire had been burning for mere minutes, and yet you claim you are hot. Perhaps you should retire and call the physician."

I stared up stonily at her. She was the maid I liked least of my three servants. She was the prettiest, with rose-gold hair and striking green eyes, but her manner often bordered on insolence, which she cloaked in an over-obsequious facade. When she thought I was not listening, she bragged to the others that she was the descendant of some ancient Welsh King with an outlandish, unpronounceable name—and I heard her say, spite in her voice, that she deserved to live in a castle such as this, with a lord…like Humphrey. I had seen her inviting him with her eyes, but thankfully he had never noticed; she was as interesting to him as the castle furnishing, which was to say, not at all. But I would keep my eye on her and see that she was married off soon and out of my way. I knew that although my looks were not those of a gargoyle, I had the long, thin face borne by many of the Beaufort line—a 'horse' my sister Nell called me once when we were involved with some girlish spat over a necklace. She had inherited the rounder, softer looks of my mother…

Suddenly I heard the blurt of a clarion down in the hall. Familiar footsteps echoed in the corridor outside the solar. I took a deep breath; my hands curled, the nails digging into my sweaty palms. I saw Eva glance over, noticing my nervousness, her full red mouth forming a moue of distaste.

Humphrey entered the solar, still wearing his russet travelling cloak though the hood with its squirrel-fur lining was thrown back. His curled hair was windswept, damp with night dew; a leaf stuck up from its tangles like a jaunty green feather—and suddenly I was choking back an improper urge to laugh. He looked nearly as wild as the woodwose graven on the priory's ancient font!

Any mirth, inappropriate or otherwise, died within me as he cast a stern, weary look towards the servants who were filing in and out, bringing flagons of warmed-up hippocras and pewter platters of meat and cheese tarts, hard-boiled eggs, demain bread. "Go, all of you!" he ordered. "I would speak with my Lady Margaret in private." The servants scuttled away, bowing, and Humphrey turned to my tiring women, his face still forbidding, even severe. "You go as well…but linger in the hall. Your mistress shall need you shortly."

The women scuttled towards the door, Eva swaying her hips ever so slightly and glancing back to see if Humphrey was watching her. He was not.

I realised then he bore evil news. I felt as if I was frozen. The heat that had afflicted me was gone and now it was as if the blood in my veins had become ice. I stared up at him with desperate eyes, my tongue dumb in my head. I tried to speak; no sound would emerge.

"Margaret…" he murmured, a worried frown creasing his brow when he saw my state of agitation.

I strove to speak again, and finally the dam burst, and my voice sprang free, the iciness melted. "Oh, husband, your face…your manner…I fear it is evil tidings you bring…but God, I am glad to see you."

My resolve broke and heedless of my dignity, I flung my arms around his waist, burying my face into his cloak with its smell of damp drizzle, horses and woodsmoke.

"Meg…" His hands came to rest on my shoulders, holding me back from him. That small distance between us brought even more terror to my being; I stood shaking, like a fearful dog or horse. "York has been appointed Protector of the Realm and Chief Councillor. His ally, Richard Neville, my uncle, has become chancellor."

"Did the Queen not protest at such an action?" I cried.

"Vociferously…but what could she say to convince great men? A woman and a French woman at that—no one would listen and she retired in great distress. As for your father…" He hesitated and then the words, the awful, dreaded words, tumbled from his lips in a rush. "York has had him committed to the Tower of London."

"On what charge?" I cried, although I already had guessed.

"The surrender of Rouen and Caen to the French," he said in a flat voice. I gazed into his eyes and saw, for the first time, that he was as disgusted as any about the losses of English territory. That he blamed my father, thought him incompetent as many other nobles had claimed. "Also, there was great displeasure over the ransom he paid…"

A little flame of anger seethed in me, although such was usually not part of my nature; 'meek as a mouse' my mother would say and it was not meant as a compliment. "You know what that ransom money was for, Humphrey? His family. My lady mother. My brothers and sisters. Me. To ensure our safety, our escape! We had gone to France with him, and it was terrible…the French surrounded us. We could all have been killed or worse…"

He bowed his head, unwilling to meet my gaze. "Although his reason may have been well-intentioned, he is to be punished for it."

Tears started, running unheeded down my cheeks. "My heart is broken in two. What if York should slay him!"

Humphrey's lip curled; he seemed frustrated with my upset rather than sympathetic. "Do not be foolish, Margaret. He has not the authority."

"Yet."

Humphrey put a hand to his brow in frustration. Weariness leached from every pore. "You talk too much, woman. I have ridden hard from London with this news. Do not burden me with problems that do not yet exist, especially when I am powerless to solve them. Whatever happens lies in the fickle hands of Dame Fortuna."

"I must go to Mother…" I murmured dazedly. "I cannot imagine what kind of state she is in…"

Humphrey's hands slid from my shoulders, tightening on my arms, the fingertips digging painfully into my flesh. "Meg, do not be foolish. There is nothing you can do for her. Write if you wish; I will dispatch a courier to take it to her. But you are a Stafford now, and one day shall be Duchess of Buckingham. Any journey would put you in danger. Your place is here at my side in Brecknock, not running off to your mother at the slightest trouble."

"The trouble is not slight," I cried, trying to yank away from his grip. "My father…"

"What help could you provide him? Be honest with yourself---from what I saw at our wedding, your mother is hardly likely to harken to your words or seek your assistance. As for your father—would you dig under the Tower walls with your bare hands to free him?"

Another bitter blow. Truth, but a blow nevertheless, and told harshly. Mother had always preferred Nell, her favourite of all her daughters. Just like she favoured her sons, Hal and Edmond, above John, who was the one closest to me in temperament and looks.

Defeated, my shoulders slumped. I could not bear to look at my husband, almost hated him for revealing my shame—that I was, despite my marriage to him, unimportant. The least of the Beauforts even within her own family.

Humphrey must have realised the upset he had caused for he abruptly released me and stepped back. "I am weary," he repeated. "Forgive me if I have spoken too bluntly. I should not have upset you so. I admit I have long been a bachelor so not used to the moods of women. You are more distraught than I imagined you would be…"

"I forgive you," I said with bitterness. "I am sure you are regretting our marriage, having realised how foolish and of little consequence I am."

His hands returned to my shoulders, gentle this time, turning me carefully back in his direction. "Meg, you are not with child, by any chance? I-I know but little of such things, but have heard breeding women become overwrought…"

Oh, how I wished I could have told him yes, and restored my favour instantly, but a lie would only make my problems grow tenfold. Miserably, I shook my head.

He sighed; I felt his fingers flex on the silky fabric of my gown. "Well…we must soon change that, my Lady. And then you will truly have Stafford duties to attend to, rather than dwelling on the fortunes of the Beauforts. The duty of raising my heir."

CHAPTER THREE

I spent much of the rest of the year on my knees praying—for both a child and for good news regarding my father. Neither arrived. Humphrey was back and forth from London and his other properties, leaving me at home. I was becoming used to Brecknock, however. The ghosts had grown familiar, even friendly. No longer did the shriek of wind off the hills wake me from rest, and the old green man on the priory's font smiled a welcome rather than unnerved with a leer.

As Lady of Brecknock, in my husband's absence, I spent time assisting the townsfolk with any grievances, and I found I enjoyed that task and that, slowly, I won the respect of the locals, if not love. Confidence growing, I dismissed my uppity tiring woman, Eva, which shocked the others but seemed to have the result of making them more diligent servants. Her leave-taking resulted in better manners, as they recognised that I was not quite the timid mouse they first thought me.

In November, Humphrey, home for the past month, announced that together we would go to London where he would meet up with his father and discuss with the King's councillors what must be done in the King's incapacity. I chewed my lip nervously at the thought. I had never seen that great and fabled city with its magnificent palaces and churches, the buzz of foreign voices, the merchants' shops where a wealthy man or woman could buy their heart's desire. I longed to savour its reputed delights, even if only once, but I also felt uneasy, for court would be full of the very men who railed with each other over power and position. Men who could turn on you in a heart's beat. Men like those who put my sire in the Tower.

"I thought you would be pleased, Meg," Humphrey said, noting my unsure expression after his announcement. "I fancied you thought Brecknock a backwater and would find gladness in a great town like London."

"Brecknock…it has grown on me," I said, casting him a weak smile, "but when I think of London, I try to imagine all the pleasures it could offer, but can only envision the King in his sickbed, staring blindly at the ceiling, and Richard of York parading about the halls of power as if he was King himself...and my poor father shut in the most notorious fortress in the land. So close, but I know I would never gain permission to see him."

"No, you would not—but come, Edmund Beaufort is a man of stature, despite his present circumstances. He is not starving to death or bound in chains." Humphrey sighed. "If you truly do not wish to come, you may stay here and I will accompany my Lord Father and Lady Mother, but..."

"I will come." I quickly reached out to take his hand. "It is my duty to be at your side. You must forgive me for my over-cautiousness; it is just the way I am made."

"There is no shame in it." Humphrey reached forward to brush a stray wisp of hair from my face. "I prefer your meekness to the bluster and imperiousness of Queen Margaret. I have seen too much of it in recent months. What a termagant she can be! As others have stated, she is a manly woman, use to ruling and not being ruled. She will listen to none, even those who would counsel her well."

"Humphrey!" I was startled; the Staffords were ardent supporters of the royal family. "You shock me to speak so of our Queen!"

"My words may be unwise and not very gallant, but through these hard months, that is how I see it. How many see it. The woman could have gathered more support for herself and for her son had her manner been more pleasant with a willingness to listen and negotiate. Instead, I fear she has shot an arrow into the heart of her own cause, with her haughty conceit ...and her...her *Frenchness*."

"I must admit I would like to see this terrifying French Queen, if only from a distance."

"Maybe you shall, Meg. I have no idea if she will attend the traditional feast as she is currently at Windsor, keeping watch at the King's bedside, but she likes to keep a watch on the conduct of the court, so who knows?"

Dirty grey snow mounded the streets on the approach to London's Newgate and stench rose into my nostrils—a rancid mixture of damp, decay, dung and smoke. Nonetheless, I gaped like a wondrous child through the silk-shrouded window of my chariot as our retinue squeezed through the crowds toward the jagged portcullis of the broad gatehouse with jutting twin towers that guarded the inner sanctum of London. Sentries patrolled; the captain rollicked out, a burly man in black, and asked our business. We were granted immediate access, and our cavalcade progressed under the gloomy double arch and past the barred windows of Newgate prison into the fabled streets beyond.

Those streets were definitely not paved with gold as some moonstruck youngsters claimed. Animal dung and offal clung to the cobbles, deeply trodden in, and the gutters spilt over with wastewater, melting snow and piss. A rat, belly up, floated by in one glutted conduit, and a decayed cabbage rolled, kicked by straggle-haired children in rags. The vegetable came to rest beside the drowned rat, greenish-brown and tattered, reminding me of the black-tarred severed heads spiked above the gate as a warning.

All around, commonfolk, tradesmen, hawkers and merchants trudged, wet by the sleet, many singing and laughing and whistling nonetheless. Some pushed barrows from which they sold dried Carlin peas, leeks, turnips, parsnips and other seasonal foods; others shook handfuls of coiled, coloured ribbons, or saints' relics strung on thongs—yellow bones, polished and engraved, that rattled in macabre fashion. Old dames flogged cheese wrapped in linen from wooden barrows; women and men carrying boxes of pastries and pies pushed through the crowds, calling out. A man in threadbare jerkin whose face was distorted by the pox had an array of knives spread out on the ground and a thuggish crowd around him, haggling over the prices. Shuddering, I averted my gaze, lest any of the miscreants objected to being watched and reacted with violence. But Humphrey assured me the watch was very diligent and violence in full daylight was unlikely, and none of the thuggish men even bothered to glance in our direction.

Taking a turn, we swept by the beautiful House of the Greyfriars with its conventual church, university buildings and the library founded a few years ago by former London mayor, Dick Whittington. Several Queens lay at Greyfriars—the heart of Eleanor of Provence; Marguerite, the second wife of Edward I; Joan of the Tower, Queen of Scotland; and Isabella wife of Edward II, who was buried in her wedding gown despite the unhappiness of her marriage. Then we passed the famous sanctuary of St Martin le Grand, a college of secular canons who rang the London curfew bells each night, and trotted down Bread Street, where the scent of the bakers' wares and their continuously blazing ovens sweetened the air and roused hunger. Almost immediately, the street wound round again and the air changed, growing rank with the smell of fish from the fishmongers' stalls. Everywhere stood booths and stands gleaming with the catch. Scales shone like coins, not only on the dead fish with their staring amber eyes, but on the hands and faces of the fishwives and their customers. I saw my two ladies, tucked into the chariot next to me beneath a sheepskin, grimace at the pungent smell and hold kerchiefs over their noses.

Leaving the fishmongers quarter, our entourage re-joined a tail of ancient Watling Street and we descended towards the Thames. A church spire speared through the falling sleet. Humphrey slowed his mount and bent down to my window to speak to me. "The house I rent for London stays stands near St Magnus's church," he said. "That is the church whose spire you can see. It is very near the river, and when the time comes, we will take a wherry to Westminster, rather than fight our way through the streets. Faster—and safer."

We continued in the direction of the river. Before us lay the expanse of London bridge, crossing the dull waters with their floes of brownish slush. Houses fanned out across the arches, some towering to an immense height, and bells rang from a wayfarer's chapel on the span. Traffic clattered noisily through the formidable gatehouse with its grisly decorations of traitors' heads and other body parts.

"Nearly there, my dearest" Humphrey informed me, quite cheerily. His breath smoked in the chill air. "It has been a long, cold journey and by God, the fires had better be stoked and tuns of wine in the cellars when we get there!"

We trundled past St Magnus's church, its corner sticking out oddly into the King's Road as if the building attempted to trip travellers up, to remind them to pray for safety on their journeys—and to leave some coins on the altar. The Guild of the Company of Fishmongers were patrons, Humphrey said, and the Confraternity of Salve Regina sang there every eve—a glorious sound we would hear from our house.

As the church fell behind us, our entourage entered a narrow stony lane, so tight the horses had to walk single-file and the sides of the chariot nearly scraped against the porches of the nearby buildings. When we emerged from this claustrophobic jam, the lane opened out again and we were facing a wide-open cobbled space with a high wall and wrought iron gates that gaped open. Beyond the gates, through a garden filled with bare-branched fruit trees, stood a handsome mansion facing onto the river, with jagged crenels along the roofline and large oriel windows full of shining leaded glass.

Humphrey dismounted his horse and came to personally hand me down from the chariot. "The tight little lane is known as Duck's Foot," he said. "It is our private entrance to the city—the Duke's Footpath. Before you lies the House of the Red Rose, which I have let out from the Duke of Exeter when he is not himself in residence. I pray you will find it comfortable."

I entered the house. There was a long hallway darkly panelled, and a small hall with a minstrel's gallery. It had new fireplaces, all decked in holly boughs for the upcoming Christmas season, and the window embrasures were hung with blood-coloured red velvet. Immediately, I warmed to it—so different from brooding Brecknock on its steep hill, where the roar of the wind and the grind of the river hung ever in my ears.

"Oh, Humphrey, it is beautiful!" I cried, as a shaft of late sunlight, deep yellow from the shortened winter day, pierced the central window and lit up the tapestries with their Lancastrian gazelles leaping, the Bohun Swan lifting its wings, the huntsmen in green pursuing a white stag...

He seemed pleased that I was happy. "I am glad you like it, Meg. You have not smiled or shown joy for far too long!"

We dined together that eve, and my head felt light as if it was full of air, and I laughed in the tinkling way I had heard other women laugh when teasing their spouses or their lovers. I felt almost not myself...not like dowdy Meg who feared too much and spoke too little or who spoke awkward, embarrassing words.

Humphrey called for more wine and additional fuel on the fire, and into the hall strolled a troupe of musicians, all clad in matching red doublets and tall felt hats. Standing before the table, they leaned together and sang,

> *"This endless night,*
> *I saw a sight,*
> *A star as bright as day;*
> *And ever among*
> *A maiden song*
> *Lullay, by by, lullay."*

When the candles burnt down and we were sated on wine and on sweet and savoury mincemeat pastries, which we could consume without guilt, for it was one of the Advent days when fasting was not required. Tomorrow we would eat fish. We then retired to our bedchamber and our union was happier and more ardent than it had been for some time—although, really, as devout Christians, we should have abstained from such passion in this holy month. But almost no one ever did...

Afterwards, when Humphrey lay with his face on the mounded pillows, softly snoring, his gold-brown curls damp with the sweat of his ardour, I slipped silently from the bed and pulled a long robe about my shivering nakedness. I could not sleep. The constant whisk of water, the boatmen's cries, the faint sounds of merriment and music—all were too unfamiliar, too intrusive.

Padding over to the window, I peered out. As it had thick glass and heavy poison-green curtains, the shutters were not securely fastened and I was able to push one aside and gaze out across the night-furled Thames. Lanterns bobbed on passing barges and wherries, eerie in the foggy darkness. A bell was tolling somewhere, sombre, sounding an almost funereal knell. And then I saw it, or was it merely my imagination?—a night funeral upon the breast of the great river, a catafalque set upon a barge, ringed by sputtering torches and cowled monks kneeling in prayer. I was too far away to see the deceased clearly, but imagined through the blurry haze of the torches, that I saw the edge of a gold-trimmed pall flapping in the breeze. Someone of high status lay dead, carried on the ever-moving river on his or her journey out of life, out of memory…

I shuddered, the pleasure of the evening dying away, the sweat of Humphrey's love-making drying on my skin. Gazing back down the expanse of the river, the funeral cortege was lost in the gloom, hidden amidst swirling waves and bouncing lanterns on boats. Instead, I caught a distant glimpse of the high white turrets of the Tower of London, with sleepless birds wheeling around their tips. The Tower where my father was imprisoned, his fate uncertain, beyond my reach, unaware his daughter was near at hand.

The shadow of the Tower descended over me, even from that distance, and all of a sudden, the joy of the evening was sucked from my heart, and I was left a dry, empty vessel about to shatter.

"Meg?" Humphrey rolled over, realising I was gone, his voice heavy with sleep. "Is something wrong?"

"No, no; I just felt restless and wide awake. So many bells in London, and chanting, and cries in the night…."

"Come to bed if you cannot sleep," he laughed, raising himself on one elbow. The light from the solitary taper burning in a holder on a table cast a golden shimmer over his hair, his bare chest. "We do not have to get up early in the morn."

I slid into the bed, placing my hand in his while trying to hide the fact that I was shivering. Even as he drew me into his embrace, dragging the thick coverlet over us as he kissed my neck, I could see in my mind the mist-muted torches of the funeral barge drifting down, down to the deadlands, like the ferry of Charon.

Over the next few days, Humphrey went to meet his father the Duke, discussing men's business regarding lands, fees, tariffs and political strife. I used the opportunity to explore London—and to shop!—in the company of my ladies and a handful of stalwart retainers sworn to keep us from harm.

As we neared Christmas Eve, I bought luxurious cloth from Bulstrode of Candlewick Street—*tiretaine* and taffeta—and silk from the well-known merchant Thomas Bernway, and ordered Leonard the Tailor to make me a gown of fine sarcenet. I fared to St Paul's, ignoring the marketplace atmosphere of the churchyard and the noisy yammering of a Dominican monk preaching from Paul's Cross, to slip inside the church to pray—and to scrutinise the wall-paintings of the Dance of Death, commissioned by the King before his illness. However, their macabre subject made me think of Father in the Tower once more and I did not linger but went on with Jennet and Anchoret to admire the gold and silversmith's shops near the church. There had to have been over fifty of them, selling salt-cellars, ewers, chalices, necklaces, collars, goblets and reliquaries. I brought my husband a gift of a goblet with a swan engraved on the side, its wings holding up a fluted rim embedded with small green stones.

I avoided the grocers' streets, which were too busy for comfort, although I sent a servant to obtain a pot of honey flowered by meadowsweet and some sugar loaves. Then, as the air began to cool and the sun slipped behind the buildings, I turned back towards our accommodation at The Rose. With the approach of sundown, the mood of the streets had changed—bawds and harlots in striped hoods, and bawling drunkards and scabrous beggars, were beginning to appear as if emboldened by the thought of encroaching darkness.

"Stop! Thief!" My litter came to a jarring halt that almost threw me into the road, as an angry, scarlet-faced man dashed in front of our party, fists flailing at the air. A scrawny child in rags, so filthy I could not tell the poor creature's sex, raced before him on thin but fleet feet, holding his prize aloft—the man's leather hood.

"I can scarcely imagine a child will have much use for that hood," I said, rather naively as the urchin and its roaring victim vanished into the growing crowds. "It is much too large; it would fall over his or her face."

"The little hellion is unlikely to keep his ill-gotten goods, my Lady," said one of the soldiers guarding my party on our travels. "It will soon end up sold on; it looked to be of decent make. No doubt the man the brat stole it from will find it for sale in some shop tomorrow—and will have to buy it back, at a hefty price, if he wants it badly enough."

We continued to little Duck's Lane, leading down to The Rose. The sun was now setting and London's skyline turned to blood and the river surface to molten gold. In St Magnus the Martyr's, the Confraternity of Salve Regina were singing their nightly hymns, the sound of their mingled voices drowning out earthy shouts from the streets and wharves.

In the trembling golden light, I could almost forget the shadow of the Tower—not a shadow I could see at this distance, but one I could *feel* enveloping my heart, my senses. But as darkness fell, what ghosts would fly from those ancient walls?

The dread reached out for me, as it did so often…but then was in The Rose's courtyard, with radiance spilling from the open door and the servants were bowing as I entered and made my way into the hall. Humphrey was back from his business with the Duke; he must have also visited the merchants, for he was directing a servant to hang a large counterfeit tapestry—a painted cloth rather than a woven one—to replace a wayworn Arras of a unicorn. The beast's virginal whiteness had turned, over the years, to a dirty grey, like the slush in the gutters of the London streets.

I motioned to my tiring woman to make away with Humphrey's gift, which he would not see until the day we celebrated Christ's birth. It was, fortunately, in an inconspicuous oak box and could be easily smuggled away into the wardrobe chamber.

"Ah, Meg, I was beginning to wonder where you were." Humphrey turned from hanging the tapestry. "I hope you have not over-extended my finances today."

"Lord husband, I assure you I would not do…"

"Margaret, I was jesting with you! Every word I say you take so seriously. I am not always a serious fellow, you know." He walked over, placing his hands on my shoulders. "Have you a gown for the Christmas feast at Westminster?"

"I do. Or I shall soon! Violet sarcenet and lined with yellow cendal. Leonard the Tailor is making it for me."

"And it will be ready so soon?"

"He assured me."

"Good. I commend your choice of colour…for I have brought you a gift. You may have it now." He snapped his fingers and one of his squires dashed out, returning with a small red velvet bag.

"Open your hand, Meg," Humphrey ordered and taking the bag, he opened it and poured its contents onto my palm.

It was a necklace with golden links, set with amethyst cabochons, some pinkish-violet, others reddish-purple. It would indeed fit with my new gown. "Oh husband, it is lovely…"

"I would not have my wife fade into the background at a court banquet," he said.

A little cold shiver went through me. I had known we would dine with the good and great at least once, but it had seemed a distant dream when we were still at Brecknock.

"Do you think the Queen will attend?"

"I cannot say for sure; I have not heard she's left the King's side, but she is paying from the royal coffers as is traditional and I hear no expenses have been spared. She is a strong soul, Margaret, but if she is there, do not fear her—as a man, I admit I've spoken ill of her ways, but she remains on good terms even with the wives of men who are not known to love her."

"And the King? If she does come, will I see him too?"

His smile faded. "That seems unlikely. Meg, he cannot even rise from bed. She would not put him on show, drooling like a babe."

My voice dropped lower, to a whisper. "What about York…the Duke of York who despises my father and bears him so much ill will?"

"He will be there. It is part of his duty. He is, after all the Lord Protector."

York. The enemy. We would be face to face. Again, the Tower's shadow reached towards me, black and cold as the grave.

Christmas Eve passed in midnight prayer and contemplation. Early the next day, Humphrey and I took a barge to Westminster from the wharf directly behind The Rose. I had never before ridden in a boat and the thud and thump of the waves against the bow brought both exhilaration and fear. Under a lowering sky, with the wind cold and smelling of nascent snow, the craft was poled out into the swell, its captain calling instructions to the rowers in a booming voice. As it was a nobleman's barge, the craft was decorated and covered by a canopy for Humphrey and me to sit under, protected from winds and spray and curious passers-by in other vessels on the Thames.

Surprisingly swift on the river's swell, the barge bobbed along past Ebgate, Dowgate and Queenshithe, then Baynard's Castle, one of the homes of Richard, Duke of York. I shivered and drew my warm woollen mantle, red as cherries, close around my shoulders, scarcely believing that I would soon be in the presence of my family's enemy. I fought to keep my mind serene as we drifted by the House of the Blackfriars, Bridewell Palace, the House of Carmelites, the Middle Temple, Whitehall, and finally saw the walls of Westminster Palace loom out of the grey winter's day.

On the river side of the huge courtyard stood an arched gateway leading to a wooden landing. Above the arch soared an immense tower with a thin lead spire resembling a rapier.

Humphrey gestured toward it and I followed the motion of his hand, blinking—flakes of snow were beginning to descend, sticking irritatingly to my lashes. "That is the Clochard. It has three great bells housed within, the biggest and loudest you can imagine. Their sound is so strident that tavern-goers say it turns their ale to sour pi…I mean, water."

I continued to stare at the Clochard, its open gate with rows of metal portcullis teeth and two round-arched upper windows almost giving the stone edifice semblance of a gigantic louring face. "Will…will the bells toll when we enter?"

Humphrey shook his head; snow fell from his curls onto the patterned dark velvet of his cloak. "No. Coronations, princely births and funerals only."

I continued to stare, my breath fogging before my cold lips. What if those huge, brazen bells were to start to chime now, telling me of death…the death of my Father in the Tower?

But mercifully, the bells remained silent.

"Come, Meg." The barge was drifting into the dock, thudding softly against the wooden struts thrust into the water. Once the craft was moored in its dock, Humphrey clambered up and disembarked, waiting to guide me over a wooden ramp the rowers had placed down, bridging the gap between the craft and the dock. Murmuring excitedly, dressed as colourfully as peacocks, our little company of personal attendants followed us onto the wharf.

"Where are we going now?" I craned my head about, trying to take in all the sights as we emerged into the courtyard with its myriad buildings, tall and pinnacled and golden despite the snowy dimness.

"Westminster Hall," said Humphrey. "Where else? Unless you would like to sit on the King's own seat in the Court of the King's Bench? His Grace is not in it, after all!"

He laughed but I could not; how small I felt sometimes, how backwards. For all that I was the daughter of a Duke, my education had always paled before the greater needs of my brothers—they learned of history, I learned to sew. Thus the sexes were divided but although we women were the 'weaker sex', why did we have to be the 'foolish sex' too?

Near the Hall, I noticed another Tower near the gate that led out into the street. "More bells?" I asked

"No, this time a clock...a modern timepiece," replied Humphrey. "It strikes every hour."

"Every hour! What a noise that must make."

"It can be quite irritating at times, but it is useful for the courts that take place here almost daily. One day, Meg, I am convinced such clocks will replace bells for telling time."

"How extraordinary," I whispered, half-wishing the clock would chime. "But what would happen to all the bell ringers all over England!"

Humphrey shouted with laughter. "I am sure they could become...become clock-repairers," he grinned. "But the future is not ours to see. Only time will tell." He peered through the drifting snow as if waiting for my response.

"Oh...oh *time*," I gibbered, realising with a blush that he was trying to be witty. I was no good at jests or banter, and no one in my family was much inclined to any form of humour, save perhaps my younger brother John. Even when my sire had been home, our Christmases were austere occasions, dedicated solely to celebrating the birth of Christ. The feasts were glorious but the dances subdued, and the carollers sang the most doleful-sounding of the Christmas songs. The hall would groan under the weight of verdant boughs, but there were seldom mummers, no Lord of Misrule, no Lord of the Bean...

We came to the hall doors and the steward welcomed us in with a bow and delegated our bench. I tried not to gape like a ninny as we walked the hall's length, reminding myself that I was a Duke's daughter. The hammerbeam roof soared overhead, archway upon archway of oak timbers supported on huge buttresses of stone. Golden angels peered down, faces beautiful and serene, wings battering the shadows away. Heraldic Beasts roared and menaced from cornices near the raised dais where the King's seat stood.

Our designated seat was near the dais in a place of honour, yet outside the most esteemed seats, which were those reserved for Humphrey's parents, John Mowbray, the Duke of Norfolk...and of course Richard, Duke of York and his wife, Cecily Neville.

Other nobles had already arrived, Salisbury and his son Richard, Earl of Warwick, York's supporters; the Earl of Wiltshire, handsome James Butler and his wife Avice; Lord Egremont, Lord Bonville, seated far away from the Courtenays, with whom he had a long-standing feud, and still more notables were entering the hall, the men in houppelandes and great coats of various hue, their breasts draped with glimmering livery collars appended by gems, and their wives in tall hennins, cow-horn headdresses or jewelled crespinettes. The air was warm, rich with the scent of burning firewood, sweet tallowy candles, cinnamon and exotic spices, and the greenery spread on the linen tablecloths and wrapped around the pillars.

I glanced furtively towards the high table. Buckingham had just arrived, dressed from head to toe in blue cloth of gold. Beside him, Duchess Anne walked like a Queen, wearing a pearled gown the colour of the dawn's blush and a hennin with long silk veils. Following were the King's half-brothers, Edmund Tudor and Jasper Tudor, the former sullen and dark-haired, the latter gingery-red with a slightly roguish smile and freckles on his face. With them was their ward, Edmund's future bride, my little cousin Margaret Beaufort, still tiny as a doll but now dressed in womanly attire. I was surprised to see her at Westminster but then she was Edmund's future bride. I got the impression that, despite her young age, Margaret *liked* the world of politics and nobility far more than she liked the feminine arts, and that she wanted to miss nothing of what was happening around her. I found that unusual but admirable.

A clarion sounded from the farthest end of Westminster Hall—so far away I could scarcely see the newcomers in the bustle of servants and servers but guessed they must be of great importance. A herald in a vivid tabard strode to the foot of the dais. "Arise for his Grace, Richard, Duke of York, Lord Protector of England," he cried in a strong voice.

My heart hammered against my ribs and my head felt light as I rose alongside Humphrey. The persecutor of my father, his bitterest enemy was here…the Duke who in my nightmares had taken on an ogre's semblance, ugly and threatening.

The man who walked down the centre of Westminster Hall did not seem so fearsome; it was almost a disappointment. Of middling height, York was subdued in black velvet—a rich man's colour but dull amidst the swaggering peacocks in their swirls of scarlet, crimson, tawny, sapphire and emerald. His livery collar, pure gold, bore at its heart a white rose—the emblem of his House. As if he realised I was watching him, he turned slightly in my direction with a little frown, and I was surprised to see, not a monster's visage, fiery-eyed and harsh, but a slightly careworn man with a firm jaw and solemn greyish eyes.

He took his place in his allotted seat at the high table, joined moments later by his wife, the famous Cecily Neville, my Humphrey's aunt. Cecily was, I had to admit, far more lovely than her sister, Anne. Her face was fuller, her skin smoother, her nose gently up-tilted and her mouth a rosebud. She was dressed more sumptuously than any of the other ladies in the Hall, in a gown of silver and gold brocade, decorated with stitchery of pineapples. Her headdress, I surmised by its shape and size, was a Burgundian import, modern and frightfully desirable at the royal court. She lacked height but with her regal bearing and air of importance, she seemed taller, a lioness who ruled the pride. A jewelled girdle straddled her midriff and her hands, long and smooth with white, slim fingers lay lightly on the almost imperceptible swell of her belly. I realised with a surprise that she was with child—again. She had already given York a huge brood, bearing the last child, a son, but two years ago.

She was drawing attention to her belly, I thought, almost flaunting her fecundity to supporters of Queen Margaret, who had borne only the one child in all her years of marriage. Despite this, it was claimed that in the past, the relationship between the two women was fairly amicable. However, if there was ever even the slightest traces of amity, they doubtless had vanished when York became protector and Cecily's star rose alongside his until she began to be seen almost as a rival Queen…

The Duke and Duchess of York sat down, Lady Cecily with great elegance and assurance. The Duke's worried, tense expression never left him, however, and he stared towards the door as if fearing an armed assault, even on Christmas Day.

However, the only assault was one upon the feaster's eardrums. Seven trumpeters clad in tabards bearing the varied Arms of the Queen—the Arms of France, England, Hungary, Naples, the Kingdom of Jerusalem, the Duchies of Bar and Lorrain, and, of course, Anjou—stepped from the corridors into the body of Westminster Hall and, lining up against the tapestry-hung walls, played a tremendous fanfare that rang up to the very rafters.

A thrill passed through me. There was only one person it could be. The Queen had indeed decided to head the feast, despite her woes!

"All rise for her Grace the Queen!" called out Lord Beaumont, the Steward of England, with fervent zeal.

The chatter in the hall dimmed and the nobility got to their feet, almost as one, myself included. Into the chamber strode Queen Margaret, newly arrived from Windsor Castle, where she had sat watch over the ailing King. It surprised many that she had come to the Christmas feast, but I assumed, as Humphrey had said earlier, she was taking the wind out of the Duke of York's sails. She would take her rightful position; he would not feast at the head of the table as if he were a King.

Over the years, hearing of her astuteness and unwomanly toughness, Margaret of Anjou had taken on almost legendary proportions in my mind, much as Richard of York had. If he had assumed an ogre's guise, she had become an Amazon, a flame-eyed warrior-woman, manly in her bearing, hands itching to wield a sword. In person, she surprised me, though she was not diminished. Rather than an armoured virago, I gazed upon a tall, slender woman, in royal purple skirts threaded with gold, her headdress set back on her brow to reveal a patch of sleek dark hair. Like York, she looked a little worn by life, lines beginning to show around her sombre mouth, but traces of faded beauty still clung to her features.

An Amazon, no, that had been capricious fantasy on my part—but formidable, yes. A brittle strength radiated from

Margaret's person as she swept by in a haze of jasmine and orange scent, exotic and wonderful.

The Queen sat down in one of the empty royal thrones on the dais, near the huge silver salt cellar, fashioned into the form of a Greek sea-god, and decorated with pearls and agates, which stood on tall gilded legs. At her side, the King's chair remained vacant, its emptiness a conspicuous reminder of the parlous state of our land. "*And I am this day weak, though anointed king; and these men be too hard for me…*" How true those Biblical words seemed of King Henry!

The first courses were served—fish mortrews, *salat*, chicken and a civit of hare. Spiced wine, malmsey and hippocras flowed and subtleties appeared, frosted with sugar, depicting the Queen's Arms and those of her baby son, Edward. Dancing commenced to the sound of plucked lutes, horns, the rebec and the drum, and then the second, third, fourth courses arrived—an enormous silvered pie shaped like a crown, a kid goat, salted venison, goslings, capons, chickens basted with spiced egg yolks, and an immense sturgeon steamed in vinegar and sprinkled with ginger. The last course consisted of wafers, slices of pungent cheese, gilded sugarplums, marchpane cakes and fruit stewed in hippocras.

Everyone ate heartily since Advent was now over and we were hungry after a month of prescribed self-denial—and fish, lots of fish, washed down by almond milk, even fish roe stuffed into eggshells to make us believe we were eating real eggs. Now we had meat, glorious meat, and sweet milk and egg in unlimited abundance—and some of the men, lower down the tables, were attacking their trenchers like wild beasts long held at bay, juice and sauces running down their chins. I glanced at Humphrey, glad to see him eat in a more refined manner, wiping his mouth with the bleached linen napkin left on the table for his use, but I could not truly have blamed him if he tucked in with the rest.

As the celebrants finished with the sweets and fruits, troupes of mummers and Moorish dancers arrived in magnificent and sometimes humorous or sinister costumes—ash-smeared Disguised Men, ribbons on their knees; a gigantic Spirit of the

Greenwood, muscle-bound and bearded, heavily-decked in holly wreaths; a burly St George, helmeted and carrying a vast wooden sword, the red Crusader's Cross a blood-bright slash on his white tunic; a Doctor and a Moorish Prince wearing outlandish dark robes and sporting long and quite clearly false beards.

After the maskers and dancers had performed and received payment from the Steward's purse, the Queen rose from her seat, gesturing to her ladies-in-waiting, who fluttered like butterflies behind her seat. It was late and we thought she was preparing to depart, leaving us the freedom to stay and converse with old friends and family or leave the Palace for our own lodgings.

But she did not move, standing like a statue in her shimmering ermine. "Before this feast ends," she said in a voice deeply accented, even though years had passed since she arrived in England, "I show you one given to us all, as Christ was given. A miracle also, and one to whom you one day must kneel."

Out of a passage that ran to the apartments behind the, a nursemaid in pristine cap and apron appeared, walking swiftly but steadily. She held a large, well-grown child clad in a robe of cloth of gold, a small cap on his head. Margaret took him from the nurse and held him aloft like a trophy. He kicked the air and bawled, the golden cloth trailing down like the tail of a shooting star.

"Behold your prince!" Margaret cried. "Edward, son of Henry, your sovereign lord. Do not forget that even though his Grace lies incapacitated, he has, by Grace of God Almighty, a strong and healthy son to rule after him!"

On his side of the high table, I could see York frowning. His Duchess was ice-cold and pale. It was common knowledge that while the Queen was barren, York had pushed to have himself named as heir. Father had railed against such an action, stalking around his solar and shouting, 'If York can claim the throne—why not a Beaufort? I too descend from Edward III.' Mother, seeing how this subject consumed him, had sighed in exasperation, 'We have been over this before Edmund. It is a sad but true fact that your grandfather was not married to your grandmother at the time of Lord John's birth, and that although John of Gaunt's children were legitimised, it was decreed they could not inherit the throne.'

Father's teeth had ground in rage. "There is doubt that the codicil added to the legitimisation was properly ratified, Eleanor! Why should York take precedence if the King has no son? I am the one the King prefers…"

Why, indeed? But it was a moot point now, for the long-awaited heir was here, screaming the hall down…and York was Lord Protector while Father languished in prison.

Suddenly a messenger wearing the royal badge of a chained antelope skidded into the hall, sliding on the rush mats and almost falling in his haste. The Queen glared, her brow lowering, and handed the baby to the nursemaid, who clutched the precious infant. The babe stopped screaming and began to grizzle fitfully instead.

"Your Grace…" panted the newcomer, racing up to the dais and dropping heavily to one knee. "News! News from the King's bedchamber! A physician has sent me…"

Queen Margaret paled but stood all the straighter. A gasp ran through the room and a terrible silence fell. Richard of York and his wife glanced at each other, expressions unreadable; York had gone ashen.

"Speak, sir," said Margaret, her voice surprisingly steady. "What tidings do you bring from Windsor?"

The young courier's mouth worked as if he could not quite expel the words. The Christmas celebrants held their breath. We were all expecting in those dreadful moments to be told that his Highness the King, bedridden for so long, had departed the circles of the world; that he, ever pious, now ascended to the Throne of God.

Instead, the courier burst into tears and pressed his glove against his sodden face. At last, his words flooded forth: "It is a Christmas miracle, your Grace! The King…the King has woken from his stupor! First, he moved his eyes then opened them wide. They no longer stared like one blind; he recognised all around him! He did not know the day or year but he remembered faces and names! He then struggled to sit upright! He says he is…hungry!"

The Hall burst into violent cheers, thunderous after the deathly silence. Men and women, lords and ladies hugged and kissed and cried. The Queen, a hand to her throat, looked as if she might faint. Her ladies were fanning her madly, one of them even daring to clasp her shoulder as support.

York and Cecily Neville sat like statues, along with a few others such as Salisbury, who had been made Chancellor under York's direction. Then, knowing that they must react with joy or look treacherous, they joined in with the cheering.

"God Save the King!" shouted Jasper Tudor, and the cry was taken up by his brother Edmund. Others followed, including Humphrey and his father, the Duke of Buckingham, and then the ladies of the court joined in.

"God save the King!" I cried with the rest, overwhelmed by the good news. God had spoken that Christmas Day.

The Queen's colour returned, red roses blooming on her cheeks. It was as if a wizard's wand had passed over her; she suddenly appeared years younger, less harsh of visage. Pushing aside her still-fussing ladies, she stepped forward and lifted a hand for silence.

The shouting and jubilation receded. Raising her arms on high, Queen Margaret gazed heavenwards. The angels on the hammerbeam ceiling smiled back. "This is truly a Christmas miracle!" she cried, voice heavy with emotion. "Praise be God on High…and God save the King!"

Like most of the other feasters, Humphrey and I spent the remainder of the night in a second celebration. The Yorks and their closest supporters had vanished, quickly and silently. And me—my heart was leaping and I felt as if I walked on air, for I knew that the King's revival would soon trigger the release of Father from the Tower.

As Humphrey talked with the Duke of Buckingham, whose face was a glow with both thankfulness and relief, I retreated to the open door to take a breath of night air. It had grown hot in the Hall, between the crowd's excitement, the fireplaces, and the candelabras, while the noise of so many jubilant voices had become overwhelming, a roar that hurt the head.

As I stepped out and entered the palace gardens, I saw a shadow move, silent as a bat or a nightbird. To my surprise, cousin Margaret emerged from behind a shrub white with hoarfrost. "Margaret," I said, "it seems we are always meeting in gardens at times of great celebration!"

She smiled, her mouth drawn thin and long. The year since my wedding had matured her slightly, but I doubted she would ever be described as pretty, let alone beautiful. Yet there was a strange, compelling power about her, despite her plain features and small size. Perhaps it was her eyes, large and dark, deep-set and intelligent, or perhaps it was some strange aura she radiated. Whatever it was, I knew I possessed none of it. Horse-faced Meg, with her megrims and her strange moods and fears.

"Edmund and his brother Jasper are preparing to ride to Windsor, to join in thanksgiving at the bedside of their brother, the King," she explained. "Once they have arranged a chariot for me, we will all depart together. For now, though, I will offer up my own prayers of thanks, in my own manner."

"Would not St Stephen's Chapel be warmer?" I asked, unable to quite believe she was here to speak privately to the Lord, no matter how pious she was.

She peered at me, lips quirking upwards to reveal small, rather irregular teeth. "Do you doubt me? Oh, you are clever, my cousin. I *did* come here to offer prayers of gratitude—one can speak to the Almighty in any place, not just in his House! But I will be frank with you—I believe I can trust you—mostly I slipped out to spy on the Duke of York and his stuck-up wife."

"You—you do not think they will try anything, like raising an army?" I gasped. *Or seeing that Father meets an unfortunate 'accident' before he can be released from the Tower.*

"It would seem not. They both hurried away, calling for their servants, looking like they had sucked on Spanish lemons. Salisbury and his son followed them, equally scowling, but the two parties did not leave together, so if there is any conspiring, it is not taking place yet. As long as there is little delay, now that the

King is recovering, I am sure we will soon see the over-mighty fall."

"My father…" I breathed.

Margaret patted my arm in sympathy. "Poor Uncle Edmund—but I do not think he has suffered overmuch in the Tower, except perhaps with boredom and frustration. In any case, the King will free him soon, I have no doubt. Uncle Edmund will want his revenge on Richard Plantagenet then, I should imagine."

Shuddering, I stared at her, light and dark, her face a pale moon in the dimness. I had not thought of what Father might do upon release. He had been cast low, imprisoned, his honour sullied. He would indeed desire revenge.

Margaret changed the subject, perhaps noticing my distraught expression. I surmised that there was very little this slight, plain girl missed. "My wedding date is set now, cousin. I will marry Edmund Tudor late next year."

I was slightly taken aback for she was still terribly young; next year she would reach the age of consent in England, but it was rare for girls to be wedded and bedded at such an early age. More often they were fifteen or sixteen. "A…a *true* marriage…living together as man and wife?"

"Yes," said Margaret. "Edmund, you see…" A brief shadow crossed her face, her mask of confidence suddenly slipping. "Edmund is afraid something…might happen to me, some trouble drive us apart before the marriage is perfected…and he is so desirous of this wedding, he does not wish to wait any longer."

For the first time, she sounded like the little girl she was, rather than studious, sombre Margaret. *He wants your lands, Margaret; you are most likely the richest heiress in England. That's why he wants the wedding done so swiftly, even at the expense of your wellbeing…He is afraid you will die before the marriage is consummated and he will end up with nought…*

"I pray it all works out as you wish, Cousin Margaret," I said solemnly. I was sure I could not keep the doubt from my voice.

"It will. It has been prophesied by St Nicholas."

So Margaret still believed in her vision…Well, who was I to say it was not true? Such things were well-attested, especially in days of yore.

"And how is your Humphrey?" asked Margaret. "How does it go with you?"

"He is often busy… Brecknock can be lonely and isolated when he is not there," I admitted, "but he is a good husband to me, and I hope he sees me as a good wife."

"There is no child as yet, I take it?"

My face grew heated, despite the chill in the wintry air. "No, not yet, but he has been away much, with his father Buckingham. Soon, God willing…"

"Yes, God willing," said Margaret. "I pray such a happy event happens quickly for me, too—once I have wed Edmund."

Again, I could not help but shake my head. "Have you spoken to your mother of this?" I said gently. "Maybe she could advise you. Margaret, having a child is the most fearsome thing we will ever endure as women…it…it is like a knight facing death on the field!"

She burst out laughing. "You jest, Cousin Meg! Yes, the travail is awful, as God willed it because of Eve's Sin, but so it must be…"

"Do you have any idea what childbirth entails? Are you even…ready?"

Perplexed, she peered at me through the gloom, resembling a small dark crow with its head cocked to one side. "Ready?"

"You know…" I spoke low, in what I believed was a sisterly fashion. "Your flowering…"

"Oh, *that*…" she said dismissively. "Eve's curse. Yes, twice. As for childbirth being fearsome, I put my trust and my life in God's hands. St Nicholas would not have appeared to me if I were doomed to die giving birth!"

She fixed me with a steady gaze as if daring me to contradict her. My cousin, despite her youth, seemed like she was not happily contradicted.

Then she smiled, a little girl again albeit a solemn one. "Wouldn't it be wonderful if our sons became good friends, Meg? More like brothers than cousins?"

"It would be a fine thing."

"Maybe it will prove so." Margaret touched my sleeve. "If you have a boy, what will you call him?"

"Oh...Humphrey and I have not discussed it. Another Humphrey, perhaps; it's a preferred name of the Staffords. Or Henry after the King. It is always prudent to name one's eldest boy after his Grace."

Margaret nodded enthusiastically. "Yes. Edmund had already said our son will bear his Highness' name. He loves his brother dearly as does dear Jasper."

*So obsessed with this idea of this prophesied son when she is not even yet wed....and she so young and small...*I fought the urge to cross myself. There *was* something about Margaret; whether it was truly Godly or not, I could not tell. Such conviction, such confidence. It was vaguely unnerving.

"Margaret!" We both whirled around as a male voice rang out. Into the garden marched Edmund Tudor. "Your transport is ready—we must be away without further delay. The King cannot be overburdened by visitors; he needs to recoup his strength after such a long illness. That's why we must get to Windsor first, before all the sycophants and untrue minions arrive and start begging. What are you doing out here anyway? Stop slipping away, girl—you enjoy your solitude, but if aught were to happen to you..."

He cast me a hard, frowning stare as if he thought I was some panderer ready to sell his intended bride to a pack of ravening Hanse traders. The very thought of being thought to have such wicked inclinations made me want to laugh, but Edmund did not appear the kind of man to take a jest well.

Margaret pursed her lips and sidled up to Edmund like a sleek black cat. He towered over her, yet oddly, she seemed to be the one in control. "I came outside to pray for His Grace before our departure. I did mention it...but perhaps you...*misheard*, my

Lord. Do you not think my prayers a worthy thing, dearest betrothed?"

Edmund mumbled inaudibly and then extended an arm to her, awkward, as if not used to women's company. A soldier rather than a courtier, I suspected. "Goodnight, Cousin," said Margaret, inclining her head in my direction.

It was only then that angry and suspicious Edmund appeared to realise who I was—the wife of a future Duke and daughter of a present Duke. "My Lady Countess," he gave me a tiny bow from the waist. "The night is chill. You must go inside at once. It is not fitting for a lady to be out here alone. I know you are not used to the ways of the wicked world—and neither is Margaret, for all that she is headstrong! We are behind firm stone walls here but the palace staff are many—and who can one trust in these days of doubt?"

Sharp as lances, his eyes pierced me, a stormy dark grey, and I wondered if he thought that I was one of those who could not be trusted, my loyalties questionable. He seemed an overly suspicious man, this Edmund Tudor—my family were the most loyal Lancastrians and so were the Staffords.

And some even think... I blushed, glad that the redness of my face was hidden by the shadows—*that he is my father's son, not Owen Tudor's*. That would make this saturnine, abrupt man my half-brother, but thankfully I could see nothing of Father in either Tudor's manner or his appearance.

"Thank you for my concern, my lord." I forced a smile. "I will take your words to heart and return to the Hall at once."

Margaret had lost interest in me, her attention solely focussed on Edmund Tudor. She latched onto his arm as if he might vanish like smoke; she appeared to be nearly as worried that their projected marriage might never take place as Edmund himself. I felt a little sorry for the son she wanted so desperately, should a son be born indeed. Henry. He would have a mother who would do anything for him, I surmised, even if it was not altogether savoury. But who knows? Mayhap he would think that a good thing.

Margaret and Edmund left the garden and hurried, almost running, toward the busy courtyard with its array of horses, groom, chariots and departing nobility. I entered Westminster Hall, and Humphrey, happily drunk, staggered towards me and threaded his arm around my waist, pulling me close against him. "What a magnificent night this has been," he breathed in my ear. "What a Christmas gift to all of us…I have some good news for you, Meg."

"Yes?"

"Certain factors have already decided to petition for York's removal from the Protectorate…and to release your father from the Tower. It won't take too long. The King was apparently most distressed to find out his dear Somerset was incarcerated. He promised that his position as Captain of Calais shall be restored as soon as he is well enough to deal with such matters."

Tears rushed to my eyes; my head felt light. "Ah, Meg." Humphrey wiped my cheek with his sleeve. "So many tears. Hopefully, soon, there will be no more reasons for you to weep."

We returned to The Rose on our barge as the morning sun ascended over the River Thames. Bells clanged from abbey and priory and parish church, and sky and water were blood-hued, beautiful and yet terrible at the same time. Humphrey's gilt curls turned to flame, as did his visage; a man of blood and fire in the face of the dawn.

Upon return to the Red Rose, we retired to our bedchamber—a most decadent decision at that hour of the day, when the rest of the household were rising to start their daily tasks. Laughing, we threw ourselves onto the linen sheets and consumed more malmsey, more sweetmeats. The door was barred and I lifted the headdress from my brow to let flow my waist-length tresses and then turned my back so that my husband could release me from my gown. It fell, rushing like water, to the floorboards with their imported Turkey carpets, and my chemise followed.

On that sweet, glorious, happy morning, with the sun piercing our bedchamber through the glass window, circling us with a nimbus of golden light and bringing promises of a new day, a renewal of fortune, Humphrey and I conceived a child.

How did I know such a thing, so soon? I *felt* it, as I lay sated, breathing heavily amid the tangled bedclothes, just as if there was another presence hiding deep within me, new to the world, waiting to emerge. I could say nought, though, until the time was right; I would sound moonstruck. I was not Cousin Margaret with her talk of saints and destiny, after all.

Instead, I merely smiled a warm, secret smile and cradled Humphrey's head against my belly.

CHAPTER FOUR

Back in Brecknock, it was cold and snowing, the land heavily mantled in white. Winter lasted long in Wales, far longer, it seemed, than in my old home in Devon. Ice crackled on the river and the town streets were filled with bowed figures facing into the bitter winds, kindling strapped to their backs for their fires.

The instinct I had about being with child had proved correct. My courses had been regular since I was thirteen and now—gone. Food made my stomach churn and I spent mornings with my head hanging down the privy, heaving up the sops I had just consumed. I wanted to rush and tell my husband the good news at once, but the midwife my maids brought from the town shook her head.

"I am certain you're breeding, milady," she said, "you have all the signs, but best wait a month or two more. Often they don't stay…especially the first."

"Don't stay? What do you mean?"

She pursed her lips, clearly thinking I was ignorant. And so I was; I had no knowledge of such mysteries of womanhood. "Sometimes a child does not stay in the womb, Countess. It passes out before a woman even grows round in the belly."

"You mean…the child is dead?"

"Well, it never really was a child, was it? It never took the first breath of life."

Cold fear consumed me and my hand fell to my belly. Oh, I could not bear it…

"Rest yourself, my lady, and wait a bit longer before you inform the Earl. Once the third month is behind you, you may safely tell him."

So I swore to keep my silence, although it was difficult to keep both my joy and my fear to myself. If there was a visible change in me, Humphrey did not appear to notice…for he was much consumed with news that reached Brecknock from London.

The King had recovered his wits but spent most of his time on his knees, thanking God for his recovery. At least, he had finally declared the little prince his son, putting paid to any ambitions of York. But that, of course, brought new problems. No one thought Duke Richard, so close to the throne, would take his demotion lying down…Added to that, Father had been released from prison and was restored to all his offices—another affront to York.

"The King has summoned all the nobles to a Great Council," Humphrey informed me. "It will take place in Leicester."

"And you will attend."

"Of course; it is my duty. York is no longer Protector, and your father and Percy of Northumberland have forced Salisbury from his position as Chancellor."

"Percy? When was he ever friend to the King?"

"Whatever he was in the past, he swears loyalty now. He regards the Duke of York as an enemy and has feuded bitterly with the Nevilles. He will be a watchful eye in the north for his Grace, for it is from the Neville lands the threat will come. From Middleham and Sheriff Hutton."

"What is the King's intent by holding this council?"

"What do you think, Meg?" He looked solemnly at me. "He will imprison the instigators of trouble in the realm…or rather, your father will see that their malice is subdued on the King's behalf. York will be his first target."

I chewed my lips nervously and stared at my feet. I imagined father was eager for retribution and a restoration of his honour, but this action—it seemed too soon, too obvious, not subtle. I blinked, and behind my eyes, saw images of men fighting, falling, dying. Banners lay strewn about, torn and bloodied, and gore sank into the soil of England. In the heavens hung multiple suns, like some vision out of Revelation predicting the end of the world, and above them spun a golden crown…

"Oh Humphrey, I am afraid!" I cried, so loudly that my husband jumped in alarm. I wrung my hands together. "There will be war, Humphrey, I am sure of it. A bloody war that will rage for decades, causing the flower of manhood in England to wither and die…No family will be spared, otherwise; cousins shall fight cousins, brothers fight brothers…You must seek out my father, tell him that he must sue for peace!"

"Meg!" Humphrey caught my shoulders, shook me lightly as if trying to wake me from slumber. "What has come over you? You've always been prone to fancies, but this…I have never seen you so distraught. Put away your fears, and leave the business of men…to men. York may be troublesome, but he lacks enough support to be a real threat, especially with Percy now supporting his Grace."

My head throbbed, lightning bolts streaking in my vision. Biles swelled into my mouth. "I pray you are right. We need peace in England…we must have peace. For our son…"

"We do not have a son…yet!" he jested, and then his face grew serious and he stared at my wan face, my eyes brimming with tears. "Meg, are you…?"

I nodded weakly. "Yes…it must have happened around the time the King regained his wits. I was told not to tell you so soon, but now…"

"Come, Margaret, sit…" He was solicitous, guiding me with a gentle hand to a window seat. I could tell how he was overjoyed; his eyes glowed with pride. It made me happy too, but I could not forget.

He knelt down beside me, hand on my knee. "You must not talk of calamitous events that will not happen…You are merely having the fancies of a breeding woman. I will see that you have the best midwife sent to you—not some crone from Brecknock—and I will apply to the Pope for a dispensation so that you may eat meat on Fast Days. Often, I think you look far too pale and thin, Meg—you must endeavour to guard your health, for the sake of our child…our son…"

"I will, Humphrey, I promise." I clasped his hands; they felt so warm, while my own were freezing. "But I beg you tell me…will you stay with me in Brecknock? Or must you go to Leicester?"

"Of course I must go to Leicester," said Humphrey, blinking as if shocked that I should suggest otherwise, baby or no. "It is important. My father will be attending the King…"

"Can you not leave it in his capable hands, just this once?" I murmured, meek, head hanging.

"I am the Duke of Buckingham's eldest son. His heir. I must be seen to support my sire and the King, not dawdling at home with my breeding wife. If any of the courtiers got word of such a thing, I would find myself the laughing stock of the court." He glanced at my dejected face and softened his words. "It is not that I would not prefer to stay with you at Brecknock, but remember, one day I will rise from earl to duke. I must make sure all men respect me."

"I understand, Humphrey," I forced an insincere smile. I could hardly see his face through the flashing lights of my megrim. "I-I will await your return with great eagerness. May you come home soon bearing good news."

"York and his Neville accomplices in the Tower would be good," said Humphrey. "My poor mother, seeing her brother Salisbury and nephew Warwick leave the Lancastrian cause to attach themselves to such as Richard of York—son of a traitor who lost his head in the time of Harry Five, the King's esteemed sire. May it will end up like father like son." He laughed, clearly amused at the thought.

As my head continued to throb, I envisioned battle again. I took a deep breath, shuddering as I thought I smelled the iron tang of spilt blood. It was likely only coming from the kitchens where the butcher had brought fresh meat that morn—I'd spied a great bloody haunch hanging by the door—but nevertheless the odour sickened me. I leaned back against the stonework of the window, fixing my blurred gaze on the carved angel corbels looming above. I tried to focus on them, ancient and tangible, to bring me back in touch with reality.

"You have grown pale again," said Humphrey worriedly. "Best you rest, my dearest. I must get ready to ride to join my father and the King. If I see your sire, shall I give him any message?"

"Inform him of my happy state," I said, in a faint voice. "Tell him I fain would see him after his unrightful captivity."

"He is a busy man, Meg, and will be even more so now that he has been released," said Humphrey, smiling at me as if I was some kind of simpleton. "I doubt he will ever find himself at Brecknock. But who knows how things will pan out with York in disgrace? If we can rid the land of these malcontents, who knows how far your sire might rise? Oh, the little prince Edward is here and invested as Prince of Wales, but the King is frail—if anything should happen to him? Who better to be Lord Protector than Uncle Somerset?"

He went away then, leaving my ladies, who had been discreetly sewing behind a painted screen in the corner of the solar, to fuss and cosset me before leading me to the supposed serenity of my chamber.

But the old ghosts were haunting me, and the sharp spring winds were screeching like demons round the towers, and the clouds that scudded by the windows assumed the shapes of armoured knights with sharp lances rising stampeding horses down the storm.

As spring bloomed from grim winter, the skies over Brecknock brightened, sunshine stippling the hurrying clouds. Flowers bloomed on the riverbanks, sun-bright Lent-Lilies, early Umbellifers, Kingcup and Lady's Smock. I had received the dispensation to avoid fasting and I was filling out in every way, my belly beginning to slowly grow round. The child had stayed, safe and secure within my belly, my fervent prayers to Our Lady, St Anne and St Elizabeth bearing fruit. A few times I even felt him—I was convinced it would be a boy—move inside my womb, a vague fluttering, a tickle, a tap. I imagined him, fully formed, playing at my feet, gambolling with the hounds, a strong boy like his father pounding his way into the world, eager to take his place amongst his great ancestors, the Stafford and Beauforts. A child of the blood of Kings.

Lent came and Palm Sunday, where I brought newly-cut Yew into the castle chapel and my ladies brought armloads of river-reeds to represent the palm leaves that signified Christ's walk into Jerusalem. Maundy Thursday followed and I went into Brecknock to perform acts of charity to the poor, giving them new garments and shoes as was customary. My old dresses were also given to my ladies and other articles of clothing were doled out to the castle servants. I sent Jennet to the tailor in Abergavenny to fetch a dress in silver brocade that I had ordered for myself, and a deep damson doublet as a present for Humphrey upon his return.

Then it was a special, solemn Mass, repeated on Good Friday and Holy Saturday—the *Tenebrae*, when all the candles were extinguished slowly, one by one, to remind the faithful of the darkness that fell at the time of the Crucifixion.

Easter Sunday itself dawned a blessed day indeed, the weather fair, the sky cloud-free. A grand procession ranged from town and castle to the doors of the priory, singing hymns that filled the air with beauty greater than birdsong. The priest admitted the flock into their section of the nave, separated from the monks' area by the bridge by the Rood, and a joyous Mass was read, and the Eucharist, forbidden in the days of the Triduum, returned once more.

I stood at the forefront of the congregation with my attendant, all wearing our new raiment, and I marvelled that the priory seemed a place of light and splendour, sacred to the Lord, all imagined darkness of the past driven away forever.

Returning to the castle, the Great Hall was lined with tables for the Easter Feast. Eggs in abundance lay in woven baskets, some waiting to be eaten, others for decoration, painted red for Christ's blood and bearing murals of the Cross or coverings of thin gold leaf. A few were hidden in nooks and crannies for the servant's children to find, reminding them how Christ had risen from the tomb on Easter. "Remember, Huw, this egg is not just a plaything," I heard one of the kitchen staff say as his young son held up a red egg in triumph after finding it inside a niche. "Remember that a great rock was rolled out from our Lord's tomb, just like this big round egg that you've pried from that hole in the wall. The tomb beyond was empty, meaning that our Lord had risen."

I smiled, as I imagined telling my own unborn child of the sacrifice that Christ made for us all. To worship the King of Kings before any earthly King…

Abruptly my thoughts went to King Henry, wrapped in his none-to-clean robes, sitting in Leicester with Father, who whispered imprecations against York into his ear, heart burning with constant anger over his shaming imprisonment. I desired York gone from court as much as any, and by any means, but I did not want war. Humphrey had chided me for expressing my fears, but it was impossible to pretend the situation in England was not still volatile. One day, this battle of cousins might well impact my unborn son…

My smile fading, I seated myself on the dais, with notables from the area on the benches near me. I resolved to keep my spirits high, despite my sombre thoughts. It was Easter. It was a time of both prayer and rejoicing. I curved my lips in a forced smile as a trumpet sounded and the servers entered carrying bowls and platters full of food.

Three courses were served, the attendees eating ravenously after their time of deprivation during Lent. First course was a mushroom soup with shredded leek and heavy spices, saffron colouring it a vivid daffodil yellow. This was followed by mutton with minced onions, stewed in a broth of wine, vinegar, pepper, salt and cinnamon. Last was the sweet course—fried bread pudding, heaped with raisins and dripping with sugar and golden honey.

After the banquet was over, I felt pleased, the author of a great success. I had finally shown myself to be a lady of quality like my mother. At nigh on eighteen years, it was time I stopped hiding in the background like a witless young girl and took my place. I only wished that Humphrey was not away at that unhappy council meeting in Leicester. Still, I must fight my tendency to worry, for the sake of the babe—my womanish fears must not transfer to him. He must grow strong and proud, the perfect blend of Stafford and Beaufort.

Shortly after Easter, which had fallen late in that year of 1455, came May Day, a feast day sacred to St Phillip and St Jacob. Now the town of Brecknock truly erupted in to life, but any saintly associations with this Holy Day were swiftly forgotten. By chance or design, the Saints' feast fell upon a day the locals called Calan Mai or Calan Haf, and it was a time of unbridled frolics and celebration amongst the ordinary folk of the town.

All through the streets surged dancers and fiddlers, men with straw effigies upon their shoulders, women in tall hats and gaudy ribbons, green-clad archers who resembled Robin Hood of the old legends.

I walked out with my ladies and several servants. Anchoret followed closely at my heels and Jennet behind her. In the last few months, Anchoret and I had developed a friendliness that had not been there at first. I had grown to trust, she to respect.

"I have heard they dance the Maypole in the village where Father held his manor," I told her, "but my nurses and my lady-mother would never let me even watch, let along join in. I assume this festival is much the same in character."

"Calan Mai is one of the *Ysprydnos*, the spirit nights of the year," said Anchoret gaily. She was clad in green, rich as grass, setting off her fair skin and dark hair and eyes. Her cheeks were flushed with colour. "A girl can divine her future husband on such a night …"

"Divination? But surely that is wicked!" I said, shocked.

Her cheeks darkened and she glanced away. "Even so, folk will do what they always have done. It stops none going to church and praying the next day."

We meandered on through the town. The air was smoky, blue, heavy with the scent of fires. Many fires.

"They were burning the bone fires last night and they'll do the same tonight," murmured Anchoret, sniffing the air.

"And where do they do that?" I had been so timid the prior year that I had never stepped from the castle gate unless absolutely necessary, so still knew little of what took place beyond the sturdy walls. "In the town square?"

"Oh no, no…." She shook her head. "On the hillside in the dark of the trees. I do not think the priests would much like what goes on."

I shuddered with good Christian revulsion… but in truth, I found it almost a delicious fear, to learn such wickedness had survived the centuries.

"If there's been sickness in the flocks, the men might make…a sacrifice. To the flames." Eyes glistening, she leaned close. "Kind of like they did with Moloch, but not with children, of course. Not *now*…"

I shivered again, clasping my hands over my stomach. "Now I believe you are just trying to frighten me, Anchoret," I said sternly. "That is most unkind…in my condition."

Contrite, she bowed her head. "My Lady, I have a foolish, quick tongue. Forgive me."

Up ahead, I heard shrieks and uproarious laughter, and as the crowds swept apart, I saw two men facing each other on opposite sides of the town's market cross. One wore black rags and carried a hefty blackthorn club and a wooden shield covered in bleached lamb's wool. His visage was smeared with black ashes. His opponent's face was whitened by flour and blossoms decked his hair; his long tunic was bleached linen, and he carried a willow withy tied with bright ribbons. The two shouted mocking insults at each other as they circled like a pair of angry bulls. They spoke in Welsh, so I could not follow them.

"What on earth is going on?" I whispered into Anchoret's ear.

"Have you not guessed, my Lady?" She grinned, teeth white pearls. "One represents Winter, the Other Summer, and they must fight for supremacy on this day. Summer always wins, though…"

In the square, Summer and Winter began to smite each other with club and willow withy, re-creating the wild battle of the seasons, railing against each other just as storms often railed against the walls of Brecknock Castle. Round and round in circles they went, battering and pummelling, Summer darting away before Winter's onslaught, Winter throwing up his shield to protect from the sting of Summer's flailing withies.

Suddenly, Summer discarded his weapon and grasped Winter's fleecy shield in both hands. A loud crack rang out across the marketplace, the townsfolk shrieked and clapped, and the shield clattered to the cobbles in two halves. Winter gave a bellow of despair and fell to the ground, drawing one-half of his broken shield to cover his face. He then kicked his legs theatrically before lying still.

"Winter is slain and Summer is here!" cried the victor, dancing around his foe's fallen form, and as if by some sorcery, the clouds that had hung over the town since dawn ripped asunder to reveal a glowing sun.

More cheers burst from the surrounding crowd, and maidens hurled petals into the air that fell like springtime snow. Flutes were blown and harps strummed, and the May festivities continued.

I began to feel a little tired and my back had started to ache. Even though my pregnancy was not all that advanced, I was definitely growing rounder—I wondered if my baby would be huge, a thought rather fearsome for a first-time mother. Yet if he was, surely it would mean he was strong, and like to grow into a great warrior....

"I think it is time to retire to the castle, Anchoret, Jennet." I gestured to my maids. "The cobbles are hard on the feet and back."

The women nodded in agreement and we headed back towards the river and the stone gatehouse, my other household attendants trailing in the rear, some munching on cakes or pastries they had purchased from hawkers at the festival.

As we neared the drawbridge, an old woman shuffled in front of the party, grinning. "Hey, my pretty lady, all dazzling as the sun that shines!" she croaked. She spoke in clear English so her comments were obviously directed to me.

Confused, I halted. Was she wishing to petition me, the lady of Brecknock? Or was she expecting alms? She looked poor, her garments stained and ragged and her hair matted beneath a filthy linen wimple.

"You bear a treasure, don't you, milady?" she croaked, hobbling closer while leaning heavily on a knotty walking stick. I noticed it was blackthorn, like the club born by Winter in the ritual fight. Blackthorn was a tree of ill-repute, even in England. A tree of death, of witches, of binding and blasting…

"Treasure? I have no coins to give you, grandmother," I said. "Today is not a day for almsgiving. You missed that at Easter. If you need a crust or bread of place to rest your weary feet, the priory is close by…"

"The treasure is what you carry beneath your belt…" She stared hard at my midriff, making the hair on the back of my neck rise. With a little gasp, I crossed my arms defensively across myself.

"I knew it," cackled the old woman. Her teeth were ragged, the top ones missing through decay or fighting, leaving but one yellow stump. "Would you like me this Calan Mai to tell the babe's fortune…and yours?"

Anchoret paled to the roots of her hair. She clutched at my sleeve. "My Lady, come away. Do not go near her. Do not look at her. She's not a fortune teller, she's mad…"

I heard Jennet, protecting my back, mutter in a fearful tone, "*Gwiddonod…*"

Then the two maids were hustling me at some speed over the lowered drawbridge and towards the gatehouse. Scorned, the old woman, began to screech and shout, calling out imprecations. "He'll grow up as proud…and stupid…as his forebears, mark my words. Then they'll cut him down…cut him down, and your pride will be cut down too, and you'll be no one…All that great high and mighty royal blood and it will run red…"

"Do not listen!" cried Anchoret, pushing me on. "She raves, that is all."

"But-but she is cursing my child…my baby!" I sobbed. Overhead, the sun, so bright in the marketplace, was wrapped in ever-darkening clouds yet again. A drizzly rain began to descend, soaking out garments and hennins.

"Pay no heed; let us get inside!" Anchoret and Jennet dragged me, half-tripping on my long hem, under the gatehouse arch and into the bailey. Behind, I heard the guards call out, ordering the mad old woman to stay back. I heard the inner doors clang shut—a comfort—and stood in the tower's gloom, breathing heavily.

When I had recovered, I turned to my ladies. "You said a word when that crone was after me," I said to Jennet. "What did it mean?"

The girl hung her head. "Nothing, milady; it meant nothing."

"Anchoret?" I turned sharply to my favourite maid. I trusted her not to lie to me. "You must have heard. What did Jennet call the old woman?"

Anchoret took a deep breath. "*Gwiddonod.* She called her…a witch."

I could not get the old woman—the witch—out of my mind, no matter what I did. My tiring women sang around me, trying a tactic of distraction—I sent them away, my skull aching from the noise. Instead, I went to the chaplain and relayed my fears. "She was not a witch, Lady Margaret," he told me solemnly, with a shake of his head. "Just a poor tormented old soul whose mind wanders…I have seen her here before; she comes down from the mountains to beg. She deserves Christian charity…"

"Not when she threatens my family," I said. "If I see her again, I will see she's bound to a ducking stool or goes into the gaol."

He bowed his head and, face burning, I stormed out of the castle chapel, angry that the chaplain had not leapt to my defence and called for a hunt to find and punish the witch. Beneath my belt, the baby kicked. I leaned against the wall, feeling suddenly dizzy. Oh Jesu, how I wished for some word from Humphrey!

Over the next few days, disturbing tidings began to reach Brecknock borne by wanderers, carters, journeymen and mendicant friars passing through towards Abergavenny or Pembroke. The King and his councillors had not reached Leicester. York's army, swollen by the forces of Salisbury and Warwick, had blocked the road and was advancing towards

London. Henry had departed the city with his own forces, but no one had any hope this encounter would end well or peacefully.

At night in the chapel, I cast myself onto the floor, the cold flagstones biting through my robes, and begged God to spare my husband and our King. Although he was no warrior himself, King Henry had stalwart men around him—Buckingham and Humphrey, my father Somerset, my brother Hal, newly come to court, Lord Clifford, Lord Percy of Northumberland, and Jasper Tudor. Surely, he would prevail against his enemies. Once the Royal Standard was unfurled, to ride against him would be considered High Treason, deserving of death.

The news of battle came as May died away in a blaze of summery heat. The May-trees still bore white blossoms, although they showed signs of decline, and their fragrance hung sickly on the air. Like the blackthorn, these hawthorn trees were considered unlucky by many folk, and their rancid, cloying scent, to my offended nose, bore the faint tang of the abattoir.

I was on the castle walls, savouring a spell of rare sunlight, when I noticed a cloud of dust in the distance. Riders, galloping at great speed, nearing the town walls. A premonition of doom swept over me. Hastily I descended from the wooden wall-walk and went into the solar, where I summoned my two ladies. "I saw riders," I warned, "soon they shall be at the gate."

"Surely it is good news, my lady?" said Jennet, with a forced smile. "I am sure the King, with Lord Humphrey and the Duke, will have prevailed against his foes."

"The horsemen galloped at great speed. They bore the air of urgency—not victory."

"Did you see any devices on their cloaks, my lady?"

I shook my head. "Too far to see, but there were no banners."

"It may be nothing," said Anchoret, but I heard the doubt in her voice. "They may not even be from England, for all we know."

But I knew they were, as sure I lived and breathed. I closed the window shutters, despite the brightness of the day, and motioned for a servant to light some candles. Taking a deep breath, I sat in my chair and waited.

Time passed; minutes felt like hours. Sweat made the back of my neck clammy and moist. Then…commotion in the hallway. Raised voices. Men's heavy feet. Anchoret glanced over, expression caught between pity and concern. I focussed my attention on the door.

There was a brief silence before the Steward entered, flustered and pale. "My Lady…" His voice shook. "Messengers have arrived from the Earl…"

From the Earl. So he is alive…Perhaps the King is victorious!

My heart leapt hopefully, but then I saw the courier, standing outside the door, caked with mud, face drawn and sorrowful. This was not the appearance of one who brought news of victory.

"Enter." I nodded in his direction.

The man limped in and went down on one knee. "My Lady Countess, I bring news from the Earl. A battle has been fought at St Alban's between the forces of the King and Richard, Duke of York…"

"Bring this man some bread and wine!" I ordered a loitering servant, as the courier swayed on his knee, looking as if he might drop to the floor in a faint. I motioned Jennet to bring him a stool. "Speak on, sir, if you can," I said to him as gently as I might. "First, tell me of my husband, the Earl of Stafford."

"His lordship is injured, Lady Margaret. The monks look after him in the Abbey there, alongside Humphrey, Duke of Buckingham, and the King himself."

"The King is wounded?" I cried, and a horrified murmur rippled between the ladies at my back. I waved my hand for them to fall silent. "How has this come to be? Start…start at the beginning, sir."

The man took a gasping, strained breath and lifted his head. His eyes were a pale, washed-out blue, streaked by red veins from exhaustion. "My Lady, I will tell you, but the tale comes hard to my lips." At that moment, the servant turned up with a mazer of wine; the man took a grateful slurp, wiped his mouth on his sleeve, and continued his story. "The King was not prepared for York's swift approach and his available forces numbered at least a thousand less than his enemy. There had been some…discussion…about who might lead the royal forces; first, the King gave the position to your noble father, Countess, but then he changed his mind and reassigned the captaincy to his Grace, the Duke of Buckingham."

I was astonished at his words, but perhaps it should have come as no surprise. My father was the King's 'dearest cousin' but even in his addled state, he must have recognised that my sire's hatred of York might lead to rashness. No, solid, dependable Buckingham was the better choice…although Father must have fumed to have been passed over.

"York sent messages to the royal army from Roystone," the courier continued. "One letter was to the Lord Chancellor. York said hostilities would cease if Somerset were removed from all his posts immediately."

"The knave!" My cheeks flamed. "How dare he issue such an ultimatum!"

"The letter was ignored, of course, but Duke Edmund's position was not entirely secure. Some of the King's advisors and other lords believed his Grace should parlay with York and hear his grievances. As Richard of York's army arrived and camped in Key Fields just outside of St Alban's, heralds came and went, bearing messages between York and the King, who was now encamped in the town centre. I fear to tell you of the viler contents of the Duke's letters…his demands." He hung his head.

"You need not be ashamed of a traitor's actions. What is your name, sir, so that I can call you by it?"

"Rufus, my Lady. Rufus Gray."

"Well, Rufus, I ask you again to speak plainly. You are amongst friends here. For all the bad tidings you bear, you must fear no censure or punishment. You are loyal to Lancaster, are you not?"

"No one is more loyal, my Lady", said Rufus Grey. He pushed back a fold of his Great Coat to show a battered swan badge. "I beg you doubt me not. But I am loathe to offend your ears, to wound the tender heart of such a high and noble lady."

"Please, put your fears aside. I must know all. It is my duty."

He took another deep breath, his eyes fixed at some spot on the wall beyond my shoulder where hung a tapestry of knights engaged in the melee. With a jolt, I realised that not only was Gray reporting from the field…he had witnessed the battle, maybe even participated in it.

"The Duke of York, Salisbury and Warwick sent out stronger demands that Somerset be surrendered to them or they would commence with hostilities. They wanted him to face a trial—my Lady, I think you understand what that would mean."

The blood turned to ice in my veins. "It would have been a sham trial. They would have executed him then and there."

Rufus Gray nodded. "The King refused, as expected. However, he made a dreadful mistake. He still believed York would not attack, that he would continue to press for terms. Instead, at mid-morn, the Duke and Salisbury attacked, each one assailing the barricades set up across the main thoroughfares during the night." He sighed, put down the mazer, and closed his eyes, remembering. "For a while, the Royal Army held them back. It looked as if they could gain no purchase—but the King's men had forgotten about the Earl of Warwick, Richard Neville. He led the reserve, amongst them a contingent of five hundred archers. Like cravens, they crept through the back lanes and alleys and gardens of the town, hiding behind fences and walls. Eventually, they broke into Hollowell Street, where they sprayed the men defending the barricades with arrows before storming on into the market square."

"And…and where was the King then? And Buckingham? And…and my husband the Earl?"

"The King was in the Square, not even in his armour." Gray let out a piteous groan, his hands shaking as they lay on his knees. "An arrow grazed his neck and he ran for aid into a tanner's shop. Buckingham made to accompany him, but an arrow struck his face and he fell. The Earl of Stafford…" Gray swallowed, his Adam's Apple rising and falling… "he went to defend his father and an arrow hit him in the arm. As he stumbled, a pikeman stabbed him in the thigh…"

I choked back the scream forming in my throat.

"But he is alive, my lady, as I told you. Members of the Buckingham retinue bore both Duke and Earl into the abbey where the monks treated their wounds."

I was desperate now, for there were yet others unaccounted whom I loved. My brother Henry—Hal—had gone with Father to fight his first battle. He was only nineteen and accounted one of the handsomest knights in England. He and I were close in age, only a year apart, and had in earliest youth spent much time together, where he teased me with worms and mice…but with jollity, not with malice. "My brother…the Earl of Dorset," I gasped. "Have you word of his fate?"

Gray's eyes flicked nervously around the chamber. "I am glad to say he lives, Lady Stafford…but he was also sore wounded. He had to be carried forth in a cart."

A cry tore from my lips at the thought of brave, comely Hal lying pale and bleeding in some slovenly cart. But he lived…*he lived*….

"What about my sire, the Duke of Somerset?" I suddenly blurted. "Hal would have fought at his side."

"And so he did, Countess," whispered Rufus Gray, voice hoarse and tremulous. "The Duke and the Earl were in the Castle Inn and had bolted themselves inside, but Somerset…he knew he could not stay there forever, trapped like a rat. The foe would break in or burn him out. He vowed never to be taken in that manner. Instead, he flung himself out of the door with the Earl of Dorset at his side, sword in hand. The Duke cut down four men before the forces of York overwhelmed him."

"O-overwhelmed…" I stammered, unable to believe the worst. Surely they must have captured him…taken him for ransom. He was worth money…

The messenger crossed himself. "My Lady, his Grace the Duke of Somerset died there outside The Castle Inn, fighting for his sovereign. God rest his soul."

I sprang from my seat, an agonised gasp tearing from my lips, and then collapsed upon the floor in a swoon.

They brought Humphrey back to Brecknock Castle in a litter. I watched as the servants and squires carried him through the door on a bier, swaddled in linen, his face a pale moon on the cushion they had placed beneath his head. He did not move as he was carried past me as I stood watching, horrified; his eyes were screwed shut. He looked like a dead man awaiting his burial.

In silence, I followed the bier to his bedchamber, prepared for his arrival over the last few days. I had rushed about, trying to make the room as pleasant as possible, tearing down old tapestries and replacing them, throwing warm rugs upon the floor, adding candelabras for extra light, scenting the draperies and the bed curtains and linens with bags of fragrant herbs. I had made sure there a jug of watered wine stood beside the bed and had placed a carving of the Virgin made from Nottingham alabaster in a niche in the wall, where she glowed pale honey in the candlelight.

Humphrey did not even look around as he was lifted into the bed and the coverlet pulled up to his neck, although I saw his eyes flicker beneath the lids. He had lost weight as if everything he had endured had sucked his strength away. His attendants had washed his flesh with rose water, but underneath I could smell a vague scent that reminded me of the sickly aroma of the faerie blackthorn—the smell of putrid flesh.

Stepping forward, I told his squires and body servants to leave. They crept away like mice, downcast. I sat on the edge of the bed with its tester patterned with silvered antelopes and clutched his hand—his uninjured hand—in mine. The fingers did not engage with mine and his palm felt damp and sticky. The other hand, wrapped in heavy bandages, lay at his side.

"Humphrey?" I said quietly, releasing his hand, which flopped onto the coverlet like a dead fish. "Are you awake? Can you hear me?"

He stirred and his lids flickered. The eyes that gazed on me were dulled by illness, lifeless. "Meg…" he muttered.

Emotions overwhelmed me and I wept openly. I could find no words.

"Why...why do you weep?" His voice sounded like gravel. He barely sounded like the man I knew.

"For joy, my dearest lord—that you are alive and returned to me." It was not the entire truth, but I *was* glad. The situation could have been much worse.

"Alive..." he spat, and his lips pulled back in an unnerving death-rictus grin, "but maybe it was better I had died at St Alban's."

"How could you say such a terrible thing?"

He struggled up on his elbows; his hair was matted against the side of his head, darkened by sweat. "We failed the King..."

"But Henry lives. York did not harm him."

"I failed my own father...and your father too, Meg. I know what they did to him at the Castle Inn. He was...unrecognisable..."

Bile burnt my mouth. How could Humphrey speak so coldly? His face was contorted, twisted, almost as if he enjoyed the pain he brought with his words. He felt agony and shame, and he sought to infect me with his own grief. "I beg you, do not speak of the manner of my sire's death. It is enough to know he is dead."

"Christ..." Suddenly, he collapsed back against the bolster, an unhealthy flush creeping on his cheeks. A bead of sweat trickled down his neck. "At night...sometimes I wish I had died with him and I pray God to release me from earthly bonds."

"I-I do not understand." I grabbed a linen napkin from the bedside and wiped the sweat from him. "Yes, you are wounded, but you are young and strong. You will heal in time..."

"Do you think so, woman?" His brows raised. "Look you at this..." He struggled to lift his swaddled hand. "I have lost two fingers. I will not hold a sword again. But that is not the worst of it..." He tore back the bed coverings with his uninjured hand and yanked up his long nightshirt. He had more bandages below, wrapped tightly around his right thigh. Blood and matter oozed from the wound beneath, and that rank smelt of rot rose up, making me gag. I could not help myself; I turned away, retching.

"See?" he shouted, almost triumphantly. "Even you, my wife, turn from me now. I shall be lucky if the leg wound does not kill me—and if it does not, I may be a cripple all my life!" His visage suddenly crumpled and he began to weep harshly, a sound that appalled me. I was not used to seeing men cry and never had Humphrey wept in my presence.

"A doctor is coming from the town." I leaned forward, steadying him, hoping my touch would bring some small comfort. "The best in the region. He will heal you."

"Some things never heal."

"You must be strong," I said, desperate. "You must not give up hope. Remember, soon you are to be a father…"

Reaching out, I drew his good hand to my belly. "He kicks strongly every day…your son."

He jerked away as if my very touch hurt him. "If I am a cripple, it would better I died ere he came to know me. Now go, Meg; I want no one around me to witness my shame, my weakness. No one, do you understand? Now get out!"

I was too stunned to even cry. It was as if he had stabbed me to the heart.

In a daze, I left him, lying corpse-like in that bed. Outside the door, I slumped against the wall and the tears fell, while inside, my unborn babe kicked out strongly, new life amidst all this injury and death…

Humphrey improved but little. A physician came, re-bound his hand and cauterised the gash in his leg. I blocked my ears against my husband's screams by having Jennet and Anchoret sing in Welsh as loudly as they could. Ugly events could scar the infant in the womb and I did not wish to risk my child. If anything should happen to Humphrey, the babe was all I had.

After finishing the cruel treatment and drugging Humphrey with poppy-juice, the doctor was escorted to my solar, funereal in black robes that swished on the rushes. "I believe he will live," he said. "The thigh wound was not as badly infected as I feared and the bad flesh has been burnt away. His hand knits well; I can do nought for missing fingers but the bones that were broken by the arrow's strike are joining back together."

"He still seems so ill…so desolate," I said.

"His Lordship's bodily fever has broken, yet, in mind, he remains fevered. He blames himself for all ills at St Alban's, but with luck, if he regains his feet, that may pass. His fear of becoming a bedridden cripple holds him back also."

"And your assessment?" I asked. "Will he walk again?"

"He might, but it is in God's hands, my Lady. I fear he will always have a limp and may need to use a crutch."

I moaned in despair. "He is a proud man. To be so incapacitated will destroy him. He is the eldest son, set to inherit a Dukedom one day…"

"You must convince him that he has much to live for." The physician nodded towards my rounded middle. "Watching his own heir grow tall and strong may yet bring him pleasure."

*Or envy…*I thought. Or sorrow that he will never spar with the boy using wooden swords or joust against him in mock tourneys in the castle yard. Nonetheless, I dared not say such things aloud. I must believe all would turn out well.

Humphrey, at least, would not die.

As my pregnancy progressed, Humphrey's melancholy grew, as I feared it might. He had tried to rise and collapsed, unable to walk further than the door. He had returned to his bed, where his muscle wasted, leaving his thighs stringy, his chest hollow. I tried to tempt him with delicacies brought in from the town but his appetite was poor.

His father the Duke visited once. He had healed well, although his cheek was badly scarred from the arrow that had struck him. He tried to cheer his son, but Buckingham's avoidance of news regarding the situation in London only made Humphrey wild. "You must tell me all, Father," he cried, pounding the bed with his fist. "I do not want to be mollycoddled. What has transpired since that dreadful day at St Alban's?"

"It is much as you would expect," the Duke said drily, giving in to his son's demands. "The King was not much hurt, a mere scratch despite the blood, and he was escorted back to London by

York, Salisbury and Warwick. Young Dick Neville even had the temerity to ride in the front of the procession, bearing the royal sword...Since then, York had been made Lord High Constable and Warwick appointed Captain of Calais..."

Humphrey gritted his teeth, his eyes hot and angry. "I would strike all three of those traitors down, without mercy, if I could!"

"Let us talk no more of such things," said Buckingham, his visage suddenly grown weary, old. "At least not now. The Lancastrian faction is down but not beaten—remember what a strong woman the Queen is. She will not forget...or forgive, I deem. But you need to rest..."

"Rest, rest, I do nothing but rest," shouted Humphrey. "I rest more than my wife who is heavy with child."

The Duke of Buckingham looked over at me as if he had forgotten I was in the room. He smiled sadly. "Margaret, you must grow tired of our conversation..."

"No, I do not," I said, with surprising force. "My father was killed at St Alban's, and although I am merely a woman, my desire for retribution runs as deep as any man's." I put my hand on my stomach. "Even if I can never seek justice with a sword in hand...my son may well someday."

"Margaret, Margaret, ease yourself," soothed the Duke. "Remember, your health is precarious at this time. Let us hope all such retributions are bought through the courts and *not* on the point of a blade." He touched his cheek, the scar tissue still livid red and purple. "I never thought I would gain such a wound from a fellow Englishman. We do not want this country to descend in Anarchy as in the time of old Empress Matilda, hundreds of years ago."

"Where is the King now? In the Tower?"

"No, York and his followers insist he is not a prisoner, merely being kept from the influence of 'evil councillors.' York has installed him at Hertford Castle. He may not be long there, though."

I raised my eyebrows. Buckingham grinned. "The Scots are causing trouble in the north."

Humphrey, lying on his pillow, groaned in angst. "Not the bloody Scots, too!"

"Hush, my son," said the Duke. "This time, their depredations may prove a boon."

"How so?" said Humphrey, propping himself up on his elbow. "They loot and burn."

"So they do. York and his cronies have many holdings up north and will not wish to see them go up in flames. They will sally forth to beat the Scots back. When that time comes, I believe the Queen will show her own strength and take the King back into her keeping. Never underestimate her, for all that she is a woman. If not for the King, she will fight tooth and nail for her son, the young prince."

Later, when the Duke and I had left Humphrey to the ministrations of the physician, my father-in-law walked with me in the gardens. The bees buzzed in the lavender and crawled on the sun-baked castle walls. Hollyhocks nodded, Columbines were a riot of colour. Passing under a trellis wreathed with fragrant roses, we came to a turf seat embedded with herbs that, when sat upon, would be crushed, releasing their sweet fragrance into the air.

"Do you mind if I sit, Margaret?" asked Duke Humphrey. "I am getting old, and my back is stiff—and the wound in my face still pains me. I must see your physic for a sleeping draught tonight, I fear."

"Of course, you must rest," I took his arm and guided him to the seat.

"You must sit too, my dear." He patted the seat beside him with his sword-calloused hand. "You carry the hope of the Stafford family."

I sat next to him, the scent of the herbs rising about me, clean and pungent. "I worry that you put so much on me, your Grace—Humphrey is surely still your 'hope.'"

"He is crushed at the moment," sighed Buckingham. "His first battle, and it ended in disaster. But he will rise again, I am sure...."

"You are not sure, though are you, your Grace?" I murmured. "I saw it in your face when you looked at him."

"One can never be certain, Margaret. You must be the one to give him encouragement, so that he might live again, no matter how his wounds heal."

"Maybe your 'hope' might better lie on the shoulders of your other son, Henry…"

"Ah Henry…" Buckingham leaned back against the intertwining greenery shading the seat. "He has issues of his own. Almost thirty summers, and still not wed…My younger boy, John, too—hawks and hounds are all he can think of, not domesticity." He smiled wryly. "I have a pretty little ward, Constance Green, who I think might suit, but he shows no interest as yet. So it really is up to you, my dear, to keep this old man happy."

"What if my child is a girl?" I said, half-teasing. "I feel in my heart that it is not, but I am not a soothsayer to predict."

"Nor should you be. If the child be a girl, Margaret, I will be just as happy, and secretly I think my Anne would like a granddaughter, especially now that our girls are growing up, with Nan and Joanna already wed and plans for Katherine's nuptials slowly progressing." He gave a theatrical sigh. "It has proved painful to have so many daughters—their dowries hurt my coffers just as their departures hurt my heart."

Despite being a great magnate and statesman, the Duke always managed to make me laugh. At first, I had been nervous in his presence, having heard he had an ungovernable temper, but if he did, I had never seen it. Perhaps he had mellowed with age as some men do. Perhaps Humphrey's moods would decrease with time too—but first he had to be healed, body and soul.

"And how are you, Margaret?" inquired the Duke. "After all, you have taken a grievous wound to the heart, not only Humphrey bedridden, but you have lost…"

"My father," I murmured. "I know so little, only the horrors Humphrey told me. I wrote to my mother, but as yet she has not written back. Now she is a widow…I am sure I am last in her thoughts." *I always seemed to be last even before…* "My Lord Duke, will you at least tell me if you know—where does my father's body lie?"

"Fear not, my dear, Duke Edmund safe lies within the abbey of St Alban's, honourably buried by the monks in the Lady Chapel."

I bowed my head, tears springing to my eyes against my will. It was so hard to imagine my sire, so haughty, proud and active, cold clay beneath unloving stone. "It was so strange," I mumbled, half to myself, "where he was killed."

"An Inn called The Castle. Why is that strange?"

I feared my explanation would make me sound foolish but grief loosened my tongue. "When I was small, Father came into the hall, angry and bemused. 'You know what happened today?' he asked my mother. "I was at the trial of the noted witch, Magery Jourdemain, the Witch of Eye. She waggled a finger at me and warned me to 'shun all castles.' Can you imagine, a man of my estate shunning castles? Would she have me live in a barn, the vile old fool?' Everyone laughed, but it seems Jourdemain's prophecy was true, though it was not a fortress he needed to fear, but a tavern of that name. If only Father had listened…."

"Life is full of 'if onlys'." The Duke's face was sombre.

"Yes, if only I were a man, I would ride out against those responsible…."

"I have put aside my enmity with York, as much as is possible." Buckingham stared at the sky, watching a hawk swirl over the tallest tower of the castle.

"My Lord Duke?" I blinked, surprised, feeling slightly disheartened and let down. I thought he might want revenge as much as I—for Humphrey's sake. It was not a feeling I thought I would ever know, but bad or good, the urge for bloody retribution was strong.

"I am near enough an old man. I will support and serve my King and his family but will not enjoin in any further blood feuds if such can be avoided. I put any grievances with York to rest. I will not bear a personal grudge."

"But…but what you said earlier to Humphrey…the Queen freeing the King…the Scots in the north…"

"If the Queen wants revenge for St Alban's, she will be the one to plan it—with young hotheads like your brother Henry and

Clifford's boy. Let them enact their vengeance. If a direct threat is made to the King or the prince, I will act to protect them, as I always have, but this inner fighting and bloodshed that is tearing up England…no."

He shuffled up from the turf seat in his rich, heavy robes and bid me a good day. I remained in the garden, wearing my uncomfortable mourning black, wondering what would become of us all.

The baby kicked, hard, almost painfully Yes, the Duke was right—he would have to be the hope, not just of the Staffords but the Beauforts. "Be at ease," I whispered to the unborn child through gritted teeth, my mood dark and not of womanly gentleness. "Your time will come; you will make sure our Houses rise again." I thought suddenly, unexpectedly of Joan of Arc, the Maid of Orleans, whom the Duke of Buckingham had interrogated before she was burnt at the stake—some said she was of God, some of the Devil, She certainly fought like the devil for her cause.

I would have to fight for mine in more subtle ways.

CHAPTER FIVE

Humphrey continued to brood, possessed by despair. His leg was improving…I had spied him out of bed peering longingly out the window when he did not realise I was hiding outside his door, keeping watch over him. But still he refused to come down to the Hall and had his stewards and chamberlain do all his duties He even summoned the chaplain to him for private prayer rather than attending normal mass.

I felt disloyal watching him secretly and learning the truth of his weakness, but I had to know. In order to help him, I had to. I was determined to have my husband back again as much as possible.

I asked my ladies if they knew of any healing shrines where we might take Humphrey for treatment, both for his actual wounds and for the other affliction that had grown in his mind. "But, milady, you dare not go…" Anchoret's warm brown eyes fastened on my expanding midriff. "It is not long ere you must go into confinement."

"And well I know it, but you have also seen how it is with your lord. He is afflicted in body and mind, and I would do anything to return him to his normal self before the child is born. Remember how it was when Queen Margaret birthed little Prince Edward? I would not have such a shameful start for my son."

"I do not think the Earl will think his child born of the Holy Ghost!" tittered Jennet. "He is not so ill as to have forgotten…"

"Jennet, mind your tongue," I frowned. The last thing I wished was this chatty girl to spread talk throughout the town. Undoubtedly rumours about Humphrey's health had already reached the townsfolk, but I wanted to keep the gravity of the situation as quiet as I could. Humphrey was a marcher lord and there were still many in Wales who saw us as unwelcome occupants, a hated reminder of the loss of their own kings and nobles.

Jennet bowed her head to hide her sulky expression. I glanced at Anchoret, always the best of my maids, the most faithful and intelligent.

"There *is* a place," she said thoughtfully, "at Merthyr Isiw, or Patrishow in your English tongue, a small village not too far from Abergavenny. A holy well sacred to Saint Issui lies on the hillside below the church."

"Issui? I have never heard of him."

"A Welsh saint from ages past who lived there in a cell. He was robbed and murdered by a pagan traveller, who begged for food and shelter but refused to listen to Issui when he sought to tell him of Our Lord. Issui was buried where he died and the church raised over his grave. An altar with six consecration crosses marks the spot."

"And the holy well?"

"It is rumoured to have strong healing properties. The locals leave gifts—mostly bouquets of flowers but sometimes coins, brooches or other trinkets."

"I will go there," I said. "If I can persuade the Earl."

Humphrey was not impressed at the thought of a journey. He argued with me, claimed his pain was too great, and sent me from his bedchamber like a naughty child. Again and again, I returned, unwilling to drop the subject, acting the dutiful wife and speaking in meek tones, with downcast eyes…yet I was determined to get what I wanted.

"People might see me if I went to your 'healing well'," Humphrey snarled. "I cannot ride, Meg; I would have to lie in a litter like a decrepit old woman."

"We will ride together in a chariot," I said. "The windows will be curtained. No one except our closest servants will know who is in the carriage or what our purpose might be."

"I still do not like the idea."

"If we make an offering at this shrine, maybe God…"

"I have already said a million prayers if not more!" He thumped the feather mattress as he always did when he was frustrated.

"But not at Patrishow. This Issui is a Welsh martyr…and we are in Wales. Maybe we need intercession from a Welsh saint since we live in that land. Humphrey…" I reached out to clasp his uninjured hand. "Will you not even try? For our son…Henry?"

He gave in, although with sullen face and aggravated air. Before the week was out, we were riding in a chariot towards Patrishow, accompanied only by a few soldiers and Humphrey's squire, Lewis. Anchoret came with me too, but she rode a pony at the rear of the carriage, wrapped in a heavy travelling cloak to disguise herself. Every now and then she would ride up to the chariot's window to tell me where we were. Occasionally I let Humphrey sleep and would peer out of the curtains at the landscape beyond.

Patrishow lay within the Black Mountains, in Coed Grano, the valley of Grwyne Fawr, the Great Wet River. The slopes of Rhos Dirion rose up, bald and misted, while forest cloaked the flanks of Mynydd Dhu, the Dark Mountain. It was a dim, mysterious place, heavy with an air of loss and loneliness, and I found myself running my fingers over my rosary beads, quietly praying that we would reach our destination unharmed. A beautiful land…and yet dangerous, a land where I was not truly welcome, where I did not really belong.

Anchoret was gazing around as she trotted near the carriage on her sturdy white pony. Even she seemed more nervous than usual. I cast an inquiring look in her direction. "We should reach the village soon," she said.

"I did not ask that. Why do you look so uncomfortable, Archoret?"

She gazed into the distance, squinting into the bright sunlight. "Long ago, around three hundred years, the Earl of Hereford was murdered here by Iorwerth and Morgan Ap Owain… They say the memories of evil events can linger in the land itself, fading with the years yet never fully vanishing…"

"Such foolish talk," I said, overly shrill, not wishing to hear any Welsh tales—which were often bloody and always tragic. "Next you will tell me King Arthur himself lies sleeping in a cairn on the hilltop!" I yanked the curtain back over, not wishing to see this blighted, benighted landscape any longer.

Humphrey, who had been dozing, struggled into an upright position. "Are we not there yet?" he snapped with a cross frown. "The struts of this ox-cart have made stripes across my back, I am sure of it."

I rushed to his side, trying to plump up his cushions and wrapping a rich green quilt around him. "It won't be long now, according to Anchoret," I soothed.

His face suddenly softened. "I have not been a good husband to you of late…You should not be away from the castle in your condition. We should turn around…"

"No, not when we are so close. Humphrey, I will try anything to make you better."

We reached Patrishow, a cluster of slate-roofed huts on a wooded hillside. I peered out to assess the situation. Nervous faces of women peered from slanted doorways; I assumed their men were out with flocks in the mountains and was glad of it.

A short way from the huts, down a muddy lane, stood Saint Issui's church, a tiny grey building huddled against a stand of trees and surrounded by a crumbling wall. The church's sides consisted of packed rubble, its roof of slate slabs. A preaching cross stood in the churchyard, the figures on it eroded beyond recognition by centuries of exposure and the touch of countless hands.

I called to Humphrey's squire, Lewis, who dismounted his horse and helped me to get his lord down from the chariot. Humphrey's expression was one of anger mingled with anguish at being so handled; I prayed he would hold his emotions in check and not start roaring or causing difficulty. If there was one time in his life when his pride needed to be kept in check, it was now.

"What is this Godforsaken place? Where is this bloody well?" he cried, head snapping around, his curls blowing wildly in the wind, giving him a fierce leonine appearance.

"First, the church," I said firmly, "so that we may pray before your immersion."

With my husband leaning on my shoulder, I crossed the churchyard to the church door. I opened it one-handed, my other arm around Humphrey's waist. Together we entered a fusty dimness. The church smelt cold, unused, and I wondered if they even had a priest in this remote place. Perhaps he had died and the villagers had to attend church elsewhere or wait for a priest to come in.

The outside of the church was plain but the interior as we walked up the aisle took my breath away. Smooth-sided and austere, a robust stone font stood at the heart of the nave. Words were carved in ancient script on its flank—*Menhir made me in the Time of Gelinnen*. A little further on, a Rood screen of rich red wood stretched across the chancel, adorned with images of dragons blowing, not fire, but foliage from their open jaws.

Slowly, with Humphrey's leg dragging on the floor, we approached one of the three altars within the church. I helped my husband to kneel; he winced in pain. Then I knelt at his side before the Rood, shimmering through a haze of dust motes. I tried to keep my attention on it alone, and on all that I asked of Christ and his Mother...but I found my gaze trailing around the unfamiliar building, its walls rimed with faded paintings, some with green patches of mould growing on the ancient paintwork. One stood out brighter than the others, however, as if it was continuously scraped clean while the others were left to decay and disappear—skeletal Death bearing a scythe in one hand, a dagger in the other.

I could not look away; it was as if I was entranced. My prayers became jumbled. Fortunately, Humphrey did not appear to have noticed; his head was bowed, shrouded by his hair.

Death grinned down at me as if saying, *I almost had him and maybe I still shall take*...I almost imagined I heard a whispery, grating voice, from a throat long devoid of flesh...

"We must go, Humphrey."

Next to me, my husband grunted. "Meg...what? Surely to rush is not respectful. It was your idea..."

"If the day grows too late, the water of the well might become too cold for bathing," I babbled, realising how silly I sounded.

I dreaded that he might argue, chastise me further for my inappropriate behaviour, but with a groan and a rolling of his eyes, he held out a hand. "Help me rise…if you can."

I got him up without much effort; he had lost so much weight since his injury at St Alban's. Hastily we exited the church and returned to our entourage. "We have prayed to God for hope and healing. Now we will seek the well," I said, gesturing to Anchoret and Lewis.

Surrounding Humphrey, the three of us guided him down the muddy path that led from the churchyard to the hillside below, supporting him so that he would not take an embarrassing and painful tumble while also trying our best to make it look as though he walked mainly on his own so that his dignity would not be compromised overmuch. Passing through a gate, I heard the sound of water gurgling and churning borne on the breeze.

"I hear the song of the stream Nant Mair," murmured Anchoret. "We are almost at the holy well."

I saw the brittle grey stonework of the well-covering first. As we proceeded towards it, the long grass whipping our legs, a sudden gust of wind tore apart a wreath of flowers some supplicant had laid on the stones, showering us with brown-tinged petals. Approaching from the front, we faced a deep trough of greenish water, fed from an underground source, its surface strewn with leaves. A tree overhung the well, giving a veneer of privacy; its boughs were tied with ribbons in an offering not quite holy, but as ancient as time itself. Little pebbles were laid on the three shallow steps leading down into the pool—more offerings. There were also handfuls of rusted pins, beads, trinkets.

I glanced at Humphrey's face; it was like thunder. tension in Tension knotted his back beneath my steadying hand. I caught my breath. What if he were to pull back and shout at me for bringing him hence? I could not bear the shame, the defeat…

"My lord?" his squire, Lewis, queried, anxiety written across his guileless young face. "Shall I help…"

"Yes, yes, let's get this mummery over with!" snapped Humphrey, his eyes narrowing. He pulled away and began tugging at his garments; Lewis ran to help him untie his points. Anchoret turned modestly away, admiring the view down the valley while Lewis and I helped Humphrey onto the steps descending into the healing well.

Lewis, fully clad, entered the water first until he was almost up to his waist; Humphrey joined him, taking a staggering step forward while leaning heavily on his squire's arm. "Jesu…the cold…Agh, it hurts!" he cried, his face screwed up with pain.

I leaned in, my own feet and my skirts sopping. The water was indeed like ice, biting into my calves. "I need to get out," said Humphrey, as cold as the frigid well-water. "Now."

"Just endure one moment more," I begged. "Let me say a small prayer."

"God has turned his face from me!" barked my husband and he pushed past me back onto the grass. Lewis slipped and slid after him, throwing a cloth around his lord to wipe him dry before rearranging his garments. I turned on the step into the pool and suddenly my foot landed on a submerged leaf stuck to the stone; my leg went from under me, and with a cry I plummeted forward, trying to protect my belly as I fell.

Anchoret turned and rushed towards me. Humphrey went white as milk, the rage and frustration in his face transforming into naked fear. "Meg! Oh, Christ…" He pulled away from Lewis, limping awkwardly towards me. "I should not have…"

"I-I am all right!" I gasped, struggling up from the damp earth. Inside, though, I was angry beyond words. I saw Anchoret glare at Humphrey, but of necessity she held her tongue. "Let us get back to the carriage."

Anchoret helped me up the slope towards the church while Lewis tended to Humphrey. "Are you truly hale, my lady?" asked Anchoret, with concern. "That was a nasty tumble."

"I think so," I muttered, but I felt a pulling tug in my side, slightly below my hip-bone. It was like nothing I had experienced before, but surely it was from the jolt of going down and nothing more.

"You look pale," said Anchoret. "I do not like this."

We climbed into the chariot, Anchoret leaving her pony to be led by Lewis so that she could keep an eye on my condition. As we journeyed on, Humphrey turned sullen and gloomy, glowering ahead into the carriage, gaze fixed on the canvas roof. Ignoring him, Anchoret fussed over me, bringing out candied violets and the like. Suddenly I winced; a tightening sensation crossed my belly now, running across the front, while a slightly uncomfortable pressure began in my private area. I shifted uncomfortably on my furs and quilts.

"Something is wrong; I know it!" cried Anchoret.

Now I had to agree. Tears welled in my eyes. "My back is hurting terribly and I am cramping."

"You should not have come out here. You are but a few weeks away from your lying in," said Anchoret. "It will be a long journey back…Oh Jesu, we need a proper midwife to examine you…"

Humphrey's head snapped around; his expression was so full of remorse and misery it was almost frightening. "This is my fault. Where is the closest town to this church?"

"Abergavenny, my lord," answered Anchoret.

"We will head there then…The monastery."

"The monks won't see to an expectant woman!" said Anchoret, shocked.

"No, of course not…" Humphrey ran a hand over his tormented face; sweat began to bead on his brow. "The castle then."

"The castle?" I said shakily. "Humphrey…have you forgotten who holds it now. Warwick!"

"Yes, I know, but he is not there—it is in the care of a constable. Warwick would not turn us away anyway, although he's a black-hearted bastard. York claims he wants peace. Neville is kin to you after all, though his own Beaufort heritage."

I was not so sure of a welcome greeting as Humphrey seemed to be, considering that the true Lord of Abergavenny castle was Edward Neville…but Warwick, his nephew, had taken control of it under dubious circumstances. Edward Neville had received royal licence some six years ago to enter the lands and castle, but Warwick claimed it in the right of his wife, Anne Beachamp. Edward was still known as 'Lord Bergavenny' and summoned to parliament as such, but Warwick was unwilling to let the fortress go. The Earl clearly showed no favour to *that* kinsman—although it was true that Bergavenny made little complaint, perhaps because of obtaining other rewards from within the Yorkist party.

Nonetheless, I knew I must decide. The cramping was worse, coming in slow, incessant waves. Abergavenny town was closer than Brecknock, so there we must fare.

"Anchoret," I called to my maid. "Tell the guards and drivers that we must hasten to Abergavenny without further delay. This is the will of their Lord, the Earl of Stafford."

Anchoret thrust her head out of one of the narrow windows and shouted at the top of her voice to the rest of the party, her tone full of stark insistence and surprisingly authoritative. I felt the carriage begin to rock as the drivers cracked the whip, the bumps in the rutted track adding to my discomfort. Humphrey had grown quiet again; clearly disturbed by both his own pain and the unease all men felt about womanly matters. At that moment, I cared nothing about how he fared—I cared only for the safety of my baby.

By the time we reached Abergavenny, my discomfort had become mild pain and dampness wet my skirts. "Will it be all right, Anchoret?" I clutched my maid's hand tightly. "The birth was not expected quite so soon."

"Babes can come early or late," she reassured. "Although you had a little jolt that may have woken him up before time, you are not so early that we might expect…problems."

The entourage came to a halt outside Abergavenny Castle's large barbican, added on to a simple gateway after the battles with Owain Glyn Dwr earlier in the century. Above the two towers, one round, the other a polygon, fluttered the Neville saltire. Enemy territory, but what choice did I have but to trust the inhabitants?

Lewis, acting on his master's behalf, walked boldly to the gate, which at this time of day stood open, allowing folk from near and far to go about their business in the bailey. He called to the gate warden, "Summon your Lord Constable. The Earl of Stafford and his lady-wife are without your walls."

"Oh, are they now?" asked the warden, a fat man in a leather tunic, jingling his ring of keys as he wandered over to peer into the chariot. His broad face filled the window as Anchoret hauled back the curtain, and the man leapt back in surprise. "God's teeth, so it is! My Lord, my Lady—what brings you here?"

Humphrey had dragged himself into a dignified upright position. "My wife is with child and it seems her travail has come upon her. I beg your master take pity on a woman in her condition. For all the enmities that have burst into flame across England, Lady Margaret is still kin to Richard Neville and his sire Salisbury, and to Lord Bergavenny…Treat her well, and it shall not be forgotten…" His lips thinned, his eyes narrowing, telling the man without words that if I was ill-treated *that* would not be forgotten either.

"I shall go find the Constable at once," huffed the warden, face red, and he stomped away into the castle grounds, the clatter of his keys growing fainter and fainter.

It seemed an eternity before he returned, this time accompanied by the Constable. A well-dressed man with a dark, earnest face peered into the carriage as his predecessor had done, assessing the situation. A Yorkist rose gleamed on his collar. "I am Richard Herbert, Constable of Abergavenny castle; I have sent the servants to prepare rooms for you both in your time of need."

"You'll need midwives too," Anchoret interrupted, pointing at my belly.

He looked at her seriously. "It shall be done. I'll send my own lad Gwillym to the town to find the best midwife for the Countess. Now come inside, and we will get you to your chambers."

Lewis signalled to the drivers and the chariot rolled into the bailey of the castle, coming to a halt by the main apartments, which looked small and rather mean even compared to Brecknock. However, beggars could not choose at such a desperate time!

"Do you wish for a litter to carry you inside?" Richard Herbert asked, looking at me.

"I-I think I can walk," I said.

"It may be better you do so now," said Anchoret. "Stay up on your feet as long as you can, milady."

Gracelessly, I climbed from the chariot, Anchoret my sturdy support. Pain lanced through my body and I clutched her shoulder.

"And you, my lord Earl?" Herbert turned to Humphrey. "You have a wound…"

Richard Herbert clearly knew that Humphrey had taken injury at St Alban's through the agency of his master. The whole castle household most likely knew. High colour stained Humphrey's cheeks. "Certainly not, sir. I can—and will—walk."

Stiffly he rose, not calling for Lewis to assist, and climbed down the four wooden steps from the chariot. I could tell every step pained him but he struggled to hide his agony. Richard Herbert shouted for a boy to guide my husband to his designated rooms, while a woman in a dark red dress of good quality approached me. "I am Sir Richard's wife, Margaret," she said. "Follow me."

"I am Margaret also," I said.

"So many of us. I am Welsh born though, so, you may call me by the Welsh form of my name, which is Marged. It is like my son—when he is around high English knights, he is William but here, Gwilym."

She took me and Anchoret to a small chamber at the back of the castle apartments. The wooden shutters hung open; beyond I saw a bare, bald, green hill with clouds scudding over its summit. A watercourse twisted, serpentine, below.

"The Blorenge Mountain with the River Usk at its foot," said Marged. "Look at it while you can, my Lady, and take in sweet, clean air, for propriety says we must soon close these shutters for your lying in."

I went to the window, braced my aching body in the frame, watching distant birds of prey soaring on the wind currents, the flicker of sunlight on the swift-flowing waters of the Usk. Would I survive this birth to look upon these sights again?

With a sigh, I turned my back on the sun and the wind, facing into the gloom of the chamber. "Close the shutters, if you will. It is time to begin women's work."

The shutters were closed. A servant girl scuttled in and stoked the fire. It was not cold, being early September, but so it was always done. Heat was prescribed for a safe birth. I lay on the bed in my shift, my headdress gone and my long hair falling in soft damp waves about me. My belly rose like a whale's back beneath the shift's thin fabric. Across from me, Anchoret had loosened her girdle and unbound her own hair, long and dark—another birthing tradition. Marged had done likewise. It was a ritual of unbinding, I had heard, a magical thing to coax the infant to safely and swiftly leave the womb and emerge into the world of the living.

A knock sounded on the door. Marged went over to admit two women in aprons and hoods. "The midwives are here, Countess," she said.

She had hardly ushered them in when another knock rang out, and a pretty maiden in a green kirtle entered the room, carrying a large, gilded harp.

I raised an eyebrow, wondering.

"It is customary for the expectant mother to have friends and family to keep her mind occupied in the hours before the birth," said Marged. "But we do not know each other and you only have your tiring woman. So Eilian shall play the harp and sing. It will be soothing for you."

Eilian sat on a stool in the corner and began to play. The music that her long slender fingers spun was indeed soothing but also filled with sorrow. Tears threatened and a sense of longing filled my being…though for what I did not know.

I told Anchoret, adding, "You will surely laugh at the follies of a woman with child."

She shook her head, dark curls tumbling around her face. "No, my lady. You experience what the Welsh called '*hiraeth*'."

She laughed. "I am not surprised. You have dwelt a few years amongst us now."

The midwives came to my side, one old with long tawny braids streaked with grey, one a younger assistant who might have been her daughter or niece, as she looked similar. They examined me as I tried to concentrate on the harp music of Eilian. Marged sidled over and pressed a worn shard of jasper into my hand. "This was given me when I birthed my son Gwilym. Now I give it to you. Stroke it when the pain comes hard and fast."

I clutched the stone close to my heart. The pain was not yet significant and I could only imagine what was to come.

Day dragged on into dusk. Darkness flooded the chamber and female servants shuffled in, heads bowed, to stoke the fires again. I could hear pattering noises against the shutters and glanced in their direction.

"The weather has changed; it is raining," said Marged. "Hear how the wind howls?"

I held my breath. Over the crackle of the fire and the slackening thrums of Eilian's harp, I heard the rising gale sobbing amongst the castle towers, wailing over crenels on the wall.

A sharp cramp took me and I grimaced. Something skittered across the roof tiles far above; it sounded like tiny feet but I told myself I was being foolish; it was nothing. However, fear reached its hands out, winding dark fingers around my heart.

There were things I had heard about Abergavenny Castle. Things more fearsome that the Neville owners. I had tried to put the old stories from my mind, but they flooded in as night fell—and the pain in my belly increased, spreading in a dull ache into my thighs. Abergavenny was a castle known for treachery…and murder. Anchoret had once told me the tale, though she had since forgotten. But I remembered. Centuries ago, its master, William de Braose—those ill-starred Braoses again! —invited a Welsh lord, Seisyll, his son Geoffrey and other Welsh nobles to a conciliatory feast at Christmas. Unfortunately, William had revenge in his heart, for years before Seisyll had slain the father of

William's wife, Bertha. As the Welsh lords feasted and drank till their senses left them, Braose signalled to his waiting soldiers, who leapt from the shadows and slit their throats, throwing their bodies upon the floor of the Great Hall where the dogs licked up their blood...

A great pain took me, almost as if I had been stabbed. A gush of wetness soaked the bedclothes. "Your waters have broken, Countess Stafford," said the older midwife, hovering at my side.

Overhead, the pattering continued on the tiles and the wind gave another powerful screech and then another—the cries of doomed men, struck down in an act of infamy?

I closed my eyes, wishing I was back at Brecknock, where at least the ghosts had proved friendly....

In the early hours of the morning, I rolled and writhed, gripped by endless pains and spasms. Marged had called her tiring women and they brought in a birthing girdle she had used herself. It was painted with mystical symbols—a heart, a hand, an eye—and the more familiar prayers. "This girdle is very old, and has been blessed, Lady Margaret," she said. as she wrapped it round my body. It smelt old and strange, a residue of honey and stale milk. Its touch on my heated skin was oddly comforting.

The young midwife handed me a little pewter cup full of soft yellow cheese. Words were written into the surface of the cheese, *sator arepo tenet opera rota.* "What is this?" I asked.

"Sustenance to keep you strong," smiled the midwife, "but more besides. Gathered around the 'n' in the middle it spells out the words of the Paternoster. It will help protect you and the babe, my Lady."

I ate the cheese, although my stomach was in knots and I felt nauseated. The older midwife was examining me again. "Up, let's get you onto a stool."

They had brought in a birthing chair and bundled me onto it as gently as they could. The spasms in my belly were coming more frequently, over and over in waves. Dizziness made my head spin, and Anchoret was holding me, muttering soothing words.

Marged began rubbing the jasper on my skin. The lower part of my spine ached unbearably as if it was being torn from my body. Curse Mother Eve for landing all women with this agony!

"It won't be long, I think," said the senior midwife, nodding. "Stay strong, Countess—and push when I tell you. And take deep breaths, also when I tell you…"

I did as I was bid, eager for this ordeal to end…I wanted to go home, I wanted my baby, I wanted my husband. In the agonies of travail, I even wanted my mother, although she had never shown much interest …

And then, suddenly, it was all pain and blood and flurry and excitement from the midwives, Anchoret and Marged. I screamed against a thick wad of cloth I had been given and the next moment, I had a sensation…or freeing? Being freed? And then the lusty screams of a newborn infant filled the chamber.

Struggling to keep from fainting after such extreme exertions, I saw the midwives lift the babe, wipe it, wrap it in linen. It was large, red-faced and howling lustily.

"Is it…" I gasped, striving to look closer but too weak.

"It is a boy, my lady," said the young midwife with a smile. "A fine, handsome boy."

I was placed back into the bed, my bloody shift stripped off and taken for burning, as was that matter which came from me along with the babe—important, for the birth-cord could be used in witchcraft, just like discarded nail parings or hair caught in a comb.

I lay back against the bolster and Anchoret wiped my brow with a rosewater infused cloth, and for a few blissful minutes, the baby was laid in my arms. He snuffled at me, searching. "He is hungry," I said, suddenly worried and protective. "He needs a wet nurse…."

"I sent for one earlier," said Marged. "She is waiting in the Hall; I did not want her milk to curdle because she heard your screaming. She is healthy, plump and of good character. She will do well for you and you can take her to Brecknock…as long as you send her back eventually."

Weary beyond words, I nodded my agreement, and Marged Herbert called in the wet nurse. Soon I was watching my baby, my long-awaited son, suckling strongly. "Humphrey," I murmured. "What of my husband…"

"He cannot come into this woman's space," said Marged, "as that would be most unseemly, but he will be informed he has a son."

I sank into the sea of cushions surrounding me. Maybe the birth of his heir would bring healing to Humphrey's tormented body and soul…

The next day they baptised the baby in the castle chapel, giving him the name of Henry after the King. As the mother, I could not watch, for I was not allowed to re-join public life until I was churched and no longer considered 'unclean'. Anchoret and Marged were permitted to attend, along with Constable Herbert, and Humphrey was there to witness the immersion of our son in the caste's ancient font.

"His lordship beamed!" giggled Anchoret, sitting on the edge of my bed afterwards. "He looked to be in awe of his son."

"Henry…our Harry," I breathed. "And how was my sweet babe when the priest dipped him into the font?"

"Oh, he shrieked and roared—what a great voice the little mite has! A good sound set of lungs on him!"

I laughed, gladness warming my heart. Everything would come aright now, surely. I only wish young Harry's grandsire, my father Edmund, might have laid eyes on him. I was certain he would be proud.

I certainly was, and for a time, the darkness that had gathered around me lifted to allow the light, and I walked gladly towards that brightness…

My constitution was hardier than I believed, and I recovered quickly from Harry's birth. At the end of my month's wait for Churching, Anchoret dressed me in a clean, simple gown and a modest veil fringed with white damask, ready for the short journey to the nearby priory for the *Benedictio mulieris post partum*, the blessing laid upon a woman after giving birth. Humphrey wanted the rite to take place in the priory rather than the castle chapel; it was a famous place and a good announcement to the world that the Earl of Stafford had a son. Although he did not say it openly, he also wanted to be away from a Neville-held castle, no matter how well we had been treated there.

Under a canopy and holding a lighted taper in a cup, I walked through the town to St Mary's. Inside the priory, it was dark and smelt of candle wax and Frankincense. In the gloom, lay effigies of the notables of the town—John de Hastings, once lord there, wearing a hood of chain mail; Eva de Braose, daughter of the untrustworthy William, holding a heart on her palm; and, most poignantly Margaret, daughter of the great Edward III and Queen Philippa, who had married John Hastings. She was depicted with a stone squirrel attached to the chain linked to her girdle. Anchoret had earlier told me Margaret had died young, falling from the castle walls while chasing her pet squirrel, which had escaped its collar.

I looked at her worn stone face. So sad to die so young…but today I could not be sad, for my son lay in his cradle, sound and healthy, and soon I would walk in the world again.

My gaze turned from the pitiful effigy to the mighty Jesse Tree that stood within the side chapel. Never had I seen such a massive wood carving before, hewn from oak and rising to the ceiling in a riot of colours. Jesse, a true patriarch, wise-eyed and bearded, towered above, with branches twisting out from his broad shoulders, showing the descent of Jesus and David and Solomon through all the great kings of Christendom.

The priest emerged from the vestry and walked in my direction, the candlelight shining on his bald head. As I knelt, he uttered the blessings, with Jesse, a wooden giant, looming over my kneeling form, his shadow black across the tiles as the sun swung behind the window. Another branch on the tree had indeed blossomed.

At length, the priest made the sign of the cross over my brow and finished with a ringing prayer, *"Almighty, everlasting God, through the delivery of the Blessed Virgin Mary, Thou hast turned into joy the pains of the faithful in childbirth; look mercifully upon this Thy handmaid, coming in gladness to Thy temple to offer up her thanks...*"

And I was thankful, I was whole and clean, and now I could go home with my husband and son.

I returned to Abergavenny castle and was surprised to see the chariot in the courtyard, ready for departure. Humphrey was waiting outside, leaning on a crutch that someone must have found for him. "Margaret, it is time to go," he said curtly. "Get in. Henry is inside with the wet nurse."

"What has happened? Why is there such a rush?"

"You are churched and free to walk amidst men again—why should we tarry any longer here, amidst enemies?" he snapped, glaring up at the castle towers.

"Enemies?" I reddened, hoping none of the garrison had overheard. Marged had thankfully already retreated inside the castle. "Surely the actions of the Constable and his lady showed you that they were far from enemies."

He looked at me and the blackness in his eyes made my heart sink. Anchoret had told me he was happy at little Harry's birth and christening; I saw no happiness now. "You have forgotten so soon? Your father, and *this*..." He gestured to his leg.

"None of that has anything to do with the hospitality we have received, which has been exemplary," I said. "Humphrey, please..."

His lips thinned. "I will discuss it no further. Get in before I look a fool. I will leave you here if you are going to stand and make a scene."

Anger and fear mixed within me. It galled me to come like an obedient dog, especially when I had done no wrong, and yet if he kept to his threat I would end up stranded in Abergavenny, looking like an abandoned wife. But worse than that, my baby was in the chariot. I stalked towards the carriage, my hands clenched at my sides, unable to even look at my husband.

Anchoret followed me, daring to touch my sleeve. "It doesn't matter, my lady. Please do not fret. He is not himself."

I climbed in, Anchoret following me. I sat by the wet nurse who cradled my baby in her plump arms. I stroked his downy head, his soft cheeks and refused to look at Humphrey who crawled into the pillows and furs on the far side of the carriage, aided by his squire.

Halfway home, I heard him complaining that he felt feverish and his leg hurt. Still, I refused to look at him. I just prayed it was indeed his wound paining him and not some other malady, not while my child was so young and vulnerable.

By the time we reached Brecknock, Humphrey was clearly ill, taken with chills and shaking, his brow awash with sweat. He was taken to his quarters and the physician called from the town. I went to the nursery to sit with my son.

Hours late, near Evensong, the doctor found me. "My Lady, we must speak."

"Then speak." I was in no mood for long speeches dancing around the truth of the situation.

"The Earl's battle-wound on his thigh was grave, as you know. When I first tended him, it was cauterised and packed, and I thought this would be enough. But the flesh of his lordship's thigh has not welded one side to the other as I had hoped. The edges have torn loose and become infected once more. I cauterised it again and cleaned it, but I must be honest…"

I held my breath. The wet nurse clung to baby Harry, her face white and doughy.

"He will live as long as the infection does not continue to return or worsen…but in my professional opinion, he will have a severe limp, perhaps need support to walk. "

"Permanently?" I whispered.

"Yes, my Lady. Permanently. I am also dubious as to whether he could endure long rides when mounted…and it would be dangerous for him to fight in anymore battles, the danger being to his squires and captains as much as himself. They would doubtless try to protect him when they needed to look to their own defence and that of their fellows."

Breath rushed between my teeth. "Thank you, Sir, for your honesty. I would rather have that than false hope."

Bowing, the physician left. I kissed baby Harry to sleep and with heavy heart went to Humphrey's chamber.

My husband lay on his bed staring at the ceiling. "H-have they given you a draught for the pain?" I asked tremulously.

"Nothing they give me will be to any avail," he said, hoarse with suppressed emotion. "What did the physic tell you of my condition?"

I could not repeat the doctor's words; they tasted of wormwood in my mouth. However, Humphrey neither sought nor expected any answer. He pushed himself up, shaking with effort, rage and despair. "I won't ride my mount again, I won't wield a sword again...I am but half a man, bringing shame to my family honour."

"What shame is in fighting for your king and being wounded for his cause?" I cried, and tears fell from my eyes, a river that would not cease. I crawled onto the bed beside him, burying my face in his sweat-soaked linen shirt, sobbing—for him, for both of us. For a while he would not even touch me, lying like a corpse save for his poppy-slowed breaths, but then, slowly, one arm went round my shoulders.

The hour was dark but my battle for my husband was not over yet.

CHAPTER SIX

A letter arrived for me at Brecknock Castle. I thought it might be a rare missive from my mother or one of my sisters, but to my surprise, it had come from my cousin, the other Margaret Beaufort.

Dearest beloved Cousin, she had written in her own hand, spidery and childish still, with loops and threads abounding, and a determined but barely readable signature, *I pray God sends you wealth and happiness. I heard that you were safely delivered of a son—Henry, after his Grace the King. I trust you find maternity a pleasant state. I have heard, with sorrow, about Earl Humphrey's grievous wounds. So brave, in defence of our noble and pious King. I pray every night that he, and all others harmed, shall soon recover, and the guilty be sorely punished—in this life or the next! But it is not of such evils I wish to speak—but a happy occasion, the happiest of occasions. The date for my wedding to Edmund Tudor has, at last, been set. He wants to delay no longer; as you know when last we met, he was very eager! The place has been chosen, Lamphey Court—in Wales, not so many miles from you. I would be most delighted if you, my dearest kinswoman, and Earl Humphrey, would attend upon this happy occasion…Margaret B"*

After all that had transpired, I did not know if Humphrey would accompany me to Margaret's nuptials, but I asked him anyway, hoping it might rouse him from his malaise to join with others of our rank and allegiance. Alas, he stared at me as if I had lost my wits. "No! A wedding is…is for celebration!"

Not understanding, I blinked like a big-eyed loon.

He grew agitated, waving his arms—his ruined hand, healed but missing two fingers. "Margaret…no one wants to see a cripple! I do not want to sit at table amidst the Tudors and their friends and have everyone smile to my face then go away laughing at my plight."

"Why would they do such a thing? They are our friends and kin. I am sure they feel sorrowful that you…" I choked on my words, realising I had spoken amiss. He did not want anyone's sympathy; he wanted life to be as it was.

Humphrey's cheeks purpled. "Sorry! You stupid woman; the last thing I need is false commiserations from the fucking Tudors, born of the scandalous union of a whorish queen with her minion, a humble food-taster who himself might have been the bastard of an alehouse keeper or a murderer!"

I gasped at his harsh words, and realising how his temper had got the better of him, he jerked away from me, dragging the coverlet over himself. "I will speak no more of this matter. If you wish to travel to Lamphey to see your cousin wed, I grant my permission. I will not stop you…but I will not go."

For many days I determined to tell Margaret I must stay in Brecknock, fearing my departure would make Humphrey even more wroth with me. But the castle walls seemed to press in and life, save for the time I spent in the nursery with little Harry had become bleak—no feasts brightened our days, no musicians sang in the halls, no merry hunting parties set out into the woods.

With shaking hand, I wrote back to Margaret. *I will attend your wedding, dearest cousin…but I pray you will not be scandalised, for I come alone.*

Margaret's wedding at Lamphey Palace was set for the first of November. An ominous day and not one I would have chosen had the choice been mine. Yes, it was the Feast of All Saints with All Souls the next day, so blessed to all the holy martyrs and to our own lost ancestors, but one could not dwell in Wales, or for that matter in the English countryside, without knowing that darker, older rites underlay the feast of All Hallows or Hallowmas.

"I don't like being on the road at this time of the year, milady," said Anchoret, as we readied to depart in my carriage. "It is another *ysbrydnos*, a night when the graves open and revenants step forth to haunt the living."

"Oh, nonsense," I mocked, more confident in my words than I truly was in my heart. "If you are frightened, say your prayers. All Hallows is a sacred time, not a devilish one. Besides, the feast does not begin for five days yet. It is a long way to Lamphey, for all that it lies in Wales."

Jennet, who was also accompanying me, took a deep breath. "Even so, we must be careful. I suppose if we avoid stiles, crossroads and churchyards, we should pass unharmed. That's where spirits and witches are wont to congregate."

Our party set off at a brisk clip, the chariot pulled by three dappled greys with bright plumes attached to their bridles and a contingent of soldiers in Stafford livery protecting us from any harm. I stared from the carriage window as Brecknock castle vanished into the distance, its thin red-stoned towers shrouded by mist. Was I wrong to feel a frisson of excitement at leaving, when my baby was back there on his own? Well, not *alone*…but without my presence. I touched the silver and enamel crucifix I wore and said a silent prayer for him…and Humphrey too, of course. Poor Humphrey.

The day became dim; light was short and twilight rushing in early. Red leaves swirled in the wind and the air was heavy with the acrid scent of burning, a pleasant enough fragrance redolent of the coming of winter.

"You haven't plucked any ground ivy, have you, my Lady?" asked Jennet, sidling up with a bowl of candied violet and wafers.

"Ivy? No. Why should I touch such a plant?"

"Just making certain," she said. "If touched or smelled around the Feast of Hallowmas, ivy will make you see evil hags or mares in your sleep."

Anchoret made a dismissive noise which Jennet ignored. However, soon the pair of them were chilling each other's bones, and mine, with local tales of All Souls, each more lurid and fantastic than the last.

With eyes big and round, and voice hushed, Anchoret told the story of a great Black Sow and a headless woman who would roam the countryside on the Night of the Day of the Dead. "The Sow has no tail," she said, "but eyes red as fire, and 'tis said she eats the flesh of liches…"

"Pigs will eat anything," said Jennet, giving Anchoret's waistline a hard look.

It was just silly banter and Anchoret slapped her companion's arm playfully. "I'll feed you to her if Old Piggy should materialise. I think, though, she might get sore indigestion."

"I have a more fearsome story than an old wife's tale about a smelly pig," said Jennet. "This one is true; I swear it on the Rood."

"Do you now?" I made a disbelieving face.

She nodded, her expression deathly serious. "In many of the cottages in the wilds, families build fires to keep the dark—and all that lurks in it at *Calan Gaeaf*—away from their door. Every family member from the oldest crone to the youngest bairn is given a stone marked with their name or their symbol if they could not write. The stones are placed in the fire and then the family bolts the door and retreats to bed. In the morn, everyone then scrambles in the ashes of the dead fire to find their stone. If it is gone or cracked in two…" her voice dropped. "Without fail, they will die within the year."

"That's a horrible tale," I said, with a delicate shiver, pulling a shawl around my shoulders for added warmth. "Worse than Anchoret's sow."

"But it is a true tale. Saw it myself… saw a healthy young lad whose stone went missing carried to his grave within the year."

I began thinking of Harry back at Brecon, and Humphrey too, ailing and full of grief. "No more tales," I said firmly. "Soon we will reach our night's lodgings at Kidwelly Priory."

When we reached Kidwelly, the daylight had failed. The air was cold and smelt of the sea, and there was an old castle, partly wrecked by Glyn Dwr's rebellion, standing in the Old Borough section of town, its shattered gateway gaping like a dragon's maw. The priory was situated in the New Borough, and it was a thriving place, for many sea journeys ended or began here, and pilgrims abounded as they headed for St David's down the coast.

The priory church itself was handsome and clean with two new Rood screens heavily painted with gilded saints, and a life-sized alabaster figure of the Blessed Virgin and the Christ Child in a wall embrasure. I left offerings, although it was not officially a shrine, and asked the Blessed Mother to guard my son and to bring me safely to Margaret's wedding. I said a few swift prayers for Margaret too—she was glad to be married, a willing bride, but her youth still troubled me. If the protection of the Blessed Virgin could be invoked to guide her, so much the better.

The next morning my party went down to the harbour to commence our journey to Lamphey, leaving our horses and carriage with the monks, waiting for our return. The rest of the way would be by sea rather than road, in a sturdy little cog which would let us alight at Tenby before ferrying a clutch of pilgrims on to St David's. It was safer, Humphrey had assured me, than riding through lands where the roads might be haunted by lawless Welshmen, but I was not overly familiar with boats, having ridden them only on rivers. This was the sea, wild and unpredictable, and as we set off my stomach lurched wildly. Anchoret and Jennet were even worse; they screeched louder than the gulls overhead and clung to each other like children.

"I am going to be sick!" moaned Jennet, a shade of yellow-green. "Why, my lady, did we ever come this way? Could we not have continued in our chariot?"

"We could have, but the journey would have taken far longer, and we might have been waylaid by rogues. Surely you would not want your honour compromised?"

"I think that ship has sailed many a year hence." Anchoret nudged Jennet in the ribs, and the two of them fell to friendly taunts and bickering. Their noise was irritating, but at least it took their minds off the rolling of the boat. I was able to concentrate on some embroidery and have a little peace.

The boat docked at the town of Tenby and fresh horses awaited us to ride on the final three leagues to Lamphey Palace. As we reached the palace, the steward of Bishop Del Mere came out to escort me and the maids to my chambers in the hall block, a handsome building whose walls bore a fine chequerboard pattern in purple local stone and limestone. Once I had been given time to settle in, I received a message that Cousin Margaret wished to meet in one of the Palace's two Great Halls.

Just before Evensong, I sought her in a hall painted a rich creamy yellow with overlays of hundreds of red flowers. Margaret emerged from a side corridor, tiny as ever, but more mature than I remembered. Grasping my hand, she kissed me swiftly on either cheek. "I am so glad you are here, cousin. At last—someone not too far from my own age! Is not the Bishop's Palace beautiful?"

"Fair beyond words," I agreed, "though I have not had much chance to see it as yet."

"I will show you when there is time," said Margaret. "After he officiates my marriage to Edmund, the Bishop will move on to St David's and leave us to establish our household here. Is that not kind? So, Edmund and I shall spend our honeymoon in this wonderful place. There are orchards, gardens and forests, ponds and dovecotes. If the weather is inclement, forcing us indoors, there is a fine library with collections on philosophy and religion."

"I am glad to see you so happy," I said, a trace of wistfulness in my voice. I had to admit, other than Harry's birth, happiness had slipped away as autumn slips to winter.

"You look…older, Cousin Meg." Margaret's keen bird-bright gaze ran over me, missing nothing. "Even though you have birthed a child, you have lost weight."

"Worry quells my appetite," I admitted. "Humphrey still ails. I even tried bathing his injury in a holy well, to no avail."

"It is God's will, then," said Margaret, her tone grown so pious and blunt that I felt a little jolt of irritation. Although one could not doubt God, her words seemed almost flippant, callous. If she had not been so young, I would have answered back, but decided instead that forgiveness was a beauteous thing.

A bell rang out, booming through the palace complex. Margaret's pointed little chin lifted. "The bell for Evensong tolls. Will you accompany me, Cousin Meg, on my last night as a maiden?"

Nodding, I reached out and took that tiny, thin arm. We crossed from the hall to the priory church, as the clouds above, darkened by night, oozed out a freezing drizzle that clung to our lashes like tears.

The marriage ceremony and subsequent feast were well-attended, but mostly by those who were friends and kin to the Tudors—local Welsh knights and landowners in a jumble of dazzling robes and gaudy gold, resembling the characters in the tales they told round the fires. Jasper Tudor was there, smiling and merry, his shock of red hair ablaze, a counterfoil to dour, dark Edmund, who seemed glum even on his wedding day. Margaret's mother had ridden in from Northamptonshire with her third husband, Lionel, Viscount Welles, and a few of Margaret's St John half-siblings from her mother's first marriage, Oliver, Edith, Agnes and John. They were all older than Margaret by some years and looked somewhat bored by the proceedings; I assumed they had only attended after their mother had cajoled them and would rather be elsewhere.

I was seated next to Edith, a pale woman with grey, speculating eyes. "She is special, you know," she suddenly blurted.

I almost choked on my wine. "Who?"

"Our little Margaret. God has touched her. She tells us that often." She suddenly burst into laughter and I flushed for she was teasing. I was one of those unfortunates who could never discern a well-told jest, told with a straight face, from a statement of utter truth—a quirk in my personality Humphrey, in happier times, had found deeply amusing.

"But perhaps I should not laugh," continued Edith. "Margaret *is* different. On the rare occasion we saw our little half-sister, she always behaved like a little queen. She was so aware of her ancestry from John of Gaunt and old King Edward. I once caught her trying to draw her own genealogy tree, with a wobbly Adam and Eve above, and the vines snaking down through the old royals to wrap around Margaret herself."

"She forgot about the Beaufort bastardy, that is clear," said the other half-sister, Agnes. "I am glad we hold no such taint."

"Agnes!" Edith rolled her eyes at her sister. "Hold your tongue. Remember, you speak to the Countess of Stafford who is…"

"A Beaufort," I interjected dryly. "Margaret is my cousin; our fathers were brothers."

Agnes coloured to the roots of the reddish hair revealed at the top of her plucked forehead. "I-I do beg your pardon, Countess," she stammered. "I must have had too…too much wine. I should not be gossiping like some old village crone."

"I am not concerned," I said. "Being of bastard stock did not concern my father. One may be raised high or laid low despite the actions of one's forebears. In my sire's case, it was both."

Both women looked abashed at that and Edith crossed herself. "God assoil him, Countess Stafford. It was a shock to all, that terrible battle."

I nodded. "But let us be merry now. A wedding *should* be merry. You may call me Meg if you wish. I am another Margaret—there are far too many of us."

"All named for Blessed Saint Margaret, who escaped from a dragon's belly," said Agnes.

"I think our Margaret would have liked to become a saint as much as a queen, thinking more deeply upon it." Edith went back to her musing, despite herself. "However, most saints are virgins, and after tonight …"

She inclined her head toward the high table where bride and groom sat in ornate gold-hued chairs, a canopy bearing both England's lions and France's fleur de lys stretched overhead—King Henry had granted Edmund the right to carry such emblems, integrating him into the royal family despite his father's lowly birth. Edmund was as taciturn as ever, smiling thinly only when his brother, Jasper, bent over to tell him some jest or other anecdote. Sitting at his side, Margaret wore a bride's traditional blue with her long, poker-straight mousey hair falling over her shoulders to her waist. She was so small her tiring women had propped her up on a multitude of velvet cushions so she could easily reach the table. She picked daintily at her food, barely glancing at her new husband. During the marriage ceremony at the chapel door, she had brimmed with confidence, reciting the vows with conviction and clarity, but I surmised such boldness was waning now that the unknown loomed.

"She's too young." Suddenly solemn, Agnes was shaking her head and gazing in her sister's direction. "It's not right, Edith; I have said it before. We don't…don't do things like that anymore. She should be at least fourteen if not older. Jesu, it's not like it's still the year 1200, when King John carried off a twelve-year-old to make his Queen."

"Hush," Edith warned again, gazing sliding to me as if gauging my reaction. "You really need to drink no more tonight, Aggie. I do agree about Margaret's age, but what's done is done. Those with royal ancestry sometimes must endure what others do not. Is that no so, Countess…Meg?"

"It is so," I murmured. "With God's aid, we endure."

The banquet was coming to an end. The servants brought in the voiders and started busily scraping bones and half-eaten food into them, while chasing away any of the hounds, banished to the yard earlier, who had slipped back into the hall. Edmund's companions clustered around him, well in their cups, bursting with ribald mirth. As musicians played on pipes and tabor, Edmund was guided out of the chamber, the sound of crude jests growing ever louder, while a minstrel sang in high, wavering tones,

> *For her love I cark and care,*
> *For her love I droop and dare*
> *For her love my bliss is bare,*
> *And all is greatly won.*
> *For her love in sleep I slake*
> *For her love all night I wake,*
> *For her love morning I make…*
> *More than any man…*

Margaret's tiring women gathered around her and her half-sisters hurried to join the group. I followed, finding myself between Agnes and Edith as we guided the young bride up the spiral stairs to the wedding chamber above.

There, as the men made merry in the hallway, whooping and shouting and singing bawdy ditties, we took Margaret aside and removed her raiment, combing down her long hair to form a flowing veil. She had become like a statue, still and white scarcely breathing. Meekly Edith guided her to the bed and put her beneath the covers, while Agnes and the others strewed dry rose petals on the bed to give fragrance. I threw some too…but they felt like dust against my palm. I held back a sneeze.

"A pity these blossoms are not fresh," Agnes whispered to me when her sister Edith was not looking. "A dismal time of the year to hold a wedding, don't you think, Countess?"

I made no response. My gaze was drawn to the shutters, which were still open to the night. It was All Soul's, and the moon hung like a vast eye or a raddled skull over the trees on the nearby rises. The air was crisp and smoky, the stars shrouded. Suddenly I heard a whirring, and there, hovering, was a huge moth, the largest I had ever seen. It fluttered in, seeking the light of the torches, its long wings beating madly. The women began to shriek and run about like mad things. Only Margaret did not move, staring transfixed as the moth settled upon her broidered coverlet.

I moved first, hurrying to the bedside. Staring down, I watched the creature crawl across the fabric. Close up, it had a strange, primal beauty, and on its furred back were markings that resembled a human skull… I bent over to look closer, the women's shrieks fading as I concentrated on the moth before me. I had been of a mind to kill it, to strike it with a book or a candlestick…but I found I could not bring myself to do so.

It only sought the light, after all. Is that not what we all should do? *Seek the light…*

I scooped the insect up, cupping it in my hands. It moved, frightened, its wings battering my fingers.

"Oh, what if it bites you?" cried Agnes, like a ninny.

Surprisingly calm, I went to the window and tossed the moth out into the hazy night-air. Its wings glimmered, shining golden as the light from the chamber flooded over it, then it circled around once before fluttering away into the darkness.

I grasped the sides of the wooden shutters and yanked them shut with a loud thud.

I turned around to see the women staring at me as if I was a brave knight who had saved them from some monstrous beast. I choked back a giggle.

But then I saw Margaret's face, pinched and pale. She sat upright, the coverlet grasped tightly in her hand. "You should have killed it," she rasped. "Have you not read your Leviticus! The moth has wings and walks on all fours—therefore, it is unclean!"

I smiled weakly. "At least it is gone now; I will lave my hands with water to clean them…"

One of Margaret's women, a matron with a large gleaming cross about her neck, as much nursemaid as helpmeet, I thought, was shaking her head. "It is worse than unclean, my Lady Countess. On a night such as tonight, when dead ancestors rest lightly in their graves…it is said such a creature can betoken death."

After the wedding, I stayed three more days at the Bishop's Palace. Margaret kept to her room for the first day with only her close-faced tiring women going in and out of the chamber like dark, silent wraiths. Edmund Tudor went hunting, however, with Jasper at his side, and returned with a good-sized buck suspended on two poles, blood still dripping from the carcase.

Agnes St John, walking alongside me in the palace gardens, gestured in the direction of the returning hunting party. "See how Jasper laughs? He is always the more amiable of the two brothers by far. In some ways, I wish Margaret had wed him instead of Edmund. Edmund is too dour and too rash, always thinking of his finances. He could have waited till she was older…but no, he must have his own way. Margaret agreed, though."

"She dreams many high things," I murmured. "She revealed some to me. A child's thoughts, maybe, but only God knows."

"Oh, I know of what you speak. Her visions and whatnot. I dare say she will forget about them as she settles into married life and the realities she will face. But, as you say, only God knows the future for any of us."

Before I departed for home, Margaret herself sought me out. She was wimpled like a good humble wife and wearing a sombre but rich brocade robe. "Cousin Meg," she said. "I fear I have not been a good hostess. I hardly spoke to you other than the first day; I thought we would have time to embroider together, to pray... But Edmund demands much of my attention, more than I ever imagined, and I-I want all to be...be *perfect.*" She peered at me, clearly seeking understanding and looking even younger and more vulnerable than ever before.

"No apology is needed. I have spent my time with your half-sister, Agnes. Of course, you must do as Edmund wishes—he is your husband, after all." I smiled wanly. "In any case, I must return to Brecknock and my little son. And Humphrey." I added, almost as an afterthought, blushing at how easily I had put him from my thoughts while away. In my heart of hearts, I dreaded spending time with him now; he had no desire to spend time with me, either. He merely lay abed and stared at the ceiling or out the window, and occasionally played chess with a squire.

"May the good Earl of Stafford be healed by the Lord," said Margaret piously, folding her hands. "May we meet again, in the future, Cousin. Perhaps, by then I will have a child to play with yours—two little Henries, named for his Grace the King." She laughed.

"Maybe," I said, but could raise no mirth. The hard truth was that although Henry was still King of England, he was a weak ruler and York and the Nevilles were ascendant. My child's father was maimed in York's rebellion, and one grandsire lay dead, hewn outside the Castle Inn. I did not think the Duke of York's faction would smile overmuch on Edmund Tudor, uterine brother and stalwart supporter to the King that Richard Plantagenet wanted to replace...

The road back to Brecknock was travelled in silence. Wintry weather had gathered over the Beacons and the wind's breath was bitter. A dusting of snow touched the heads of the bald hills. The Night of the Dead had gone past but now the dead season was upon us.

Upon entering the castle, I rushed straight to the nursery where a cosy fire burned in a brazier and deep, imported carpets and hangings made the room warm and hospitable. Little Harry lay in his cradle, plump and content. "He's been ever so good, milady," said the wet nurse Alice, a local lass who had replaced the nurse who first tended Harry in Abergavenny. "And he's feeding well. Look how he's fattening out! He never misses a feed—screams down the place if I am a moment late getting to him!"

"You keep my son well, Alice," I said, full of genuine gratitude. "I will see you have extra meat and a rind of cheese delivered to your cottage…oh, and fresh cream too. I will have a portion sent to your husband too; I am sure he is missing you."

She glanced down, reddening, giving a slight nod; a wet nurse to a baby of high status like my Harry was not expected to lie with her man until the child was weaned in case the milk was spoilt. "He knows what's, what, my Madoc," Alice said. "Don't you worry. He comes home too tired every eve to bother me much. Can't really when I mostly up here at the castle."

I smiled wanly. "And your own babe, Muriel, is it?"

"Oh, she's thriving. My older girl Elen and my own old mam, look after her while I am here. If she cries when I'm here with Lord Harry, they get her goat's milk in a horn."

"You may bring her in," I said, thinking of how awful it would be to attend to someone's child at the expense of your own. "I have no objection. Some in olden times would have called her Henry's 'milk-sister.' Just make sure her swaddling is clean and you may bring her in a basket to lie at your feet."

"Oh, thank you, milady," said Alice, "and thank his Lordship the Earl, too."

My own smile faded a little. In my rush to see that Harry was well, I had not given Humphrey a single thought. Indeed, I was almost reluctant to entire his bleak chamber, to see his hopeless face, to smell the faint tang of the sickroom that clung to everything around him. But I had to. It was my duty. And soon, otherwise he might think I was avoiding him.

"I must go now, Alice," I said, "to see the Earl."

I must have sounded uncertain for Alice said, stoutly, "I am sure he missed you, Countess Margaret. I am sure of it."

I was not so certain…but I would soon find out.

The wet nurse curtseyed, clumsily and I exited the nursery and hurried down the corridor to Humphrey's bedchamber. His squires were lurking around the doorway, whispering; I sent them packing, along with his five favourite hounds, who had been begging for titbits.

Inside, Humphrey lay propped against the bolster, much as he had been when I left. He wore a similar white shirt, or mayhap the same, though laundered of course. The barber had shaved him and combed down his hair, so he had made some effort, but his expression was still wan and bleak.

"Meg," he said, raising himself slightly, "you have returned. I almost wondered…"

"What did you wonder?"

"If you would come back. If perhaps you would have found reason to stay on with your cousin."

"What…on her honeymoon? Do you think I would be invited for endless rounds of merriment and dancing, without a care in the world, in the new household of a child-bride?"

"You do not approve of the match?"

"No, I do not. Yes, if she were older. As things stand, not so much…although she is happy with the marriage or at least claims to be. But it is not for me to question, despite those gossips far and wide are shocked at Edmund Tudor's unseemly *hastiness*…."

"As you speak of inappropriate hastiness, I must also put in a word," said Humphrey. "*I* was hasty, shouting at you before you left for Lamphey. I should have accompanied you there. It was my duty to do so."

"You could not; not when you are ill."

He heaved a great sigh. "I may never heal, Meg, and that is the truth of the matter, but I must do what I can to rebuild the fragments of my life. How will the people of Brecknock see me as their lord, if I do not seem lordly? My father was wounded at St Alban's too, and the scar has wrecked his looks, but he has assumed his life…he goes on as before with my mother at his side. I will endeavour to do as he does, and hopefully you will…"

"I will," I said softly, clasping his hand. His fingers trembled. "You know I will."

That night we shared a bed for the first time since Harry was conceived. Humphrey was clumsy, and in pain with his leg, so close to his vital organ, and I was pliant and meek and willing, offering soothing words, speaking not of discomfort when he lay too heavily upon me, crushing me to the bed because he could raise himself no more.

"I need another son, Meg," he whispered in my ear as we sprawled together in the tangled sheets, sweat commingled, lip to lip, frenzied heartbeats easing. "To ensure my line continues. One child is never enough. You and I both know how fragile life can be. Every night I want you here with me, till that is accomplished. Another healthy boy…and then the physic can cut off his damned, ruined leg, should he think it might ease my pain."

Our couplings from thereon were not the loving unions of our first months of marriage, but grimly determined melding with but one thing on Humphrey's mind. Another son to fully secure the Stafford inheritance.

I was relieved when, shortly after the Feast of Candlemas, I discovered I was with child once more. From the moment I announced the news to my husband, he no longer touched me. I know it is considered by some to be immoral or even dangerous to enjoin in conjugal union when a babe was on the way, but before—it seemed centuries ago—he had laughed and said such tales were either old wives' stories or the presumption of celibate priests. But now he resumed life as chaste as one of those priests he had mocked, and his mood turned strange and sour again, though at least he made no more wild statements about having his leg amputated.

Knowing something of my sorrow, Anchoret fussed over me, finding sweet meats to tempt my jaded palate and obtaining the biggest eggs and freshest meats for me to dine upon. Jennet did her best as well; she was an expert seamstress and she made beautiful gowns to hide my growing roundness, as well as princely raiment for little Harry. I took delight in seeing my son grow in size and strength. I would take him from the nursery out into the clean air of the bailey with Alice and his other nursemaids trundling behind, and although he could not possibly understand, I pointed out the brightly-hued flags on the turrets and the soldiers in his father's livery and the caparisoned horses, and said, "This will all be yours, my sweetling, one day. This and so much more. There's a wide world out there beyond Wales, and one day, God willing you will take your rightful place in the King's court. Prince Edward will likely be our ruler then—let it be many years hence! And remember always, my precious boy, you are not just a Stafford, you are a Beaufort too—and your blood is royal in two lines."

As the year progressed, the troubles that afflicted England began to simmer again…but the tide was turning for those who supported Lancaster. The Duke of York was still in a position of importance but had resigned his Protectorship in February, no doubt under pressure from the Queen's faction. In August, the court moved from London to Coventry, a city known for its loyalty to the House of Lancaster. Richard of York would find few friends there and Queen Margaret knew it. I smiled to myself when I heard that Salisbury had gradually stopped attending council meetings, leaving York to face suspicion and hostility almost on his own.

I also received a missive from Cousin Margaret, who was with her new husband Edmund at Caldicot Castle, having left Lamphey Palace behind. *'Glad news, beloved Cousin!'* she had written. *'God has smiled on Edmund and me. I am with child. Maybe all those girlish plans we made for our sons will someday come true. I am indeed blessed by God's bounteous goodness…'*

I was glad for her but fearful too; not only for her continued good health but because unrest began to stir in Wales. Edmund

Tudor had fallen into enmity with one Gruffudd Ap Nicholas and his sons who had taken Carmarthen, Kidwelly, Aberystwyth and Carraig Cennen upon its high rock. Edmund had marched against Gruffudd at Carmarthen, quickly recapturing the castle for the Crown.

But that was not the end of it. York held lands in Wales and his own faction was waiting to pounce. Sir William Herbert—yes, the very one who gave me succour in my most desperate need—marched through Wales with Sir Walter Devereux, another of York's supporters, and managed to capture Edmund, throwing him into a dungeon in Carmarthen Castle.

I could only imagine how frightened and frantic Margaret, pregnant and alone, must have been shut up behind the walls of Caldicot Castle. Humphrey said little on the subject, but extra guards were set on the town walls and before the castle gates. Fortunately, none of York's men ever attempted to harass us, but we were prepared if they did

Rumours swirled about, brought to the castle by tradesmen and pilgrims heading for the priory—Edmund was wounded, Edmund was ill, Edmund was about to be freed.

This went on for months, and then one day, in early November when the trees were bleak and the clouds piling across the sky like grey waves, a lone rider reached the castle, dressed in heavy black mourning garb. He was brought before Humphrey, who had shrugged himself into a robe and forced himself down, with much wincing and grimacing, onto a cushioned seat in the solar.

"Who are you and why do you come here?" asked Humphrey, not terribly polite.

"I bear grave news that affects all in Wales," said the man. "I serve…served…Edmund Tudor."

My breath hissed between my teeth. "Served…Do you tell us that he is…he is…"

Bowing his head, the man crossed himself fervently. "God rest his soul. He died at Carmarthen upon the 1st of November, just as his gaolers prepared to free him. The plague, it was, or some other deadly malady…it is hard to say. Some have spoken of poison or unseen murder…"

I pressed my hand to my mouth. "No, surely not!"

"It is unlikely," he admitted, "but an inquest shall be held nonetheless to keep tongues from wagging."

"Where—where have they buried him?" asked Humphrey, frowning. "Has he been returned to his widow at Caldicot?"

The messenger shook his head. "Since he died of disease, his body was hastily chested and entombed in the Church of the Greyfriars in Carmarthen."

"My poor cousin!" I cried, thinking of Margaret, so young, widowed to the day she was wed. Alone, a child in her belly, her enemies circling around her like wolves. "Humphrey, we must do something to help her!" I cried, impetuously.

A shadow swirled over my husband's face. He glowered and for a moment I felt a hot, unworthy flash of something akin to dislike. "What would you have me do, madam?" he asked, his tone chilly. "You know how things stand. Would you fain bring those Yorkist dogs to Brecknock next?"

"Your sire, the Duke, is not on bad terms with Richard of York," I blurted—a truth, though not one Humphrey savoured. He thought his father's loyalty to the King should preclude any concessions to York, especially after the carnage at St Alban's. But the Duke was of vastly different temperament to his son, a statesman in a way Humphrey could never be. "Perhaps he could intervene…"

"No," said Humphrey. "We keep out of this, Margaret. Even if we were spared any grief because my father refuses to utterly condemn that great traitor York, remember who *your* father is…*was*." He put emphasis on the *was*, sending a sliver of grief shooting through me. "Edmund Beaufort, York's most hated foe."

It was useless to argue more. Defeated, I turned to the messenger, concern and sorrow clear on my face.

The man gazed at me in some alarm. "Do not fear overmuch, my Lady," he said kindly. "It is a sorrowful burden for Countess Margaret but Jasper Tudor is on his way to assist her. He plans to take her from Caldicot to his castle of Pembroke, which is far greater in strength and defence. She will be safe there in the care of Earl Edmund's most loving brother."

I thought of flame-haired Jasper; in my mind, the superior of the two brothers. Yes, for all the heartbreak, I believed he would do his best for young Margaret.

I gave the courier some coin and he departed to the kitchens to rest and be fed. After he had departed, I faced Humphrey, who had risen and was leaning heavily on a cane his squire Lewis had brought. In my belly I felt the new infant squirm; it was not long now before he–or she—would make an entrance to the unhappy, fallen world.

"I have thought deeply on our situation these past few days—long before the messenger reached us," Humphrey said, his eyes lifeless in his drawn face. "Once the child is born and you are duly churched, I propose we retreat to one of the other Stafford properties, back over the border in England. Thornbury is not too far, near Bristol. I can, perhaps, have greater commerce with my parents and their affinity there. It is time Brecknock castle was cleaned from cellars to towers anyway; in my chamber, I can smell the stink of the privies every day."

Perhaps if you endeavoured to move, even if only to take the air and the sun you would not notice so much, I thought, but did not argue. In truth, his decision pleased me; I had a great longing to see members of my own family again—even mother and sharp-tongued Nell. And Hal, my eldest brother, close in age. After recovering from the wounds he took at St Alban's, he had been given into the 'care' of the Earl of Warwick since he was not of full legal age. He had not forgotten this insult once he had finally assumed his title of Duke of Somerset; not two months earlier he had attended the royal council in Coventry, where he had quarrelled with Warwick and failed to control his men, who caused outrage by fighting with the town watch. I wanted to soothe him in his passions, although I understood his rage—I did not want him to meet our father's fate through rash actions.

"I would be happy to go to England," I told Humphrey, reaching out a hand to him. "Once the child is born."

He did not take my proffered hand. "Good," he said curtly, and then, hunched like an old man, he limped off to his apartments without even a backwards glance.

I gave birth to my second son that winter, within the warm confines of my chamber with the knuckles of the ice-cold rain slamming the turret above and the gale shrieking through cracks in the shutters. Anchoret tutted and frowned, pulling heavy tapestries over the offending shutter to block the icy draughts. Jennet knelt on the floor, thrusting more wood into the brazier and jabbing it with a metal poker until it leapt and hissed and crackled like a living thing.

I had another sacred girdle on my belly, daubed with milk and wreathed with magic words, and a sard-stone clasped in one hand and coral in the other. The midwives hovered and the waiting wet nurse, another village girl called Gwenllian.

If Harry's birth had been fraught, taking place in a castle held by those considered enemies, my second child's entrance to the world was comforting and quick, despite the roar of the inclement weather outside the chamber.

Within less than half a day, my second boy-child slithered into the world, red and yelling. As the midwives cleaned him and held him up for me to view, I burst into laughter. His red wrinkled face… was Humphrey's in miniature.

"Humphrey!" I called to the babe, taking him carefully from the midwives and holding him, snuggling and grizzling, in my arms. He would share his father and grandfather's name; I could call him nought else. However, to avoid confusion, I gave him, as a name of the heart, the diminutive nickname—Dumph or Dumphkin. Little Humphrey Stafford.

Humphrey's eyes lit with joy when he saw his newest son, and a warm flush of pleasure ran through me to see his rare gladness. I beckoned to Gwenllian to place the child in his lap so that he could examine him closely.

"He looks like…"

"You," I finished.

"Yes." He grew thoughtful and then that hated, dreaded cloud descended on his brow once more. He frowned, a deep furrow stretching between his eyes. "Let us hope he is more fortunate than I. He is hearty, I take it? Able to travel? I will tell the servants to begin packing our possessions. Once Christmas is over and Twelfth night is past, we will begin our move to Thornbury."

Shortly before the household departed for England, a messenger reached us from Pembroke Castle. Margaret, aged but thirteen summers, had been delivered of a boy child. My Humphrey's birth had come easy and Harry's was not so dreadful either—but for Margaret, the birth of her son nearly cost her life. At one point, the infant had ceased to move, stuck within the birth channel as her hips were so narrow and undeveloped, and she had bled so much the sheets were drenched and the flagstones ran red like a slaughterhouse. The midwife had fallen to weeping, thinking she would lose both mother and babe, but then she took a breath, prayed to God Almighty, and grasped hold of the child and pulled him shrieking into the world. Margaret was mightily torn and had fainted dead away, looking as if death might claim her, but, almost miraculously, the midwife said, colour returned to her cheeks and the bleeding slowed then ceased.

"It was as if an angel breathed the breath of life into me," my cousin had written in a shaky hand; I was surprised she had not used a scribe, but she was intelligent and accomplished and preferred to pen her own missives. 'It is not my destiny to die yet, dearest Cousin. God had other plans for me, he must—and for my baby. Henry...named for the King, a kingly name." Her writing had faded after that, descending into an unreadable scrawl save for her name; I deduced she was still drained and unwell from the trauma of the birth.

I will pray for you, Margaret, I wrote back. *And for the health of little Henry. He will be the star that shines in your darkness...*

CHAPTER SEVEN

The manor house of Thornbury was comfortable but not ostentatious, unlike some of the other Stafford properties with their adamant walls and bristling towers. Hidden away in Berkeley Vale, its vast deer park separated its frontage from the nearby town that had once, centuries before, been held by Queen Matilda, wife of the Conqueror.

It was as if Humphrey desired to hide, to retreat, to remove himself from the world as much as he could. After showing some mild interest when we first arrived, walking around the property with his stick and delegating repairs to roofs and walls, he regressed into further melancholy and took to his bed.

"My great grandfather lived here for a while," he told me on one of the rare nights where we bedded together in his solemn chamber, decked with holy relics for luck, full of poultices and potions against his bodily afflictions. "Hugh de Stafford…"

"I do not know of him," I murmured sleepily.

"Went on the French campaigns," he murmured. "Gascony. Spain. He fought in the retinue of the Prince of Wales. Glorious fellow."

"And he had a wife and many children?"

"Philippa Beauchamp, daughter of the Earl of Warwick, who his enemies called 'the Devil Warwick.' Nine children, including my grandsire, Edmond. Sailed off to Jerusalem on a pilgrimage after his wife and heir died."

"Oh, how sad. The deaths, I mean; the pilgrimage was…noble." I had hoped Humphrey's story would not be one of sorrow. I felt happiness draining from the chamber as light drains from the sky when the sun falls behind the hills. I did not mention that the 'Devil Warwick' was an ancestor of mine. But then the present 'Devil Warwick' was also kin, galling as it was.

"Hugh died before he got to the Holy Land—he met his end in Rhodes, under the care of the Hospitallers. But at least he tried to reach the sacred city, even as health and hope failed. He would feel shame to look upon his sorry descendant, lying here, a half-man, a burden."

"He would *not*." I clasped his hand. "You are no failure. You are a good lord to your people. They know you are faithful to the King. You know they stand by you."

"Will their loyalty last forever, though? Ten years hence…young men will not look to me with admiration for my deeds, but see only my injuries and laugh behind my back. The 'crippled lord'…."

"Oh, Humphrey." I had not the skills to soothe his mind and his troubles made my heart sore. I kissed his brow and he rolled onto his side, facing away into the dark, and began to snore softly. I waited a while, chilled despite the heavy quilt, then pulled on my robe and sought a taper in a cup to light my way from the chamber.

My own chamber awaited, with Anchoret and Jennet on the paillasses just outside the door; at least there I could weep if needed and did not have to pretend a strength I did not truly possess.

My brother Hal Beaufort came to visit early in the summer. He rode in through Thornbury's gates looking grown-up and handsome; not at all the gangling boy I remembered. My heart leapt at the sight of him; so like Father in many ways, his mannerisms, his height, his expressions. Tears stung my eyes, both of sorrow and joy.

After Hal had eaten and spent some time talking in private to Humphrey, he arranged to meet me in the manor gardens. I waited in the arbour, apprehensive and yet exhilarated, amidst beds of purple betony, hyssop, rue, chamomile, and Oculus Christi, the Eye of Christ. All of these, although flowering herbs, were also medicinal and were used by the herbalists for Humphrey's ever-growing list of ills. I often drank the chamomile myself, brewed in boiled water, finding it calmed me when thoughts of my poor husband would make my hands shake, or when either of my babes contracted childish maladies—what if death should reach for them?

"Meg?" I turned around at the sound of my brother's voice and then I was in his strong arms, sobbing against his shoulder. The heavens seemed to swirl overhead and he half-carried me to a seat beneath a spray of blood-red roses. Petals cascaded down and at first, I cried, "No, no!" for they reminded me of droplets of blood, but then I took hold of myself and sat up.

"Forgive me, Hal. I was overcome. It has been so long since last we met and so many dire things have happened." I wiped my eyes with a kerchief. "You…you are back with mother?"

"Yes, I was let out of that beast Neville's 'care' last February and went home."

"How is she? She never writes."

"She is well enough, considering. Ever practical, is our mother. She is busy making marriage alliances. If she had not written, you will not have heard…Our sister Anne is to marry Sir William Paston…and at last Nell is to wed."

"Nell? Mother's precious shining jewel," I said, with some bitterness. "I was beginning to think she would never wed despite her being the eldest. Who?"

"James Butler, Earl of Ormond. A staunch Lancastrian if ever there was one."

I chewed on my lip, waspish. "Truly? I heard he ran from St Alban's. Was afraid of ruining his pretty face since his main claim to greatness is in the beauty of his features."

Hal slapped his thigh with his hand and burst out laughing. "He is a comely enough fellow, I suppose…and vain, but I think you do him wrong."

"Handsome is as handsome does," I said. "Anyway—how can this be? He is wed to Avice Stafford of Hook, a distant cousin of my husband."

"Avice is dead," said Henry. "The Earl cast his eye around for a new, high-ranking bride almost immediately. Nell expressed an interest—probably thought his beautiful face and hers together would make beautiful children! Mother agreed—so the wedding will take place next year, after a decent mourning period for Avice, of course."

"Of course," I mocked. Nell was an impatient girl, and at her advancing age, probably more so than I remembered.

"But let's not talk about Nell—she would love to think our tongues wagged about her doings. I have news of my own."

"Are you to marry too? I am surprised no match was ever made for you when father was alive."

"I have found favour with the Queen, Meg. She has suggested I marry Joanna, sister of our cousin, James, the King of Scotland."

"Is Joanna not in France? I thought she was to marry the Dauphin."

"Returned a few months ago. They were incompatible."

"I am not surprised—you are aware she is deaf and mute? They call her *Muta Domina*."

"As long as she still has her wits, I do not care if she has no speech. I cannot say it would not be a relief to have a wife who could never turn into a scold. She is royal; that is of utmost importance. But nothing may come of it. Indeed, I am not convinced I want the match or any match."

He began to pace around the garden; his vexation was almost palpable, yet I had to restrain inappropriate laughter as butterflies sprang up around him from the disturbed flowers and bees shot by his head, angrily buzzing. "I have less inclination to marry than to make war," he said. "I cannot let Father and the Beaufort honour go unavenged! Why do you smile, Meg?"

I put my hand over my mouth. "I was not, I just made a face because the sun…the sun hurts my eyes. Continue, Hal."

"You have heard what happened at Coventry? I attacked York with my bare hands in the council chamber, flung myself across the table reaching for his throat. They pulled me off…"

"And you caused trouble in the streets of the city and men of the Watch were killed. The locals were ready to lynch you, but Buckingham stepped in with his men to calm the fray. Oh, Hal, I understand your rage but such action is not the way. It will end up with you being killed like Father—I could not bear that!"

"I won't be silent on the matter and I will never seek friendship with the enemy." Hal's colour was high. "Do not even suggest it, Meg. I have good stout fellows on my side, who also lost their fathers at St Alban's—Lord Clifford being the main one. The Duke of Exeter, Henry Holland, has become a close friend and supporter too, despite that he is wed to York's daughter, Anne."

"I just fear for you, Hal; for all our family. We have suffered enough."

"Do you not think more indignities will be heaped on us? They shall be, as long as York and Warwick live, I can assure you."

"We must not have more war, more bloodshed…."

"I do not understand you, sister. Do you not truly care about our father's murder. Our family's honour." A sneer crossed his features, robbing him of his usual good looks. He pointed with a shaking finger at the manor house—to Humphrey's chamber, which looked out over the gardens. The great thick drapes with their traceries of antelopes were drawn. "Do you not even care what they did to him, Margaret? To your own husband! Even if you do not—think of the two sons you have and their future…"

"I do not want to hear anymore…Yes, I was angry at first; I even called for revenge, no different to you. But I have two babes now. It must stop. Differences must be wrought in the council chamber, not on the battlefield!"

I rose, the joy of the day leached from my heart. Hal was changed; angry and embittered. Overhead, the summer sun was suddenly obscured by a scudding wreath of cloud and shadows raced about the gardens, black wraiths that dusted the lavender and turned bright roses into gloomy, drooping, funereal buds. Hal's jaw tightened and with an irritated shake of his head, he stalked away, leaving me caught betwixt sunlight and shadow, my heart divided, not knowing which way I should turn.

Later that year I heard that Hal had been appointed Constable of Carisbrooke Castle and Lieutenant of the Isle of

Wight. He received these positions after a violent attack on Sandwich by the French, during which the mayor had been slain, and I hoped he might find some solace in fighting foreign foes rather than his own countrymen. Maybe it was merely womanly weakness, but although I wanted York to pay for my father's death, I did not want that vengeance to lead to greater bloodshed from my own kin.

However, it was not long before Hal tried to attack Warwick in London, with the aid of his friend Exeter and our half-brother, Thomas Ros. Warwick managed to outsmart them all and slipped away unharmed, which must have pained them no end.

I tried to put Hal's constant fury from my mind. I had no power to halt his actions. Besides, I had a wedding to attend.

To my surprise, Cousin Margaret had, with Jasper Tudor's assistance, already negotiated a second marriage—and it was to a Stafford, Humphrey's younger brother, Henry, who had never wed, even though he was past thirty summers. A dispensation was needed for the new couple, who were second cousins and related in the prohibited degree, but after the Pope cleared that impediment, they announced their intent to marry at Maxstoke Castle, one of the Buckingham properties, on the 3rd of January.

Christmas festivities at Thornbury were sombre and sparse, so I was glad to attend the wedding and glad, too, that it was a Stafford family affair, so that Humphrey would feel more inclined to come. He decided he would go, but insisted he ride upright upon a horse, his leg swathed in woollen pads to keep his wound, with its fresh, tender skin, from chaffing. As was customary, I travelled in my carriage with Jennet and Anchoret, and a monstrous mountain of silk cushions—it was over twenty leagues to Maxstoke and the journey would be a bumpy one, even though the roads in that part of the country were good.

I was stiff and sore as we neared Maxstoke, and I prayed I might have a bath drawn to ease my pains. Anchoret was peering out the slit window. "Come look, my Lady," she said. "It is a fine stronghold."

Stiffly, I shuffled over, pushing aside cushions, and took her place at the window. The castle was handsome and neat with great, red, octagonal towers set around a square courtyard. A stone bridge arched across a deep blue moat, leading to a grand entrance tower emblazoned with the arms of Duke Humphrey. They impaled those of his wife, Anne Neville, and were supported by antelopes, a Buckingham device alluding to the Duke's descent from the daughter of Thomas of Woodstock, Edward III's youngest son.

As we drew even closer, clarions calling into the wintry air and the horses' hooves clacking on the stone arch of the bridge, I noted the gatehouse, walls were also graven with Stafford cartwheels. Massive doors studded with polished strips of iron acted almost like a mirror, casting back the intense light of the low winter sun, which burned at our backs.

Once within the castle, the Duke emerged to embrace his son. His battle scar was still like a jagged bolt of lightning across his cheek but otherwise, he seemed hale and well. My poor Humphrey was a weak wisp next to him, his features aged, his complexion wan. The Duchess Anne, dressed in crimson robes and jewelled headdress, appeared shocked by her eldest's son's condition; her hand twined around the rosary of red glass beads that hung from her girdle as a frown creased her brow.

Neither Duke or Duchess had glanced in my direction. Despite having no reason for shame, the tips of my ears and my cheeks began to burn. My hands curled into sweaty fists, nails digging into my palms. God forbid the Duke and Duchess might think I ignored or even maltreated their beloved eldest son! Ankaret must have seen my pained expression and guessed what troubled me, for she crept to my side, mouth close to my ear as she pretended to fiddle with a jewelled pin in my hennin. "My Lady, you have done nought wrong. I beg you, do not ever believe you have. If they believe it, they are fools."

The family gathering continued as the groom-to-be entered the room and went to Humphrey, the two brothers clinging to each other and trying to curb unmanly tears by pretending to smite each other stoutly on the arm and shoulders. "Humph, my dearest brother," said Henry. "Glad am I to see you. A long parting. Much too long."

"I fear you will find me poor sport now," said Humphrey, long-faced. "The wounds from St Alban's—they pain me still. Not a single day passes without pain, not one night do I have in peaceful sleep. All joy has gone from my life, I fear…But I speak selfishly, for you, too, have suffered…" He raised his hand to touch Henry's face.

Henry flinched, and I then realised why he had missed our wedding, why he had not fought at his father's side at St Alban's, maybe even why he had not wed till so late in life. Like Humphrey, he was not a well man. He was of middling height, neither too thin nor too burly, but his face…a blotchy, pustulent red rash crossed nose and cheeks and chin. Skin peeled in flaky strips and his eyes were narrowed, watery and red.

I choked back a gasp. Was it leprosy? But no, it could not be, for he would surely dwell in a lazar house away from clean folk…

"The physics say Henry has St Anthony's Fire." A voice sounded at my elbow and I whirled about to see my cousin Margaret, the intended bride. She was no taller than before, seemingly locked in childhood size, but her visage was that of a woman twice her age, wracked with pain and care—although a determined set to her jaw gave her an almost ferocious look.

"I did not mean to stare, Cousin," I whispered in a low voice. "Humphrey never told me, although he often spoke of Henry." I reached out, almost instinctively to catch her bird-frail wrist. "I am sorry for what has befallen you since we last met. I heard the birth of your babe almost killed you…"

"I put it from my thoughts," she said, somewhat coldly. Her eyes became very dark as if she recalled the birth against her will—and then blotted out such evil recollection. "I am more fortunate than many—praise be to God in His mercy. He said that women must labour and bring forth in blood and pain like Eve, tainted by her sin—but he chose to spare me and my son. Glory to His name."

She seemed a little strange and fey. Margaret had always shown determination beyond her years, but now there was a peculiarity about her, as if, having stepped so closer to death's realm, she could not quite draw back to full reality. I felt concerned, as I would have for my own younger sisters had their situations mirrored hers.

I drew her slightly closer, feeling the skinny wrist turn in my hand, the vague pulse of life again frail bone. "Do you want this so soon? And…and to one afflicted, God help him."

She gave a sharp nod and pulled her arm free. "Yes, it is what I desire, Meg. I need a strong family behind me to ascertain my Henry grows up with all he needs. He is my prime concern now. As for my betrothed's illness, although it is thought St Anthony's Fire is related to leprosy, it does not spread to others and sometimes it remits altogether. I will be happy, Meg; Henry is a good man, the Staffords are a powerful family, and my baby will sleep safe…and live to fulfil whatever destiny God has decided for him. I am sure, more than ever, that my little Henry Tudor is marked for greatness…"

"Margaret…" Henry Stafford had left Humphrey and was walking towards us. He had kindly eyes for all that the whites were blood-red and the rims painfully swollen. "I did not realise you were in the hall. And you, my Lady…you must be my brother's wife, the *other* Margaret Beaufort." He gave a small laugh and grinned; his easy humour, despite his ills, appealed to my nature and I smiled back.

"Yes, there are two of us, Sir Henry—two cousins. I am more often known as 'Meg' than Margaret, though…to those who know me best."

He lifted my hand but stopped just short of touching it with his lips. My heart bled for him; he had done so deliberately to cause me no fear. "Well, it is a pleasure, Lady Meg, if I do say so. I hear that you and Humphrey have recently removed from Brecknock to Thornbury."

"For the moment, sir," I said. "You can see how it is…"

I nodded towards Humphrey, who had retired to a chair and was in earnest conversation with his mother. "He has not recovered. He does not appear to have the strong constitution of his father, the Duke."

"If you remain in England for a while, I will try to visit…I'll bring Margaret. I would like to see my little nephews—my namesake Henry---although I am sure you named the child for the King and not for me!"

I cast him another smile. "It is customary, is it not? But I would have been more than happy to have him named for my husband's dear brother."

Across the hall, the Duke of Buckingham motioned for his son to join his mother and Humphrey. Henry bowed to me, "I fear I must go. It has been a great pleasure."

He strode over to his family and aided Humphrey to rise, his hand firm as a servant took away the chair. He then wrapped a brotherly arm around his shoulders, making it look as if they only were in fraternal harmony and not that he helped support an invalid. He did it to save Humphrey from embarrassment and shame, and once more I felt a warm rush of appreciation. As Margaret had told me, he was a good man.

"I think we have been abandoned, Countess," said Anchoret, trying to make light of the fact the Stafford family had vacated the chamber without further acknowledgement of my presence.

"Ah, let them talk… they have seen little of each other," I said, pretending nonchalance, although I had felt a little stung. "Shall we go to my chambers and bring out our needlework? I am working on a shirt for little Harry and have brought it along…"

I then noticed that Cousin Margaret also still lingered in the hall. "Would you like to join us, Cousin?" I asked. "The sun is out, and I have brought a box of wafers and honeyed sweetmeats from Thornbury."

She shook her head emphatically. "I am fasting, Meg."

"Fasting? Whatever for? It is not a fast day. Do not make yourself ill, Margaret; you have not long had a baby and need your strength…You are thin as a reed."

"My body, such as it is, means nothing," she said, again seeming a hundred years old. "When I am fasting, depriving myself of earthly gluttony, I find I am closer to the angels, to God, to the Divine. It is when I am happiest."

Modestly lifting her heavy dark skirts, she swept out of the room. I saw Anchoret's eyebrows lift quizzically. "Margaret was always pious," I murmured, almost as an apology. Her leave-taking was abrupt, even discourteous; she was changed by her recent bereavement and by birthing young Henry all alone in Pembroke Castle.

"Well," Anchoret put her hands on her hips, "it would do well for her to remember in the words in Matthew if her piety is so great...*when you fast, be not, as the hypocrites, of a sad countenance: for they disfigure their faces, that they may appear unto men to fast...*" Suddenly she blushed. "I should not say such things about my betters, especially not to Lady Margaret's own kinswoman. I would not blame you if you beat me for my insolence."

"I would not beat you nor anyone else," I said wryly, as I beckoned her and Jennet towards the door. "Especially when every word you said was true."

Margaret and Henry Stafford were married in the castle chapel the next day, a sombre, swift affair. The banquet after was sumptuous, but Margaret, clad more like a nun than a bride, ate little, clearly clinging to her fast as much as possible. Lilies and roses lay strewn across the hall floor, mingled with clean cut rushes, but as they became crushed by a succession of feet, they began to give off a sickly odour...or at least so I thought. Mixed with the scent of spices and fish and hot candle wax, the aromas made my belly began to churn. Fortunately, the couple did not linger long but went to retire early, with little ribaldry in evidence.

A day later, the newly-married couple departed for their new home at one of Margaret's properties in Lincolnshire. Duke Humphrey had settled some money on his second son as a wedding gift but, rumour had it, most of their income would come from Margaret's copious lands.

Before they left for Lincolnshire, I approached Margaret, who was waiting in the courtyard to depart, swathed in grey rabbit skin and fox fur against the frigid wind, with only her pointed nose showing, a florid shade of red. I bent to kiss her cheek. "I wish you well. I am sure you will be glad to settle down and be reunited with your little babe."

She stared at me, her dark eyes growing as cold as the wind. "Henry is not coming to live with us. I left him at Pembroke with Jasper. It is safest for him behind Pembroke's great walls. I will always put his wellbeing above any wants of mine."

With that, she climbed into her chariot and was gone into the drear and hazy morning. She did not look back to wave, though I waved foolishly after her carriage.

I wondered if I would see her again. I shivered and thought of my two little boys, safe in Thornbury with their nurses. The idea of separation from them was appalling—at least for now; one day they would have to join some great lord's household as pages, then squires. But not yet, not when so young...I was certain if my sons were taken away, even to a caring household, I would seem as strange and brittle as Margaret had seemingly become.

An icy gust of wind through snow-crystal into my eyes, stinging like tears. I wanted to go home.

The King had declared his intentions of a 'Loveday'—a most marvellous thing, although an unlikely one where old hatreds would be assuaged. He had summoned the nobles to London, and Humphrey, after conferring with his father, had agreed to make the journey—and he asked me to accompany him.

"It is something I think you should also witness. All the great noble houses will be there, and you are both Stafford and Beaufort. All will be made well, the disputes of St Alban's settled—the King insists this Loveday will eradicate the roots of rancour."

I wondered if Humphrey thought I might keep a close rein on my fiery brother Hal, but if it was in his mind, it was a vain hope. Hal would never listen to me especially when it came to his thirst for vengeance. I had already heard of his movements from one of my concerned sisters, Anne—he had already reached London over a month ago with a large force of men, including cavalry, although he had been denied entry to the city by the mayor, Geoffrey Boleyn, who sent him away to lodge in Temple Bar beyond the walls.

We reached London on a blustery March day and hastily retreated to the safety and comfort of The Rose. The streets were even busier than before, heaving with the retinues of dozens of great lords. Stafford Knots and Cartwheels blazed amidst Talbot Hounds, Oxford's Star and Hungerford's Sickle. These were followed by the Ragged Staff of Warwick, the Seated Gryphon of his father, Salisbury, FitzAlan's White Horse, the Horseshoe of Ferrers, and all too numerous, the Fetterlock of Richard, Duke of York. Various badges of King Henry were in abundance—a spotted leopard, an antelope, two ostrich feathers in a saltire. Apparently, despite his lack of knowledge in the arts of war, he was wise enough to bring in 12,000 archers to keep the peace if necessary.

Buckingham brought his chariot up to The Rose to collect Humphrey, and he was whisked away to a council meeting at the House of the Blackfriars where he would participate in negotiations that would, ostensibly, bring peace between York's faction and the young men whose fathers died at St Alban's. Humphrey had forbidden me to go into the city to shop, saying that it was too full of rogues from all sides of the debate. So I stayed at The Rose and played numerous games of Tric-trac and Merrills with Jennet and Anchoret, and read to them from my book by Christine de Pisan—*The City of Ladies*.

"It is a great marvel that some women write whole books, just as men do." Anchoret took the tome from me and leafed wonderingly through its bright illustrations.

"It would be even more amazing if women *did* build a 'City of Ladies'," quipped Jennet.

"I'll wager it would be better than what we have now." Anchoret's eyes narrowed. "No drunken men allowed to fall out of taverns into the street. No stews full of sin. No fighting with swords or knives. Men who beat their wives whipped out of the city. Women allowed their free will and to determine their own fates—sounds like paradise!"

Jennet made a dismissive sound. "Such fantasies will never happen. It goes against the natural order anyway. Can you imagine a man not being permitted to chastise his errant wife?"

Later, we held a small private dinner in my solar, simple but filling—white bread with pots of whipped golden butter, eggs dripping in honeyed mustard, a thin meat pottage and a dish of strawberry soup served cold. Humphrey was still not back at The Rose. The day was failing and the sun hung blood-red over the river, the clouds flapping over spires and rooftops like torn crimson banners on a battlefield. Bells were ringing and the streets beyond the manor's gates were noisier than ever. The sounds grew in intensity and I suspected that something of import had happened today in Westminster, where the King was attempting to thrash out peace between the warring factions.

As the sun sank, making the spires and pinnacles across the river turn into black, fang-like silhouettes, I began to pace the floor with nervousness. Why was Humphrey not back? All kinds of dreadful scenarios played through my mind—my brother Hal attacking Warwick or York, Buckingham and Humphrey attempting to keep them apart, trying to act as peacekeepers and being stabbed by hidden daggers…

"Are you well, my lady?" asked Anchoret, squinting in the dim candlelight. "You look a trifle pale."

"Wine, Anchoret…I could use a goblet of wine to steady me," I murmured.

Anchoret raced for the decanter, while Jennet collected my goblet from the table. "It will be all right, madam," Jennet whispered as she pressed the stem of the goblet into my cold fingers. "His lordship will have come to no harm. He is with his father, one of the mightiest lords in the land. They are well guarded."

"But treachery is always a risk," I muttered, "and violence is never far away."

"Not in the council chamber, surely!" she said. "The King is there!"

I bowed my head. But could a King so weak, so mild, more a saint than a red-blooded man, hold back a sudden onslaught of angry young men like my brother and Exeter? Or the older, more experienced York and Salisbury?

Suddenly, outside we heard a clatter at the gate. Anchoret rushed to the window, peering out in the gloom. "I see lanterns; the guards are opening the gates. Lord Humphrey is home!"

I beckoned to my women to put on my hennin and brush down crumples in my skirts. Then I headed into the darkly panelled hall to await Humphrey, not knowing what to expect.

He stumped into the hall, leaning on his stick, aided by Lewis and another squire. He was grinning from ear to ear, his face flushed with excitement. He looked bolder, more like he was before St Alban's, which brought gladness to my heart. The Duke of Buckingham was wise to have insisted on his presence.

"What news, husband?" I waved the squires away and led him to a nearby stool before the fireplace.

"Great news." His eyes were alight. "I feared the King might cave in and deal with his overmighty subjects as if they were gentle lambs and not rapacious wolves—but no. He was stern, unyielding. I sense the hand of the Queen in this."

"What has happened?"

"A truce, of sorts. York is bound to peace for 10,000 marks—as is your brother, Hal. York looked resigned, young Hal grizzled a bit but agreed in the end. His Grace also ordered that York and his supporters send monies to St Alban's abbey for masses for the dead in perpetuity. Tomorrow, upon the feast of the Annunciation, the King has decreed his 'Loveday' will proceed to complete the new amity between his greatest subjects"

"I take it there is more here than written promises or sworn vows. What exactly will take place?"

He smiled a secret smile. "You will see, Meg. Together we will attend this great celebration, the likes of which has never before been seen on England's shores, nor ever, I trow, will be again."

Lady Day dawned bright and sunny, although there was a sharp sting to the wind, an appropriate reminder that beneath a fair appearance, there could still be things to guard against.

Humphrey and I hastened to the Palace of the Bishop of London in time to see the participants of the Loveday emerge and head on foot towards St Paul's Cathedral. First, to my surprise was my brother Hal, allowed in from Temple Bar at last, holding hands with the Earl of Salisbury, a man old enough to be his father. Even at a distance, I could tell Hal was furious, eager to take up weapons no matter what fine words he might have spoken. He would never forgive, even at the behest of his King. Behind him, strode his friend, Henry Holland, with the Earl of Warwick. Holland, a short, pug-faced fellow with a bad complexion, looked as if he would like nothing more than to tear off Warwick's arm, while Warwick smirked at him, enjoying his discomfiture whilst acting as if he was not bothered by the proceedings at all. The King followed after, wearing crown and regal robes, his footsteps shambling but his visage alight as if on this day he had contrived the most wondrous miracle. He did not note the dark furrowed brow of his Queen, who stalked in the rear, her clawed hand clutching that of Richard, Duke of York, who stared straight ahead, his mouth a grim line.

We began to follow the procession, Humphrey insistent that he could walk, as long as the pace was not too great. Other nobles crowded around us, cutting us off from the common folk, who treated this day as a festival, throwing flowers from the top floors of over-hanging houses and selling pastries and tawdry goods on street corners.

"Look!" Walking beside his son, the Duke of Buckingham nodded ahead. "The Earl of Salisbury's retainers are here. I did not foresee that." He looked uncomfortable, his hand sliding toward the dagger at his belt.

Up beyond the gaudily attired figures of Salisbury and the slimmer, red-clad shape of Hal, a horde of armoured men in Salisbury's colours filled the churchyard of St Paul's. Sunlight glittered on plate and on pikes.

"I pray those men will not cause trouble," I whispered, half to myself. "I cannot believe Salisbury's men were allowed in when Hal's were not." I knew, though, that despite my loyalty to my brother, if his forces and Exeter's were in the city, even now the streets would be gushing with blood.

The Dukes and Earls enjoined in the Loveday entered the vast church with the King and Queen. The gossipy Paul's Walkers lurking near the doorway peered and gawked, taking in every detail to pass on to curious denizens of London waiting in every tavern and inn.

We came in behind the main party, along with the rest of the nobility, the glaring young lords such as Clifford still eager to avenge the slain fathers, but constrained by what had taken place over the last few days. Earlier in the year, Clifford, Egremont and Percy had tried to ambush the Yorkist faction while on their way to meetings at Westminster but now their hands were stilled by this Loveday upon the festival of the Annunciation.

However, I wondered—these young hotheads were here now, but would the King's pretty words be enough? Oh, yes, there were monetary considerations in play—York was ordered to pay Hal 5000 marks, Warwick would give 1000 to Clifford, and Salisbury would cancel debts owed him by Egremont...but would that satisfy them? They had agreed to end the bloodshed, but by the looks upon their faces, I doubted, although my heart wished otherwise, that this peace would ever hold.

The Mass of reconciliation was read and Humphrey and I exited the church. While we had been inside, the sky had clouded over and the first drops of rain hit our upturned faces and pattered on the polished breastplates of Salisbury's men as they huddled morosely around the tombstones. Threat hung heavy in the air.

The King seemed pleased though, stepping out into the street clutching a copy of '*Knyghthode and Bataile*', which had been presented to him upon completion of the service.

We trudged wearily back through the crowded streets as the rain began to fall in earnest. Dark skies settled over London, brooding and ominous, despite the merry bells that rang in abbey, priory and church, tolling out their message: *Oh happy days, England is saved...*

Further celebrations to commemorate the truce between the warring factions took place over the next few days. Some were held at the Tower and some at the Pleasance, the Queen's waterside Palace just outside of London. Tuns of Gascon wine were downed, while the nobles of the realm feasted on oxen, venison, suckling pig, as well as sturgeon, bream and eels from the London rivers. Subtleties abounded, fashioned into symbols of the House of Lancaster, alongside heaped trays of sweetmeats and sugared almonds. Jousting took place before stalls hung with tapestries shipped from Burgundy. In the women's stall, ladies in their best gowns and headdresses, their necks awash with gems, fought to give a sleeve or kerchief or ribbon to the most handsome knights. I sat with them, but had little interest in such sport; my heart was with Humphrey, who seemed so enlivened by all the proceedings. He sat among other men of his own rank; for a moment, his pains were forgotten and he talked animatedly with his peers—and, when he had the chance, with me. Perhaps the tide *was* turning.

At the final banquet held in honour of Loveday, a minstrel in gaudy green and red, with great pointed Krakow shoes upon his feet and a hat with trailing liripipe, stood before the assembly and recited a newly composed poem about the reconciliation of the fighting factions.

"In York, in Somerset, as I understand,
In Warwick also is love and charity,
In Salisbury too and in Northumberland,
That every man may rejoice in concord and unity..." he sang at the close, to a resounding roar of approval from the feasters and the raucous banging of goblets on the tables.

This joyous cry for peace, however, was soon drowned out by even louder shouts for more wine...

Humphrey and I readied to return home at the end of the festivities. On the morning of our leave-taking from The Rose, Hal appeared at the gate, eager to speak with me before we returned to our respective homes.

"I am faring west to visit our mother," he said. "Some of the payment granted to me is also for her—and for you and the rest of our brothers and sisters."

"I do not care about such payment." I shook my head. "It is blood money."

"Nonetheless, you will receive your portion as was agreed. Use it for Masses for our father's soul, if you find it sullying. Of course, its distribution will depend on when and if we truly receive this payment."

"You think York will not pay?"

He raised an eyebrow. "I have my doubts."

"But that would mean…"

"Meg, do you truly believe this is over?"

"Well, the King does," I said uneasily.

"You know how he is—naive as a lamb."

"I beg you, do not be the one who breaks this fragile peace."

"I swear to nought, sister, but let us not argue. We see each other so rarely and once we were close. But I did not come here merely to tell you about the blood-money anyway—I came with news of a much happier nature."

"And that is?"

He grinned. "I have a son…"

"But you are not…" I paused, blushing. "Married."

He let out a peal of laughter. "No, I admit, my little son is born on the wrong side of the blanket as men say, but still, he will want for nought and perhaps grow to greatness one day, as have many baseborn sons."

"Who is his mother? I -I did not even know you had a-a…"

"Leman?" he grinned. "Her name is Joan…Joan Hill. From a knightly family, that is all, but fair of face. We have called the boy Charles—an unusual name in England, I know, and I would have preferred our father's name, but perhaps that should be held in reservation for a legitimate heir."

"Perhaps. I will send a gift for my little nephew when I return to Thornbury and can arrange something." I leaned over and kissed his cheek. "It has been good to see you. Hal."

"And you," he said, "even though our family is still bruised and battered from Father's demise. But the Beauforts will rise again; I swear they will…"

He departed then, handsome and tall on his large bay stallion, and I was left waving forlornly at his back as he trotted out into the busy thoroughfare beyond. But I could not brood for long; once he had vanished into the throng, I hurried back to the house to oversee the servants packing the last of our belongings into the waiting wains. Soon I would see my small boys again, and that thought filled me with infinite joy, making London's heady delights pallid and unimportant things.

CHAPTER EIGHT

Humphrey lay abed at Thornbury, unwell again. A boil had formed in the scar tissue on his leg and he ran a high fever that made him sweat and shiver. The physician had lanced the boil, to accompanying shouting and swearing, but Humphrey remained feverish and debilitated, his appetite poor. Harry, nigh on three years old, was proving a strong-headed handful and refusing to visit his father's bedchamber as a good son should. I thought his presence might cheer Humphrey and offered Harry sorts of treats to entice him to go—sweetmeats, barley sugar sticks, candied violets—to no avail.

"Harry no like go!" he would yell, stomping his little foot on the flagstones and thrusting out his lower lip defiantly. "Smells!"

I knew he did not understand Humphrey's illness, but his stubbornness was hard to deal with, and one day he grumbled, as I hauled him down the corridor by the arm, "Hate smelly old dada."

"Harry!" I cried. "Apologise at once or you will be punished." My words did not chasten him and only resulted in the child shrieking until his face turned crimson and big tears oozed from his screwed-shut eyes. He clawed at my arm and tried to kick my legs beneath my voluminous skirt

Weary beyond words, filled with fear and worry for Humphrey, I could endure no more of my son's insolence, young though he was. I grabbed him and pressed my hand across his yelling mouth. "You *will* be silent or you shall have no pony ride, no visiting the kennels, and no supper tonight, Henry Stafford!"

His shrieks and bellows stopped instantly, although his mouth against my palm was still open like a cavern and he stared goggle-eyed at me in white-hot rage. He hesitated for a moment, in which I feared he might bite my hand, and then he tore away and ran screaming through the manor house, tearing down tapestries and pushing servants with his hot sticky hands.

Infuriated, my head spinning, I shouted to his nurses, who hovered, embarrassed to the point of tears, in the next chamber.

"Do your duty! Take hold of Master Harry before he harms himself! Take him away to the nursery! He needs more discipline; I swear you all spoil him. I am in no mood to deal with his tantrums, nor is it my place to."

White aprons and woollen skirts flurried and a few minutes later Harry was apprehended and hauled away to the nursery which, mercifully, was on the far side of the house. My eldest son's enraged shrieks soon became muffled sobs. I slumped into a nearby window embrasure, holding my head, which pounded as if devils attacked it with hammers.

I did not know how long I sat there but the light around me grew blue and then dim. Wearily I raised my head, temples still throbbing.

At that moment, the young squire Lewis came thundering down the hall, his face a terrified white blur. Seeing me, he ran all the faster. "Milady…milady…You must come!" he cried, dragging on my sleeve despite the impropriety of touching his mistress.

"What is it, Lewis?" I asked, perturbed. "Whyever are you rushing about in such a manner?"

His mouth worked as he sought to get his words out. "Lady Margaret…please! It's Lord Humphrey. He's not himself; he keeps mumbling things that make no sense. And …and he wouldn't let me tell you ere now, but all morning he's been rushing to the privy with blood flux!"

"Dear God!" Waves of cold terror crashed over me…yet there was a sense of disaster having been averted too. I had come near enough to forcing Harry into his father's bedchamber, perhaps putting him at risk of contagion. How I regretted chastising him now; maybe the child himself had sensed his father's sickness and was overcome by fear.

"I will go to him immediately," I said. "You, Lewis, go find the physician and bring him from town without delay".

Lewis bowed and sped away, his footfalls fading into the distance. Gloom roiling around me—for no one had yet lit the cressets in the hallways—I hauled up my skirts and rushed to Humphrey's bedchamber.

I found him sprawled across the bed, tangled in sheets and coverlet. Sweat poured down his brow, soaking his curls. He shivered, though, even as he sweated, and his teeth were tightly clenched. The room reeked and my stomach churned, but I forced myself to go to his side.

"Don't touch me!" he murmured, weakly waving a hand. "Get away!" At least he was awake

"What has happened? Tell me what's wrong! I won't leave—I'm your wife."

"I have some ague…on top of my other woes. Ah…the pain." He grasped at his belly with his hand. His fingers were trembling like those of an old man with palsy.

"Let me get you into the bed." I sought to move him into a more dignified position and draw the cover over his shivering form. "You need to keep warm."

"But I burn…I burn!" he cried, sweat rolling down his cheeks. Yet at the same time he trembled. "You must go, Meg—I command you to go. You might catch this blight…and our sons…"

"I won't leave till the doctor arrives," I said. "I sent Lewis to fetch him with all speed."

Humphrey heaved himself upright, gasping, and suddenly vomited bile down his chest. His face twisted in disgust and he made to rip his soiled nightshirt away but collapsed backwards, his eyes rolling in his head.

I did not know what to do but stood gaping like a mooncalf, helpless tears starting from my eyes.

Humphrey writhed and began to mutter and rave, "The abbey…must make it to the abbey. Father…father, you must come with me, even if the King won't…."

I gasped. In his illness, he was reliving the battle of St Alban's.

He flopped over, tearing at the sheets. "The King's neck is wounded…so much blood. And my leg…I can't walk….and my hand is useless. Father's face; an arrow has struck him, yet he tears it out and still lives! But oh God, the blood, the smell of it, the screams…and Somerset is rushing forth from The Castle

Tavern...the fool. *The fool*! He swings his sword; foes fall...but he is surrounded and they are hacking...him, hacking him...oh Christ, it is butchery..."

"Humphrey, no, no!" I cried weakly. "No more. It's over. Over!"

"It will never be over!" he groaned, his hands clenched into fists. "Never till the day I die. Now get out! Out, I say!" He looked so wild then, his eyes no longer rolled back but starting from his head—red where blood vessels had burst—that I gave a sob and fled, slamming the heavy door. Outside, I leaned against it, shaking and weeping; behind its stout panels, I could hear Humphrey cursing and moaning.

Fortunately, I heard sounds of approaching feet and saw the steward marching through the gloom holding up a candle for light, the physician and Lewis scurrying at his heels.

"My Lady..." said the steward.

"Go in, at once!" I cried. "I have never seen him like this. He has the flux and he...he is not right in himself, but speaks of times gone past with great torment."

I moved aside, keeping the wall as a support for I did not trust my legs to hold me up, and the doctor and steward entered the chamber. I began to make my way along the corridor, clutching at the wooden panelling with my fingers. I was of no use here. No use at all.

Anchoret appeared at the end of the passageway, a vision of angelic mercy. I croaked her name.

"Earl Humphrey..." she murmured, drawing near. "I saw the physic enter the bailey with Lewis."

"He's very ill, Anchoret." I fell into her arms. "I have never seen anyone so ill. What if...he...what if..."

I sagged against her in a half-faint, my vision blurred and my ears ringing. "You must not think such dark thoughts," said Anchoret. "Pray, my Lady; you have always been a pious woman. Surely God will heed you."

In that moment I wanted to laugh, wild and bitter. I was conventionally pious, but although I loved Our Saviour and his Mother, I was nowhere near as devout as my Cousin Margaret, and yet God turned his face from her when Edmund Tudor died, leaving her pregnant and alone…If He did not smile on Margaret, he certainly would not smile on a weak, unworthy creature such as me.

"Anchoret, I…I do not know what I'll do if…"

"Well, I know what I am going to do right now. I'm getting you into bed and sending Jennet to the herbalist for a sleeping draught. We cannot have you falling sick like his Lordship."

She placed a comforting but firm arm around my waist and led me towards my bedchamber. Once inside, I crumpled weakly in a heap as she and Jennet untied my gown and put me to bed. Then, as Anchoret fussed and set my rosary beads in my hand, Jennet hastened off to obtain a sleeping potion from the town apothecary.

She returned with *Dwale*, a powerful anaesthetic used upon the battlefield when men must have their flesh cut and sewn, though much diluted as to not overwhelm my weak female constitution. The fluted bottle contained wine mixed with pig's gall, bryony, and pulverised lettuce, and a spoonful each of white poppy juice, the fearsome hemlock, and henbane, loved by witches who claimed it made them fly.

Normally, I might have baulked at such a brew in case I never woke afterwards, but today, I grabbed it with both hands and raised it to my lips, downing it in one.

Soon the room began to spin and my heart to slow. "I hope it wasn't too strong," Jennet whispered to Anchoret, not realising I could still hear. "Hemlock…Wicked men use it for self-murder."

"Hush!" admonished Anchoret. "No more talk, Jennet. We must keep an eye on her ladyship, and devote ourselves to her wellbeing…and pray, for both her and for poor Lord Humphrey."

I turned my head away. It was a May night and warm, and the window was slightly ajar. I fixed my blurry gaze on the Evenstar, burning above the peaked roof of the hall—Hesperus, son of Eos the Dawn, who in the morning would reappear as Lucifer, the Light Bearer, the Enemy of mankind…

As the star's brightness waned, so also did I slip away into a deep, dreamless darkness, near as deep as death itself.

A single tear trickled down my cheek.

Candles burned brightly in the castle chapel. Blinking like an owl, I stood within the ring of light. On the wall the Rood loomed, Christ's face in tortured agony, His eyes cast heavenward, His side rent and bleeding from the stab of Roman spears.

My own torment twisted inside me, threatening to spill out in wails of grief.

Humphrey was dead. He had died when I lay asleep under the influence of the *Dwale*. In the morning, a tearful Anchoret had given me the news, and I am told, I had gone mad, attempting to leap from my chamber window, pulled back only by the efforts of fleet-footed Jennet. Both my ladies had pressed me down upon the floor, kicking, thrashing and screaming...or so men say. I remember nought of such distress.

I was given more *Dwale*, in a higher dose—I slept the sleep of the dead, without dreams.

But when I woke and the light hit my eyes and the truth struck my mind, I again became witless and wandering. More *Dwale* was brought in, and empty darkness beckoned...

The physician said I must rise and so I did. There were no more screams, though they lie locked within my breast; a heavy stone of grief. I stared at my hands, white and bony; I had eaten little through my sickness and my clothes hung off my frame as if I were a skeleton.

I *felt* dead. Maybe I *was* dead and walking this world as a revenant...

Humphrey was still lying in state before the high altar, Anchoret told me. It had been what...two weeks? The air of the manor house was flavoured with tallow, frankincense and myrrh, but the taint of death defeated the perfume, sickly and cloying. It would cling to my raiment and hair for weeks, no matter how often they are washed.

"He...he must be buried." I tried to push past Anchoret. I did not know what I thought I would do—scratch a grave out with my hands?

"Milady...it is taken care of. The Duke and Duchess of Buckingham have been informed. They have sent a party to gather him up and bear him to the Stafford vault."

"I-I must go to him...before he is gone forever!" I croaked, pulling free of her and stumbling towards the chapel. My feet on the floorboards were bare. Gasping, I flung open the chapel door and fell to my knees.

Humphrey, wrapped in a heavy shroud threaded with silver, lay upon a bier within a funeral hearse draped in banners bearing the symbols of the Staffords and the Bohuns. Long candles stood at the hearse's foot and more candles at the head. Smoke trails curled up round painted corbels and the Rood.

Humphrey was only thirty-three. I had not foreseen this—but whoever foresees death in the young, save prophets and the morbid? Once again, my life ran parallel to that of my Cousin Margaret—both of us made widows after a brief marriage. Would I have to wed again, quickly, like Margaret? Sickness rose in me and I dabbed my mouth on my sleeve. I could not...*could not*. My sons...

The door behind me creaked open; light slashed the floor. In came the men sent by the Duke of Buckingham, clad in dour robes of mourning black. They would, upon their lord's order, take the hearse to Pleshey, which Duke Humphrey had decided would serve as the family mausoleum.

I flung myself down, begging on my knees to go with the cortege, but they gazed at me with horror and pity and said no word. The physician arrived and Anchoret, and they pulled me away. "You are too unwell, mistress!" cried Anchoret, her voice unusually shrill. "Think of your sons—they have lost their father; they must not lose you too."

I ceased to fight. The awful truth was clear. There was no more parts for me to play in Humphrey life's—or in his death. The Duke and Duchess would reclaim their son.

The mourners bowed respectfully in my direction. I stood, frozen, a statue, as they drew the lid of Humphrey's coffin over his body and sealed it. His squires filed in, weeping, carrying his armour, some of it still bearing dints from the fray at St Alban's.

Reverently they placed it atop his coffin—breastplate, gauntlets, helmet, spurs, then stepped away, giving their lord one final bow.

The Buckingham mourners stepped close again and lifted the hearse, carrying it from the chapel and out into the courtyard where a wain waited to bear Humphrey to his final rest. I followed, tottering like an old woman, still bare-footed, head bowed, Anchoret and the physician holding my elbows to give support

In the yard, monks from the priory joined the mourners, the one in the lead ringing a mournful bell. Folk from the household gathered around and coins were distributed amongst them.

The chief mourner, waiting beside the wain where he would ride with the body, walked in my direction. As he drew close, I saw that it was Humphrey's brother, Henry. "Madame…" he gave a little bow, "may God assuage your grief."

"And yours," I replied, voice quivering. "He had great love and respect for his brother. Never forget that."

"Margaret sends her heartfelt condolences, and words of solace," he said. "They are from…Isaiah, "he paused, thinking, "…yes, Isaiah…*Thy sun shall no more go down; neither shall thy moon withdraw itself: for the Lord. shall be thine everlasting light, and the days of thy mourning shall be ended.*"

Everlasting light? I wondered if the darkness that beat at my mind would ever disappear again. I was not as holy as Margaret. But I was polite, as I had been taught by my mother and nurses and governesses. "Tell her thank you," I said meekly. "Her words are of great comfort."

Henry returned to the wain, taking his place behind the hearse with its precious burden. I motioned to Lewis the squire, standing forlornly with his fellows, and he brought forward a wreath made of Rosemary—for remembrance. He set it into my hands and I laid it gently atop Humphrey's coffin. *Remembrance…*

For a moment I stood locked in my thoughts and memories. Images from the past tumbled through my mind like dying autumn leaves.

Henry Stafford cleared his throat. I stepped back, knowing that he signalled his desire to leave. It would be a long road, long and full of sorrows.

The funeral procession made its way out through the gates, heading towards Bristol. Already there were crowds on the road, waiting to see the spectacle and maybe t get one of the coins traditionally handed out to the poor.

I watched, bleak and empty, as the hearse vanished into the distance. Humphrey was lost to me.

Once again, I became frozen, a woman of ice. I could not speak or move. People were staring and pointing—especially at my unshod feet. I realise too—vaguely—that I wore no headdress and my hair blew out in a tangled cloud, unseemly and undignified. I felt nought as Anchoret and Jennet took me by the arms and led me, like a tethered sheep to my bedchamber. Their mouths moved but I found the words were just a formless mass of noise, like the grunting of pigs. The idea was amusing, and like so many times in the past, I began to laugh at the ridiculousness of my thoughts.

I laughed and laughed until my throat closed and I choked on my laughter. I laughed until I cried, and my tears fell like the rains that brought the Great Flood to drown the earth.

I recovered my wits within a few weeks, but I never felt quite the same again. People believe my malady was caused solely by grief, but it was more than being a widow. I had always been a nervous, frightened child, but now that fear swelled up again, threatening to consume me at every turn. Worry consumed me at every turn; I feared for my children, for my family, for the future. At night when I lay abed, I fretted for hours, sweating beneath the covers, fearful that a spark from the fire might set the house alight or that raiders would encircle us in the midnight hours and kill us in our beds.

Baby Humphrey was too young to notice a change in his mother, but Harry was different. He had already shown signs of being difficult when his father was ill but now he turned his scowling wrath on me. He sulked in my presence, he pinched the servants, he kicked the shin of the steward. If he was reprimanded, he would scream until he was hoarse. Punishments and denial of riding his pony did nothing to stop him.

Eventually, I gave up and let him howl and bellow. Once he even grabbed my stitchery from my hand and threw it into a horse trough, but I turned my face away and said nothing.

Occasionally, my brother Hal rode in from his Somerset properties, which eased a little of my loneliness. Aged twenty-three, he was growing in confidence as he moved, like a figure on a chessboard, into the innermost court circles.

"You should have seen it, Meg," he sneered, lazily leaning on a table after we had dined together in the hall. "Back in October, in London. Warwick was summoned to court to face charges of piracy. One of the cooks of the royal household attacked him with a spit …and Warwick's men took the opportunity to brawl with the royal cooks, believing there was a plot to kill their master. Warwick ended up fleeing to the river and took off like a craven on his ship."

"And *was* there a plot, Hal?" I cast him a knowing glance.

He shrugged, a sly smile tugging the corner of his mouth. "I was there, Meg, doing my duty to the Queen. I will say no more."

"Have a care, brother. The Loveday is not long past."

"And what foolishness that was. No, Meg, there can never be peace with York and his allies—especially Warwick. I admit only to you—I dream of revenge every night. You would not understand. We argued over this matter before."

"I must be honest," I said bleakly. "All has changed. Sometimes I have begun to feel the same as you, despite my earlier stance. If Humphrey had not been so sorely wounded at St Alban's, perhaps the illness he had would not have killed him."

"Never forget that, sister." He reached forward to touch my cheek. "Jesu, you look so drawn and wan. You must eat more. I shall send you some fine wine and salted fish."

"We truly have enough here, Hal."

"But you are not taking care. You must marry again, soon."

Horrified, I stared at him. "No."

"In these times, it would be for the best."

"I—I cannot. Not yet. My sons."

He made an expressive shrug. "Meg, Meg...your young Harry—he is now the Duke of Buckingham's heir. Has Stafford or Duchess Anne not spoken to you of his future?"

"I—I cannot remember," I mumbled. Letters had arrived after Humphrey's death; they had fallen, crushed from my hand—I could not read them. Anchoret had retrieved them from the floor and read them aloud but the words had made no sense.

"Well, undoubtedly they will soon," Hal warned. "Be prepared, Meg."

"I will be," I said, my voice thin and tired. Be prepared for what? A small creeping suspicion crawled into my brain. I would not countenance it. Would not.

Weakly I smiled over at handsome, dashing Hal, the light of the flambeaux glinting on his silken mane of hair.

"Would you like more wine, my dearest brother? And tomorrow, could you show Harry some hawks? He has been...of strange temperament since Humphrey died."

"Of course," Hal said. "It is hard to lose one's father...at any age." His mouth tightened and there was steel in his eyes.

The year continued, with tension growing and tempers fraying amongst the great of England. The court retreated to Coventry, the Lancastrian heartland. I kept my gates shut and set guards upon them. Only those known to me were permitted entry. The locals began to call me the 'Weird Widow' and rumours abounded that I had gone mad and walked on the walls watching for a husband who would never return. The latter, I did not do. The former—mayhap they were right. I was unquiet within myself; the fear I'd always kept in check from early childhood rushed forth, consuming me day and night. Sleep eluded me and oftimes my heart would pound so swift I thought it would explode from my chest and I would die—but every dawn I awoke in my lonely bed, alive but exhausted.

Word came from Hal that a Great Council was slated for June—but York had made an excuse not to attend. *Sister, I fear war is coming. Her Grace the Queen will not tolerate much more from her most unruly and treacherous subjects. She presses the King to indict Richard of York for treason, although Henry, as ever, dithers in this duty. York has put himself behind the walls of Ludlow and is gathering forces, as no doubt are his twin creatures, Salisbury and Warwick. I think 'twill all come to a head near summer's end..."*

I threw his missive onto the fire and watched the parchment blacken and curl. More fighting—where would it end? I glanced over at young Harry dancing around the solar with a wooden hobby horse. Humphrey was gurgling on the lap of his wet nurse, a happy baby. In his innocence, he was probably the only one truly happy at Thornbury manor.

In July I received a letter from the Duchess of Buckingham. She gave little details, other than a wish to see her grandsons and asked if I were in a position to receive her at the manor. I made no answer. Like Hal's letter, hers went in the fire. I hoped she would think better of her journey and not come till the troubles were over, but, deep inside, I understood that those troubles I feared were the very reason Anne would come to Thornbury.

The Duchess arrived in early August. The summer heat, stifling and sticky for weeks, had dissipated with a storm that had wreathed the night sky with tangled clumps of searing lightning. The thunder was so loud and terrifying that I could not sleep; Anchoret sat miserably with her hands pressed over her ears. Uneasy, I made my way to the nursery; inside, the children were screaming with fright, their nursemaids at wit's end trying to calm them.

Harry flung himself sobbing into my skirts and I lifted him up and carried him out into the little chapel. Set at the heart of the building, behind the thickest section of the manor-house walls, it was a little quieter, and the dazzling brilliance of the lightning was muted by a couple of thick panes of *grisaille* glass.

I sank down beneath the Rood Screen, wiping tears from my son's face. "Do not be afraid, Harry. I am here and God is here too, looking after you."

"Where is He?" Harry sniffed, his gaze roving the vaulted ceiling with its paintings of trumpet-blowing angels.

"All around us, Harry, protecting us. It is written in the Psalms, of which you will learn in a few years: *The Lord is my light and my salvation; Whom shall I fear? The Lord is the strength of my life; of whom shall I be afraid?*"

'Tell Him—STOP!" Harry grumbled as another particularly loud burst of thunder made the walls of Thornbury Manor judder as if a giant, heavenly hand had struck it.

"He brings the storm to smite the wicked," I said, "but that is not us. We must endure. It is just noise."

Harry began to whine and grizzle, displeased that his rather demanding prayers would not halt the Almighty's fury.

I rubbed his hot flushed cheeks, still attempting to soothe his disquiet. "Another Psalm, Harry, that you shall find is true...*Weeping may endure for a night, but joy comes in the morning.*"

But it was not joy that came in that muggy, damp morning with its overhanging black clouds and eerie stillness. Shortly before the hour of Sext, the steward called me to the gatehouse. Standing high on the towers, I shaded my eyes and stared into the distance. A retinue was making slow progress towards Thornbury Manor. I picked out banners bearing the Stafford Chevron and the Neville Saltire.

"It is nothing to fear," I told the man. "It is my mother-in-law, Duchess Anne of Buckingham."

He gave me a sharp glance; my voice was full of wretched despair. Nothing to fear? I had *everything* to fear...

Returning to the Great Hall, I sat down and waited. The house was hardly in a fit state to receive a highborn duchess. I had grown slack, consumed by my mourning and other woes, and the rushes sorely needed changing and the dust beaten from the tapestries. Soot stains from the flambeaux marred the walls, ashes clumped in the braziers, and vaguely I smelt the tang of the privies, pungent in the summer's heat. Even as I watched, one of the hounds trundled in and lazily lifted its leg and pissed against the wall. A servant grabbed its collar and dragged it away.

Soon a herald emerged to announce Duchess Anne. She walked in before he even finished announcing her, glancing about her. Immediately her expression darkened.

"Duchess Anne." I rose from a bench to greet her.

She brushed past me and seated herself on the dais—now that Humphrey was dead, she had full right, for Thornbury was a Stafford property. At present, I was only a tenant and would remain so till my Dower lands were granted.

"Why did you not answer my letter, Margaret?" She gazed at me with piercing hazel eyes. "I waited so long for a reply I thought my messenger had fallen afoul of murderers upon the road."

"I—I…" My voice was weak and shaking. What could I tell her? A lie would not suffice. The truth would make me appear weak and witless.

It seemed her question was rhetorical, for she waved a hand as if to brush it aside, and proceeded to cast her stern gaze over the hall. "The place is in disarray," she said. "Thornbury was always pleasant before. I saw the outbuildings as I arrived; some are missing tiles from the roofs. Soon they will begin to leak if they haven't already. The outside wall is crumbling in places—before you know it brigands will come in to carry off you and yours. And this hall—it stinks like the hall of some filthy little garrison on the Marches. Do you not have any reliable, competent servants, Margaret?"

I swallowed. "I-I am sorry. I will soon rectify all the damage, and have the house cleaned top to bottom. It was difficult when Humphrey was ill; he did not like noise and disturbance…"

Her plucked brows rose beneath her jewelled hennin. "You blame my dead son for this disgrace?"

"No…no, of course not." Words caught in my throat.

"Where are my grandsons?" Anne asked. "It is them I have come to see."

I gestured for Jennet to run to the nursery. An uncomfortable silence fell while Anne and I waited for the children to arrive. Sweat gathered at the nape of my neck, uncomfortable in the heat. Anne looked like a block of ice, unruffled, full of judgment.

The nurses entered the chamber, one carrying Humphrey in a white shawl, the other shepherding Harry, who was trying to bound on ahead, eager to see his grandmother.

When Anne saw the boys, her face softened and the hint of tears dazzled her eyes, hastily blinked away. She stepped forth, first to baby Humphrey who was newly out of swaddling and wearing his first cote, a long gown reaching to his ankles. I prayed that it had freshly been washed.

"What a winsome child," the Duchess exclaimed, touching his golden curls. He made a gurgling laugh. "So like to his father…"

"Am I like fada?" Harry, breaking loose from his embarrassed nurse, rushed to Anne's side and tugged on her hanging vair-lined sleeve.

"Yes, you are too. Both perfect little Staffords. Let me take a close look at you, Henry." She scooped him up; he was a stocky, well-made child and she struggled a bit beneath his weight. Like his brother, he was gold-curled and bright-cheeked with deep blue eyes, and his cote was wrought of fine cloth, embroidered with the Stafford cartwheels.

Now Anne did weep a little. Harry stared at her quizzically. "You have gift for Harry?"

I blushed. Why did the child come out with such things? I hope he would not start to roar if no presents were forthcoming.

Anne, thankfully, seemed unperturbed. "As it happens, yes, I have brought gifts. Gifts fitting for the heir to the Dukedom of Buckingham."

She motioned her servants, standing in an orderly queue at the end of the Great Hall, and one by one they approached Harry and displayed a variety of wares before him. There were robes of velvet and silk, fancy leather shoes with gold buckles, puppets of fighting knights, a whirling *scopperel*, a miniature boat on a pulley, and, lastly, a real dagger, in a sheath decked in cabochons, with red gems that shouted the name 'Stafford' and below it the Duke of Buckingham's motto '*Humble et Loyal.*'

"This is from your grandsire, to the one who is now his heir and destined for greatness," said Anne, placing the dagger into Harry's hands.

He began to tug on the hilt and with a gasp, I strode forward, fearful that he would pull it free and come to some harm.

Anne put out her arm, stopping me with a scowl. "Margaret, do not fuss. The Buckingham heir must never grow up a milksop. Besides, it's quite safe; I have bound the blade into the sheath with peace-thongs."

Harry had lost interest anyway. Handing the weapon back to one of the Duchess's servants, he had grasped the two puppet knights and mashed them together in frenzied combat. Watching, baby Humphrey crowed with laughter and kicked his legs in excitement.

"They are fine children," said Anne, turning to me. "As I would expect of their lineage—Stafford, Neville and Beaufort. But we must speak of them…in private while they play. Your solar, perhaps?"

Mutely I nodded and led Anne up to my private quarters. They were a mess. Gowns that needed washing were thrown about over screens; the bathing tub was in need of emptying, the water muddy and filled with a scum of Castilian soap.

"Would you like some wine, Duchess Anne?" I asked, trying for friendliness, although my heart felt heavy as a stone. I picked up an ewer, half-full, and nodded towards a goblet on the bench. Anne examined the goblet and her nose crinkled. "I think someone has got to it before me. A fly has drowned in the bottom."

My face burned. "My apologies…"

"No need.' She thrust the goblet aside. "I do not intend to stay long. I will leave tomorrow. I shall be heading to our castle of Tonbridge. It is a fair castle, Margaret, with a very strong gatehouse, and is not so far from London…"

I found my voice. I could no longer endure. "I can guess what you want, Duchess. That we remove to Tonbridge from Thornbury."

She cleared her throat, for the first time looking uncomfortable. She would not meet my eyes. "Not…quite," she said. "The children."

"No, you cannot take them!" Anger and fear boiled within my heart; my hands drew into balls.

"Be reasonable, Margaret. They are not the children of some merchant, some farmer. They are grandsons of two Dukes, they bear royal blood, and Henry is now heir to his grandfather. It is not safe for them to remain at Thornbury, especially now my dear Humphrey…is gone." She lowered her head.

"You cannot do this to me; they are all I have left. All that is good in my life," I begged.

"They are boys of rank; you surely knew one day they would go to another household."

"But not so young, not both of them at once…and not so soon after my husband's demise." Tears welled then, ugly and uncontrollable. "God, if only he had not died…"

"You did not even attend his funeral," Anne snapped, cruel. "I expected you to be there."

"I—I was ill…heartsick…" I argued. "I was in no fit condition to travel. Ask Humphrey's brother, ask any of the men who accompanied the catafalque. For days after, I lay in my bed, wishing I might join Humphrey in death…"

"Yes, so I've been told." Her tone was acidic. "And that is the problem, Margaret. It is not a fitting environment for the boys. Search your heart; you know it is so."

"I refuse to let them go!" I cried.

She chewed waspishly on her lip. "Margaret, come to your senses and do not take on so. I do not want to make this a struggle…for your sake, as it's a struggle you cannot win. The King had granted the wardship of both children to me."

I gave a cry of despair, throwing up my hands to cover my face, and sank onto the dusty, dirty floor. "What will happen to me? What can I do?"

Duchess Anne peered down her long, straight nose. "I am not completely without sympathy for your plight. You may stay here for a while, till your Dower lands are sorted. However, I would give you this advice—marry again, and soon."

"Marry!"

"Yes, I know it is soon for remarriage, but these are troubled times. You need a husband, just as your cousin Margaret did. She seems well happy with my son Henry, although there are no signs of children—but there is still time for that. Yes, you should wed again, and perhaps you will have a whole new brood to bring you renewed joy. My own father had two wives and seventeen children."

Anne turned, gazing at me critically. "You are still young. You have proved fertile. Do not waste your life in mourning. It is not good…"

"Not good?" My temper rose. "A moment ago, my lady, you chastised me for not attending Humphrey's burial! I cannot, will not, be both widow and blushing bride!"

She ignored me. "A decent time of mourning is fine, but already rumours abound that your grief was…too much. Unseemly. Touched by madness. If that kind of talk reaches too far, you may never find a second husband and that would be a great pity. An unmarried woman of your birth would be a target for wicked men—Did you ever hear about the case of Margery Mallefant? Deceived by her own dead husband's advisor, she was bundled off and forced to marry the caitiff. Even the priest turned a blind eye to her screaming as the knave manhandled her to the altar."

"I know of that abomination. Was that foul marriage not dissolved by parliament?" I asked surlily. "Did not Margery get her freedom back and her attacker punished?"

Duchess Anne shrugged. "Yes…but she was fortunate she was believed. It is not always so. And would you want to endure what she did, even if you were innocent of compliance with the rogue who stole you away?"

I glanced down, shaking my head, making one last appeal. "Your Grace, I am in no fit state to make these momentous decisions. Not yet. I beg you, let me come with you to

Tonbridge—at least until the children are well settled in with their new tutors and nursemaids. My boys…"

"Enough, Margaret." The Duchess was firm. "You must stay here while they depart. Occasionally you may visit them, with my permission. Such permission will not be withheld—but let them have a good long period to settle into their new environment first." She sighed. "I am sorry, my dear, but Henry is Duke Humphrey's heir and he must grow up as such. The baby is a guarantee should anything, God forfend, happen to Henry. You may have a decent life, Margaret, if you hold your head up high and choose to do so. But it will not be with your Stafford sons."

She strode away, regally strolling towards the guest quarters of Thornbury manor. It was as if she was the Lady here, while I was no one, an incompetent tenant who had overstayed my welcome. Picking up my skirts so they would not get muddied on the dirty floor, I hurried through the passageways to my bedchamber.

Once inside, I sank down on my *Prie Dieu* and wept. Once again, my life was mirroring that of my cousin—my husband dead and my son, Henry, taken away to be raised elsewhere. But at least a fitting second husband had quickly been found for Margaret by Jasper Tudor. I wondered who might help me obtain a husband? Mother, maybe, but she was older now, less interested in her children's lives outside of her favourite Nell. My brother Hal—another possibility, perhaps a better one than Mother, but he was consumed by his feud with Warwick, Salisbury and York.

I would come last.

I wondered what fate could possibly hold for me. A chasm gaped within my heart at the thought of my sons being taken away, and for one crazed moment, I thought of throwing myself from the bedroom window.

I imagined my body falling through the air, tumbling in the hot sun, bouncing from the slate roof to land within the courtyard. Anne Neville would hear the shrieks of the servants and come running and cross herself when she saw that nothing could be done. Little Harry would see me and weep…

I shook my head, gritting my teeth against such mad thoughts. Self-murder meant Hell or, at the very least, an eternity in purgatory. It brought endless shame—I could not do that to my children.

Just as Duchess Anne said, I would have to find another husband.

CHAPTER NINE

The boys passed out of my life the next day. Duchess Anne stowed them away in a gleaming chariot of oak, painted with scenes of Christ on a rainbow. The nursemaids I had hired for the children stood in the courtyard, crestfallen. Humphrey's wet nurse was weeping, wiping her face with the end of her apron. "I thought of him almost as my own...."

Anne had let me give each boy one farewell and no more. "You must let them go now, Margaret," she admonished. "For the sake of their futures and your own."

Harry certainly seemed joyous enough as he climbed into the chariot, waving frantically through the curtained window. "Grandmama says I am to have a new pony!" he cried excitedly. "A bigger, faster one!"

I smiled, trying to find pleasure in his excitement, but sadness welled in the pit of my belly. My son's love had been bought...by an animal, a little boy's plaything, used and quickly forgotten for something shinier. I almost hated Anne at that moment.

Then the entourage moved off, trumpets blaring, wreathed in gaudy Stafford splendour. I watched, one hand upraised to shield my eyes from the sun and also to hide my grief. When the gates clanged shut and the clarion calls melted into the distance, I sullenly turned, without a word to anyone, and went to my chamber.

I ate near to nothing for the next three days and would see no one. Anchoret pounded on the door, begging me to eat but I told her to go. She pounded louder, and I screeched, like some mad harridan, "Bother me no more or I'll dismiss you! I'll send you back to Brecknock on a mule, disgraced and unemployable!"

The knocking and badgering stopped almost instantly. As Anchoret's footsteps retreated, I let myself weep for my lost sons, my lost husband...and for the travails I must face in the future.

In September, on St Thecla's Day, another battle was fought—Blore Heath. The Queen had word that the Earl of Salisbury was marching from the north to meet with York at Ludlow and sent Lord Audley to arrest him before he could join forces with Duke Richard. Audley's army was nearly three times the size of Salisbury's—how could he fail?

But Dame Fortune spun her capricious Wheel again, and once again the Yorkists were victors on the field of battle, riding high and triumphant on the Wheel's spokes. Earlier in the day, the Yorkist chances had seemed slight; the heralds reported that Salisbury's men knelt and kissed the ground on which they stood, implying that they expected to die there. The Earl then ordered all his wains and carts placed in a circle, a crude barricade against his opponents massed on the blighted heath beyond, dark and burnt with summer. Only a brook stood between the two sides, coiling like a blue serpent, reflecting the sky.

Salisbury walked out before all, armoured and proud, and made a motion to his soldiers, indicating that they were to begin a retreat. The King's loyalists responded with glee, anticipating cutting down the fleeing men from behind. With a roar, they leapt on their steeds and mounted a cavalry charge, their heavy warhorses pounding toward the tranquil blue stream

It turned out this was exactly what canny Salisbury had hoped for. As the first horses' hoofs struck the water, sending up sheets of mud and spray, he shouted for his men to turn about and commence a quick, brutal attack. Arrows whined through the air, a black rain, and men and horses fell where they were set upon by spearmen and pikemen. The Lancastrian cavalry charged had failed. Lord Audley fared on bravely, climbing over slaughtered beasts in the stream, which had gone from blue to red, and for a while his line held—but as the fighting grew more intense, he was felled by an axe-blow, and the Lancastrians were routed. Salisbury's men chased them across the heath, like fierce hounds hunting down prey.

It was Hal who told me. He had been waiting to encounter the Nevilles with his own army, but news had reached him of Salisbury's victory. "It was hard to restrain myself," he said, resting before the fire in the Great Hall, "but when my spies rode in and told me of Audley's death, I knew I could not prevail even if I marched to the field. But the die is cast now, Meg—Salisbury can no longer pretend he is a voice of reason or put his foot in two camps. He may as well have declared 'I want Richard Plantagenet to take the crown' by his actions. The Queen will not rest until the Nevilles and York are subdued. Even the King is ready to take action, not just with pretty words, either."

"What do you mean?" I frowned.

Hal's eyes glittered in the hall's dimness. "His Grace is going to ride in armour at the head of his men, with the Royal Standard raised. I shall be at his side, with my companion Exeter, our sister Nell's new husband, Wiltshire, and the Duke of Buckingham. At last, we will catch those treacherous rats in a trap. If they face us on the field of battle when the King's banners are raised, all of them will be judged guilty of treason, no more excuses."

"Take care, Hal," I said stiffly. "Do not underestimate your foes."

"They are fools," Hal waved a dismissive hand, "and soon they will be dead fools." He glanced around, suddenly, at the dingy Great Hall. I had ordered some servants to scrape out the rushes after Duchess Anne's unwelcome visit, but it still looked mean, untidy and cold, a place lacking in life, its master dead, his children gone, only his sorrowing relict left behind.

"Where are my nephews?" Hal began, then he shook his head. "No, forgive me, I forgot that the Duke and Duchess of Buckingham have taken them into their care."

"I miss them so, more than you can imagine." A little hope flickered in me; Hal was close with the King and Queen and the leaders of the Lancastrian faction—maybe he could speak for me, have my boys returned if only for a year or two. "Oh Hal, I would do anything to have them back."

"They are in good hands," he said. "The very best."

"Surely their mother's hands would be the best." Anger replaced dying hope and my hands clenched at my sides.

"Alas, it is not the way the world works, sister. Have you thought of remarriage?"

"It is all Duchess Anne spoke of. I suppose she is correct," I said, with bitterness, "but suitors are not exactly beating down the gates of my home."

"I will see if there is anything I can do," he said. "Have you written to Mother?"

"About another marriage? No. I told her about my sons, in case she should seek to visit them. That is all. She never wrote back…but Duchess Anne did, to tell me that Mother had sent gifts to Harry and Humphrey at Tonbridge."

"I would ask her, Meg. She is your mother, after all."

"Who knows best." My lips pursed.

"She knows enough. There is even talk of her remarrying soon."

"To whom?" My eyes widened, startled; I had not foreseen that. Three husbands—it seemed incredible, although I knew it was not uncommon. It was a hard truth—noble women needed a protector.

Hal shrugged. "A Sir Walter Rokesley."

"Never heard of him." I shook my head.

"Me neither," he grinned. "She must be looking for a quieter life. The marriage is really quite beneath her, but there are whispers it is a love match. She'd never admit such to me, of course."

"*Amor vincit omnia*," I murmured, vinegar-sour.

"I expect he is rich, if not of worthy bloodline," said Hal.

"Indeed. I am sure his coffers are brimming. They will need to be. Mother likes her comforts."

"You should think of doing the same, Meg. Or maybe you would wish to become a nun?"

"I do not fancy spending all that time on my knees. That was more to the taste of our cousin, Margaret."

"Henry Stafford's wife, yes. Still, she seems happy enough with Henry…despite…" he gestured to his handsome face, "his unfortunate affliction."

"She doubtless believes it firms his character and that his suffering will put him in good stead with God."

He suddenly leaned over, taking my hands and kissing my cheek. "You have grown so bitter, Meg."

"It happens. A woman's lot."

"You must soon marry. I want to see you smile again—a real smile. You are my favourite sister, you know."

"I will truly smile only when these dreadful conflicts are all over and we can live settled lives again."

He kissed my cheek again, his breath warm against my flesh. "If God grants it at Ludlow, so shall it be."

I lived the following months in dread. It was as if I waited for a storm to break.

At last, it did, and for once the flood waters swept away the darkness that had plagued England. Just outside the gates of Ludlow town, by ancient Ludford Bridge, York and his cronies had set up guns and barricades and dug a deep earthwork, waiting to join battle with the royal army. The King had approached, in full harness, banners raised and Buckingham had ridden forth, bare-headed and fearless, to offer a pardon to those who would desert York's cause. Within hours, Warwick's man, the soldier Anthony Trollope had deserted, and his company with him.

York, Salisbury and Warwick then retreated into the town, before fleeing into the wilds under the cover of darkness. It made me uneasy that these men were still free to cause their vile mischief, but their star was descending rapidly and, with any luck, would soon be extinguished forever.

Ludlow was sacked and the castle looted. York had even left behind proud Cecily, his wife, and three of their many children, one girl and two young boys. Duke Humphrey took them under his protection and shipped them under armed guard to Cecily's sister, Duchess Anne, at Tonbridge Castle.

The thought of the undoubted prideful and malicious York children around my Harry and Humphrey disturbed me, but I suspected the Duchess would not permit them to mingle—she was already furious with her sister and would deem the children a bad influence. Nonetheless…I was worried. I spent many nights anxiously running over scenarios in my mind—a York boy, the one called George, who was rumoured to be a spoilt tearaway, pushing Harry over a battlement in a 'game', the girl asking to hold the baby and dropping him headfirst on the flagstones.

It was a fraught time, in what had now become a backwater near Bristol, with its master dead and his widow not coping well….

In due time, it became common knowledge that the Duke of York and one of his sons, Edmund, had fled to Ireland, where York was greatly popular. The other son, the tall, imposing Edward, had fared into Wales with Warwick and Salisbury and the lot of them had boarded a ship and ended up in Calais.

Kneeling before the Rood every night, I begged God to let none of them return.

Later in October, parliament was held in Coventry and the Yorkist lords attainted and their lands confiscated. Hal was appointed Captain of Calais, which made him smug indeed, for it had been Warwick's position and Warwick he hated most of all.

He came to visit shortly after his appointment, eager to tell me of his good fortune. "I will have Calais," he said, as we sat within the solar, cold October winds whistling through the crenels atop the manor house. "And with any luck, I will have Warwick too, and his father. I am sailing out within the week. Exeter shall accompany me in his own ship."

"I have heard Warwick is well-loved in Calais," I said timidly. "Even if you oust him, trouble might arise with the locals."

He reddened slightly. "They will learn to love me too, and if they will not, I will teach them to fear me instead!"

It was natural for a man to have war-like qualities but I wished Hal had a few less. I could see Father in him so strongly, and I dreaded that he might endure the same fate.

"I would rather you stayed in England, brother. I am sure your…your lady Joan will miss you, and your little Charles."

He looked perplexed, as if he thought I had gone mad by bringing up domestic subjects. "Joan?" He laughed and slapped his thigh. "Married her off, Meg, with a pension. Do not look so shocked—she was only a mistress, a light o' love. I am a Duke now and have more pressing business than dandling lowborn women. As for Charles…" his face softened, "he is in good hands, never fear. I see him when I may. Hopefully one day he will be legitimised, just as our Beaufort ancestors were."

"May it be," I said, "and then he can rise to great estate…but perhaps you should also think about marrying. You are well beyond the age most men wed. You chide me about remarriage, but what's good for the goose is surely also good for the gander."

"You sound like Mother. Have you done anything about remarriage as I counselled you?"

"No. It has only been a few months since you were here. I am not ready, Hal."

"Well, I will counsel you again—do not leave it too long."

"What do you mean? I know there are issues of safety for widows; I have heard all the lurid tales of stolen brides from Duchess Anne."

"It…it's not that, Meg." He stared down at his polished leather poulaines as if embarrassed. I seldom ever saw embarrassment on Hal's face.

"Then what is it?"

"Rumours…"

"What? About me?"

"Yes."

"Jesu, who would say things about me? What could I have done, shut away in here? Surely you are mistaken." I laughed bitterly. "I would suggest that I've been mistaken for the other Margaret Beaufort—but I do not think Cousin Mag is inclined to scandal and sin, either."

"It's not scandal…well, not of that sort," he said uneasily.

"Do tell."

"The Black Widow of Thornbury…"

"Silly names made up by silly people."

"Yes, but this silliness had spread about the way such gossip spreads becoming more far-fetched as time goes on. Margaret, some gossips say you are…a mooncalf."

"They truly think I am mad?" I sat back in my chair in shock.

"You have always had a delicate…a nervous disposition, have you not? Even since that cannonball struck down before us when we were children in France, separating us from Mother."

For a man, he was decidedly astute…and, on this day, surprisingly gentle in words and expressions. It surprised me that he had even remembered that awful day, let alone how it had affected me. Mother rarely mentioned it.

"Yes," I admitted, voice thick, "I cannot deny it changed me. I saw then that life was not all pageants and feasts—that death could strike any one of us, even us children, at any moment. From that day onwards, I feared almost…almost everything, Hal. I saw death with his scythe in my dreams, menacing all those I loved. And when I did lose the one I loved—yes, it was as if a black cloud filled my head and I lay in the slough of despond."

"I do not want to see you suffer," he said. "That is the only reason I implore you to wed soon. If these tales spread, you may find you lack suitors, for all that you are a Duke's daughter."

My shoulders slumped. "I grow weary of talking of marriage, but rest assured, I will do as you say."

"That's my brave sister!" he said, clasping my hands. "Now I must away. Think of my deeds upon the wild seas, and wish me luck in ousting Warwick and York's hulking brat from Guisnes and Calais."

"I wish you luck." I locked my arms around his neck in a short, hard embrace "I will also light a candle for you every night. Do not be overbold, Hal. I could not bear it if…"

"Do not say it, Meg, please," he implored. "It will not be so. Dame Fortune has spun her Wheel and our enemies have been pitched down from their lofty perches; it is *my* turn to rise to the pinnacle."

Advent rolled around with its solemnity and fasting. The darkening days with their long nights and weak sun took their toll on my wellbeing, and melancholy gripped my heart once again. Humphrey had been dead more than a year, so a new match would not be deemed improper, but despite my promises, I had no heart for seeking a husband.

In fact, I had taste for little and no money to spare on upcoming Christmas festivities. I could barely pay my staff, and a number of those who remained were sullen and troublesome. I was not so popular in the local village anymore and I knew Hal was correct—tongues were wagging and not in a good way.

Ever loyal, a friend as much as a servant these days, Anchoret was disgusted. "What is wrong with them, my lady?" she scowled as a band of tittering children lobbed a lump of horse-dung in our direction when we were out at the market. It fell short, breaking up into smelly portions all over the cobblestones. "What have you ever done to them, save be a good mistress to all?"

"That's not enough. I am the 'Black Widow' or 'Wyrd Widow' now." I smiled ruefully. "I've heard what they say, even as you. That I poisoned Humphrey. That I have a lover who is a peasant. That I am a moon-calf who talks to the spirit of my dead husband. That latter worries me most of all—for when do they stop saying 'mad' and say 'witchcraft' instead? Then their lies would go from hurtful to dangerous."

"I will whip anyone myself who dares say such a thing!" said Anchoret. "You should be harsher on these ungrateful wretches, my lady. You are still a Beaufort, one of the great families in the land!"

"I am just a woman without a husband," I said.

Shortly after I had lit the first Advent Candle, the Candle of Hope, a courier arrived at Thornbury with a letter bearing the seal of Duchess Anne. I ripped through the thick wax, sending blood-hued fragments spraying across the solar, fearing that one of the boys had come to grief.

Luckily, my fears were for nought and the wild pulse of my heart slowed. Anne was inviting me to spend Christmas with her and the Duke. Choking back a sob, I held the parchment against me. I was going to see my children again, my darling Harry and little Dumph with his cheerful smile.

I shouted for Anchoret, my voice high and trembling. She raced into the chamber, breathless. "Is something wrong, my lady?"

"No," I said, "for once it is not. Anchoret, start packing my gowns and other garments. We are going to Tonbridge to spend Christmas with the Duke and Duchess of Buckingham."

It was with trepidation that I saw the towers of Tonbridge pierce the heavy grey threads of morning fog. The journey from Thornbury had been long and arduous, the roads rutted and wet, some filled in places by thick ice, while others had huge puddles so large ducks and geese swam upon them. Many vagabonds and vagrants were abroad on the roads too, clear indicators of the unrest throughout England, and I said my Hail Marys whenever they eyed my little entourage, fronted only by several loyal old soldiers who had served Humphrey for years and who had taken a cut in pay in exchange for lodging and victuals.

"It's a fine castle." Anchoret stuck her head out of the carriage next to mine. "You must be excited, Countess."

"I am…but I am afraid too," I said. "I understand that Dumph may not remember me owing to his age—but what if Harry has forgotten his mother?"

"That will never happen," she said with absolute conviction. "You will see, milady."

The company passed under the gatehouse, a mighty edifice faced in white that was attached to a curtain wall banded by several sturdy round towers.

Once in the bailey, the Staffords' chamberlain greeted me and took me to my quarters, accompanied by a puffing Anchoret, who was carrying my most personal possessions in a casket, not trusting them to the servants who clambered around our little baggage wain. "They had best be careful with your clothes chest," she mumbled, giving the workers a black-browed glare. "No opening it up and prying…"

"I am sure all will be fine. Come on, Anchoret, hurry your steps!" I was eager to settle in and then see my sons.

In our chamber, there was a fire burning, a warm bed and a pallet for Anchoret—I was travelling with just the one maid, as Jennet was suffering a woman's complaint. It was a relief to not have to face the creeping dampness and mildew of some of the rooms at Thornbury.

Hastily Anchoret dressed me in a deep rose gown, brushing it down to rid the fabric of folds or dead bugs. She brushed out my hair, then wound it up upon my head and placed my favourite butterfly headdress over it, all glittering with gemstones like tiny stars.

I glanced in the little mirror she held out, a Christmas gift from Humphrey one year. "I am so pale and drawn. I look like a crone. What will the Duke and Duchess think?"

"You *don't* look like a crone, milady," said Anchoret stoutly, "but I do have your cosmetics pouch near to hand if you wish me to apply some."

"Do what you can, Anchoret. I must make a good impression on my hosts." Bringing out the leather pouch, she opened it and poured its contents onto the bed. There was a box containing *blaunchet*, a snow-pale makeup made from wheat flour, a tiny jar of lip salve wrought of suet mixed with marjoram and a smidgin of musk, and another jar containing crushed leaves of Angelica. Humming she mixed the *blaunchet* with rosewater from the ewer on the window ledge, then did the same with the Angelica, which turned a reddish shade.

I sat still and she painted my face white, added roses to my wan cheeks and caused my dry, bitten lips to shine. "You look like a young maid, Countess!" said Anchoret, admiring her handiwork.

"An exaggeration, but a kind one," I said, but then there was a sharp knock on the door.

It was the castle steward, clad in fur-trimmed robes, his garments as rich as my own. "His Grace and Her Grace are ready to see you, Countess."

I followed the man through passageways festooned with Arras that gave the castle a feel of homeliness that belied its martial exterior. Leaving the hall block, I was led across a covered walk spanning the curtain wall. At the end was a door that led into the ancient shell-keep on the bloated body of its earthen motte.

Once within the keep, I was escorted to Duchess Anne's solar. Painted in green and red, and decked with symbols of the season—holly boughs and mistletoe bundles, it was a cheerful place glowing with candlelight. Anne sat on a decorated seat, looking like a queen ruling over her domain. Four ladies bustled about, bringing her food and drink and tending to her clothing.

"Margaret, how glad am I that you've come to spend Christmas at Tonbridge," she said, rising, her stately bearing and long conical hat with its trailing burgundy veil making her seem regal and imposing. She placed her hands on my shoulders and kissed me, dry-lipped, on the cheek.

"You look well," she said, "compared to when last I saw you."

"Thank you, your Grace," I said. *I feel no better*, I thought, *but feelings, I fear, mean little to Anne Neville…*

"Do you wish to see your children now, or in the morn after you have rested?" she asked.

"Now!" The word tore from my lips, sharp.

Her lips were compressed, the smile hard. She thought of me as weak, I could tell. "Very well, I shall send for them."

She motioned to one of her ladies, a tall woman with an austere expression wearing a gown of deep green velvet. She swept from the chamber in a haze of rose scent, not even glancing in my direction.

I fidgeted as I waited, the minutes feeling as long as hours. Anne returned to her seat, eating sugar plums from a platter in silence. Her maid brought me one, but the thought of eating turned my belly, such was my excitement…and apprehension.

A nursemaid clad in white linens entered the solar first, carrying Humphrey, who was wearing a tawny gown with tufts of grey rabbit fur at the hem. His cheeks were rosy, just as I remembered them, his eyes bright and merry with innocence.

With a strangled cry, I stumbled forward and snatched him from the nurse. Close, he was wonderful, smelling of creams they had rubbed into his skin, his hair silken against my face. Happy, as he had always seemed to be, he smiled and pulled at my jewelled brooch. He had a lot more teeth than I remembered.

"You can put him down, Margaret. He can walk," said Anne.

Of course, he was not really a baby anymore…I placed him down on the floor; he was wearing little tasselled slippers. He walked a few steps then plumped down on the oriental-patterned rugs and began to play with the ears of one of the Duchess's three greyhounds. He was not much interested in hugs and kisses…but he was happy.

Then I heard another voice in the corridor beyond. A child's raised voice. Turning from Humphrey, I was just in time to see two nursemaids lead Harry into the room. He was wearing the garments of a little lord…and he had grown rather round. The Duke and Duchess were feeding him well—perhaps a little too well.

He glanced at me and my heart beat faster as I glimpsed recognition in his eyes. "Mama!" he yelled, racing ahead of the nurse and throwing himself into my skirts.

"Careful, Harry…careful. You might knock me over." I reached down to him but he pulled back and glanced up, hands on hips.

"Have you bought presents?"

"Henry, that is no way to speak to your Lady Mother," chided Duchess Anne. "Her presence at Tonbridge should be gift enough."

I was glad Anne had spoken, for I had worried that I might disappoint my sons since I had brought no gifts. Money was a terrible problem and little gewgaws would mean nothing to two children brought up in the lavish ducal household.

Harry still gazed at me expectantly. Anne frowned. "Harry, did you not hear? You should show gladness that your Lady Mother has come to visit. Do not forget the word of God— *Honour thy father and thy mother: that thy days may be long upon the land.*"

Harry's lower lip shot out but mutinously, but he made an awkward small bow before me, and murmured, "Sorry, Lady Mother."

He did not seem very sincere about the apology but I truly cared little for that. I was reunited with my children and that was all that mattered. No shadows must fall upon our time together.

"Did your grandmere Anne get you that pony you wanted?" I asked,

His eyes lit up and he nodded. "Yes! He is my best friend. I called him Arrow, for he flies as fast as one. Do you want to see him? I have a puppy too; a hound called Bodkin. Dumphie has one too, Griffin; his dog has black spots while mine is pure brown. Mine is bigger and fiercer. I can show you them too, but Bodkin might try to lick your face and some ladies don't like…"

"Henry, you are over-eager and shouting again," Anne interjected. "I have told you many times that shouting is impolite. I am sure your mother will happily visit the stables and kennels with you…but not today. She is newly arrived and needs both sustenance and rest. So…tomorrow."

Before Harry could mount a protest, Anne nodded towards the waiting nursemaids. "Take the boys back to the nursery."

The nurses stepped forward and the children were duly taken from the room, Harry pouting and looking over his shoulder.

"I have missed them so," I said to Countess Anne. "Even when they are naughty."

"I know," she said, with a little more kindness than was her usual wont. Her eyes were downcast and sorrow thickened her voice. "Remember, I have sons too. The loss of them in one way or another is something we women must endure, though it breaks us inside."

The days that followed were the happiest I had known since Humphrey's death. I accompanied the boys to Mass, kneeling beside them and their grandmother, I watched them fed and little Humph bathed, and I helped Anne choose garments for them to wear during the Twelve Days of Christmas. Harry showed me his pony and his hound, and we rode out into the town together, escorted by the Duke's personal guards. Harry chattered merrily away at my side, obsessed by hounds, hawks and horses and dreams of greatness—but what young noble boy was not? With such talkativeness and advanced speech, perhaps one day he would be a great orator…

While I was in the castle garden one afternoon, watching Harry buffet the spiky, denuded rosebushes with a wooden sword, I noticed some other children lurking behind a clump of winter-bleak shrubs. A very tall girl with long, light brown hair streaked with gold, a middle-sized boy with a mop of gilded curls similar to Harry's, and a small, thin lad with sandy dark blonde hair verging on brown near the roots. The maiden was chiding the older boy, waggling her finger at him as he launched himself from a stone bench and started trying to scale the castle curtain wall, using chinks in the stone to gain purchase. He ignored her angry cries, and the smaller boy leap to grab his ankles, receiving a kick to the shoulder for his pains. The youngest lad dropped back, holding his arm and glaring balefully at the climbing boy.

Seconds later, a shout rang out and the guards stationed on the wall-walk sauntered over, laughing and pointing at the climbing child. They bunched together, grinning down, folding their arms and forming a wall of armour. "Sorry, milord," one called mockingly. "There won't be no escape today. Go on now, or I'll have your tutor tan yer arse."

The curly-headed boy screamed a profanity and began to descend. Suddenly a stone dislodged from the wall beneath his left foot, and with a blood-curdling screech he fell several feet into a muddy herb bed.

"Who is that child?" I asked Harry's nurse, a stout older woman called Oliffe who seemed able to assert a calming influence on my son. Most of the time.

"Ah, Countess, that's young George, son of the Duke of York. He's a handful; reminds me of Harry sometimes..." Her round cheeks reddened and she put her hand to her mouth. "I hope you won't be cross, madam, and tell her Grace I said that. I spoke rashly; my old mother always said my tongue waved too much for me own good. Honest to God, I am fond of little Harry, but he does have a habit of getting into mischief and speaking out of turn."

"I understand—I am aware of how he can be when the mood takes him." Smiling, I patted her plump arm. "Fear not, I am not angry and Duchess Anne will never know... But tell me, those other children. Are they also York's?"

She nodded. "Margaret is the maid; she has a keen mind and is sensible and devoted to her brothers. The small one is the York runt, Richard. Quiet...deep. Politer than George, though, and more intelligent."

"I have not seen the Duchess Cecily, their mother, around the castle," I said. I had almost forgotten the family was brought here after the sack of Ludlow so elusive they had been till now. "She's not..." I swallowed, "in a cell, is she?" As much as I hated Richard Plantagenet and much as Cecily appeared haughty and distant, she was as trapped by the vagaries of Dame Fortuna as any woman...and she was a Beaufort too through her mother's blood.

"Oh no, of course not," said nurse Oliffe. "She the Duchess's sister, after all. She is inside with her Grace's chaplain. The Duchess keeps her on a straight road now, she does. No celebrating with the family, no fancy raiment, hours of prayers and instructions on humility and loyalty...."

"Do the children...play together? I mean, *my* children...and *hers*..." I asked in a whisper.

She stirred uncomfortably. "Her Grace forbade it at first, my Lady, but you know how children are. It's not their fault. Harry wanted to play ball with the youngest York—he's only three years older. I watched; there was no trouble, no trouble at all."

"I would prefer if they stayed apart," I said. "Especially...keep Harry away from that one." I tilted my chin toward George, who was crawling from the herb bed, aided by his sister. His dignity destroyed, he was hurling both mud and curses at her.

"But Harry will sulk and grow upset, milady; he is used to it now…playing knights and such."

I took a deep breath. I was still his mother even if we dwelt apart. "No. I will make sure the Duchess knows I do not approve. Harry will have to endure. Being denied will surely build his character."

If my strong-willed son was angered by my decision about the York children as playmates, I did not notice it. As the Christmas Feast approached, he became excited at the thoughts of seeing the fire-eaters, maskers and tumblers. "Will Grandmere Anne bring in a real bear, do you think?" He walked beside me near the fishpond, tugging at my sleeve for attention. "I'd like to see a bear! Could you ask her?"

"I think a bear might be too much," I said. I took no enjoyment from bear-baiting, and although this was a different situation, most of the bears I'd seen in pits outside disreputable taverns were shabby, dispirited creatures much misused. I pitied them, even while fearing their muzzled teeth and great paws. So terrible to be trapped and abused with death the only escape…

Harry sulked, his arms crossed. "I want a bear!"

"I have heard there may be a fire-eater," I soothed. "And he walks on stilts so that he looks a giant."

That seemed to satisfy Harry. He began to run around the pond, twirling, the wintry wind ruffling his hair, his mouth open and his tongue out to capture the snowflakes beginning to tumble from the pouchy grey clouds.

"It's snowing!" he squealed. "And I am out in it while Dumphie has to stay inside. Even better! If it gets very cold and the river freezes, can I go skating, mama?"

"You must ask your grandmother," I murmured, although I knew her answer would be no. It was mine too, he was far too young for such dangerous sport, skidding about on uncertain ice with sharpened bones strapped to his shoes, but I'd let Anne deal with the sulks and tantrums. I wanted my time with my son to be as pleasant as possible.

I only wished this sojourn did not have to end. Feeling suddenly cold, with ice crystals hanging on my veil, I drew my mantle closer and reached for Harry's hand.

The Christmas Feast was marvellous as I expected it would be under Anne's hand. The Duchess was sure to make all-comers recognise the power and wealth of the Stafford family with its royal connections.

Anne sat beside the Duke under a crimson canopy tasselled with gold. Buckingham had grown heavier and greyer, the scar on his cheek from the arrow at St Alban's faded—but there were new lines, new marks of sorrow and care on his features. I touched my own cheek, carefully powdered by Anchoret—the same lines of grief marred my own face.

The Duke and Duchess had kindly afforded me a seat close to the high table, along with the wives of their noble guests. A few I recognised, but there were none I knew well—till I saw Cousin Margaret enter the Great Hall. She did not see me, however; she sat with her husband, Henry, at the right-hand side of the Duke and Duchess. I noted she still wore a black gown, as if in perpetual mourning, but the garment was made of fine sarcenet cloth with gold lining in the sleeves A red-gemmed girdle laden with a rosary of green polished stones cinched her tiny waist, offsetting the darkness of her attire. A large golden cross studded with pearls hung about her neck.

The banquet began with a fanfare of clarions followed by the singing of minstrels in the gallery. All around, hundreds of candles flared in candelabrums decorated with holly and ivy. Spiced wine sweetened with honey was served and gingerbread dusted with sandalwood and cinnamon. Plum broth came next—a warming mix of fruit, beef, mutton, cloves and verjuice, followed by pea pods wrapped in curly bacon and dipped in salted butter.

After the course was done, the hired entertainers filtered in, mummers and maskers in outlandish costumes—a giant St Christopher, an Angel with outstretched wings, a swan in honour of the Duke, St George in his crusader's attire and the mystical doctor with his black robes and long dark beard.

The children had been brought down to the hall by their nurses. They would not stay for the main banquet; the only children permitted were the page boys that clung around Duke Humphrey's high seat, but the Duke and Duchess recognised that the boys wanted to see the mummery and frolics—and that Harry would not be happy, or silent, unless he did. They were led to the centre of the hall to much clapping and cooing from the watching ladies, and I felt justly proud, for both looked hardy and strong, well-dressed in garb befitting their station. A page brought little stools for them to sit upon while the mummers cavorted before them, tumbling and shouting out jests while buffeting each other with pig's bladders on sticks.

At the end of the performance, Harry rose and stared around. "Where is the fire-eater? My mother said there'd be a fire-eater!"

Even as he spoke, a gigantic shadow stretched over the floor from the direction of the servers' entrance. It lurched and clacked, its jerky motions giving it a hideous, almost spider-like appearance. Several ladies let out little nervous shrieks. Harry's mouth fell open and he reached over to clutch Humphrey's fingers.

The figure drew closer—two long legs, or rather stilts, wrapped in flapping black rags. On top was a player, grotesquely costumed as a devil from hell, with ribbed batwings flying back from his shoulders. He wore a skull-cap made of deer antlers and in one hand carried a burning torch, waving it before him in the manner of a club. Sparks scattered through the air, to be stamped on by diligent pages and squires as they hit the rushed on the floor.

Standing before my two boys, the devilish wight swayed and teetered. The mummer's face below the skull cap was visible but was smeared with ashes to give him a sinister look; his lips looked very red, coiling back in a ferocious snarl.

Harry's face bore a mixture of fear and delight. Humphrey, being younger, began to wail, and was picked up by Nurse Oliffe and carried to the side of the hall. The giant tilted back his head and opened his mouth wide, bringing the fire to his lips—and swallowing the flame. The watchers gasped; seconds later, the flame was safely extinguished and the mummer licked his fingers as if he had just consumed a most delicious dish.

Claps filled the room mingled with loud gasps of awe.

But the fire-eater shook his antlered head and held up a sooty finger for silence. He jerked up his strung wings so that they fluttered around him, concealing his cowled figure.

"Is…is he going to try to fly?" I heard a lady next to me murmur, astounded. Across the room, Cousin Margaret looked sour and ill at ease as she fingered her golden cross.

The fire-eater took another jerky step upon his stilts. A new torch was in his hands, handed up to him by a masked assistant.

He raised it on high so that all could see it clearly and his gaze pierced every corner of the chamber, bidding all to watch. Slowly, ever so slowly, he let it descend towards his pursed lips.

But, this time, he did not extinguish the flame within his mouth. Instead, a cloud of fire belched out, red and glowing, the heat striking my cheeks even at some distance. It was as if the fire-eater was summoning the spirit of some ancient dragon like the one good St George fought.

The flaming cloud evaporated into the air and the feasters began to cheer in earnest. The fire-eater's assistants ranged through the room, their caps doffed to receive coins or any other gifts.

Harry was on his feet, flushed, clapping like mad, almost bouncing with excitement. "Do it again! Do it again!"

But the act was over. The fire-eater clambered down from his stilts, shrugged off his wings and doffed his antlered cap becoming a human man once more. "I am glad you enjoy the mumming, my little Lord," he said in a gravelly voice as he bowed to Harry, and then he went to join his fellows in the courtyard where they waited to receive the leavings of the banquet at night's end.

Harry wanted to follow him but Nurse Oliffe shook her head. "Master Harry, it is well past your bedtime, and your brother's. You must come along now.

The children were led away, Harry's pout vanishing as a servant was sent after them with a tray of gingerbread, sugar plums and a wobbling red jelly fashioned into a castle with sugary turrets.

The feast then continued for the rest of us. Brawn, fatty and dark, taken from a boar's shoulders and pickled in cider. Venison ribs in wine broth, tartelettes, roasted kid in vinegar. Flampointes adorned with pastry triangles. Geese and capons stuffed full of eggs, pork and grapes. A mallard in a mustard sauce, and more. This sumptuous fare was followed by copious goblets of clarrey, hippocras and caudle—the latter being wine thickened with eggs.

My belly, no longer used to such rich food, for my appetite was lost in my widowhood, began to rebel and I could not face the final courses of sweet things—the seed cake and sticky sambocade, the sugared pine nuts, the marchpane subtlety shaped like a chequerboard.

As the feast wound down, Duchess Anne called me to her side. "When Twelfth Night is done, Margaret, I bid you come with me to Pleshey Church, where Humphrey lies at rest. I am sure you would like to visit his grave since you were not at the burial."

I listened to her intently, wondering if there was condemnation in her final words, but there seemed to be none. Her face, as ever, was calm and revealed nothing of her inner thought.

"Thank you, your Grace. I would be glad of your company, but is it not a great distance, especially at this time of the year when the elements are fickle?"

"The Duke has decided to remove there for a while and have the privies and floors cleaned at Tonbridge while we are absent. We would like you to accompany us, Margaret."

"The children will come too?"

"Yes, Harry and Humphrey shall travel with their nurses."

The thought of spending more precious time with my sons clinched the deal. "I look forward to it, your Grace."

In the Twelve Days that followed Christmas Day, there were endless celebrations—the feast of St Stephen, when the wren was hunted, the Feast of St John the Evangelist, the Feast of the Innocents when Herod slew the hapless babes, the Memorial of St Thomas Becket, Pope Silvester's Night (he who had choked unbelievers with fishbones, hence no fish graced the festal menu!), the Solemnity of Mary, Mother of God, and finally the Feast of Epiphany, where the Lord of Misrule presided over the celebrations and the world went topsy-turvy for a time.

Throughout this time, I had spoken now and then with Cousin Margaret. She had decided to depart Tonbridge before Twelfth Night. "I would prefer to spend the night in prayer, not raucous behaviour," she said. "I cannot abide such levity. Just like on Childermass, a truly sorrowful day when so many infants were slain...Now it is filled with such disrespectful mummery as 'Boy Bishops'."

I nodded but did not answer. Since her marriage to Henry Stafford, her pious and serious nature had emerged to the fore. When Lady Margaret spoke, men and women jumped to do her bidding, and the learned flocked to speak with her and she to them, for her piety and intelligence had been noted by clergy and scholars alike. Margaret's patronage, they hoped, would prove profitable.

"Henry and I are also planning a journey to Wales," she continued, a little smile pulling at her thin lips. "We are going to see my Henry and Jasper at Pembroke."

"How wonderful! I pray your journey is safe and that no foul weather blocks your path. You must be overjoyed at the thought of seeing your Henry again."

She sighed, almost guiltily. "Every day away from him is like having thorns driven into my heart, even though I know Jasper is a jewel among men and makes certain he wants for nought—but tell no one of my womanish woes, Cousin. It is not as I would have others see me—it is a man's world and although my body is frail, I want others to see I am as strong as any man in other ways. Henry is both my weakness...and my greatest strength, the arrow on my bowstring. I expect you feel much the same about your sons."

"I am so glad the Duke and Duchess invited me to Tonbridge for Yule. I miss the children so much while at Thornbury. Widowhood has not proved easy. I do not want to return to Gloucestershire yet, but I know not if I shall remain welcome in the Buckingham household overlong. After all, Tonbridge already has other unexpected guests lodging here."

"Oh, you mean the prisoners—Cecily Neville and her brood." She laughed a little. "How the mighty have fallen. A shame she is a York—I hear the Duchess has similar interests to me, books and our faith. Had things turned out differently, we might have become friends…"

She shook her head, pondering the vagaries of fate. Then she turned to me, her small dark eyes glittering in that old-young face. "What are your plans for the future, Meg? Have you still made no marriage arrangements? I would have thought…"

"Not yet, it is barely a year since Humphrey was laid to rest," I said hastily. "Although everyone tells me I must wed soon. And so I must. It seems my dower lands are not as lucrative as they might have been, so not much for a widow to live on—and, in these harsh times, I will need the security of a husband."

"A wise decision," she said. "Remarriage was an excellent move for me. I remain content; Henry is a decent man who gives me no grief and sees my son as his own. It may well fall out that way for you too. I will surely pray for you, Cousin Margaret."

"I will do the same for you too, dearest Margaret, and I will keep both your Henries in my prayers too." I glanced at her, thin as a reed in her voluminous black houppelande, gathered tightly under her rather shapeless chest. Could she be hiding a happy condition under that loose, flowing, rather outdated robe? I usually would not ask such questions, but on this night the clarry had loosened my tongue. "Do I see signs that a new child may be on the way? I am sure your boy Henry would like a brother and your husband an heir. My two sons would surely welcome another cousin."

Her face suddenly sank in, contorting, strange and horrible, as if a demon had possessed her. Her hands scrabbled at her cross, twisting the gold links of the chain. "No…" she barked. "It is not God's will. No other child will I bear; my first travail was too much for my fledgling body, the physics say. Henry, alone, shall remain the focus of my love and…and of all my desires, all my ambitions."

CHAPTER TEN

The road to Pleshey was peaceful enough, icy but clear of snow, the sky a marbled blue vault above us. Sometimes the wheels of the carriages and carts slipped on frozen puddles, but it was still preferable to the cloying waist-deep mud that often bogged down my journeys in the West and Wales.

However, nerves overtook me as we reached the border of Essex. Unsettling thoughts crowded my mind, after being pushed aside in my desire to remain with my sons. The Duke of Buckingham was not with us. Why had he not come, if Tonbridge was up for its yearly cleaning? It may be that he had business elsewhere, most likely at the royal court, but I'd heard nothing of that. I also wondered what had happened to Cecily Neville and her children with Duchess and Duke gone. I supposed she might have stayed confined in Tonbridge while the Stafford servants busied themselves around her, ignoring her, the York prisoner. I found a certain amusement at the thoughts of such a proud woman, enduring the rank smells and fleeing vermin as the privies were sluiced down and the reed-mats peeled from the castle floors full of encased bones, dog hair, dung and other muck.

I rode astride on a placid roan gelding, preferring to travel on horseback rather than spend hours with Duchess Anne in her chariot with a carved white swan juddering on the front. The children and their nurses were in a second chariot following behind her, and mounted I could check on them every now and then. Humphrey would cling to the back window and wave, but Harry was, the nursemaids informed me, too engrossed in a game of skittles to get up and greet me. Shamefaced, they asked if they should command him to stop, but I shook my head, knowing how my high-strung child might react. Peace was the better option.

On the horizon, the walls of Pleshey Castle finally drifted into view, glaring white in the harsh wintry sunlight. Once a scene of happiness—my wedding to Humphrey. Now it seemed a thousand years ago, and my husband lay under cold stone in the nearby church.

Once Duchess Anne had been settled in her apartments, I was escorted to my own chamber. To my surprise, I was attended upon by one of Anne's ladies-in-waiting. "Where is my own maid, Anchoret?" I asked crossly.

The woman, a cool-eyed blonde creature called Annice, looked down her Patrician nose at me, her face expressionless. "Did the Duchess not tell you? She decided to send both your maids back to Wales—to Brecknock. That is where their families are. Her Grace deemed they had dwelt overlong with you through loyalty…"

"This is outrageous!" I cried. "I was led to believe Anchoret would be travelled with us in one of the wains. Why has the Duchess done this? Should have conferred with me first. Even if I had agreed—to do this behind my back is a vile, duplicitous act!"

"Were your maids not paid from the Buckingham estates?" said Annice dryly, as she began to unpack my gowns and brush them down.

Her words stunned me into silence. My financial woes were legion, but I had never thought Anne that would remove my maids without at least warning me. And yet…how could I argue with her decision? Humphrey had employed them. Ladies changed their attendants all through their lives. Nonetheless, my heart was hammering in my chest and my breath felt constricted in my lungs. Anchoret and I had grown close… the nearest thing I had to a friend, despite the differences in our rank. She had soothed me in my worst days of despair…and now she was gone.

"Is there anything more you want today, my lady?" asked Annice, finishing with the gowns.

My gaze came to rest on the tray of pasties and tartlets filled with meat, cheese or fruit. It would do as a meal. "Loosen my gown," I said coldly. "Then you may go."

Nodding, she untied the lacing on the back of my dress. "Finished, my lady. I will take my place on a paillasse outside your door as Her Grace advised."

To keep me inside? I wondered with bitterness.

"Do as you wish," I said, fear making my tongue sharp as an adder's fangs. "I will tend to myself. I am not incapable."

"As you wish." She curtseyed, stiff and exuding haughtiness. "And if the Duchess should wish to speak with you tonight?"

"Tell her I am indisposed."

Annice left and I stormed about the room in a rage, stabbing the fire brazier with a poker to get the kindling burning and slamming the shutters to keep the warmth in. I shrugged out of my travelling gown, leaving it lying on the floor, then pulled on a thick bed robe and crawled into the cold bed.

I stared up at the ceiling; above, a spider was spinning a web.

Was *I* caught in some kind of web? Why was my former mother-in-law treating me in such a way? My thoughts were in so much turmoil that I feared I would not sleep a wink, but after some hours, when the bailey fell quiet and the only sound was an owl. hooting in the trees beyond the curtain wall, I fell asleep.

The next morn I stood in the Great Hall, frozen like a deer facing the huntsmen. Mother was at Pleshey, and it was apparent she had been dwelling there for some time. Beautiful but frailer than I remember, she drifted across the Great Hall to greet me, dripping pallid blue gems that matched her eyes. Her gown was equally sky-hued, beautiful blue cloth-of-gold. I was aware that she wore no mourning black...but then nearly five years had passed since Father was slain. *Five years...*

"Oh, Meg, how glad am, I to see you. It has been so long." She peered at me, appraising me from head to toe. "Oh dear...so thin...so wan...You look almost...almost *stretched...*"

"My health is far better than it was," I snapped, annoyed. "You did not seem so worried then. But I do not wish to talk of the past."

"No, no, quite right too." Mother could be argumentative, so it surprised me that she backed off needling me and continued smiling. "I have some news for you."

"What is this news?"

"First, I have come into some money. The King had granted me four hundred marks per year to be taken from the former estates of the Duke of York. Hal has been awarded the same amount. Thank goodness too; my coffers were nigh-on empty and I had not seen a solitary penny of the 5000 marks York had agreed to pay earlier."

"I am glad to hear of your windfall, Mother. I am sure it will help you buy some new…jewels and dresses."

Her lips pursed; there were little lines fanning out from them that had not existed last we met. "You've grown so brittle. Hardly my Margaret…"

"Was I ever 'your Margaret'? I always believed that Nell was by far preferred…because she is so like you. Even my little sisters pleased you more than I, the one who never fit, whom you deemed weak and silly."

"Oh, Meg, do not be foolish." Her lips tightened even further; a hard, painted rosebud. "You know that's not true. You had the best marriage of all my daughters, to a Duke's son. Nell's husband is only an earl, Joan's a baron, while Elizabeth's but a knight…and Anne's has only just earned his spurs. Anne's husband William is one of the Pastons of Norfolk, you, know and there was a terrible rumour that they were descended from serfs! I am certain it's not so as the Pastons are such a clever, astute family—William has even compiled a manuscript, The *Paston Book of Arms*."

I listened to her rattle on with dulling senses. More than anything, I wanted to know why she was at Pleshey. I contemplated asking her outright, but had no chance, for she suddenly blurted, "Speaking of marriages, Meg…Well, this may surprise you, but I am going to marry again. Soon."

My eyes widened. Hal had mentioned this possibility but I was still surprised. "Marriage?"

"I am a practical woman. I need a protector, even at my age. And…" She primped like a young maid, her cheeks colouring. "He is madly in love with me."

"Who is he? Someone of note?"

"His name is Walter Rokeley. "

So the rich but untitled fellow Hal mentioned had definitely won Mother's affections.

"And no, he's no one of note," she continued, as if reading my thoughts. "Not even a knight. A wealthy merchant. Very, very wealthy." She gestured to the gemstones flashing sea-fire around her neck. "He obtained these for me, and much more besides."

"I-I am surprised. You, the daughter of an earl."

"I never thought you so snobbish, Margaret. You were spoiled when we betrothed you to Humphrey Stafford, that's it. Spoiled. All quickly forgotten how your father was the poorest of Dukes, despite his noble blood. Well, a lessening of position is something I fear you are going to have to accept, as I have, if you want any kind of decent future."

"Why are you here, Mother?" I asked, exasperated.

"To give you my good news, as I told you. And to see my grandsons, of course. I would dearly like them to get to know me, as is only fitting and right. And, I did come to see you too. I know times have been hard for you…for all of us. The Duchess has told me that you will visit the Earl of Stafford's tomb for the first time since his burial. I am here to support you on that day. To offer counsel and advice."

My eyes slitted. Her last words bothered me, although I strove, as ever, to curb my fears and believe she had my best interests at heart. I did not want her counsel or advice…but still, she was my mother, so I could not gainsay her. *Honour your father and your mother…*

"I've heard from Hal," she said, changing the subject. "He has sailed to Calais in an attempt to take the garrison from the Earl of Warwick. Your half-brother Thomas went with him. Unfortunately, Hal could not gain entrance to the port—Warwick fired his cannons at Hal's ships and he had to make for Guisnes instead. He was luckier there—the soldiers at the fortress had not received their pay from Warwick and let him in."

"Money can open many doors, even those of a strong castle."

She nodded. "But not those of Calais, it seems. Hal keeps assaulting it, but for some reason the inhabitants love that devil, Neville the Devil…" She chortled at her own weak jest. "The ungrateful fools jeered when Hal showed them the letters patent confirming him as the *true* captain of Calais."

"That will not please him."

"No, he was most put out, Meg, as well he might be. His father and grandsire had held the office of Captain of Calais before him and he wanted to add his name to that glorious list. But York's supporters are slippery as eels and brazen as…as brass. Has Duchess Anne or the Duke told you of their latest tricks? His Grace will have had the news, being of such importance in the royal circles."

I shook my head. "I have not, but I do not believe the Duke or Duchess would speak of such matters to me. I am not important enough now."

"Warwick has raided English ports! The traitor attacked his own country! He has burnt part of the royal fleet—the Queen must be furious! Hal certainly is—he was depending on those ships for reinforcements."

"He must be livid." I thought of Hal's mercurial temper, inflamed by desire for vengeance. The payments Mother mentioned would never be enough; only degradation of his foes and their spilt blood would assuage him.

"It is a disgusting situation. On one raid, Warwick took Lord Rivers captive, along with his son, Anthony Woodville, and Lord Scales. A scandal it is and such a pity—Richard Woodville is such a fine handsome man; I've danced with him, you know, and Anthony is just as comely and very learned…"

I had not met any of the Woodvilles but had heard of the past scandal concerning Lord Rivers' wife, Jacquetta of Luxembourg. A known beauty of impeccable lineage going back to Charlemagne, she had married the much older John, Duke of Bedford, brother of Henry V, that warrior king of endless renown. However, when John died, he had hardly been laid in the tomb when she embarked on an affair with the dead Duke's chamberlain, Richard Woodville, a common knight if of uncommonly good looks. They wed in secret, incurring the wrath of King Henry, who decided to forgive the couple upon receipt of 1000 pounds. Despite this small blot on her reputation, she became one of the premier ladies of the court—not bad for one whose descent was not only from Charlemagne but, reputedly from some fishy-tailed sorceress called Melusine.

"I do hope Earl Rivers will survive," Mother was chuntering to herself, "and Anthony too. Warwick took them to Calais and word has it that he and Salisbury and that great lump Edward of March berated them with foul insults. Shameful…"

"When will it ever be over?" A knot of frustration unravelled in me, and I began to pace the room. "It seems all of my life men have been fighting…"

"That's what men do!" said Mother.

"And that's how they die...like Father."

"God assoil him!" She piously crossed herself and stared heavenward. Her face bore an odd expression; I wonder if she was remembering any good times spent with Father—or the uncertain times, with rumours abounding that he was sleeping with the Queen. Or maybe she was comparing him with her new, lowborn but wealthy beau, Walter Rokeley.

Mother shook her head, her smile which was never a true smile returning. "Well, enough of this talk for one morning—don't you think, Meg? You…you are becoming *overwrought*. We mustn't let that happen again. Come, let us take little Henry and Humphrey to the gardens. I have missed my grandsons. Such fine lads."

At least there was one thing on which we could agree.

The church of the Holy Trinity at Pleshey stood beyond the great earthworks of the castle, part of the college founded by the Staffords' royal ancestor, Thomas of Woodstock. Duchess Anne walked sedately on my right-hand side while Mother was on the left. I had the distinct impression I was being shepherded by these two strong-willed women, and it was not entirely comfortable, but I would sound a ninny if I began to make objections about visiting my own husband's tomb.

"The church was built around the year of Our Lord 1400." Anne paused before the door, gazing up the expanse of golden stonework filled with saintly statuary. "Humphrey loves Pleshey, so much so we decided to make this humble church our family mausoleum. Better than lying for eternity in some dreary abbey far from home."

Overhead a bell rang out, chiming the hours, its deep tone shuddering the very earth. "We have very fine bells," Anne said, "made by one William Dawe. The one that tolls is dedicated to the Virgin—*Ora Mente Pia Pro Nobis Virgo Maria* is written upon it."

Entering the cruciform building, we walked in silence over the tiles filled with images of swans beaked and legged and tree stocks, eradicated and couped, for Thomas of Woodstock. Thomas's arms also appeared in a stained-glass window, flaring with jewelled brilliance—the Arms of England quartered with those of his wife, Eleanor de Bohun, which were six golden lioncels split by a silver bend upon an azure background.

As we neared the chancel, I spotted hundreds of candles burning, flickering in the gloom. Duchess Anne nodded towards the ring of brightness. "There lies my dear eldest son, with all the lights in the world to guide him to heaven."

I broke away from the other two women and walked over to the tomb, a solid chest with carved weepers on the side, and angels on the stone canopy. A brass effigy of Humphrey lay atop the chest, bare-headed and armoured. I felt my knees begin to buckle and I sank to the floor, my head resting against one of the weepers. "I am sorry," I murmured to nothingness, "that I did not come before, that I failed you…"

Mother was at my elbow. "Come now, Margaret," she said, kindly but with the hint of an order in her voice. "Compose yourself. We will all light candles for Humphrey and pray for his soul. Let this day be one of closure for you, daughter; from here onwards, a new life will await you."

I got up and did as she bid me, lighting the candles in the cresset stones around the tomb. "I…I will find the money to pay…"

"Don't you worry about that," said Mother. "I shall take care of it with the award granted by the King. I understand your plight."

Again, unease came over me. Mother's kinder actions often had strings attached, but it was not the place to argue, and she was very aware of my straitened circumstances.

Huddled together amidst the candle smoke and incense smell, the three of us prayed for Humphrey's soul. Anne's eyes were closed, her lips moving as her fingers played on her expensive rosary. Her voice was a mere whisper, yet it echoed through the arches above, echoed in my mind, *"Who can tell what a day may bring forth? Cause us, therefore, gracious God, to live every day as if it were our last, for that we know not but it may be such. Cause us to live so at present as we shall wish we had done when we come to die. O grant that we may not die with any guilt upon our consciences, or any known sin unrepented of, but that we may be found in Christ..."*

As if in a trance, I reached out to touch the tomb again, my hand flat on the cold brass, almost as if hoping in some way to connect with Humphrey, wherever he was. *Let me know what I should do next...I am so alone...*

No answers were forthcoming from that cold block of stone, the weepers' faces already black and oily from the constant burnings of the nearby tallow.

Anne's hand descended on my shoulder. "Margaret, of other things must we talk this day."

I blinked. We stood before Humphrey's tomb. The duchess looked as if she was about the deliver a lecture...or a sermon.

"Your Grace?"

"Thornbury," she said. "You are aware of its condition. The Duke wants to take possession. He may, in the future, wish to rebuild the manor house."

"I beg forgiveness that I was not a better mistress..."

"It matters not now." She gave a dismissive wave of her hand.

"I must find new lodging then," I said bitterly," on those humble dower lands, what few I have. Lands so poor they can turn no profit, and I have nought to invest in them. That is what you are telling me."

"Not necessarily," Mother interjected. "A marriage, as I told you, as many have told you, is the best solution to all your ills, monetary and otherwise."

I spread out my hands, lips tight in a bloodless smile. "That is all very well and good, Mother. But suitors are even more sparse than my lands."

"Do not demean yourself, Meg," said Mother. "When I first visited Tonbridge, after Duchess Anne took over the caretaking of my grandsons, I spoke with her about potential matches for you. Did I not, Anne?"

Anne Neville nodded. Both women were smiling at me as if they had given me the happiest news any woman could receive. I wanted to scream or cry; instead, my hands gnarled into fists as I strove to keep myself from shaking, from showing my weakness.

"And what did you decide in my absence? What type of man have you deemed suitable?"

"Margaret, why must you always expect the worst! I have thought long and hard on this matter!" Mother shook her head as if in despair at my intransigence. "You do not have to say yes if a prospective suitor does not please you. You are a widow, with more say than a young maiden. Just remember, before you make a hasty decision, that without a husband you are vulnerable, and as you've realised yourself, it may prove extremely hard to manage your lands by yourself. I too have heard they are boggy and barren."

"You have not answered my question," I asked. "Who is he?"

The sound of the church door creaking reached my ears. Dust motes flurried as light spilt into the nave. A man and a woman stood in the doorway, silhouetted against the bright sky beyond.

My breath escaped between clenched teeth, a hiss. I wanted to scream, to run. What had Mother and Anne been thinking, to bring this man here, so boldly, in some kind of unpleasant ruse?

The newcomers drew closer. The man was tall and well-made, with dark curling hair and bright blue eyes. His complexion was dark, almost like a Spaniard's, and he had a slightly arrogant, roguish look, his jaw long and square, the stubble blue upon it. I imagined most women would find him attractive enough.

The woman at his side was diminutive and wrapped in pale grey silks and laces. Her eyes were the same hue as the man's and there were enough similarities in their features to proclaim them as close kin. She was older though, much older.

"Margaret, this is Sir Richard Dayrell of Littlecote," said Countess Anne. "His father was sun-treasurer of England, and his brother George has oftimes been Sheriff of Wiltshire. With him is his mother, Mistress Elizabeth Calston. Sir Richard, Mistress Elizabeth, this is the Countess of Stafford, widow of my son, Earl Humphrey."

The man bowed, while the woman dropped a deep curtsey. She kept her head bowed, very respectful, but I could sense she was trying to get a good look at me, surreptitiously, from under lowered lashes.

"I will not lie," I said, in all honesty, "this meeting was unexpected and not exactly welcome."

I saw Elizabeth Calston's lips twitch. Sir Richard, on the other hand, seemed unphased by my coldness. "Forgive me, Countess, I was led to believe…" He glanced at Mother and Duchess Anne, who stood boldly unrepentant.

A part of me wanted to cry, "Well, you were wrong, all of you, wrong!" but I knew that would avail me nothing. If I refused this man's suit, I would soon find myself out of Thornbury and making a subsistence living on lands I was in no condition to manage. I did not even have my loyal, hard-working maids anymore. I might lose connection and access to my sons—that would be intolerable.

I stepped closer to Richard Dayrell, telling myself to look him in the eye, to show strength. I was a Duke's daughter; a prize even if the Beaufort family was not the wealthiest of the nobility—with the exception of Cousin Margaret, who inherited the bulk of the original Beaufort lands from her father, John. Our misfortune was slowly changing, though, with Hal's increasing prominence in the King's government.

Richard gazed down his long straight nose at me; he was, I had to admit fine-looking. He showed no carnal desire, nor had I truly expected to find him possessed by some otherworldly love, as a hero in an old Arthurian tale—but I saw greed and want.

"I am surprised you are not already wed, Sir Richard," I said with a little smile. I guessed his age to be around thirty; old for a first wedding by any accounts, although I could not overthink it as several men within my own family had not wed at the usual age, including Hal.

A flash of displeasure crossed his features, but Elizabeth Calston cleared her throat. "My son has been very busy, Countess. He aspires to be Sheriff someday, like his brother, and one day he hopes to inherit his father's position as sub-Treasurer of England. He is very involved with local governance in Wiltshire."

I guessed what they were about then. It was about climbing the ladder by marrying into the old blood of England. And who was I to blame them for that, as it was done by every intrepid family in the country? Girls and lands moved around like pieces on a chessboard.

"Littlecote is a fine house," said Elizabeth. "Spacious, with a fine garden. It came through my family, the Calstons, with my marriage to Sir William Dayrell. Chilton Foliat and Rambury are nearby—the Bishop of Salisbury has a palace at the latter. For the most part, it is a quiet, peaceful place far from most troubles."

Peaceful. A sensation of longing gripped me. That's what I desired most now. Peace. A life far from the battles of men.

Perhaps I could have that if nothing else. And if peace and simplicity were promised to me, Sir Richard Dayrell and his mother could have what they clearly wanted—a match that might further elevate the family in the next generation.

I took a deep breath. Mother peered at me, nervous, expectant. Duchess Anne was stern and pale, eyes willing me to make the right decision.

"If you truly wish to marry me, Sir Richard," I said, "then there is only one thing I can say—I will."

I returned with Anne and the boys to Tonbridge. Mother headed to the west, well-satisfied. Richard Dayrell and his mother returned to Wiltshire, the older woman's face smug, the cat that got the cream. I had chosen a date to go to them; September, when the summer was over, yet the weather still fair. I had thrashed that out with Duchess Anne; I told her I wanted time with the children first. She and Duke Humphrey could take immediate possession of Thornbury again if I could stay for those last few months of widowhood at Tonbridge. She agreed without hesitation, of which I was glad.

Back in Tonbridge castle, I found the floors and fireplaces cleaned and the privies slightly sweeter. So it had not been just subterfuge on the part of Anne, an excuse to get me to Pleshey to meet up with Richard Dayrell. Richard...my betrothed. I rolled his name off my tongue. It felt so strange. Soon I would give up widowhood and become a wife again. I was betrothed...

By March, however, I had more to think about than weddings. Warwick had sailed from Calais and was rumoured to have fared on to Ireland to liaise with the Duke of York. Whispers travelled, swift as lightning, claiming that soon Richard Plantagenet would return and make a play for the throne. In Warwick's absence, Hal made another attempt to take Calais. A bloody battle was fought...and he failed again. At least he escaped with his head—a few weeks later, his captain Osbert Mountford, was captured by a returning Earl of Warwick and summarily executed, his head decorating the gates of Calais, where it was picked by the ever-hungry gulls and terns.

And then came the tidings we all feared—Warwick, Salisbury and March had left the French port and were sailing for England, not to raid as pirates but to march to war. Spies brought estimates of two-thousand soldiers.

"They will try to take hold of the King and remove him," stormed the Duke of Buckingham. "Remove him *permanently*, I should imagine."

Anne made as if to protest then fell silent. She knew it was true. I knew it too but continued embroidering in the Duchess's solar, pretending I did not hear. I thought of Sir Richard. Would he fight for King Henry? I supposed he would. Maybe he would die. Maybe I would not become a bride after all. Would I feel sorrow if he fell in the service of his king—or feel nothing at all? I could not say. I kept my eyes low, watching my needle flash through cloth like a miniature sword blade.

Eventually, Anne spoke, her voice strained. "Is there any news of York and Rutland in Ireland?"

Buckingham shook his grizzled head; caught at a bad angle, his scar looked livid in the candlelight. "Not as yet, but he will come. There is no doubt about it."

"And what will you do? Humphrey, you are getting…"

"Anne…I must go to Henry's side. There is no question. I must move quickly too, for Warwick is no sluggard; his men march towards the Midlands as if demons from Hell were at their heels."

"They *are* the demons," cried Anne with more emotion than was usual. She stabbed at her needlework, then flung it to the floor with a small cry. "Is there no chance of holding talks with my misborn nephew, Warwick?" She spat his name as if it burnt her tongue. "Surely he would parley."

The Duke's visage turned granite-hard. "I will not hold talks with such as him. He is a traitor, wife. He has shown this many times. Battle it will be, and if God is merciful, his malice will be quelled forever. Perhaps the death of Warwick, Salisbury and March would keep York from returning. He could spend the rest of his days in exile."

"March…Edward. He's also my nephew," said Anne, rather unhappily, "but unlike Warwick, he is only eighteen. Surely, some mercy could be shown for him. I promised Cecily that although I disapproved of her support for Richard's folly, I would try to beg for clemency for her children. *All* of them, including Edward."

"No mercy." Buckingham's fingers twisted the hilt of the dagger at his belt. "Edward is young but not so young he has no reason! He has cast his lot with traitors to the crown and will face the penalty."

Anne bowed her head. "What will be, will be, then. When do you go?"

"The levies have been summoned," said Duke Humphrey. "I will depart as soon as possible and march up-country. The King will join me. There is no time to lose."

A few days later, Buckingham rode forth from Tonbridge in martial splendour, banners raised and clarions blaring. I stood beside Duchess Anne on the gatehouse tower and little Harry gazed between the crenellations, waving frantically. Humph whined; he was not quite tall enough to see, so a nurse held him up on high, where he laughed as if at play and beat the sky with his fists.

"Don't, Dumph," said Harry sulkily, annoyed that the attention had gone onto his little brother. "Or I'll ask Nurse Oliffe to throw you over!"

As the departing army vanished into a haze of smoke and dust, I turned from the walls. In the courtyard below I spied Cecily Neville and her children. She glanced up at me and the look on her face stopped me in my tracks. It was a look of triumph, all penitence forgotten. Her stance was bold again, and though she was wearing dour clothes at her sister's command, she had added a golden crucifix with white enamelled roses on the chain.

A cold chill fingered my spine. It was as if she had a presentiment of a return to her old life, an intimation that her husband would soon return to her side, victorious.... I crossed myself, telling myself it was only the haughty old Cecily re-emerging, flouting Anne's rules and stern rebukes in the Duke of Buckingham's absence.

Overhead a bird shrieked, the harsh cry of a bird of prey. Staring up into the brightness, I saw a wild falcon soaring on wind swells, seeking its prey in the fields beyond the castle walls.

The Duke of York's emblem was a falcon. The Falcon and Fetterlock. Below, the boy called George spotted the bird and pointed towards it. "A good omen, Mother! A good omen for us!"

May blazed with colours—cornflowers and Lady's Mantle, Monkshood and Marigold, Teasle and Honeysuckle. The fishpond stretched long and green, dragonflies skimming the surface like radiant jewels. The smell of mint and sage mingled with damp soil permeated the air.

In the garden, I enjoyed the simple pleasures of the day. So caught up in a reverie was I, I scarcely noted the sounds of horsemen galloping at speed over the lowered drawbridge and entering the bailey.

But then…I heard the scream. A terrible agonised cry, scarcely human, almost like an animal in pain. Instinctively, my hands flew up to cover my ears. There was a familiarity in the cry, not just the voice but the emotion within it—despair, loss, grief.

Oh Christ, no…the Duke!

I ran for the castle door, trampling over the herb beds, the sky tilting crazily above me. Inside, the place was in an uproar, the ill news having already leaked out. Servants wept and hugged each other, as the chaplain rushed by, crossing himself. I followed on his heels as the chapel bells pealed a sombre death knell that filled the entire castle. The priest entered the chapel; over his shoulder, I saw the Duchess Anne collapsed in a heap, her ladies clustered around her.

"Get away from me!" She thrust at them with her hands. "Leave me in my suffering!" She began to rock back and forth and keen, that odd, awful sound I had heard before.

Seeing how she resisted all comfort, I decided not to intrude on her grief. It was Harry and Humphrey who concerned me more anyway. Harry, in particular, was close with his grandfather… My breath suddenly escaped my lungs in a gasp and my throat knotted. *Jesu…my little son, not quite five, was now the Duke of Buckingham!*

Staggering, I leaned against the wall, going hot and cold, black spots dancing in my vision. While he would not enter his lands for many years, Harry was an important person and royal-blooded. By his very birth he was a danger to York and his allies. I did not think they would harm a child, but they might well want to take control of him, take him from his widowed grandmother, take him far beyond my reach.

Forcing my ragged breaths to normalise, I swept away from the chapel to the nursery. Inside, Oliffe was holding Harry who was weeping profusely. Humphrey was grizzling too, but was too young to understand any of what had occurred—he was upset because his brother was in tears.

"Oh, Countess!" cried Oliffe, tears oozing from her eyes and running over her plump face. "What shall become of us all? These poor babes…First their father, now their grandfather! Such wicked, wicked times. I swear we are coming to the End Times, as spoken of in Revelation, when the seven trumpets shall sound and the Star Wormwood sail across heaven and the sun and moon grow dark…"

"Oliffe, enough," I said, though kindly, "you'll frighten the children even more."

She bowed her head and I took Harry from her. "Harry, Harry, your grandfather was a kind man, a great man…He was loyal to his king and served him all his days. You must remember his goodness and emulate him when you are grown. Weep for him, but not overmuch, for he is with Christ now, our saviour."

"I want him back!" Harry wailed.

"You will meet again someday, I swear it…And there will be no more weeping then; it has been promised."

He knuckled away his tears. "I—I…am the Duke now, mama, aren't I? Now that he is…gone."

"You are."

His wet, blood-shot eyes grew fierce. "When I am big…when I have a sword that isn't wood…I will kill them. Those who killed grandfather. I will kill them all."

It was a terrible unnatural thing to hear from the mouth of a young child, although, in our world, children were not protected from the realities of strife or death. Amongst the nobility of England, there was not one family that had not had a relative or ancestor beheaded for treason or slain in battle.

"You must not speak so," I managed to say. "Forgiveness is a beautiful thing for Christians, Harry."

He pulled away from me and slumped heavily on the floor, the fire going out of him, a sad, heartbroken child. He said nothing but buried his face on his knees.

I went to Humphrey, my laughing boy, so unlike his brother in temperament. He cheered up instantly as I took him in my arms.

Why…why could the children not come with me when I married Richard Dayrell? But that was a foolish dream, one not grounded in reality. The matter of blood and tradition put paid to such ideas.

I pressed my face into Humphrey's tousled curls and cried my own tears for the Duke of Buckingham, who had been kind, and for my broken family.

The Duchess of York was a free woman. I watched her walk regally across the inner courtyard with Duchess Anne, her plain, workaday garments of penitence put aside and wearing a gown of blue cloth of gold, the long sleeves inlaid with tawny silk. She was soon to be on her way to Barnard's Castle in London, to await the arrival of the Duke of York from Ireland.

I noticed the tall, lanky York girl, Margaret standing to one side with her younger brothers, obviously ordered to mind them. Richard was standing dutifully near her, a spare little wraith with windblown hair and worried expression. The obnoxious one, George, was careering around the bailey, smirking merrily, I supposed, at the thought of freedom. He was the noisiest child and often played tricks on the laundresses and servants—I would not miss the shouts and yells that followed George like a cloud.

I frowned as I spotted Oliffe with Harry, who went running towards the York children. I suspected he had interacted with them, for innocent purposes or for childish rivalry, more than I knew about, my orders for separation ignored. Boys always did what they were told not to—and sometimes maidens too.

George came swaggering up to Harry, hands on hips; I saw his mouth move, but was too far away to hear his words, even if the wind was blowing in the right direction. Suddenly Harry's cheeks reddened and his hands became fists. He launched himself straight at George of York, his head driving straight into the taller boy's belly. George was taken by surprise and fell backwards onto some paving stones. He scrambled to rise, a bellow of outrage blasting from his open mouth—and Harry butted him with his head, causing his nose to stream blood.

"Jesu!" I cried, darting for the spiral stair into the courtyard. I had no doubt George would pummel Harry if no one intervened. I would have stern words with Oliffe, although I had no doubt my strong-willed son demanded to say his farewells to the Yorks and soft old Oliffe gave in.

I arrived in the yard just as Margaret of York started tousling with her brother, pulling him away from Harry as blood flowed from his injured nose to spatter on his sky-blue doublet. However, he unchivalrously kicked his sister in her shins and she released him with a pained shriek. George grabbed Harry by his collar, lifting him up off his feet. I saw my son's face turn red as his throat was compressed and began to run as fast as I could in my restraining skirts.

"Stop! Stop it, both of you!" I cried but my voice sounded no more forceful than the mewing of a gull. Even if the fighting children heard, they ignored me, even as I drew close.

To my surprise, it was the boy Richard that stopped the fracas, dragging Harry away from George. "Enough!" he commanded, his voice strangely authoritative despite his size. I narrowed my eyes; he had the look of his father about him, my sire's enemy....

Margaret, being the eldest, now took control of the situation. "George, you apologise to Cousin Harry…"

"I won't!" he shouted back. He was clutching his swollen nose. "The brat's marred my face!"

*I'll mar it further if you touch my son again…*I began to descend upon him, but Richard of York spoke again, "George, not now. Leave it. You got what you deserved. Get in the chariot and hush your mouth—Mother is coming soon, with Aunt Anne."

George released a torrent of abuse at his sibling but left Harry alone and stalked to the Yorks' waiting chariot, sent by

Edward of March and Warwick to collect the family. He leapt inside, where he could be heard kicking the walls.

"I am sorry," Richard said to Harry, "for my brother's behaviour and for the death of your grandfather."

"No, you aren't!" retorted Harry, blotchy-cheeked and furious. "You are all traitors! Go away!" He saw me then and ran to my side, not touching me, as that would ruin his boyish dignity, but wanting to show the others that he had an ally more senior than them.

The remaining York children trudged gloomily to the carriage, just as Cecily Neville and Anne began to stroll toward the carriage, still deep in conversation. If they had noticed the commotion, they had chosen to ignore it. Perhaps they had seen it before in their broods of children and did not let it disturb them over much. It disturbed me. My child was not some spare younger son—he was a Duke.

"I will pray for you, sister," said Cecily, "and arrange masses to be said for Humphrey's soul. He was kind to me and mine at Ludlow. It might have gone the worse for me had he not ridden up when I stood upon the Buttercross, death and destruction all around. One day all that blood shall be washed away and true peace will reign again"

Anne's face was pale and sharp, a carven effigy. "Will it? Not for a long time. Cecily. Not with your husband still attempting to oust the rightful King. We will never see eye to eye on this matter. As things stand, although I do still hold you in affection, perhaps it is best if we do not meet again."

"I would kiss you farewell but by your words. I do not think that would please you," said Cecily. "So, sister, we part in sorrow, with this feud of two houses falling like a sword between us. I wish you well, nonetheless."

She turned to be helped up the wooden steps into the chariot when she noticed me standing there, windblown, my shaking, angry little son at my side.

"I recognise you…" She took a few steps in my direction. "The wife of Humphrey Stafford the younger…"

"Who was wounded at St Alban's and never fully recovered," I whispered.

"It is hard the life we women lead when our menfolk are drawn to war," she said, and her face, though still fair, showed more weariness and age than I had seen upon it before. I realised it must have been hard for her—husband and one son fleeing one direction, her other son the other, with the possibility their heads might end on pikes looming large. They were traitors in my eyes…but, I had to admit, to their families they were heroes and they were loved.

I said nothing and she gave me a faint smile. "I must apologise for George's antics. He was born in Ireland, and sometimes I swear the faerie folk there replaced my true son with a changeling! No, I jest, I had indulged him rather more than my other children, I fear. I will have stern words with him about his behaviour. And fear not…" She nodded towards Harry. "In the future, I am sure, a place will be found for young Henry at court. No matter what happens, I am certain he will be treated with all due respect and come into his own as the Duke of Buckingham."

I realised then she was speaking thus because she thought that soon she would be Queen and Richard of York King. Yes, they'd want Harry there, under their gaze, watching him, moulding him into a loyal supporter, his Lancastrian roots denigrated and forgotten.

I took Harry's hand, wind-chilled, still shaking with anger. "I bid you a good day and safe journey, Madam," I said, my tone as chilly as my son's fingers, and then without acknowledging her or curtseying to her superior rank, I turned abruptly and hurried back towards the castle door.

CHAPTER ELEVEN

A wedding is supposed to be a happy occasion—or at least give the outward appearance of being so. There was little happiness when, in September, I left Tonbridge and my children, and rode to Littlecote to marry Richard Dayrell.

The house was a grand pile set amidst green fields and clustered trees; in the far distance, one could see smoke rising from the chimneys of Ramsbury. However, despite the size of the house and its verdant lawns, fish pond and flowering gardens, I found the manor had a forbidding feel, its timbers heavy, its windows dim.

The house contained its own chapel and there I married Richard. His mother, Elizabeth Calston was there, of course, prim and brittle, as were some of his brothers and other kin. Few came from my side to wish me well on my new life, my youngest living sister, Bess, and my half-brother, Sir Richard Ros, known to his family as Dick, accompanied by his wife Jane Knyvet.

Bess and I had not seen each other for years and our conversation was stiff and awkward; our ways had diverged. I knew Dick Ros even less, as we were of the half-blood only, but he had been an amiable boy as I recalled and now seemed an amiable and educated man, with an interest in foreign books and poetry and their translation into English.

At the end of the swift, unremarkable nuptial Mass in the dark, narrow little chapel, Dick joined the wedding party in the banquet hall and presented me with a handsome book with a red leather cover. "It is a poem I translated from the French," he said proudly. "*La Belle Dame Sans Merci.*"

"The Beautiful Lady with No Pity?" laughed Richard Dayrell, leaning over my shoulder, already deep in his cups. The smell of the wine on his breath tormented my already queasy belly, fluttering with nerves since day's dawning. "I pray your sister is not that—although I have heard from many that each man's wife eventually becomes that heartless Dame!"

Richard's brothers George, Alexander and the extraordinarily named Constantine burst into raucous laughter at his jest; their wives pretended to have taken no offence, though their tight mouths and snapping eyes implied otherwise, and they began to indulge in mindless chitchat to block out their husbands' insults.

Richard's hand reached out towards my gift. "I would like to look."

I dared not say no and passed the book to him with reluctance. He put down his goblet, balanced the book on one hand and roughly flipped the pages. Out of the corner of my eyes, I saw Dick wince at the rough handling. Jane Knyvet, seated at the ladies' table, looked appalled and pretend to chase a morsel on her plate with her knife.

Richard smirked and cleared his throat, ready for a dramatic pronouncement. "Listen to this, my friends!" he crowed. "A translation from the French by our esteemed guest, my wife Margaret's brother, Sir Richard Ros. *Half in a dream, not fully well awoke, the golden sleep wrapped me under his wing...*"

The words were fair but the tone of Richard's voice mocking, and his rowdy friends and family bellowed with mirth. "Can we not have something less fey and more bawdy?" one shouted. "This is a wedding, after all, not a funeral."

"Some would say the two are much the same!" laughed Richard, to another roar of mirth.

His jesting over, he thrust the book back in my hands and whirled about to join his companions in their merry-making.

"I thought those were fair words, brother," I said to Dick. "Your book is a gift I will always prize, I assure you."

"I wish you well in this marriage, Meg," he said, and I could tell by his expression that he thought no good would come of it.

Later, when the feasting was over and the dogs yapped for scraps as the voiders were hauled away to the kitchens, Jane Knyvet came to my side. "I will attend you tonight, if you wish, Meg," she said. She was a plump woman, not pretty but kindly in appearance, with rosy cheeks and clear blue eyes.

"You are kind—thank you, Jane," I said, clasping her hand so that no one could see. "My sister Elizabeth—Bess—will also accompany me to the bedchamber."

I glanced down the length of the hall; Richard and his brothers were red-faced and shouting, egging on a Fool whose hose was down around his ankles, as he sang in a high falsetto:

He took the maiden fair aside
And led her where she was not spied
And told her many a pretty tale,
And gave her well of his sweet ale!
His right sweet ale, his strong sweet ale!
Enough to make a maid grow pale…"

Jane frowned and took my elbow. "Let us retreat from this rowdiness."

With Bess joining us, we ascended the creaking wooden stairs to the upper floor, guided by a sullen old serving-woman whose silvered spikes of hair crawled with lice. Bess trailed in the rear, uncomfortable, keeping her distance from the bug-ridden servant. Mother had sent her in her absence and she appeared to wish she was anywhere else but Littlecote.

The bridal bedchamber was a large room painted green and red, but it looked as if the colours had not been renewed for a very long time. The plastered ceiling was patched with mildew, the shutters full of wormholes. There was a pottery bowl full of water, a jug of wine on a small table and several battered wooden chests. The bed, fortunately, appeared new, with a red velvet tester and plump pillows and mattress, and some kind soul had scattered fragrant blossoms across the coverlet. I breathed a sigh of relief; the dampness above had made me fear the sheets would be cold and soiled.

"The nights are getting colder now," said Jane, rubbing her hands together. "I will start a fire in the brazier."

"Are you sure a fire won't make it too hot?" said Bess. "After all, the heat betwixt two lovers…"

"Did it look to you that Richard is particularly desirous of our union?" I asked my sister, as I placed Dick's poetry book on the table and took a quick draught of wine to calm my nerves.

"You know this marriage is only one of convenience. He gets a wife with royal blood and hopefully an heir; I get a household and security."

"Oh, Meg," said Bess. "I did not know it was quite as bad as that. Mother said you found Richard Dayrell…suitable."

"He is 'suitable'," I said. "I expected nothing more. Please…I do not wish to talk of it, for the vows have been made and I am lawfully wed. Ready me for what is to come."

In silence, both women began to unfasten the ties on the back of my heavy wedding gown. The fire crackled noisily, cheerfully; shadows swept around the room. Down below I could hear the wail of bagpipes and the hurdy-gurdy, the yells of roistering men, the thud of dancing feet.

"I think they are dancing on the trestle tables by the sound of it," Jane said with disapproval. "I hope Dick stays well away… Master Dayrell and his kin seem a rather rowdy lot. I heard a story once…" Her mouth shut with a sudden snap and she tugged harder on the bindings of my clothes.

"A story? What sort of story?" I asked, curious and a little apprehensive.

"A silly old wives' tale, nothing more. You know the sort. Murder and mayhem and revenge from beyond the grave."

"This does not sound like appropriate fare for a wedding night," said Bess, primly.

"Does it not?" My brows arched as my dress tumbled around my ankles, leaving me standing in my best shift. "Well…my curiosity is thoroughly piqued. Jane?"

Jane looked a little flustered after Bess's admonishment. "One of the patriarchs of the family, many centuries ago…he was called Wild Dayrell for his wicked ways. He terrorised the serfs who worked the land, stole from the church…and had his way with the serving girls…"

"This is *not* appropriate," Bess spluttered.

Jane hesitated. "No, go on," I said. Outside the wind was rising, sobbing in the eaves of the great old manor house, making timbers creak and roof tiles rattle.

Jane licked her lips, gaze darting around if she thought unseen listeners were in the chamber. "One of the girls became with child by Wild Dayrell, 'tis said. When her time came, an old midwife was summoned from the village to tend her and delivered a healthy boy. She expected the mother to be pleased but she sat and sobbed and would not look at the child. The midwife was perplexed but 'twas none of her business; she just wanted her pay and to go home. A man-servant summoned her into a side chamber and handed her a blindfold. 'What is this?' she cried. 'Put it on,' he ordered, 'or you'll get no coin from tonight's work.' Her heart was drumming in confusion now but she desperately needed her pay. Reluctantly she took the blindfold and the man-servant tied it tightly and guided her to a seat. Before long, she heard the door creak open and the rustle of a cloak. A bag of coins was pressed into her hand. Before she could open her mouth, the door shut again, leaving her inside. Tearing off the blindfold, she jumped up, frightened now, but too afraid to run out into the hall. She felt along the walls and finally came on a wooden panel with a hole bored through; she could see straight into the room next door. What she saw brought horror to her heart. The servant girl lay upon the bed, a scarf knotted around her throat. A dark-cloaked man was holding the babe in his hands; he threw back his hood, and it was Wild Dayrell. He looked at infant and then...and then...he hurled it into the fire."

"Oh, how horrid" Bess's nose crinkled in disgust. "That is a dreadful tale; not fitting for gentle ears. I don't want to hear any more."

"I have no fear of hearing the end," I said. "What was it, Jane?"

"The midwife heard footsteps, ran back to the antechamber and pulled the blindfold back over her eyes. She was escorted out of the house and sent home. After a few days, she got up the courage to tell the local bailiffs of what she'd witnessed, but they laughed her fears away. Yes, they'd heard the serving girl was dead, but according to them she'd died of childbed fever and the child died at birth. The midwife argued that this was untrue, but no one would investigate a man like Wild Dayrell. He got his comeuppance, though. One night he was riding in a great storm, hurrying back to the manor. On the road he saw a spectral light—green, burning witchfire. Amid the cold dead flames, a ghost child hovered, pointing accusingly at him. Screaming in terror, he drew his sword and drove his mount straight at the apparition…and slammed straight into the low-hanging branch of a mighty tree, shattering his skull until the brains burst out…"

Bess's face was a picture. Jane looked vaguely embarrassed. "It probably was *not* the right tale to tell…"

"I asked you to proceed," I said, "and so you did. Don't look ashamed, Jane; it is only a tale."

"And I am sure Sir Richard is nought like his murderous forebear," said Bess.

I hoped so.

"Speaking of whom…I think the wedding party is ascending the stairs!" Jane cocked her head to one side. "We had best get you ready!"

Hastily they pulled off my kirtle and bundled me into the bed, where they combed out my hair, letting it flow free. Outside the door, feet thudded in the corridor, a drum banged and a flute gave a reedy wail. Men sang drunkenly. Although the bedding ritual was customary, my first had taken place with more discretion—and much less bawdiness—in the Duke of Buckingham's castle. It seemed so long ago, even though it was only seven years…

The door inched open. In walked the local priest to give his blessing to the bed. He sprinkled holy water on the covers and drenched me with it while intoning,

"Lord, look favourably upon this thy handmaiden, who is to be joined with the bond of marriage. May the yoke of favour and peace be upon her: faithful and chaste may she be wed in Christ. May she endure among saintly women. May she be as loveable as Rachel to her husband; as wise as Rebecca; as long-lived and faithful as Sarah. May she remain in the bond of faith and the commandments, bound to one marriage bed. May she be weighty in modesty, outstanding in virtue. May she be rich in children, and prudent and innocent. May she also come to desired old age,

and see the sons of her sons all the way to the third and fourth generation...."

Cope swishing, he then backed away from the bed as the door opened again, this time flying back with a loud bang that made the priest wince. In stumbled Richard's tipsy crew, red-faced and sweating, the dwarf amongst them, his hose thankfully tied in place once more, a small drummer boy panting as he beat out a tattoo on a great, goat-skinned drum almost as big as he. The Dayrell men were clapping Richard on the shoulders and shouting crudities that made Jane and Bess blush.

"You had best go now," I said to them. "My thanks for your assistance this night."

Heads bowed, they sidled from the bedchamber as the drunkards ogled them as if they were tavern slatterns and not married women of good family. Then they began the task at hand—readying the groom for the marital bed. Off came his deep marron doublet; the cambric shirt was flung across the room. Then they rugged at his points, bellowing and jesting as each one came loose beneath their clumsy, drunken fingers.

I took a deep breath and stared at the ceiling, willing the noise to die away. The next moment air rushed over me as the cover was hauled back. Richard crawled in, sweating, the dark matt of hair on his chest glistening. "Sit up, my dear bride," he said. "We must drink the Consecration Cup."

I wriggled upright, holding the cover as high as I could. The men in the chamber lingered hopefully. Still pressing the cloth against my chest, I reached out with my other hand to take a silver goblet preferred by the oldest Dayrell brother, George. Richard and I toasted each other and then drank the sweet, dark wine. Richard finished in a trice and flung the cup towards the fireplace. "Enough, or the night may end only in sleep!" he laughed.

I finished the wine, feeling its heat up my belly. I had drunk earlier at the banquet and was glad of it. Handsome as Richard was...he was not Humphrey, the father of my children, in either appearance or temperament. It was wrong of me to feel rejection towards him, for most widows wed again if they did not seek the cloister, but this man was so different to Humphrey and not in a way I admired.

The men, the dwarf and the drummer boy filed out of the chamber and began setting up a noise again as they departed into the hall, where, no doubt, they would drink and carouse till dawn. I was alone with Richard. My husband. How strange that thought seemed. *Husband. To have and to hold...*

"Come, wife," He leaned across me, hot spicy breath blowing into my face. "Surely no maidenly blushes are needed from a woman who bore two sons in close succession. I will do even better—I'll give you five or six, I swear."

He pulled the cover away from me, revealing my nakedness. Although I had put on some weight at Tonbridge, I was still thinner than was considered comely, my breasts hanging like flaps against my ribs. I reminded myself of those ugly carved female exhibitionists sometimes found alongside the gargoyles on the rooflines of churches—scrawny and goggled-eyed, paps withered, with only their hidden places spread to show that they were female.

If Richard felt the same, he did not show it. His wet mouth found mine, his tongue seeking, probing, his hands exploring. I endured, denying him nothing as he caressed and kneaded and squeezed, then crushed me into the feather-filled mattress, in no wise gentle but somehow radiating triumph. Eventually, he collapsed upon me, spent, heavy, bruising, then hastily rolled away. "I plan to hunt early in the morn so must get some sleep," he muttered against the bolster. "I hope you do not snore, Meg."

I did not. But within minutes, he was making sounds like a rutting bull, his eyes screwed shut and his mouth gaping wide.

I turned over, facing the opposite direction, yanked the cover over my aching limbs and stared blindly into the night.

A restless sleep had claimed me when Richard rose before sun up, flung on his crumple, sweat-stained raiment and left the house. I woke only at the sound of clattering hoofs outside the windows and then the strident shriek of hunters' horns mingled with the yelps of the hounds.

I got up, dressing myself as best I could with stiff fingers. Elizabeth Calston, my new mother-in-law, had promised a waiting-woman from nearby Ramsbury but no one had yet appeared.

A beam of sunlight, piercing the grime on the inside of the windows' ancient glass, touched upon the book given to me by my half-brother. The rich red cover glowed like a jewel, the brightest thing in that gloomy chamber, the candles burnt to wax puddles and the brazier brimming with ash. I opened it with care, as Dick would have wished, and my eyes fell upon a stanza of his translated poem:

> *Pleasure is not the same for all,*
> *What is sweet to you, proves bitter to me,*
> *Never more shall you see me in thrall*
> *To love, nor to the will of any.*
> *No man can claim me as a lover*
> *Unless the heart admits the word;*
> *Force can tame the free will never,*
> *Nor rule, ere ever it be heard.*

Tears prickled at my eyes. I was in thrall, but not to a lover—to a man I did not care for, and who, by his actions cared little for me save for what I might bring.

I took a deep breath, readying myself to descend into the hall where sharp-eyed Mistress Calston was doubtless lurking like a spider about to pounce, along with sundry members of the Dayrell family, addle-pated after the wine consumption of the previous night.

I would not shame myself, would not show weakness before them. Whatever happened, now and in the future, I was a Duke's daughter and would behave with all the dignity I could muster.

In the weeks that followed, Richard hunted, returned, and then went off again to Ramsbury or Marlborough or Salisbury on business. The long days when he was gone were a relief, since I could find my way around the estate, learning the servants' names, poring over the account books, making lists of what food supplies we would need for the winter. Mistress Calston had finally sent me a maid for my personal needs, as promised; a young plump thing called Martha. She was not Anchoret, whose company I missed daily, but she would do.

In the evening, Richard would return, tired, unshaven and sweaty, expecting to be waited on like a king, delicacies and wine brought, his garments changed. He had several man-servants for that purpose but for some reason he insisted I do most of it, although it was not very dignified.

"Tend me with your own fair white hands," he had said, mockingly the first time. "Just as if you were Iseult in that old story. Iseult of the White Hands."

I doubted that Richard had ever read Tristan and Iseult; he could read, but owned few books and what few he possessed dealt with military or legal matters. "Iseult of the White Hands was Tristan's second wife," I had told him, as I poured his wine and removed his boots like a menial. "The one he did not love."

He'd made a grunting noise and smirked. Some mud from his boot had tumbled upon my hem, sullying it. *She killed him in the end, Richard...When she learned he would never love her.*

Later, when night swept in and the candelabras burnt low, he would take my arm and almost drag me to my bed-chamber, scarcely caring that the servants saw and started tittering because his intent was so obvious. He would pin me to the bed, almost suffocating me beneath his weight and hoist up my skirts. At least the act was always over quickly and he would leave for his own, finer chamber; he did not spend time indulging in lover's caresses. Every morning he asked if I thought I might be with child, as if I might have had an unearthly revelation in the night—perhaps as the Holy Virgin did.

What a dumb ox, I thought, full of contempt as I stared blankly at him and pretended sorrow that there was no child as yet. He knew far less about women than he imagined he did.

At month's end, Richard went to Marlborough for two days—a welcome relief. But when he returned it was with a party of officials; men I had not met. I heard their voices as they dismounted in the courtyard, flinging their reins to the stableboys. They seemed stirred by some event, feverish; each one's voice drowned by the others until it sounded like the Tower of Babel. Something must have happened, perhaps in Marlborough.

With Martha in tow, I ascended the stairs to the hall. Richard and his companions were inside, the servants rushing to and fro with wine pitchers, pastries, cold meat and cheese. I slid unobtrusively along the wall, listening to what the men were saying. Richard, his baritone voice booming like thunder, did not even notice me—or pretended not to.

"It is outrageous," said one man, a squat burgher wearing an outdated chaperone that had seen better days, "but hardly unexpected. He rode straight through the heart of the country flaunting his ancestor's arms. The arms of Lionel of Clarence."

My breath drew in. *York*. Richard of York had returned from Ireland.

"You are behind the times, Lawrence," said Richard. "It has progressed further than a mere ride displaying the royal arms. York just this week processed into London, riding in like a King. It was all theatrics, of course; he knew parliament was in session, and his attainder and other charges against him were being lifted. He burst straight into the proceedings and marched up to the dais…and…he put his hand on the throne as if to put forth his claim."

Several other men gawped. "I had no idea he'd been as blatant as that…!" said the one called Lawrence, ripping off his battered headgear and tossing it on the table.

"I'd have given coin to have been there to witness it," laughed Richard, "for the messenger to Marlborough castle said it did not go as the Duke desired. He stood there, expecting acclamation, and there was silence. Stony silence. Everyone stared at him in shock—even, 'tis said, his supporters and his sons! No one had thought he was going to do it!"

"He has ballocks, I give him that," said another man gruffly. "It takes a lot to stand against an anointed King. So…what happened then? Did they sanction him…arrest him?"

Another roar of laughter from my husband. "No. He went off and sequestered himself in the King's own apartments, would you believe? Refused to leave them. The best legal minds are working on some kind of a compromise. I have no idea what they'll come up with, though. Only time will tell."

My heart beat strongly in my ears. To have York back in England was dangerous, but perhaps his popularity was on the wane. I wished I knew what was happening with Hal, still overseas in Guisnes.

"Come, Martha." I gestured to the maid. "I think I have heard enough, and Sir Richard is too engrossed with his companions to bother with us. Let us go to the solar…do some embroidery."

We crept into the solar and worked on our stitchery in silence. Before long, however, Richard's long shadow stretched over the floor. I glanced up. "I spied you two little mice listening in on the conversations of men," he said.

Martha looked terrified as if she feared she would be punished or expelled. "I heard the sound of raised voices," I said. "I guessed something important had happened. I do not like to live in ignorance, Richard. The world and what happens in it affects me, and my sons far away, not only high and mighty lords, bishops and kings."

Surprisingly, he nodded and did not gainsay me. Then he grinned nastily and said, "I have never cared much who sat on the throne, as long as my own lands and positions were secure. But now I have married a Beaufort so I suppose my star is hitched to Lancaster. So, we'd both best hope York never gets the position he craves so much. If I were to lose my job as Justice of the Peace, and hence my bid to become Sheriff one day…I cannot say what I might feel pushed to do."

He shrugged and walked away, heels clicking on the floorboards, and I was left shaking. His words almost felt like a threat. If he felt his offices or status were threatened by our marriage, rather than enhanced, perhaps he would find a way to rid himself of me. Annulment would not work unless he forced me into lying that the marriage was never consummated. We had no relatives, near or distant, in common, so consanguinity could not be claimed. I thought of Jane Knyvet's dark story of Richard's supposed ancestor, Wild Dayrell, and wondered if he would rid himself of an unwanted wife as Wild Dayrell had disposed of his baseborn child...

I pushed such unsettling thoughts away...*He would not dare*, I told myself. *He would not dare.*

By the beginning of November, towns through England were abuzz with new tidings from Westminster. A compromise had been reached and the Act of Accord passed. York was made Protector of the Realm for the third time, but now he was far more than that. He was given the titles of Earl of Chester, Duke of Cornwall—and Prince of Wales. He had become King Henry's heir and his sons after him. The King's small son Edward was disinherited, his claim cast aside. Rumours flew thick and fast once more than Edward was not Henry's get—that my father Edmund was his true sire. A slur on an innocent child; a slur on my sire's memory.

At first, Richard was angry upon hearing the news. "Damn it, why does ill-luck seem to follow all that I do? Here I am, married to a Beaufort wife these past few months, and our next ruler loathes the Beauforts!"

"His wife is of Beaufort stock and so are his main supporters too," I argued. "His main quarrel was with my father, and now my brother."

Richard harrumphed. "He won't forget his old hatred; I certainly would not! He will never trust any of his bitterest enemy's brood, especially when your brother Hal has tried to attack him and his colleagues so many times!" He folded his arms, gloomy, grumpy. How had I once thought him handsome? He looked like a petulant child. "There may be one saving grace to this situation, though. The Queen."

"Queen Margaret? What can she do if parliament has made the decision in York's favour?"

"She's a mother. Would you not do nigh on anything for your Stafford sons? She will do the same for Edward. She will fight on for his right to the throne, you mark my words. York's appointment as heir is not the end of the troubles—it is only the beginning."

"What can the Queen do? A woman…"

"What can she do? It's what she is *doing*. She departed London as soon as the Act was passed. She hastened to Wales, to Jasper Tudor, who saw her onto a ship that sailed to Scotland. She's in the court of Mary of Gueldres, widow of King James…"

"King James himself was of Beaufort blood, and hence his young heir too."

He chucked me under the chin, which I hated. "Yes, so we know that we must attach ourselves to the Queen's cause. If she does not overcome York decisively…" he sighed, shrugging, "our life here may well be in ruins. I have no problems with kneeling to York, but with you as my wife, I fear his suspicious eye would ever lay upon the household. That would not be good, Margaret. Not for me…and not for you."

Shortly after the Act of Accord was passed, I wrote a letter to my youngest brother, John, inquiring as to whether he had heard from Hal, and sent it secretly from Ramsbury without Richard knowing. I assumed it would be useless to ask Mother for details; she would accuse me of being meddlesome and unfeminine, and my sisters were busy with their own households. Edmond was my other choice, but John, just nineteen, had always been the more talkative and amenable of my younger male kin.

It was with great surprise that John turned up at Littlecote on a sunless wintry day, the blue and white Beaufort banner, mounted with the symbol of the Beaufort Portcullis, crackling in the wind. Richard was on business at the Abbey of Bradenstoke near Swindon and had warned me he would not return for several days. That was even better, in my estimation; John and I could talk unhindered without any questioning or interference from my husband.

"John…John!" I ran to my brother, who flung himself from his saddle to embrace me. "I had no idea you would come yourself."

"In these times, a visit is the only way to avoid an important message going astray," he said. "Ah, Meg, it does my heart good to see you again."

I noted Richard's steward, Roger Cowper, scowling from shadows cast by the chimneys of the house. He was firmly his master's man and had never warmed to me, remaining coldly polite in all our interactions. I wondered if he thought John was a lover, here to cuckold Richard while he was away. I almost laughed out loud at the thought.

"John," I said, "You had best come to meet Steward Cowper. He looks fit to be tied. I believe he thinks we meet for a lover's tryst."

John made a face. "Ugh, what an unpleasant little man he must be…but I will do so. I want no harm to come to your reputation, sister."

Giving his steed's reins to one of his attendants, he joined me in walking over to the Steward. "You should have come to greet my guest as is your duty, Master Cowper," I said, smiling but without warmth.

"Sir Richard did not inform me that any guests were expected," he retorted, gruff, suspicious, his gaze darting between me and John.

"Does that mean one must behave in an uncharitable manner if anyone else should turn up at the gates? Master Cowper, this is my youngest brother, John Beaufort."

Roger Cowper went red then pale. "Sir…" Finding his manners, he made a quick bow.

"John will be staying with us for…for as long as he wishes," I told him. "He has six men with him, as you can see. Find food and lodgings for them and have the stableboys tend their horses. At once."

"Yes, Countess." Head lowered, he stomped off with all the grace of a charging bull.

I took John out into the manor's grounds rather than the gardens. I did not want the gardeners, busy with pruning and planting, trying to listen in. All around us rose scabious oak trees, leaves rustling in the breeze. A green sward filled with lumps and bumps, rabbit holes and molehills stretched out before our feet. I sometimes came here when I wanted privacy, a time to think my own private thoughts. Sometimes I would bring my missal and pray; I felt closer to Our Lord here, in this quiet section of land, than in the gloomy chapel inside the manor house. This place had other secrets too, from centuries past.

"One of the gamekeepers found a ring here once, in a rabbit's warren," I said to John. "It was gold and had as its bezel a great pale gemstone bearing the image of a heathen goddess. My husband wears it sometimes, but I told him not to do it often."

"Why"

"In case it is cursed, of course. It had Latin written inside, but so worn no one can read aught but a few words: *he who steals my ring…*"

"Who do you think owned it?" John glanced about as if he too might find treasure bursting from the ground.

I shook my head. "The gardeners often find heaps of broke tiles and fragments of coloured stone that may have formed a floor once. They refuse to dig further, though; they are afraid of ghosts that would rise up if there are bodies buried below. Richard did not push them; he merely asked that any finds worth money be turned over to him at once."

We sat in the shade of one of the oaks, side by side on John's thick woollen cloak. The air was cool, rushing through the boughs. Acorns rolled along the ground; I wondered if that betokened a hard winter.

"Meg, how is it with you out here?" John asked. "That Steward…I liked his manner not at all. He should show more deference to you. And you…your eyes are not happy."

"I have not been truly happy since Humphrey died," I said, "and in truth, all was not well even for the last few years of his life. His injuries changed him; made him embittered. But that is the past now. I am content to remain mistress of Littlecote. It can seem lonely here, though, at times."

"I am grieved to hear it."

"Your presence cheers me, at least...but the fact you are here brings disquiet too. It is a long way to ride for a mere chat."

"I bring both happy and unsettling news, Meg, which is why I have come in person. Which would you hear first?"

I began to shake; I clasped his hand tightly, fingers locking. "The worst. Tell me that it may be over."

"Edmond...he has been taken prisoner on the Isle of Wight by one of Warwick's retainers, Geoffrey Gate, and is in the dungeon of Carisbrooke Castle. Hal left Edmond as Captain in his absence, but Gate, who had been ousted from the very same position, lay in wait until he rode out of the castle and overwhelmed him, even though he had sixty stalwart men-at-arms in his company."

I blanched, shaken by these tidings. "How could this have happened?"

He shrugged. "He was taken unawares. He believed Geoffrey Gate had left the island and that he was safe."

"My heart feels sore," I said. "My heart would shatter if he came to an end, so young."

"He won't." John placed a firm hand on my arm. "The family is already making inquiries as to a ransom. He has done nothing wrong; even the Yorkists should surely spare him. Please don't weep, Meg...Don't you want to hear my happier tidings?"

"Yes, but I was not expecting..."

"Hal, I can tell you of Hal's adventures!" He tried to sound excited, to lift me from my gloom. "I have received several messages from him in the past months. He was residing in Guisnes, as you may already know, having failed to oust Warwick from Calais."

I nodded. "That was the last I heard of him."

"Well, he received a letter, sealed by King Henry, telling him to hand Guisnes over to Warwick. No doubt the order was written under coercion from either Richard Neville or his father Salisbury. With no other choice, Hal abandoned the garrison...."

"He's not captured, is he?" My hands started to tremble. "I could not bear it, not again. Both Hal and Edmond, and Father before that…"

"No, no, fear not, Meg. I told you that this part was *good* news! Under the cover of night, Hal galloped off into the wilds of France, accompanied by our half-brother, Thomas. And God be praised, King Charles of France offered them safe passage!"

"Safe passage!" I cried, relief flooding me. "I never thought I would heap praises upon a Frenchman, let alone the French king, but I fear in this instance I must! I am astounded, for King Charles was never a friend to the Beauforts before."

"It is like a miracle, is it not? Perhaps Charles fears the potential reign of York more than Henry's placid rule; and as the Queen is his kinswoman, he doubtless favours her cause. Whatever his reasons for such generosity, Hal and Thom were given rooms in Montvilliers, and have spent much time enjoying the pleasures of France! Hal even befriended the Count of Charolais, heir to Phillip of Burgundy, at a regal feast in Ardres. They got wildly drunk and became the best of friends."

"I am just glad Hal is safe," I said. "If only the Queen would make her move from Scotland…"

He held up his hand. "Who do you think is with her now, offering his sword to both Margaret and the little disinherited prince? Hal, newly returned from his sojourn in France."

"H-Hal is home?" I gasped. I prayed he would return eventually, but it seemed he had been happy abroad, and safe at Charles' court…

"He is home indeed. He has gathered a force of men and even as we speak is marching towards Hull. Our cousin Thomas Courtney rides with him. He has plenty of support, including Northumberland and Clifford. Now we must wait…to see how Richard Duke of York responds."

I was shaking again, fear and excitement commingled. Hal was home, but danger ran high again and violence threatened. "I could ask for no more. This is fair news indeed, John…except for Edmond, God keep him safe in his incarceration. Our Fates are in the hands of God and capricious Dame Fortuna. Now, would you walk through the gardens with me? I will show you my house."

Richard returned to find my brother ensconced in the hall, sitting before the fire with his long legs outstretched, drinking his wine. John greeted him cordially; Richard scowled like a snappish dog but spoke him fair nonetheless. I had come to realise my husband was mean, even miserly, with both hospitality and money, unless it was to impress family members and friends. I had no winter gowns and Martha spent days putting lining into what I had so that I would not feel the cold in the draughty rooms. "It can be chilly here," she had said, sewing a moth-eaten squirrel pelt into a collar. "They say there's always a cold wind blowing, up from the site of the buried ruins and through the trees."

I could well believe it. No matter how I tried to brighten the manor, for all its size and affectation, it remained a louring pile, dark and damp.

"So Master Beaufort, what brings you here?" Richard asked suspiciously.

"A friendly visit to my sister. I am sure that is permitted?" There was a challenge in John's eyes and stance. He sat up straight, the tip of his sheathed sword banging on the flagstones.

"Naturally." A slight curl to Richard's lip showed his displeasure "But had I known I could have arranged to be at home when you arrived."

"My mistake," said John. "I will remember next time."

Richard paced around in front of the fireplace, looking like a sullen bear. "Next time." His tone suggested he would rather there was no 'next time.' "How long do you propose to stay, Master John? It is merely…well, I am ill-prepared for uninvited guests, and your horses and men have partaken of my winter stores of food and drink"

"Richard!" Embarrassed, I flushed to the roots of my hair.

So did John. "I had no idea we were coming to an inn and you were the errant innkeeper!" he snapped, and reaching to the purse fastened to his belt, he took out a handful of coins and flung them on the floor amidst the rushes. "I hope that will suffice."

As Richard stared open-mouthed, John strode from the hall and out towards the stables. He had intended to leave later that day anyway, so luckily his small entourage was prepared to go. I chased after him, puffing.

"Forgive me if I have brought disharmony into your house," he said, as he swung up onto his bay destrier. "But I find your husband insufferable. I know not what he must have said to Mother to convince her that he'd make you an adequate husband."

"What's done is done," I said. "I told you—I am content enough. It is a woman's lot to make do. Please…do not tell Mother, or Hal, or any of the others what he is like. I will work on making my husband…less offensive. If…if I give him a son, he might well change his ways."

"I hope you are right, Meg," said John, gathering up his reins, "but some can never change, no matter what."

John rode out through the gate and down the long, treed avenue that led to Ramsbury and beyond. He did not glance back. I tearfully stared after him until he became a misty blur in the distance.

Shoulders slumped in defeat, I trudged back to the house. The path was wet, slimed with dead leaves; mud oozed over the tips of my unsuitable shoes. Entering the house, Richard was in the chair John had vacated, throwing back the contents of a mazer.

I paused, feeling a rebuke on my lips, but bit it back. I realised I was…had grown…afraid of him.

He flung the mazer down; the head of the ale whitened his stubbled upper lip like froth around the muzzle of a crazed dog. "Do not let anyone in here without my permission, Margaret," he said. "Do you hear me?"

I blinked at him, appalled.

"Hear me?" he shouted, leaping up.

I nodded quickly, head jerking like that of a marionette, and fled the room. How I loathed him sometimes, whether that was against God's laws about woman's obedience or not. As I huddled in my bedchamber, I took comfort only in one thing—*Hal was home.*

Winter trundled on. I tried to forget the possibilities of war and dwell instead on Christmas and its festivities. Richard was riding around the shire and then taking a break of several days to hunt with his brother George in Savernake Forest. While he was gone, I set to the duties of a good housewife—checking on supplies and ordering food for pantry and butlery, hiring a new girl to assist in the kitchen, replacing one who'd fallen pregnant, finding the cheapest good fabrics for the spinsters and weavers.

Richard returned shortly before Christmas Eve. The main bulk of winter food had been delivered from fleshers and cheesemakers, although untouchable till Advent was over. Fish would have to suffice. I desperately wanted to ask him if he had heard any news from the north, but he did not like me to ask questions. He liked to do the telling, when and if he saw fit.

Christmas and its Twelve Days came and went. Snow fell, the heaviest I had ever seen it. White dunes filled the countryside, fashioned into fantastic, glittering flutes by the lash of the wind. The sky hung brooding, a grey pall. Church bells and the harsh grackle of crows and rooks in the trees were the only sounds save the rush of the gale. Richard was miserable, glancing over his accounts. "Christ, you purchased too much food, Meg," he glowered. "You'll make a pauper of me at this rate. You are not living with a Duke's son anymore."

I tried to look chastened, but resentment showed in my stance. If I had kept the pantry empty, I would have been equally damned. My choices, I thought, were fairly frugal and sensible. He had not complained on feasting days of the roast goose or venison or the Great Pie filled with spices, fruit and game, nor had he declined the savoury cheese tarts or the plum pudding or pears in honey. Indeed, he and his brothers had wolfed the lot down with great gusto and drained most of the manor's wine stores.

"I will try to do better next time," I said, "but you must be clearer at how much you want spent—or not. I am not privy to the contents of your coffers."

He reddened then to the tips of his ears. I wondered if I had spoken too rashly. He slammed the ledger shut with a thud. "Do not worry about what's in my coffers. Worry about what is in your belly…or isn't."

I recoiled as if he had slapped me. So cruel…so unfair. Only a few months had passed since our wedding. I wanted to voice a retort but knew it would only further inflame the situation.

The uncomfortable silence that fell was broken by the whinnying of a horse. We both stared towards the window. I was closest, and pulling the draperies aside, peered out. A stocky man wrapped in a ragged black cloak was dismounting a weary-looking mare, its mane and tail heavy with clumped snow. The man's shoulders were frosty-white; his breath blasted out in a pale cloud as he talked to Steward Cowper.

"Someone has arrived." Unease crept through me. "It must be important if he has ridden out in such vile weather. His horse looks half-dead."

"I will go and see." Richard rose from his bench. "Have the servants bring some warmed wine for the newcomer."

While my husband hurried to the courtyard, I went with Martha to the kitchen and ordered spiced wine, bread and salted beef. With a servant in tow, carrying a platter and a mazer, I returned to the solar, just in time to see Richard enter with the rider.

The man crashed down onto a proffered bench, rubbing his cold-reddened face with gloved hands. He wheezed as the mazer of wine was handed to him, then downed its contents in one go. His hands were trembling.

"I have ridden through many shires, Sir Richard," he said, "visiting all the notable manors…"

"Yes, yes, get on with it," said Richard impatiently.

"I bring news from the north. A battle has taken place outside the walls of Sandal Castle near Wakefield."

"One of York's castles," I breathed.

"No longer," said the man. "The Protector is dead, killed in the fray. His head has been sent to decorate Micklegate in York by order of the Queen."

I felt my knees weaken, the room shivering around me. Martha clutched my arm, steadying me. *York was dead…my father was avenged!*

"Tell me more, man!" Richard huffed, his eyes bright with excitement. "This is news indeed!"

"How it happened is unclear. However, it seems the castle was running low on supplies, and a band of York's men went on a foraging mission in the nearby woods. While there, they were attacked by the forces of Henry, Duke of Somerset."

Hal! Hal was there, exacting his long-desired vengeance. And this time he had succeeded…

"When York realised his men were beleaguered, he donned his armour and rode out with the rest of his army to give them aid. As he did, Somerset and Northumberland attacked from the front, with the Duke of Exeter and Lord Ros coming in on either side, so there was nowhere to flee. Lord Clifford slipped behind the Duke, so no retreat to the castle was possible. York was trapped like a fish in a net. He had no chance of survival; he was dragged down by many men, suffering grievous wounds—and then his head was smitten from his shoulders."

"What of his fellows, Salisbury and Warwick?" I asked. "And his son, Edward of March. Are they dead too?"

"Salisbury was taken alive and delivered to Pontefract, but the townspeople there had no love of him and his high and mighty ways in the north. Despite offering to pay a great ransom, he was hauled from his prison and 'headed just like York. As for the Earl of Warwick and March, they had not reached Sandal in time to do battle; they were still in the south. One of York's lads did die, though—Edmund, Earl of Rutland. Clifford took him down on the bridge crossing the river into Wakefield town. It was not well done, for at the end of the day he was but an unblooded lad—only seventeen."

Edmund of Rutland dead. I shuddered, having pity for a life cut so short, even that of an enemy's son. I thought too of my brother, Edmond, who Geoffrey Gates had transported from Carisbrooke to the Tower. One Edmund dead, the other, well, still in a serious situation, but now a lot less likely to die. A capricious spin of Dame Fortuna's Wheel yet again.

Richard gave the messenger a few coins, seeming actually glad about it, which surprised me, knowing his meanness. Then he sent the man off to bed down in the stable. He was unusually bucolic, pouring himself drink after drink, despite his earlier avowals that the wine was almost gone.

"Are you not celebrating, Margaret? Your brother was victorious against York. Surely he will be rewarded by the King and Queen. The Beauforts shall rise in esteem through his actions, and with any luck, that luck shall run onto us!" He caught me in his arms, rough; his big hands nearly spanned my waist. 'I am glad now that I wed you, Meg," he breathed against my ear, his breath drenched in alcohol. "So, so glad."

Any gladness in our household soon disappeared. York was dead, but his son Edward was now seeking revenge, just as Hal had sought revenge. Warwick was firmly at his back, asserting even to the Pope that 'All would be well'…for the Yorkist cause.

At Mortimer's Cross, Three Suns had appeared in the sky, and Edward had crushed the forces of Jasper Tudor, capturing the aged Owen Tudor and executing him in Hereford market square. They say an old woman sat on the market cross, cradling his severed head while ringed by hundreds of burning tapers. I thought of Cousin Margaret and her son Henry, whose grandsire was Owen. She was close to Jasper, who had escaped—but where was the boy and what would become of him? She surely would be frantic. I prayed for her and for the safety of young Henry Tudor.

Meanwhile, the Queen had marched from Scotland, bolstered by Scottish mercenaries, and joined up with Hal, burning and pillaging as they hurried towards London. Warwick met them at St Alban's, scene of his earlier infamy…and this time he lost, but, slippery as ever, managed to escape. He had taken old King Henry with him for 'safety' rather than leaving him secure in the

Tower but had left him behind while making his escape. Hal found the King wandering outside his tent, under a tree, where he was singing to himself and trailing his robes through the mud.

However, despite reaching the outskirts of London and having the King in her possession once more, Margaret and her army could not proceed. The Londoners refused to open the gates, no matter what threats were uttered. They feared they would find themselves looted by the Queen's Scottish mercenaries. If only Hal had succeeded in convincing the King to hand his throne over to his son, Edward! A child maybe, but England had grown tired of Henry's weak rule. If he abdicated, the stern and war-like Margaret would surely make an excellent regent for Edward...

Instead, the Lancastrian forces retreated North, while the Yorkists, ever-popular in London, entered the city unimpeded and hastily proclaimed the usurper Edward as the new King before setting off in hot pursuit of their foes. The King, Queen and little Prince locked themselves up in the city of York, behind immensely stout walls.

Hal led his soldiers to a field near Tadcaster, blocking the route that led straight to the King and Queen. If Edward of March wanted to capture the royal family, he would have to force his way past my stalwart brother first...

Nigh crazed with worry about the possible outcome of this encounter, I stalked the corridor and grounds of Littlecote Manor, while the servants whispered behind their hands. Richard prowled about looking like a shambling bear—he had gained weight over the winter, his belt straining. Also ill at ease, his temper was as bad as a bear's too.

It was in Holy Week that the great, decisive clash took place, on a field called Towton, near Tadcaster. Within days of the battle, my brother John rode in, ignoring my husband's former inhospitable words. Richard made no complaint now that my brother had information he desperately wanted to hear.

"It was a disaster for our cause." John hung his head, almost in tears. "I came here because I could not let others bring you the bad news. The Lancastrian cause is crushed, Meg; Edward of York will be King."

I had sat down, for his pained white face had already told me what I needed to know. "And our brother?"

"Thank God Almighty." His voice choked in his throat. "He lives. So does Tom, but they are on the run with Exeter, a price on their heads as if they were common wolfsheads. He reached York before Edward had the chance and informed the Queen of the massacre at Towton, for such it was. They say hewn corpses are strewn for miles and that Cock Beck runs red with blood...Margaret took the King and Prince and had fled toward Scotland—pray Mary of Guise opens her hand in charity again..."

Haggard, Richard leaned forward. "What went wrong? How could this have happened?"

"The weather, the bloody weather," John groaned, "and the harsh northern landscape. It snowed, a blizzard that blew straight into the faces of our archers and made their arrows fall short of their marks. The line held, nonetheless, until the arrival of Edward of March's ally, the Duke of Norfolk, who ordered his infantry to attack Hal's flank. Norfolk pushed Hal's soldiers towards a ravine where the Cock Beck ran, breaking its banks from winter rains. They panicked then and the line broke. They ran for their lives and were mercilessly hewed down. Christ, Meg, it is rumoured that captured men were scalped and mutilated, their ears and noses cut..."

My stomach lurched at the thought and John pressed a hand to his own belly as if he might heave. "As for the lost—Northumberland is dead; also, Lord Clifford, Lord Dacre and Baron Welles..."

"Our cousin Margaret's stepfather," I murmured unhappily.

John nodded. "Yes, and our Cousin Thomas of Devon was taken alive—only to be executed a few days later, along with Nell's husband, the Earl of Wiltshire. Our poor sister is now a widow."

"Wiltshire?" Richard spat into the fireplace, making us both glare at him. "James Butler, the damned Irishman? Heard he was a coward so afraid of spoiling his pretty face in battle that he turned tail and ran at every opportunity."

"You are disrespectful, sir," chided John, "but...' he heaved a sigh, "I cannot say you are wrong in your assessment. Butler fled twice before in the face of enemy action, and he tried again at Towton, but this time, his luck ran out. He made it to Cockermouth, where he tried to take ship, but he was captured and summarily beheaded. My sister Nell made the wrong choice of husband." He cast Richard a hard look, as if telling him without words that he deemed him a poor choice for me, too.

Oblivious of the slight, Richard slurped down another goblet of wine. He had not shaved in many days and now not only did he behave like an angry bear, his resemblance to one grew by the day. "Well, things are what they are," he slurred after a few minutes. "I guess we must all say 'God Save King Edward'."

John and I both stared at him in silence. Richard shrugged, his lips red-jewelled from the wine. "I am if nought more, a practical man. God Save King Edward, Fourth of that Name."

CHAPTER TWELVE

In the early days of the Usurper's Reign, Richard cast himself into his work, eager to appear a diligent bailiff deserving of a higher promotion, a scion of his late father who had served as sub-Treasurer to the old King. He avoided me and there were fewer of his battering-ram advances in our loveless marriage bed, which I had come to dread. Getting a son suddenly appeared less important than making sure his official records were faultless if inspected by ministers of the new regime.

The thought crossed my mind, as it had before, that he might seek an annulment of our marriage, now that my family was once more in disgrace—Hal hiding in exile and Edmond still locked up in the Tower. I cared little for whatever brewed in Richard's hidden mind, for my own thoughts were solely on my sons. Would the new King gaze harshly upon them, as they were of a Lancastrian family? They were his own cousins, the Duchess Cecily and Duchess Anne being sisters, but as such, they were also risks to his throne, carrying royal blood even as he. I imagined at the very least he would want them where he could keep an eye on them, where he could gradually mould them into loyal Yorkists. The thought niggled at me night and day, disturbing my already troubled slumber.

In November of that year, King Edward convened parliament—and tore apart the lands and holdings of my family. Impassioned, he spoke of how he had brought 'redemption from the tyranny of his insatiable enemies' and accused all loyal followers of the former regime as extortioners, murderers, rapists and rioters. Hal, above all, was excoriated for his part in the demise of the Duke of York before the King placed him under Attainder. "Henry Beaufort acted against all humanity!" Edward had thundered. "He cruelly murdered my father with insatiable malice and violence!"

All the Beaufort estates were then assumed as Crown possessions and doled out like toys to Edward's faction, including his young brothers, George and Richard—mere children but now destined for great things, while my family faded into despised obscurity. Away in Scotland, Hal was not entirely passive in the face of adversity—he continued to lead border raids into Northumberland, while Exeter attacked Carlisle castle with such ferocity that Edward sent Warwick to raise the siege. Then Hal was sailing by night to France, sent to appeal to King Charles for aid on behalf of his kinswoman, Queen Margaret.

More disaster followed, however, dogging Hal's every step. King Charles died unexpectedly and his heir, Louis, deciding in a fit of perversity to favour the Yorkist cause, had Hal and the other ambassadors imprisoned, as they carried no official papers to guarantee their safe passage. Luckily Hal's friend, Charles, the Count of Charolais, came to my brother's rescue and saw him freed, taking him to his lavish house in Bruges, where he spent the winter.

By March Hal had returned to Scotland, and for a while I heard nothing of his whereabouts from any source. He might have been dead, for all I knew—but I forced such dire thoughts from my mind. I managed to convince Richard to let me leave Littlecote—perhaps he hoped I would not return—to visit Henry and Humphrey at Tonbridge. I spent a month there, with Anne's permission. Both boys had grown in height and strength, and ran about battering each other with wooden swords and riding around the bailey on their ponies. It was hard to believe Harry would be seven in October; his grandmother had given him his own hawk from the mews and he would strut about with the bird gripping his glove, looking very grown-up indeed. Too grown-up. Both children, unaware of the politics, chattered endlessly about how the new King was young and strong and killed all his enemies.

"Old Harry was mad; I heard a stableboy say so!" I overheard Harry telling his brother when they were visiting the kennels. "He was a lunatic!"

"What does that mean?" Humphrey asked.

"The moon turns him all funny in the head! The Man in the Moon puts him under a spell!"

Humphrey giggled. "What does he do?"

Harry chewed his lip, looking thoughtful. "Well…I think he acts silly, like a Fool. Dances around and waves his arms, while his eyes roll like this…" Harry careered around the kennels, milling his arms and making grotesque faces, while Humphrey crowed with childish laughter and all the dogs began to bark.

The urge was in me to tell Harry to hold his disrespectful tongue, that Henry was still the rightful King, no matter what had transpired—but I was not foolish enough to do so.

It was a new world, a Yorkist world, in which we lived—at least for now.

In the Autumn, Queen Margaret, with forty French ships, landed on the coast of Northumberland. She had managed at last to persuade her kinsman Louis to cease his brief Yorkist flirtation and fund her invasion. Hal had emerged from hiding and together they captured Alnwick Castle, the stern fortress of the Percys, and Bamburgh, a massive coastal stronghold crouched like a lion on white dunes overlooking a rushing grey sea. Immediately on hearing of this development, King Edward raised a vast army headed by the Earl of Warwick and his brother, John Montague—and for the first time ever, I felt resentment and anger toward Queen Margaret, who I had always seen as brave and forthright.

Hearing that Warwick was on his way, she left Hal in charge of Bamburgh and nearby Dunstanburgh, packed up King Henry like a simple child, and attempted to depart back to France. Unfortunately for her plans, a great storm descended, bringing wild winds and waves as tall as hills—and her ship was driven ashore on Lindisfarne, the Holy Island, only a few miles up the coast. She ended up resuming her flight in a humble fisherman's boat, seeking the safety of Scotland.

Hal was alone, defending the Queen's cause.

He stood fast for a long time but he could not hold out forever.

Warwick took the castle of Warkworth, said to be weak in wall and earthwork, and used it as a base for attack. Daily he rode to the castles of Bamburgh and Dunstanburgh to oversee their sieges, assailing walls with grappling hooks and stone-flinging engines, and striking the gates with an iron-headed ram.

By December, a rumour ran about that Hal and his captains, locked within Dunstanburgh, had no supplies left and had been reduced to eating their own horses to avoid starvation.

Capitulation to the Earl of Warwick was the only option left.

Negotiations began on Christmas Eve—and the greatest Christmas miracle that year, at least to the families of the Lancastrian soldiers, was that King Edward, recovering in Durham from an unexpected case of the *meazils*, decided to offer clemency to the defenders of the northern fortresses. A pardon or safe passage into exile for a peaceful surrender.

After all his years of burning hatred, Hal began to have a change of heart. He felt abandoned by the Queen and it rankled.

Humbly he laid down his sword before Warwick and swore that from then onward he would be faithful and true to King Edward. Oath accepted, he then journeyed beside the Earl to Alnwick Castle, still holding out for King Henry, and the embattled garrison, seeing him riding beneath the banner of the Bear and Ragged Staff, immediately opened the gates and laid down their arms.

When Richard found out that not only was Henry pardoned by Edward, the two bitter foes seemed to be forging a strange, unexpected friendship, he was thrilled. Crowing with delight, in fact. He no longer had to fear that he might find the King's eye fixed suspiciously on him because he had wed the daughter of Edmund Beaufort. He began to thaw a little towards me, and treated me with greater respect, returning to my bed more regularly, but with a less pugnacious manner. When Hal invited us to a joust King Edward was arranging in his honour, he jumped at the chance to attend, buying himself a fine velvet bonnet and a doublet inset with yellow silk, and giving me a new gown of cherry-red brocade with seed pearl on cuffs and bodice.

I was excited, embarrassingly so for a woman my age. Many of my kin were going and it was the first time I had attended such an occasion for years. "You look so much happier, milady," Martha said, brushing my hair out till it shone like pale brown silk. "You smile more these days and your cheeks are rosier. Master Richard picked out a fine dress for you, one that flatters your colouring; you'll fit right in with the other high and mighty ladies of the court."

I hugged her wordlessly for her kindness.

Dame Fortune had smiled on me, for once. Maybe the tide was turning, even if the House of York now held the throne. If our family could be reconciled to the new King, perhaps the Beaufort's Portcullis would rise again.

London.

It seemed so strange to set foot there again, without Humphrey at my side. Journeying by river, our barge moored at one of the many wharves along the banks of the Thames. The grim stronghold of the Tower was visible; I thought of poor Edmund, still inside but now certain of release unscathed.

Everywhere was bustle and noise; a Venetian ship bobbed in its bay, its crew unloading huge bales of damson velvet; next to it, a Prussian ship unloaded sacks of grain; a Spanish cog arrived bearing oils and iron. Further on along the river, one could just see the edge of the great, castle-like enclosure of the Steelyard, where the men of the Hanse worked on huge cranes that looked almost like fantastic monsters along the quay.

I noticed that Richard's eyes were round and his mouth hanging open, wide enough to catch flies. For all his worldly pretension, I suspected he had never set foot in London ere now. He was a little man in a big, oftimes dangerous world.

On the water-side, we were met by one of my brother's servants, the Beaufort Portcullis fierce on his tabard. He had a chariot waiting in which Richard and I would ride to one of the city's Inns—not, in truth, an inn at all, but a great mansion. Edward, showing his largesse to his former enemy, had granted Hal permission to stay there awhile.

"Not sure if I want to ride in that," grumbled Richard, nodding toward the carriage. "A chariot's for women and...invalids."

"The streets are busy here," I chided, "far more than any street or market in Marlborough or Salisbury—and they are dangerous streets for the...*inexperienced.* By the time we reached our destination, the footpads would have your dagger, your purse and maybe even the rings on your fingers, most likely without you even noticing."

He grumbled but the thought of losing any of his valuables vexed him sore and so he clambered into the chariot without further complaint.

Up Thames Street our little party proceeded, past fortress-like warehouses and merchant's towering abodes. A rush of humanity seethed in the street—dark-faced foreign sailors with flashing teeth and golden earrings, one carrying a monkey dressed as a lad; mercers and grocers pushing their wares in barrows or dragging them behind dray-horses; tall, haughty yellow-headed Germans from the Steelyard thrusting their way through the crowds, their eyes blue ice.

Reaching London Bridge, its central drawbridge raised to allow the passage of ships, we journeyed through the crush of carts to Crooked Lane, where the finest inns were situated, half-timbered and white-walled or stone-built with frontages massed in wooden carvings—saints, flowers, mermaids. We were taken to a house with mighty iron gates enclosing its courtyard where we disembarked, the gates clanging after us, locked against incursions of ruffians or the merely curious. We entered the house by a stone staircase and came into a long hall paved with polished marble. The mansion had large, modern, glass-filled windows, allowing extra daylight, and chandeliers suspended on iron chains gave off additional brightness that illuminated the fine vault of the ceiling, arrayed with angels and squinnying foliate heads. The walls were hung with a mixture of tapestries, one depicting the Annunciation, another the Roman Emperor Julius Caesar, yet another the great general Alexander on his steed Bucephalus, and, above the dais, a vast hunting scene in which both noblemen and ladies hunted down a slavering Boar.

Richard's gaze was now full of envy, and I could tell he felt slightly ashamed by his rumpled travelling doublet and the worn knees on his hose...

Footsteps sounded in the hallway and through the curtained door near the dais strode Hal. I had imagined him wind-battered and gaunt after his privations and misfortunes in the cold bleak north. However, if he had ever suffered, such suffering was not in evidence now. Hal was dressed like a prince in tawny velvet with white *diasper* lining the sleeves and gleaming at his throat. His belt gleamed with cabochons and he wore fine poulaines with gilded tips. Most striking, however, was his livery collar. Gone was the S-collar of the House of Lancaster, replaced by a heavy golden chain bearing King Edward's Sun in Splendour and wreaths of enamelled White Roses. In the centre hung a pendant of the Lion of March, its lips curled in a snarl, its eyes twin rubies.

"Meg, you have arrived at last." He swept towards me, catching me in a hard embrace. He smelled of rich and exotic spices—a courtier's scent rather than a soldier's.

"At times I thought I would never see you again," I said, a wave of emotion sweeping through me.

"And I thought the same of you...but all is come right now." He smiled. "John is here already, and Thom Ros, who has also been pardoned. Not Edmund, alas; these things take time but the King assures me he will have his release soon. Mother shall join us for the joust, along with Joan, Anne and Bess, but Nell, alas, is beside herself with grief and wishes to stay at home."

"I cannot believe it. It has been so long since our family has gathered together. I-I never thought that it would be Edward of March who joined us."

An unreadable expression crossed his face—then, quick as summer lightning, it vanished and his smile broadened. "I had not foreseen any reconciliation, as well you know, but..." He shrugged. "Perhaps I should have done less fighting for lost causes, and more careful *thinking*..."

He did not appear to wish to speak more on the matter but turned instead to Richard. "So, you are my sister's new husband. Richard Dayrell Speak up, man, I want to hear from you—stop standing there gaping like an over-awed man-servant."

I had to bite back my mirth as Richard continued to gawp at his brother-in-law, and Hal clapped him on the shoulder in brotherly fashion, almost sending him spinning to the floor.

The joust was held at Westminster. In the ladies' stand, seated beside my mother and sisters, I watched the jousters thundering down the tiltyard, dust flying from beneath the horses' hoofs, plumes on the knight's helms swaying, their lances shattering with hideous cracks against their opponent's armour. Men were unhorsed, tumbling through the air before landing in crumpled heaps, while the crowds screamed and women fanned their faces. Some jousters clambered up immediately, to roars of approval, even though they had lost; a few unfortunates were carried off senseless by their squires, their fate to be determined by the physics.

The King sat in his own stand, painted with suns and roses. He was immensely tall, seeming near enough a giant, and as rumoured, was of great beauty for a man, with a fine pale skin, straight nose and a surprisingly delicate, yet resolute mouth. His hair was long and a darker shade of brown, but when he leaned over to speak with the marshal or the victorious combatants, his hair had a copper-gold sheen, creating a halo around his head. He wore ermine and a fine bonnet with a jewelled cross of St George pinned to its brim. It was hard not to admire him, no matter that he was a usurper. I thought of sad old King Henry, unable to even recognise his own son, standing in dirty, stained robes and singing like a loon...I could no longer pretend he was fit to reign.

Beside King Edward, I recognised his mother, Cecily Neville, proud and serene, wearing a vast butterfly headdress and purple befitting a Queen—she now apparently called herself 'Queen by Right,' which had caused something of a stir amongst gossips. To my surprise, she must have felt my gaze upon her, for she looked in my direction with burgeoning recognition, remembering me from her imprisonment at Tonbridge. She nodded in my direction, acknowledging my presence, as I flushed in surprise and embarrassment.

My attention was drawn away by my husband. "Now comes the more exciting part!" he said, gleefully rubbing his hands.

The contestants had now dismounted and held battle axes. They would fight for supremacy afoot, and later repeat their battle with daggers. The clash of steel on steel and the grunts of the knights rose to my ears. Richard was rapt, leaning forward, agog, but I was rapidly losing interest.

My gaze wandered to Hal, who was sitting near the King in a place of honour. When Edward's eyes were not on him, his face bore that same unreadable expression I had briefly seen when we met. For someone newly accepted into grace by his monarch, after many years of enmity, he looked visibly disgruntled, his mouth curved downwards. Hal had a temper and sometimes his mood could be melancholy, and I saw both emotions in his visage.

The King leaned in Hal's direction, and my brother forced himself to assume a cheerful demeanour. "Henry, my friend," said Edward, reaching out to clap him on the shoulder. The King's voice rolled like thunder, even reaching us in our stand. "As this event was devised for our new amity as brothers, I should like to see you ride in the lists as we discussed."

Hal shifted uncomfortably. "Your Grace, I am satisfied as a watcher and not attired correctly to ride in the lists. Let others who wish to fight go forth."

"Nonsense!" said Edward. "Do not be shy, Somerset! I want to see you in harness. I trust you will not disappoint me."

Again, I saw Hal's face freeze, his eyes momentarily icy. His right hand curled as if he might strike. My heartbeat flip-flopped at the base of my throat. "*No, no!*" my mind screamed, fearful of what might ensue should his temper override common sense—but then the voice in my head switched to another, stronger, Beaufort voice, a voice redolent of my father, "On, Hal, *ON!*"

The moment was over. Hal's arm dropped to his side and he rose, bowing. "I would not disappoint you if you desire it so much, your Grace. I shall ready myself."

Hastily he removed himself to a pavilion on the edge of the enclosure. Before long, he emerged, clad in polished *whyte* armour that blazed like the sun. A horse was brought, caparisoned in the Beaufort colours, and Hal swung up into the saddle, still helmetless.

I squinted into the sun, frowning, wondering where his helm was. He could not fight without it.

A squire ran out, carrying an object in his arms. It was large but flopped as he ran, and it did not shimmer in the light.

It was a vast straw hat. Hal snatched it from the child and thrust it on his head. Its brim hid all his face save his mouth, which was drawn in a hard line. The crowds were laughing.

The King had planned some kind of jest by having Hal appear thus attired—and this was a worry, for Hal was a proud man and would never consent to such mummery. Perhaps he had not realised what he had consented to until it was too late to back out.

Sullenly, he rode out onto the tiltyard, scowling under the flapping hat. The mirth of the crowd grew even louder and catcalls rang out.

Hal faced the King's stand. "I cannot proceed, your Grace. I am a knight, not a mummer."

I expected the King to grow incensed at his bluntness but instead, he heaved a great sigh. "Ah, Henry…Hal, my friend, life is not always so dour and joyless. I pray you, this one day be merry—for me. For your merciful sovereign lord…"

Hal remained silent and Edward sighed again, shaking his leonine head. "Mayhap a small token of my affection may make you smile again, Hal." Taking a ring from his finger—gold, embedded with many stones—he called over a small, snub-nosed page and pressed it into the child's hand. "Take it to Duke Henry, I bid you."

Fleet-footed, the child ran from the King's stand out into the tiltyard, presenting the ring to Hal. He took it, staring at its glitter, then he held it aloft so that the crowd might see. Then he tucked it into a small pouch on his belt and began to ride.

The challenger came out to meet him—and he too was clad as a humorous figure, his helm also made of straw and his horse a swaybacked nag. There was much playing to the audience, and Hal, now appearing more relaxed, played along with the false knight and gently tipped him from his saddle onto the hard earth, where he pretended to be dead. A squire rushed up and splashed a bucket of water over him—the spectators were on their feet clapping as he returned to life. He bowed to Hal as the victor and departed the yard, leaving Hal to ride up to the King's stand.

Edward stood, hands planted on his hips, a towering and princely figure. "It is good, at last, to see you smile, Henry Beaufort," he said, and he snatched the ridiculous straw hat from my brother's tousled head and hurled it away into the watching throng.

King Edward held a banquet that night to complete the welcome of my brother into the inner circles of his court. Mother glittered in her taffeta and huge headdress, clearly trying to outdo Cecily Neville, whose garments were wreathed in cloth of gold and whose hennin was like a jewelled steeple.

"It is so wonderful that Hal's been pardoned," she chattered to me and my sisters, "and the attainder was lifted and his inheritance returned. The King, well, I hardly know what to say now, but he has shown generosity to me, too—an annuity of £222!"

"So…we are to be Yorkists now?" Joan looked dubious.

"Hush, Joan," Mother frowned. "We will never forget what had happened in the past, but it is time to move on. For our own sakes."

"But Edmund…he's still in the Tower!" my sister complained. "And were there not rumours, too, not so long ago, that you were suspected of aiding Hal and Tom in their 'treason' against King Edward?"

"I told you—hush!" A line deepened on Mother's forehead. "Edmund shall have his freedom soon enough, I have it on great authority…and His Grace is going to pardon me in due time."

"Oh, so it's 'His Grace' now," muttered Joan, still argumentative. "What about the other 'His Grace', King Henry, fled who knows where, our rightful…"

"Joan, I swear you have had too much to drink." Mother shook her head angrily. "I will see you escorted from the Hall ere you spoil it all for us. No one must hear the barest whisper of anything that might be deemed treacherous talk, do you understand?"

"Yes, Joan, you are indiscreet," said my other sister Bess, daubing her mouth with a linen kerchief. "The world has changed and our family has the chance to rise to prominence again—so do not ruin it for the rest of us…"

Joan, who as a girl always had a fiery temper like Father and Hal, looked positively thunderous.

I could not bear to listen to any more of the wrangling and excused myself from their presence. The musicians in the gallery had begun playing a lively air and dancers were gathering between the trestle tables. I paused for a moment, watching as they moved through rings of candlelight, beneath the shadows cast by the huge chandeliers. Rustle of taffeta, swing of brocade, slither of silk, in all the colours of the rainbow, the men peacock-bright to match the women.

Suddenly I felt a presence at my back—smelt the scent of sandalwood and musk. Breath touched the back of my neck. I surmised it was Hal…but as I turned my head with a smile, a gasp tore from my lips and my smile faded. It was King Edward himself, so tall and broad the lion pendant on his ornate collar was at my eye level. I glance up, shyly, carefully, averting a direct glance, for to meet the sovereign's eyes was forbidden unless given permission to do so.

Edward grinned, white teeth gleaming in his lightly tanned face. "You may look at me, madam. Would you join me in the dance?"

I dared not refuse. Indeed, in that heady, mad moment I did not know if I *wished* to say no. I nodded, and the King guided me onto the floor. Out of the corner of my eyes, I saw Mother and my sisters gawking, green with envy despite the past history of our family. The previous dance had finished and the musicians began playing a statelier tune, that of the Basse. It had been so long since I had last danced, I prayed that I still recalled the steps.

All around me swept the court, resplendent, dignified. Across from me was Edward, head and shoulders above the tallest, the warrior-king, the shining Sunne in Splendour. He was watching me keenly to the point I felt my cheeks begin to burn.

As the Basse dance wound down to its completion, he leaned across, coming closer to me, almost uncomfortably close. "You dance well, madam. You remind me of another lady I...*know*...A widow of a Lancastrian knight...The eyes..."

I froze, wondering if he mocked me, but he was shaking his head and staring over my shoulder into the far distance. It was as if he was wishing himself somewhere else, with someone else. A lover? Many said the young King took his pleasures amongst numerous women, but none had spoken of a special leman. But perhaps he had one secreted away...

"Can you name this lady? Maybe she is my kin if we resemble each other?"

He seemed startled that I had spoken, and I was startled at my own presumptuousness. Like Joan, I must have imbibed too much wine.

"No, I cannot...little Margaret Beaufort," he said, sounding bemused. "Mayhap one day, or maybe never. But thank you for your company this night. I might ask for more of it, if you were here alone, a widow...Were you not the Earl of Stafford's bride?"

My ears felt as if flames engulfed them. "Yes, I was. But I am here with my second husband, your Grace. Sir Richard Dayrell of Littlecote."

"A most fortunate man," said the King, his gaze still lingering on me, warm gold and green, and then he spun around and strode to the dais and his begemmed mother and sisters and his brother George, now grown into a coltish youth but still brimming with arrogance and devilment that hung around him like a miasma.

I glanced over to where Richard was seated, wondering what his reaction would be to my dance with King Edward. He must surely realise I could not refuse, but his temper often overrode common sense. Or, who knows?—perhaps he would feel pleased and flattered. As it turned out, he was nursing a capacious goblet and talking to his betters, who politely listened with bored expressions to his slurred rambling about events in the backwater of Wiltshire. He had not even noticed.

I had no wish to return to the women in my family with their pointless chatter and bickering. How estranged I had grown from them over the years. I felt like a changeling, fairy-touched, brought in to replace the true daughter of Edmund Beaufort.

As I walked away, out into the corridor, I heard the whisper of silk. "Meg! Cousin…"

A voice I had not heard for many years sounded in my ears. Turning sharply, I saw Cousin Margaret, her white face hovering in the shadows, her dark gaze intense and probing as ever. About twenty years old now, she was still small in stature, but no longer appeared frail and child-like. Indeed, she seemed far older than her age, almost ageless. Her air of confidence had increased to the point it radiated around her, clear in her stance and her expression.

"Margaret!" I cried, genuinely pleased, for I had often wondered about her and Henry Stafford. "I did not see you before now or I would have sought you out."

"Henry and I were delayed upon the road," said Margaret. "We arrived late…but come, come with me so that we might have some privacy. I do not much like being in the hall—with Edward of York's courtiers ever watchful. Some of them would like to pin treason on us all, I'd wager."

Halfway down the long corridor was a curtained window embrasure. Margaret stole behind the velvet drape, reaching out to take my sleeve and pull me in beside her before drawing the curtain over. There were two window seats, cushioned—beyond the cold, misted, window-glass the night was dark save for the torches of those moving about the palace grounds.

"No one will bother us here, I deem," she said. "These hiding places are usually sought out by secret lovers."

I sank into the cushions. "It seems such a long while, a world away. How do you fare with Henry?"

"I was right in my assessment. He is a good man. Even the new King saw that at once—and so he was pardoned, even though he fought against Edward at Towton. And you, Meg? How do you fare?"

"I am perhaps not so fortunate as you…but many have worse lives." I hung my head. "Richard might be happier if I bore him a son. He talks of it often."

"If it is not God's will, he must accept it will never be," said Margaret severely. "Henry has and is content. He sees my Henry almost as his own. If only he could come to us."

"Your son, Henry…Where…where is he now? I heard Jasper fled into exile. He did not take the boy?"

Margaret shook her head. "No, he thought it too dangerous and he was likely right. He knew not what reception he might get amongst strangers. My Henry was placed with William Herbert, to whom King Edward granted Jasper's title of Earl of Pembroke. He gave him wardship of Henry last year, and he now lives at Raglan Castle with Herbert and his wife. I am permitted to visit on occasion…"

"Thank God for that small mercy."

"The new Earl has children of an age with Henry, so that is a positive thing, although Henry now has no lands of his own—Edward gave them to that popinjay brother of his, George of Clarence." Her nostrils flared slightly; the first time she had shown strong emotion since we met. "Your sons are still with the dowager Duchess of Buckingham, my husband tells me."

"Yes. I saw them not long ago, but I wish they could abide with me at Littlecote."

"I am sure," said Margaret, eyes narrowed, "that the King will make them wards of some great lord soon, even as my son. They are too important to leave with their grandmother overlong. Selling wardships of royal-blooded wards can be *profitable*…."

"I-I cannot bear to think of that day. They might even be separated."

"Ah, you are still so tender, despite all that has befallen." She cocked her head on one side, a mixture of pity in her countenance and something I could not quite identify. Scorn?

"You look down on me for my weakness. I feel it." I was not so much accusatory as sad.

"No, you are wrong, Meg. But I am a practical woman. For my own sake, and more importantly my son's, I will play a game of necessity. I will smile at the new King, curtsey to him and to his family. No taint of treason shall lie upon me and mine. I will serve dutifully—until the time comes that God may reward me for my many sacrifices. I am convinced that day will one day come."

When Margaret and I parted upon our return to the Great Hall, I had the odd feeling of another separation, another loss. Our lives had diverged utterly. She still walked within the upper echelons of society and would continue to do so, courting Edward's favour no matter her true feelings, while I, wife of a mere knight, faded into obscurity, far away from the splendour and intrigue of court. The Wheel of Fate had turned again for Margaret Beaufort, my cousin.

Glancing towards the dais, I saw the King with Hal, arm draped companionably around my brother's shoulders. "It has been a good night, has it not, Hal? Ah, I am glad in my heart that we have become firm friends—I do love you well, despite the past! Tonight you shall sleep in my bed in the royal apartments, and tomorrow we shall go on a hunt in Greenwich Park. How say you, Hal?"

All around, the King's loyal courtiers strove to hide their shock. It was a great honour, heard of but little in this age, for a lord to share the royal bed with a loyal companion. It was even more extraordinary because the King and Hal had been enemies for so long, and their fathers before them.

Mother was sitting at the ladies' trestle table, mouth agape, watching as the King made to retire for the night, Hal walking sedately at his heels as he left the chamber. "How high my son has risen, how high!" she breathed, her eyes damp with emotion.

I kept my peace. Before Hal had left the room, I had spied that unreadable expression crossing his features once again, quickly masked by close-mouthed smiles and courteous nods of his head. A look that did not savour of joy but something else…distaste?

CHAPTER THIRTEEN

Back at Littlecote, life went on much as before. Word reached us that Queen Margaret had sailed from Scotland, taking her precious son to her father, Rene, in France. My half-brother Thom Ros went with her, having fallen out with Hal over his defection to the Yorkist cause. Jasper Tudor was with her, and the hot-headed Duke of Exeter, and a wily cleric called John Morton. The only one left behind was King Henry—it had become obvious he could rally no men, so he was now almost discarded. The hopes of the Queen's party now lay on little Prince Edward.

England was not altogether peaceful, despite the new youthful Warrior King. Strangely, though, their ire was not directed towards Edward, but at my brother Hal. In Northampton, as Edward progressed north to win the love of the people, the locals hurled rocks and dung at Hal and attempted to drag him from his horse to his death. Edward managed to protect him from harm—by giving the ravening mob a tun of wine. They hastened away, preferring the spilling of drink to the spilling of blood.

"I suppose they did not like a turncoat," said Richard slyly, always full of belittling digs. "Is he still travelling with His Grace?"

Miserably I shook my head, the letter sent me by my brother John trembling in my hands. "No, John says the King sent him to Chirk Castle for his own protection."

"Wales? Lucky him?" crowed Richard.

My shoulders slumped. "Worse...Chirk was his own castle once. Edward granted it to his youngest brother, who is just a little boy. I know Hal...he will be furious. No matter what else he may think of Edward, he will feel the King is rubbing his face in his misfortune."

Richard scratched his nose and dug into the stuffed quail on his platter with his knife. "Hope he doesn't fall out of favour. It's been rather nice saying I'm wed to a Duke's sister...the Duke who oftimes shares a pillow with Edward. Hmm...but it's easy come, easy depart, I guess."

Easy come, easy go indeed. I felt that to be true of my husband's limited affections. I prayed in the chapel every night that even if Hal and Edward's friendship cooled, Richard would never return to his rough treatment of me in the earliest part of our marriage.

I prayed for a miracle.

And one happened. I realised, with both joy and trepidation, that I was with child again. One of our rare couplings had borne fruit.

Richard, at last, would have his heir.

He was ecstatic, and although I could never truly love him, I was gladdened to see his face light up. He opened those tightly bound coffers of his, paying for a carved oak cradle and a christening robe of silk. He even purchased some dried fruit for me and made sure I had a dispensation to eat meat when I wished and did not have to fast on Ember Days during Advent.

Christmas that year was a merry one—as Christmases seldom were at Littlecote. Even my mother-in-law, Elizabeth, managed to crack a smile and admit how she looked forward to the birth of her grandchild. "My *royal*-blooded grandson," she sighed. "Do you think I could ever be invited to court, Margaret?"

I doubted it but humoured her to keep her temper sweet. All around me, the joys of Christmas unfurled, somehow sweeter and more poignant than they had seemed for years—the scent of the red-berry holly, cut down from Ramsbury's woodlands, the crowns of mistletoe, the wreaths of evergreen ivy with their vaguely acrid scent. Happily, I lit the beautiful rose candle on *Gaudete* and then the white candle on Christmas Day.

We supped on partridges, herrings and a fat goose slathered in mustard sauce, and later devoured such fancies as *chewette* tarts and gingerbread and some sugared sticks called 'pennets' The latter had been Elizabeth's treat. "They can be medicinal," she told me, "and might ease the sickness that comes when a woman's growing a child. They certainly help *my* indigestion!" She let out a rather indiscreet belch, half-muffled by her napkin.

Around Twelfth Night, the weather began to grow bitterly cold and snowy. Clouds of white flakes tumbled from the sky, making lacy patterns on the windows, coating the bushes in pale cloaks, hiding the dips and bumps where the old lost ruins lay hidden. The world seemed strangely muted and distant, the noises of normal life muffled save for the distant bells of Ramsbury church. If there was a time that I came close to knowing happiness at Littlecote, it was then—Martha embroidering next to me, Richard silent at his ledger with no hint of temper in him, and the first signs of my rounding belly straining against my gown. Soon I would have to have Martha let it out for comfort.

And then, as in the past, I heard the unwelcome sound of hooves on icy courtyard stones and the raised voices of men, and the sweet peace was broken. Turmoil filled me, as Richard, cursing under his breath, flung on a cloak and thumped out to the courtyard.

As I waited, laying aside my own embroidery, the threads hanging, a sense of doom washed over me. This last little while had been too good to be true…

Richard returned to the solar a few minutes later, snowflakes melting on his hair. "Come!" He grasped my arm and propelled me from the room, leaving a gaping and worried Martha behind.

"Stop…stop…You are hurting me," I cried. "Think of the babe!" He dropped his tight hold then, but his look never changed. He thrust out an arm, gesturing me into his private closet, darkly panelled and dim, lit only by a few glowing embers in the iron brazier, smelling faintly of stale beer, old paper and woodsmoke.

"It's your brother…"

"Which one?"

"Who do you think—the so-called 'Duke.' He has only gone and defected back to the Lancastrian cause again. The King is furious; he's renewed his attainder and given all his lands to Richard of Gloucester."

"I must sit." My head began to spin.

He kicked a stool towards me. "Sit, then."

"Where is Hal now?" I asked.

"In the Godforsaken north, hiding in the keep of Bamburgh Castle. He has convinced Ralph Grey and Ralph Percy, who the King was good enough to keep as constables of their respective castles, to rebel." He reached up, grasping his own hair as if to tear it out in frustrated anger. "How will this affect us?"

"Probably not at all," I said boldly. "We cannot control the actions of others, only our own."

He strode across the room, hitting his fists against the panels. *Boom, boom, BOOM*! I jumped at every loud thud. Such loud noises always terrified me, reminding me of my past, that awful day in Rouen as a child when the cannonball landed near me. I began to sweat.

"I...we were rising in the world," Richard raged. "At the joust, the great lords treated me as an equal."

I stared at my hands, shaking. *No, you were never an equal, Richard...*

"Now, they will shun me...married to the sister of a traitor. A traitor who made a fool of the King, which is even worse than most acts of treachery. Edward will never forgive this outrage."

Sickness gripped my belly. For all his foolish ranting words, Richard was right in one regard. Edward would not forgive Hal a second time.

This time he would hunt him down...till one of them was dead.

"Go to your bedchamber!" Richard ordered, as if I were an errant child, pointing at the door. "I do not want to look at you. You remind me too much of him..."

In a daze, I went and sat stiffly by the window. The direction of the gale had changed and now the blowing snow made a mocking hiss as it struck the panes. Gusts of wind chuckled in the eaves like malevolent laughter.

My heart fell dead inside.

As winter receded, the days became lighter and milder, but my burden increased both in mind and body. Battles raged in the north—King Edward had sent John Montagu, Warwick's brother, to hunt down Hal, who had started taking other castles such as Norham and Skipton. At Hedgeley Moor, the two opposing sides engaged—and Hal's soldiers broke ranks and fled before the charge of Montagu's vanguard. Hal again slipped his would-be captor, though. And vanished into the wilds.

May danced in, the trees heavy with blossoms, the sickly scent of hawthorn hanging in the air. My heart also hung heavy, and my belly; the babe stirred fitfully, its flutters and kicks keeping me awake at night. But at least, its movements filled me with hope, the promise of the future.

Where was my brother...and what future would he ever have now?

I prayed that perhaps Hal had left England, faring to his friend, Charles of Burgundy, but I knew such self-imposed exile was unlikely. He had set his course for good or ill and would not step aside. Hal was hiding in the harsh lands of the north, waiting for the chance to make a brutal and decisive strike against Edward.

By the end of the month, the weather worsened, as if spring turned its face back towards winter. Gales blew the blossom, ripped branches from trees, sent roof tiles spinning. The house creaked and groaned, its walls shuddering. I felt almost as if it breathed—laboriously, dying breaths.

I waited.

The winds escalated. They boomed, smashing into the house's framework. I tried to block my ears. The noise brought back that awful old recollection—the blast of cannons in Rouen, the cannonball crashing on the ground before me, earth and grit flying, followed by the smell of smoke and fire, Mother's hysterical shrieks, Hal darting forward to reach me...

Where was he?

Soldier, warrior...*traitor to his King*. I saw skeletons dancing in my head, the painting of the Three Living and the Three Dead that was in one of my prayerbooks. So it came to pass for all, and death did not stop for even the young, hence the picture of young bravos crying out and covering their faces at the sight of imminent death...

Oh Hal, Hal...think better of your actions and go! You cannot win. Edward is unbeatable. You cannot win...

A magpie came tapping at my window. Tap...tap...tap...Its beak darted around the glass as if demanding entry. Weak sunlight shone on its glossy feathers, a black so rich it almost looked blue, mingled with streaks of milky white.

One for sorrow...

"Shoo, shoo!" Martha flew towards the window, waving her arms. "Get away, you dirty creature."

Magpies were ill-luck, birds that hovered, along with the ever-hungry rooks and crows, around the battlefields and the gallows, seeking to pluck out dead eyes like soft plums and rip out hair to make their nests.

I watched as the magpie soared away to land in a nearby tree where it made much angry chatter, sounding almost human.

"My brother Hal is dead," I said, to the air, to the babe in the womb, to myself.

Martha paled and crossed herself.

When dusk fell that eve, filling the air with grey-blue haze, Richard rode in from a journey to Hungerford. His eyes glittered and his colour was high, almost purplish. Right away, I knew something had occurred.

Dismissing Martha, I sought him in the solar. "Well?" No more would come from my lips.

"Hexham," Richard murmured. "A courier heading to London spread the news throughout Hungerford. A battle took place at Hexham. Montagu and Ralph Greystoke. They cut the Lancastrian force to pieces. Your brother...was taken prisoner."

"Prisoner..."

"Briefly. He was tried before Montagu...and found guilty. They dragged in a block of wood and beheaded him in the town square of Hexham. He was accorded a decent burial, though, considering he was a traitor. The King did not demand his head for London Bridge, allowing him respectable interment in Hexham Abbey..."

Inside me, the babe kicked as if it realised its kinsman was dead. *Life...Death...*

"I have more evil tidings too." He drew closer, eyes pouched and heavy, the smell of drink and sweat and horse rancid in the air. "Your half-brother, Thomas Ros—he was 'headed two days later in Newcastle."

"Oh, no...not Thomas too." The world tilted.

He nodded grimly. "Baron Hungerford died with him...Christ, I knew old Hungerford well. Sir William Tailboys too, almost thirty others. Your family dragged them all to ruin. Ruin!" He suddenly screamed, spittle blasting into my face. "You'll ruin me too, goddamn it. If it wasn't for the child, I'd have you put away...There's a curse on your family, I swear it—a curse!"

I looked into his red, angry face, thinking how ridiculous that he howled at me as if he had borne a great loss when it was my brother who had died. I began to laugh, great, wheezing gales of humourless mirth. I folded my arms over my big belly, laughing and sobbing together, as tears streamed unfettered down my cheeks.

"Have you gone mad?" Richard leapt back from me as if he thought I had shape-shifting into a witch and would blight him with my malice.

"Go to Hell, Richard!" I cried, and I whirled about and rushed for the door, flinging it wide with a crash that alerted all the servants.

I raced out of the house into the dusk, zigzagging between the shrubs and flowering bushes in the dark. A hard, cold Man in the Moon grinned down at me, visage a bleached and pitted skull. Black iron rails on the gates rose like spears, peaks winking in the starshine. The fishpond rippled, stars milling on its surface, fronds waving on the edge.

I fell to my knees beside it, tearing off my modest headdress and shaking my hair loose. It trailed in the water like slime. I saw the reflection of my own face, white, luminous, ugly—distorted by the ripples on the water.

Hal was dead, Thomas was dead, Father was dead...and of course my husband Humphrey, ruined by battle, felled by illness.

They were all gone.

I wanted to be gone too. Trembling, I placed one hand into the water—cold, slimy. Should I throw myself in, force myself to take great gulps until I sank to the bottom of the pond like a dead fish? I thought of my boys and wavered, but then, they rarely saw me, hardly saw me as a mother. They would forget; they were halfway to forgetting now. As for the babe in my womb—it had never taken the breath of life. If my family *was* cursed, the babe was doomed no matter what …

I leaned a little further forward, both arms sliding beneath the surface. The mud and muck and leaf mulch on the bottom sucked on my fingers, my wrists, drawing me down, down to death…to everlasting peace.

But no, there would be no peace if I committed an act abhorrent to both God and man! I yanked my arms free and fell backwards onto the lawn, gasping and shuddering. Self-murder was an unforgivable sin—I remembered well the whispers, the scorn, after Cousin Margaret's father, my Uncle John, had been suspected of taking his own life. Gossips had condemned him roundly, without pity, called him weak and sinful; they had raved of hellfire and the torments of demons for eternity. They had said it was folly for Margaret to inherit his legacy, as his taint lay upon her. I could not doom my own children to taunts and cruel smears…

Dragging myself to my feet, I glanced around in the blackness. Distantly, I heard Richard yelling my name. Torches flared as servants ran out of the house doors, searching for me.

I did not want them to find me. Especially Richard. I began to breathe heavily, my eyes adjusting to the dimness of the garden. Stealthily I began to feel my way along a row of bushes, towering over me like black sentinels. Thankfully, my gown was midnight-blue which helped to conceal my presence.

I slunk from the garden, following the line of shrubbery and then along the retaining wall. I passed through the archway that led into the manor's capacious grounds and began to run as best I could. My stumbling feet bore me towards the site of the old buried ruin, the Roman place. The moon seemed to guide me, casting a long white path across the dew-drenched grass. Trees lifted, swaying, their limbs moving like clawed arms…

And suddenly, there were arms and faces and foxes with sinister green eyes, and my brother's head upon a pike, his own eyes flat discs reflecting moonglow. I pressed a hand against my brow, my body flaring hot and cold, and I knew I had either fallen under some malign spell…or I had gone mad. Madness or a fevered brain had been implied before; the fears and fancies of my youth, my debilitating *megrims*, my bedridden, fevered state after the death of Humphrey. *The Weird Widow of Thornbury…*

Now I had lost everything and everyone. Why should I continue to live in a hard, uncaring world? I would not drown myself nor cause myself harm…but if the chill and the night were to take me, so be it!

I flung up my arms, embracing the shadows. Mist had begun to curl from the ground, twisting into vast wraith-like figures with yawing mouths that dripped green darkness. Their chill touch affrighted me and I began to run again, but my foot slipped into a rabbit hole, and with a cry, I pitched forward. I managed to break my fall at the last moment, my wrist cracking beneath me as I sought to protect my belly.

I rolled onto my back, head spinning, arm throbbing, the world rotating about me, the lumps of earth that shallowly covered the old Roman ruin pressing against my back through the fabric of my dress. And then amidst the coiling mists, I saw them—wandering across vanished floors, between painted columns, striding towards my fallen form. Beneath my body stretched a vast image—Orpheus, the pagan God of the Underworld, in a sun circle surrounded by goddesses and sacred beasts: goats, bulls, panthers, hinds.

A man in a crested helmet stained with verdigris gazed down at me; he had no face, just shifting shadow where a face should be. Beside him stood a woman in a white robe, her hair piled high, exquisite earrings dangling; She wore a theatrical mask that changed from smiling face to weeping.

"Who are you?" I cried out, attempting to squirm away from these grave-wights, these revenants.

The man bent over me, cold white hand reaching out, and I saw a ring on his finger. The same ring that had burst out of a molehill and which Richard sometimes wore…

I let out a high-pitched scream, and suddenly light struck my face, blinding torchlight. I screwed my eyes closed against the dazzling brightness, and when I dared open them again, I saw a circle of torches and the familiar faces of the household servants. Richard was leaning over me, hand gripping my shoulder—and on his small finger gleamed the Roman ring, the stone in its bezel a dollop of blood. The spectres from the past had vanished and I was shivering uncontrollably. And wet. I feared I might have shamefully loosed my bladder, but the wetness was rain—the moon had hidden its face in an incoming bank of clouds and a heavy drizzle fell, soaking me, Richard and our staff.

"We must get her inside—at once!" Richard bawled. His rage had abated and I could hear true fear in his voice—not for me, but for the child inside my womb.

I felt myself lifted; a cloak was thrown over my inert form. Then I was inside the house and carried to my bed. I uttered no word; at the bedside, Martha was snivelling and tearful.

"Be silent, girl!" Richard scowled at Martha, before leaning over me. I stared past him, at the fraying canopy above, willing myself not to focus on his face. He waved a hand in front of my eyes; I remained as still as a corpse.

He stormed away, shouting to his manservant, "Go to the village; get a midwife so that she can be examined. Get someone else to ride to Marlborough and summon the castle physic. Tell him it's for the bailiff's wife; they know me there…he'll come. And…and send someone else to ride to my mother's manor and tell her to hasten to Littlecote as fast as she may!"

The physic stood to my right, a crow in his ebon robes. His beard hung to his waist, a tangled bird's nest that looked most unwholesome. On the other side of the bed stood Marjorie, the Ramsbury midwife, hands on her hips.

They two were arguing.

"It is known," said the doctor, stroking that matted beard with a bony yellow hand, "that a shock, such as hurling the afflicted into cold water, can restore the wits."

"You cannot hurl the Countess into a river like some evil witch!" countered Marjorie. "She is with child. She is fragile. It would likely kill her and the babe."

The beard tugging went on. "Yes...I can see your point, mistress. Perhaps we should bleed her..."

Another noisy harumph from Marjorie. "She'll be losing enough blood when she gives birth as it is. No, no, no...this won't do. Do not even think it, Master Doctor. You'll have to get past me before you get your knife near her veins!"

The doctor took a step back as if he feared short, stout Marjorie might attack. "She clearly showed mania, so that means yellow bile or choler, but from what I hear, she also suffers melancholia, which is *black* bile... I must conceive of a way to balance her humours, but there are few methods suitable for her present condition..."

"Leave her be. You doctors seem to have no knowledge of women anyway." Elizabeth Calston's crisp, sharp voice sounded from the doorway. Elizabeth strode briskly into the chamber and stared down at me. "Margaret...Margaret...Can you hear me?"

I nodded dumbly.

"Will you speak to me?"

I did not wish to do so and shook my head with vehemence.

"Have you eaten?"

Martha, standing in the corner, crept forward like a plump grey mouse. "I've spooned some soup into milady's mouth...but not enough, really, Mistress Calston."

The doctor cleared his throat, phlegm crackling. Elizabeth shot him a vexed stare. "I would suggest," he said, "that the recent death of her brother overwhelmed her mind. When she ran out into the moonlight, she then turned into..."

"A lunatic," said Elizabeth. "You are telling me my daughter-in-law has become an imbecile."

"I cannot say with absolute certainty, but...perhaps."

"Do you think it is possible she can recover?" asked Elizabeth.

"She may; such is known. Remember how the old King was? Sometimes he knew himself not at all, and at other times he was almost like any other man?"

"Almost," sneered Elizabeth.

Another scuffling from the door. Richard appeared behind his mother. "I heard what you said, Doctor. Mania, leaving her an imbecile. I cannot have it—my future role as Sheriff or in local government will be jeopardised. Men will laugh at me." Fists clenched, he rounded on his mother. "You were the one who persuaded me to wed her. Good for the family, you said. Proven fertile. An Earl's widow. Royal blood in our line forever more. And now...now...she is moon-mazed, and Christ only knows what will happen to her child! *My* child!"

"Oh, stop your bellowing!" Elizabeth's finger shot up into his face, warning. "It solves nothing. I will take her to my house at Paulton and care for her there, far away from Littlecote...and away from you."

"Mother!" He looked horrified as well as angry.

"It is the most sensible thing to do, Richard. Whilst the girl has turned out not to be quite what I thought, she is still your lawful wife and her child, by you, still carries royal blood. I will try to put things right. You will have to pay me, mind. I cannot feed and care for an extra mouth all by myself. Do you agree?"

Gloomily, he folded his arms. "Yes. I agree."

"Then have a chariot readied for Margaret. At once."

The Dayrell manor at Paulton in Hampshire was smaller than Littlecote but Elizabeth Calston ran a tighter, more efficient household, demanding the highest standard of work from her household staff. The kitchen floor gleamed, the rushes were always fresh, herbs hung in bags everywhere to sweeten the air. The privies were always sluiced down, and no room lacked for light despite the expense of candles.

I was given a small chamber in the rear of the house overlooking the garden and walled orchard. Pear and apple trees stood outside in neat lines and the scent of rosemary and lavender drifted in when the shutters were open.

"You will stay in here to convalesce," said Elizabeth, pointing to the bed, a close stool, and a *prie dieu* set before a carving of the virgin in Nottingham alabaster, pale and glowing with the radiance of a full moon. "You are not to go out without my leave. Is that understood?"

I nodded. I had not spoken to her since Richard had sent me here. There was no impediment in my speech, but I had not wanted to talk. What could I say? I was too tired to talk…I wanted nothing more than to seek slumber, where for a short while, I could escape the reality of Hal's death.

After about a week, Elizabeth bought in an old woman from the village. She was not only a midwife but a herbalist and village healer. She tended my wrist first; it was broken but not badly so did not need to be set, merely swathed in bandages while it knitted. Then she poked and prodded, nodding and mumbling as she examined me. She asked when the baby was due according to my accounting. "Late July, I think," I told her.

"Oh, so you *can* still talk," said Elizabeth, who insisted on staying in my chamber with the midwife. "I thought you'd been struck dumb."

"I have nothing to say to you or Richard," I said simply.

"You are insolent…as well as hare-brained," she snapped. "You are lucky I am such a kind-hearted soul, looking after you here and keeping your reputation intact as much as I can. Hopefully, the folk of Ramsbury and Hungerford will have moved on from tales about 'Mad Meg' by the time you return to Littlecote."

She sidled over to the midwife. "Is she healthy, Alma?"

"She seems so, Dame Calston. A little thin…."

"I suppose I must feed her up then."

Alma nodded. "No water—but the best wine you have. If she has cravings for strange things—give her beans cooked with sugar to calm the desire. Poultry is recommended rather than beef, which digests not so well, along with kid, partridge and soft-boiled eggs. Fried fish on Saint's days and Fridays will also suffice. Quinces, pears, sour apples, roasted chestnuts and hazelnuts can be given as treats."

Elizabeth sighed. "I shall have to write up tallies. Richard must pay me back for providing so much. Is there anything else she might take…to cool her heated humours?"

Alma chewed her lip. "Taking medicines is not a good idea when carrying," she said, "but some camomile and mint might help. Baths, too, in cool water. I trust you have a tub? Cool water, not freezing, which might do damage, but most definitely not hot."

Another pained sigh from Elizabeth. "Very well. I will have a tub brought as soon as possible."

"I would have thought you would have supplied one already. I am sure you won't want me to smell up your fine room with my tainted Beaufort presence."

Alma pretended to cough into her sleeve, hiding a smirk. Elizabeth gave me a daggered glare and stalked from the bedchamber.

Months stretched on, dull and dreadful in turns. At one time Elizabeth spoke of 'treating me' by cutting my hair and rubbing cold oil on my scalp. I knew she would not dare do it without my permission or Richard's; she just meant to be cruel, to show that she was in charge.

With relish, she also informed me of the further misfortunes of my family. "Your younger two brothers… Do you wish to know of them?" she asked one day when she took me on a rare trip into the garden. Butterflies were fluttering over the flowers but there were horrible flying black bugs too, which had flown in from the fields where the local peasantry was threshing the grain. The insects clustered on walls, greenery—and on one's skin.

I made no reply, not wishing to give her any more power over me. Of course I wanted to know…

"So, you are 'mute' again," she said sourly. "Well, I shall tell you. They've left England; gone into exile."

A small moan broke from my lips. Mother would be heartbroken to lose John and Edmund so soon after Hal's execution, even if it was safer for them abroad.

"Such is the fate of traitors," Elizabeth said, waving an imperious hand as the black flies buzzed around her face.

"They are not traitors—my younger brothers have done nothing wrong!" I spat out with sudden fury, my fists clenching. The vehemence of my retort made Elizabeth jump away.

"They share your tainted ancestry; is that not enough?" she snapped, and then—"It is too hot out here…and these godforsaken flies! I am minded to send the steward to ask the workers to cease threshing. This is the worst I've ever seen these bugs—it is like the plague of locusts in the Bible out here!"

"Cease threshing? That would mean no bread before long, for them or for us," I said. "Or maybe you think the innocent farmers are traitors and should be punished for nothing, too?"

She sputtered at my insolence and grasped my arm, her fingers biting into the soft flesh of my underarm. "Back to your room, Margaret. I do not want to walk with you any longer and listen to your ridiculous ramblings. My head is spinning. I want to lie down. Lord help me, I think I am getting one of those *megrims* that afflict you—only mine is through the stresses you've brought me, not from a fevered mind!"

I smiled to myself. Although I longed for the garden's freedom, it was not freedom while my mother-in-law was there.

During the night, though, my mood faded from rebellious to melancholy. What would happen to me? Would Richard find some reason to have our marriage annulled once the child was born? Would he and Elizabeth continue to claim I was a madwoman, an imbecile, and have me taken to some awful place like the Hospital of Bedlam in London? I thought of being chained within that grim building, never seeing any of my children again, held like a criminal although I had committed no crime…and terror raked at my heart, setting it beating so fast I thought it might burst.

On the last day of July, the child decided to come. It was a sweltering day but overcast, thunder grumbling in the distance, and the sky and air held a sick, yellow shimmer.

Alma trudged up from the village with an assistant called Claris. Elizabeth and her maid, Amye, entered the bedchamber as well, making sure the shutters were tightly sealed and covered, for sunlight was said to hurt a birthing woman's eyes. They both undid their hair and their girdles as was customary, and seated themselves on stools at the end of the bed. The latter was not customary—usually the mother would have friends and family to sing to her, to chatter of pleasant pastimes, to hold her hand in her travail and bring ease. Neither Elizabeth nor Amye was inclined to do any of these things; my only reassurances came from the two midwives, who gave me a drink of minty hyssop and some sweet wine from a bowl with the Paternoster written around the brim.

If the births of my other two children had been surprisingly easy, this one was not. I pushed and groaned, sweat beading on my brow and running down my body. Waves of excruciating pain coursed through me, and though I pushed with all my strength, after many hours, it seemed no progress was made.

A worried frown on her brow, Claris began rubbing my trembling thighs with rose oil. "I wish I had an eagle-dung poultice instead," she murmured.

It sounded a horrific remedy but, at that moment, to ease the excruciating pain, I would gladly have swallowed such a nauseating concoction had it been offered.

Alma inched round the bed to examine the progress of the babe. She glanced up, her florid cheeks slightly drained. "I fear the child had turned—it cannot come out."

Elizabeth leapt off her stool, almost stumbling over Amye. "No...no! That means you could lose the child...lose its mother too."

"Be calm, Madam," said Alma with firmness. "You will frighten Lady Margaret. I have experience in rectifying this problem, but I will need silence so that I may concentrate."

Elizabeth fell back, hands pressed to her chest, long grey-streaking hair fanning out around her wan face. She had no love for me, but I could see that she already loved this grandchild that struggled to emerge into the world.

Alma took some pots and bottles from the basket Claris has brought with her. She washed her hands in a rose-water bowl, then opened one bottle and then another, pouring the contents over her fingers.

"W-what are you going to do?" I gasped, struggling to push myself up on my elbows.

"I must turn the babe; it is the only way. I have done it before, with both women and ewes. I have put flaxseed oil and chickpea on my hands so that they will slide easily toward your womb."

I shut my eyes, trying not to think about what Alma was going to do, and what the consequences would be if she failed in her task.

As if to remind me, Elizabeth, ignoring Alma's earlier admonishment to be still, scuttled in my direction and whispered, "Have you written a will, Meg? It is customary and…"

Claris glared, and despite the disparity in their ranks, Elizabeth fell silent and hunkered down by Amye. Both women started to pray, their combined voices a dull buzz.

Alma continued to work, being as gentle as she could be while rivulets of sweat dripped from her nose and chin. "I-I think it is coming," she grunted, after what seemed a pain-wracked eternity. "May the Holy Virgin give the poor mite protection so that it may be born alive. Now push, Lady Margaret…push!"

I did as she bid, crying out, wailing, my cries almost bestial in my agony. Suddenly there was a hot rush and I fell back, panting like a dog.

"It's born!" cried Alma, elated. "Claris, get it up and clip the cord. Get it crying. It's quiet, too quiet!"

Alma's last words filled me with terror. Both my sons had screamed lustily the moment they were born. Oh God, please let this infant be alive…Don't let it have suffocated inside…

Claris pulled the baby up, all slippery and beslimed, her practised fingers clearing mouth and nostrils. She held it almost upside down, giving the child a slight tap on back and buttocks. A moment later, a thin, high wailing filled the chamber.

"Alive...the babe is alive!" I gasped, half-crying, half-laughing. "Is it a..."

"It's a girl," said Claris. "A comely, well-made girl-child."

"A girl!" cried Elizabeth, disappointment clear in her tone, but nonetheless, she abandoned her stool and rushed over to the bedside. She stared down and as she looked at the babe, her expression changed. "Bless her; I think she resembles me."

She took the child from Claris, still red and blue and sticky and cradled it. Relief flooded me; at least she loved my daughter, even if I, mad, unruly and unwanted, was the infant's mother.

"What is her name to be?" asked Elizabeth. "Had you and Richard spoken of it?"

I nodded. "It is was a boy, it was to be named for Richard; if it was a girl, for me."

Her mouth turned down. She must have wished the child to bear her name. "Hmph, there are so many Margarets about. It shall become all too confusing, I fear."

"The name Margaret means 'pearl'—let that be her nickname if you find the confusion is too great."

So 'Pearl' my daughter became, and a fair shining pearl she was with tufts of thick dark hair and skin like lilies. Claris swaddled her and a wet nurse arrived from Ramsbury to give her first suckle. Elizabeth and Amye bustled off to arrange the Christening and to send Richard word that he had a baby daughter, while Claris burnt the afterbirth and birth-cord in the fireplace.

Alma bent over me, examining my torn intimate places. "It has been a hard birth. We must pray there are no complications. There is tearing, which is unfortunate. I will do what I can."

She brought out another jar from her basket. "Dried roots of comfrey, ground up with powdered cumin and cinnamon. It will solidify in your wounds."

Kneeling between my upraised knees, she applied the potion. I gripped the sides of the bed with my hands. "It was never as painful as this before," I moaned.

"As I said…it was a very hard birth, Lady Margaret." She gazed down sympathetically. "Try to get some sleep."

I slept…and when I awoke, I found, beneath the coverlet, I was bleeding. I cried out, alerting the wet nurse who had been drowsing in the corner, relieved of her small charge, who was in the chapel with her grandmother. The woman ran from the room and returned with Alma, who was still on the premises. The midwife examined me again, her face grim. "Claris!" she called to her assistant. "Find someone to bring more linens…*now*! And not just ones to change the sheets, but ones we can tear into strips that we can wad together to stop the bleeding."

Once more, she rummaged in her basket. "I have here goat's milk mixed with linseed and honey, said to thicken the blood. I will also give you something for the pain."

Gratefully I took what she offered, but my hands felt shaky and cold. I was giddy and nauseous. "Midwife Alma, am I going to die?" I asked. "I feel so strange."

"No, if I have any say in the matter," she said with false cheeriness, but I could see the worry and doubt in her eyes.

"Call Mistress Calston," I said, reaching out to catch her wrist. "Tell her to bring the priest—just in case."

But I did not die. I was sick for many days, weak as a newborn kitten, but Alma's cures worked and the bleeding stopped and I avoided the dreaded childbed fever that claimed so many women's lives. When my time for churching arrived, I could only enter the chapel with Amye on one side and Elizabeth on the next, holding me upright. At first, in that period of weakness and malaise, I feared they would take my baby away, send her to Littlecote to dwell with her father. But Richard had not asked such a thing, perhaps because of disappointment at her sex, and he rode to Paulton Manor instead to see his daughter. He spent minimal time at my bedside, brooding and uncomfortable, but I did catch an unwilling smile when he looked at Pearl sleeping in her cradle.

I also heard him arguing over money with Elizabeth in the corridor outside my room.

"Have you brought the payment, Richard?"

"No, I have been too busy to sort such things. Why so eager? You are hardly impoverished, mother."

"I may be soon, with two extra mouths to feed—although I do not regret feeding my granddaughter, so do not give me *that* look… I have had the pay the midwives, the wet nurse…It all mounts up!"

"If it is such a burden, Meg and the child must be brought to Littlecote soon."

"Margaret is still unwell."

"She's not like to die if moved, is she? If not, I will send a carriage to bring her and the baby home."

There was a long silence. I lay in my bed, stock-still, straining to hear what Elizabeth would say—if anything. Eventually, she spoke, "Do as you will, Richard, but I still want what is owed me and do not forget it."

"I am sure you will never let me forget." I heard his boots making large angry thuds as he tromped down the stairs.

Alone in my chamber, I struggled with my emotions. Elizabeth cared nought for my wellbeing, but she loved Pearl. My daughter was safe here, well cared for. I did not want to return to Littlecote, especially in my frail condition. But it was my husband's will, therefore my duty.

Duty. How I had grown to loathe that word.

The chariot to bear me hence arrived at month's end. I stumbled out, using a cane Elizabeth had lent me, and climbed in, every bone aching with the effort. Baby Pearl came next in the arms of the wet nurse, Gillian, who had agreed to remain with the Dayrell family until the babe was weaned. I sat in silence, wrapped in my blue muslin cloak, gloves on my hands, feeling every jolt as the carriage rattled over the rutted road.

It was the dead of the year now, and Littlecote House looked very bleak as the chariot rolled up the heavily treed drive, the great oaks and elms swinging their fleshless arms as if in combat with each other.

"Oh!" I heard Gillian mutter, rocking Pearl on her knee. Her face showed consternation at what she had come to. Elizabeth Calston's manor had at least been warm and bright.

In the hall, Richard emerged to greet me and Pearl. The servants had been ordered to attend, standing like a child's army of wooden soldiers around the great chamber. Many stared at me as if they were waiting for me to dance like a lunatic or roll about the rushes chewing bones with the hounds. Such is the power of rumour and suspicion. My husband bent and gave me a dry kiss of welcome on the cheek. Then he turned to Gillian and took the baby, holding her up, while the wet nurse looked flustered and I felt my heart thump against my ribs.

"Give welcome," Richard shouted, "to my daughter, Margaret, my heir—until I have a son, if that day should come."

The crowd mumbled noisily, making silly obeisance to my child. The baby began to cry.

Richard stepped back in surprise, not expecting the howls next his ear. Hastily he handed Pearl back to Gillian, who hugged her close.

"The nursery is ready," he said to me, "as is your old bedchamber."

The bedchamber had been cleaned and aired and someone had decorated the arch of the windows with Christmas Holly. I had hoped Martha might have assumed her position as my maid; instead, there was a strange girl—Lucie—all gangling legs and large teeth. Martha had left Ramsbury to marry a merchant near Devizes. I was sad to think I'd not see her again. It was nearly as hard as losing Anchoret and Jennet.

Lucie for all her gawkish looks was efficient enough in her duties and soon the fire was burning merrily, a platter of bread and pastries set out beside the bed, and I resting under the coverlets in a new red robe that smelt strongly of the lavender it had been stored in.

"This was not one of my garments," I fingered it suspiciously, wondering if my husband had taken a mistress in the months I was gone. I would not wear raiment tossed aside by some trull.

"Master Richard had it brought in specially for you, Lady," said Lucie. "It's a lovely shade of scarlet…"

"Yes, yes, it is." I felt ashamed; my thoughts of my husband's faithfulness, or lack of it, were unworthy…but such thoughts raised another unwelcome realisation. Soon, no doubt, he would want to resume relations as man and wife. I dreaded the idea after the battering my body had taken to birth Pearl. Richard had never shown himself a gentle lover, and it was unlikely he could appreciate how the birth had damaged me.

When Lucie left later, bidding me goodnight, I hunched down in the bed, breathing heavily, listening for the creak of boots on the stairs with dread.

They did not come, and eventually sleep claimed me.

Elizabeth Calston never did receive the money Richard swore he would pay her. A mere fortnight after I returned to Littlecote, Richard received the news that she had suddenly collapsed and died after coming in from visiting a local market. She was over sixty, so her life had been long, and one could not mourn overmuch.

Richard's brother, Alexander, was eager to claim the monies due on her behalf. He rode up to Littlecote in a great flurry, demanding that Richard pay up. "I am the executor of Mother's will," he said, bursting into the Hall with hair and cloak swinging, his face full of righteous fury. "You promised to pay her for your wife's board and keep but not one penny of it did she see. What kind of a creature are you to first foist your moon-struck wife on our aged, ill mother and then diddle her out of what was owed!"

"How dare you speak so to me in my own home!" Richard roared back.

"Your own home. I have no idea why George handed this place over to you. It's too good for you," sneered Alexander. "Not that you've done much with it—cold as a witch's tit and barely staffed owing to your miserly ways!"

"Get out!" Richard lumbered toward him, snarling, hand on the hilt of the dagger at his belt. "Never darken my door again, Alexander."

Alexander strode towards the door, turning halfway as he reached the brass ring. "I will see you in court, brother. And you had best appreciate the house because that is all you will have that came from Mother's family. She has cut you out of the will!"

"Just go!" Richard grabbed a brass goblet from a sideboard and hurled it after Alexander. The younger man ducked out the door and the goblet hit the frame and bounced back, clanging onto the flagstones.

Richard dived after it, cursing, and I thought he would pursue Alexander and the day would end in bloodshed, but he merely picked up the goblet and walked back in my direction.

I feared I might bear the brunt of his rage, since, ultimately, I was the reason he owed money to his deceased mother, but he merely said, "You should not have heard that. Alexander is a fool; always has been."

Leaving me staring after him in surprise, he left the hall.

Months flew by. My strength grew, both body and mind. Richard did not seek my bed, of which I was glad, and I spent much time with baby Pearl, who grew fat and winsome and pink-cheeked. I trailed around the gardens with Gillian and Lucie carrying Pearl in a basket, and sat on the manicured lawn, showing the babe her own reflection in the pond and pointing out the frogs and jewel-bright dragonflies that skimmed on the water's surface. She was too young to appreciate any of it yet, but I did not care. It was wonderful to have my child with me and made me think, more than ever, of Harry and Humphrey with their grandmother Anne. I did not even know where they dwelt, whether at Tonbridge, Pleshey, Maxstoke, Penshurst or somewhere else. I wondered if I would even recognise the boys after all this time—doubtless they would have grown like weeds as boys often did.

Then one night Richard, newly returned from Winchester, summoned me to join him for supper. I frowned as Lucie helped me into a rose-hued brocade gown and tucked my tresses under a modest hennin. He seldom called me and we usually dined separately; we existed side by side yet apart, which, I was coming to realise, was something we both preferred. Apprehension dulled my appetite as I descended the stairs, and entered the hall, sitting at the end of the trestle table.

The servants brought out frumenty and mortrews and poured claret into our goblets; Richard then dismissed them, leaving us alone together. I ate quickly, tasting nothing; he had shooed the staff away so that we might have privacy.

At length, I could bear the waiting no more. "Richard, what is it? Why are we dining together like this?"

"Is it a crime to dine with my wife?" he asked, but then his expression changed, became serious. "I have spent the last week in Winchester, as you know. Lots of news filtered in from King Edward's court. You will never guess. The King is married!"

"Married!" I put down my knife. "That is sudden and unexpected! Why was there no great wedding?"

"Because it was done in secret," said Richard. "In a little chapel with but the priest and a page for a witness. Oh, and the bride's mother—you'll never guess who that is!"

"Who?"

"The notorious Jacquetta, Duchess of Bedford. Jacquetta Woodville. The bride is called Elizabeth; she is the widow of Sir John Grey and rumoured to be exquisitely beautiful. She is older than Edward, though, and already has two sons."

I had not met Dame Grey, though her mother's tale was known throughout the old blood of England. "How extraordinary!" I exclaimed. I remembered King Edward's comments to me about a 'widow' when we danced…but if this Elizabeth was the woman mentioned, she must be fair like her mother and I was not. So if he had seen a similarity, it could not be one of looks.

"Infuriating, more like. Especially for the Earl of Warwick. He is most unhappy about Edward's choice of wife. He was negotiating a match with King Louis's kinswoman, Bona of Savoy and made to look stupid at the French King's court when word came that Edward already had a wife."

"So all is not well between the King and Warwick." I could not help but grin coldly, amused by this news. "Richard Neville is an overmighty subject; I cannot say I am surprised their friendship has failed."

"I think Warwick thought he could control Edward because of his youth, but he found Edward was no puppet to be pulled this way and that. The young Lion of March is asserting his authority."

"We have seen him do that in the past," I murmured. "When my brother went under the axe. But why are you telling me this? I shall never go to court again. I have little care for the activities of the men who destroyed my family. I will say 'God Save King Edward and Queen Elizabeth,' if I must, and let that be an end to it."

Richard cleared his throat. He was not in any wise a gentle man but I thought I caught a hint of pity in his eyes. "Meg, have you received any messengers from Anne, Duchess of Buckingham?"

The usual panic rose in my heart; the candles shimmered as my vision swam. I clutched the table. "I have not. Richard, has something happened to my sons? Oh, God help me if…"

"Hush, hush!" He waved his hand furiously. "Both are well, Meg. Well. But they are no longer in the care of the Duchess."

"No longer with Anne? Where are they?" I half-rose from my seat.

"Sit…sit, I beg you. I cannot speak when you are distressed like this…"

I sat, heavily, plucking at my collar which suddenly felt too tight. Beneath my brocade gown, my chemise clung to my flesh, sweat-drenched, uncomfortable, a sticky shroud.

"Your sons are with the King."

I made a choking noise; I reached for my cup to take a draught to steady me, but my hands shook so much that I knocked the goblet over, splashing red like blood across the table. Harry and Humphrey…in the hands of Hal's killer, the man whose father hated mine beyond all others, the man who fought and won his first battle on the day Humphrey Duke of Buckingham was slain. The children's grandfather…

"What if he harms them?" I cried.

"No, no, I doubt he would do that," said Richard.

"Why not? Look what he has done to the Beauforts; him and his sire, York!"

"Meg, Edward is a warrior, but not an outright brute, or so I'm told. Besides, the children are worth more to him alive. He legally purchased their wardships from the dowager Duchess of Buckingham…"

"So they were not wrested from her by force?"

"No. It was a straightforward business transaction by all accounts."

"Curse her!" The words spit like venom from my lips. "How could she do this without my consent?"

Richard leaned back in his chair, pouring himself another goblet of wine. My upended cup continued to drip, drip, drip on the floor, like gore from a deep wound. And wounded I was, to my very core.

At length, Richard spoke slowly. "Anne was their guardian; she had every right to sell their wardship. Who would dare deny the King anyway? But as it happens, he has now given their wardship to his wife, Queen Elizabeth—a gift. She is a mother and will see they come to no harm, I am certain."

A small rush of relief replaced the cold hand of fear. If Elizabeth Woodville had been widowed, even as I, and had two small boys to care for, surely she would find it in her heart to be kind to my sons and not see them merely as pawns to increase her wealth…

"Harry…Humph, they must be so upset at this sudden change, " I said, a faint hope burgeoning in my heart. "Do you think, if I wrote to her Grace, she might permit …"

"No, *no*, Margaret," Richard said, shaking his head. "That would not be impossible or even desirable. With your…frail health, you need to stay at Littlecote, away from all the intrigues of court, away from all that unhealthy stimulation... You need to stay with Pearl. If Henry and Humphrey want to visit when they are able to travel on their own agency, then no doubt they will."

Life can be perilous and short. I could be dead before that day comes…

I hung my head, hiding the treacherous, threatened tears. "I understand, husband. Maybe someday."

CHAPTER FOURTEEN

More time passed at Littlecote. Pearl grew into an amiable and inquisitive little girl who resembled my mother in looks but not in temperament. Richard had mellowed with her birth, and although our marriage would never be more than an alliance, he treated me with slightly more respect than in the beginning of our days together. Or, perhaps more accurately, he left me to my own devices. Several times he had crept into our bed to claim his marital rights, but when no pregnancy resulted, these not unwelcome visits ceased. I assumed Pearl's difficult birth had made me barren, as had my Cousin Margaret's birthing of her son Henry Tudor, and I supposed Richard did as well. I had no idea if he had a mistress elsewhere, but as long as he did not flaunt her under my nose or treat me ill, I did not much care.

In 1466, I received word that Harry, away in Queen Elizabeth's household, had married the Queen's sister, Katherine Woodville. This shocked me, not so much for their youth—Harry being ten and the young bride, Catherine, perhaps six—but, in truth, Harry's bloodline was far above that of his little Woodville wife. She was sister to a Queen Consort, yes, but merely the daughter of a knight; ideally, Harry should have wed into the 'old Blood', the Mowbrays, FitzAlans, Percys, Beauchamps…or even the Nevilles. Still, Elizabeth was known as a beauty, so perhaps little Catherine would have similar looks to bring to the marriage if not much else.

Harry, it turned out, was quite displeased by his marital arrangements. I received a rare letter from him, written in his own rounded, sprawling hand, with *Harry Duc of Bokingham* daubed in smeary black ink across the lower part of the parchment.

Reading his missive, I found my ten-year-old son was most indignant about the situation in which he found himself. *Dear beloved Lady Mother*, he wrote, *I have news of a great ill and evil that has fallen upon your unhappy son. I have been made to marry the Queen's sister Catherine. I call her Kate…or sometimes 'Cat' which she does not like as I always make the mewing noise of cats to go with it. She is fair enough to look upon, I suppose, with lots of curling yellow hair, but she is very silly and likes dolls and other fripperies. I took her doll once and pretended I was beheading it and I was too rough and the head fell off and broke. Cat cried and I got a birching and Dumph laughed. I know there is little you can do about this horrid outrage, mother, for it is what the Queen wants, but I wanted to let you know of my indignation and shame.*

Your Loving Son...(Humphrey sends his love too, but is too lazy to write himself, which is fine for my writing is better than his....)

Despite his obvious pique and dismay, I had to smile, if a little sadly. Harry would soon learn about the vagaries of Dame Fortuna and her ever-spinning Wheel...

The following year another loss descended on me, more exquisitely painful than any other I had borne. King Edward held an elaborate tournament at Smithfield, where the Queen's brother, Anthony Woodville, would battle Antoine, the Bastard of Burgundy, in the joust. Harry was there, acting as squire to Woodville, carrying his helm alongside that wretched Clarence, once an obnoxious child and now an overbearing youth by all accounts. Humphrey had stayed back in the palace, for he had acquired an ague, perhaps from a miasma off that dirty river that winds through London, stinking of ordure and dead things when the water level sinks.

Humphrey died, quietly and alone, and was buried in one of London's priories under a little stone that bore no image or brass. I fell into one of my periods of despair again, wondering if I should live or die, but the presence of my daughter Pearl made me fight for the recovery of my senses. I could not bear to leave her, my youngest child, merry and innocent of the sorrows of the world.

I did ask permission from Richard to go to London to see my son's tomb, and he granted it with no argument. In mourning black, I stood beside that cold grey slab, my hand resting upon it, scarcely able to believe that my smiling, bright-eyed boy lay beneath it, stilled forever, extinguished like a candle blown out in the night...I wished Harry could have stood beside me, and I could have held him, and we could have wept together for his brother—but he had, I learnt, gone on a hunt with the King, an event he dared not miss, "For how shall I ever become a great lord one day, if I do not bask in the presence of the great,' he had said, his face mutinous, daring me to argue with him. "I will go to Humphrey's grave later, Mother...*later*." I refused to argue, although I raged inside at his refusal, and as soon as I had seen my boy's tomb, I returned home. I could never look upon my sovereign with anything but distaste now, blaming him for Harry's cold manner, and of course his Queen, who was not a sympathetic woman, but a vain, cold one caring only for the advancement of her family.

The next year was hardly better. This time it was my Mother who passed into God's keeping while staying with her third husband at Baynard's Castle in London. She was not young, but her last years had been filled with sadness, with all her male children either dead or in exile. She had written once before she died, a rarity, so perhaps she anticipated his own demise—*I am old now, Margaret, and have many regrets. Forgive me that I was not a better mother to you in your times of need. I wish I could see my granddaughter; send me a lock of hair if you will. I am too frail to travel; carriages make my bones rattle. Jesu, Margaret, if only I could live long enough to see your brothers return and Edmond assume his rightful title as Duke of Somerset...*

The following June the King's sister, Margaret of York wed Hal's old friend, Charles of Burgundy. Chroniclers called it the Marriage of the Century for its opulence. I worried less about the elaborate crown the bride wore over her hennin and the feasts, pageants and exploits of young Mary of Burgundy's pet monkey than about my brothers who, I suspected, were staying with Charles as pensioners. Sure enough, I soon heard that Edmond and John were seen vacating the city of Bruges the day before the Yorkist princess and her entourage arrived.

In the spring of 1469, England's old troubles erupted once more, like pus from a suppurating wound. Rebellions led by men calling themselves 'Robin', suspiciously redolent of the tales of the outlaw Robin Hood, broke out in the north. As it turned out, the Earl of Warwick was behind these insurrections, his friendship with the King damaged beyond repair.

"It's not just Richard Neville," Richard said over his evening wine. The sun was setting, red rays piercing the glass windows and drenching our solar in bloody light. "It's his brother George, the Archbishop of York—and, you won't believe this, the King's own brother, George of Clarence! Not only has Clarence risen in armed rebellion against Edward, he has also defied his orders and married Warwick's daughter, Isabel."

"Oh, I well believe any ill I hear of Clarence, husband," I said, remembering the arrogant little boy I had seen at Tonbridge Castle. "That one was trouble from the day the Duchess Cecily birthed him."

King Edward sent Humphrey, Earl of Devon and William Herbert, Earl of Pembroke, to deal with the northern rebels, who were marching down country to rendezvous with Warwick and Clarence. The two leaders fell to arguing over lodgings (and some said a harlot!), which meant Herbert alone took the field near Banbury. His men were slaughtered, and he was captured and dragged to Northampton where Warwick executed him and his brother before a baying mob in the town square.

But Warwick went even farther—the man was always unstoppable in his malicious violence, from St Alban's onwards. He hunted down Queen's father and one of her brothers and ferried them in a prison-cart to Kenilworth Castle, where he beheaded them without trial. And then he took the King himself prisoner, not daring to slay him but hoping to rule through him, a puppet king with Warwick pulling the strings. Well could I imagine what Elizabeth Woodville went through when she heard the news, for I had known such agony too, and even felt brief sympathy, but only brief—for I had never quite forgiven her marrying Harry to her sister...or for blithely heading to the tourney when poor young Humphrey lay dying.

"It is war now, for sure," I said to Lucie, as she sat brushing and braiding my hair in the solar. Pearl was playing on the woven Turkey rug, running a toy horse with wheels around in circles. "I had thought the fighting was over after Edward won Towton, but it seems it will never be over."

"No, Madam." Lucie shook her head sadly. "Do you suppose King Edward will be deposed if he does not bow to Warwick, and the old King returned to the throne?"

I had not truly thought of old King Henry for years. I imagined he must be almost in his dotage, if even sane. "I doubt it, Lucie. It will be the young Prince."

"The people might not like that," said Lucie. "He's been in France so long he's near enough French himself! As for Queen Margaret—no one misses her much, truth be told."

A few months later Edward broke free of Warwick's hold, riding forth from Pontefract as if nothing untoward had happened and taking back control of the country. Harry had ridden with Gloucester and other nobles to accompany him back to London, which gladdened me even as I worried for his safety—he was finding his place in this ever-unstable world. The Earl, having lost control of the situation, fled England with George of Clarence and Clarence's wife, Isabel, who was heavily pregnant. She gave birth on board the ship when the garrison of Calais prevented them from entering the port, and the child died and was wrapped in linen and consigned to a grave in the sea. The Earl left the harbour and fled down the French coast, eventually finding succour from King Louis, who was ever eager to cause mischief in England.

I knew many Lancastrian supporters were exiled in France and Burgundy, including my two brothers. Would they join Warwick's rebels, now that the Earl had left the Yorkist fold? Could the House of Beaufort rise from the ashes like a phoenix, following the man who had aided in bringing it down?

I dared not hope for such a thing and was not sure if I wanted it so. Warwick would always have my hatred, no matter who he served, and I trusted him not at all.

The world had gone topsy-turvy once more. Events were almost beyond belief. King Henry was back on the throne again and men called his unexpected resumption of power the 'Readeption.' And who was behind this return—not loyal Lancastrian lords, but a turncoat Richard Neville, Earl of Warwick, aided by George of Clarence, and with the financial aid of Queen Margaret. The man who had brought our family down to remove the sad old King had now raised him back into power—although all men knew who truly governed England. Warwick could not manipulate or order Edward of York to do his bidding, but a grateful Henry was clay to be moulded in his hands. It was said Henry was so feeble when Warwick released him from the Tower, he had to lead him by the hand like a child.

And the usurper Edward? He had fled into exile with his faithful followers…and was said to be in Bruges, in the house of Louis de Gruuthuse.

"I can scarcely believe that Queen Margaret has made her peace with that traitor," I said to Richard while we sat at table. "She loathed Warwick above all others."

Richard chewed on a chicken leg, juices running down his bristly chin. "She made him grovel on his knees for a good long time, I heard," he said cheerfully between mouthfuls. "I'd have paid to see that. Clearly, she knew she would never see her son on the English throne someday if she did not make some kind of deal, as abhorrent as she might find it."

"It is the marriage that has stunned me even more—the young Prince to Warwick's daughter, Anne. I cannot believe the Queen truly approves of such a match, even if Warwick had helped get her husband back on the throne."

Richard flung the denuded chicken leg bone down onto the floor, where it was crunched upon by one of the hounds. "Oh no, she despises the very idea…but she wants Warwick's army and his military skills. I've heard the marriage between the Prince and the Neville wench hasn't been consummated and won't be till Her Grace is sure of Warwick—when Edward is either dead or in impoverished, friendless exile. His head on a pike where she can spit on it would be her delight. Her uncertainty of Monsieur Warwick is why she still lingers in France with Louis the Spider for now."

"Edward of York will not give up easily," I said with unease. Edward had fled only when Warwick's brother Montagu had turned on him, nearly trapping him when he halted his army in Doncaster. He'd sailed for Flanders with Richard of Gloucester, his lackey Hastings and the Queen's brother Anthony…leaving a heavily pregnant Queen Elizabeth to seek sanctuary at Westminster with her little daughters.

Hearing of that flight had caused me immeasurable distress, because I knew not whether Elizabeth had taken Harry to sanctuary with her, as her ward…or whether in self-serving panic she had left him alone when Warwick's men took control of London. Fortunately, within days I had a scrawled letter from Harry himself—he had been sent back to his grandmother Anne and was at Tonbridge.

Richard picked at a bowl of fruit, choosing the ripest apple. He looked thoughtful as he polished it on his sleeve. "You may be right, wife, but the tables have turned and no matter what Edward manages to do, he is likely to find himself outnumbered by his opponents. The supporters of Lancaster are once more pre-eminent in England."

"But is not George of Clarence," I wrinkled my nose, "still supposed to be heir to the throne? Another York?"

"Yes…but no," he grinned. "Warwick had to drop that idea when he grovelled to Queen Margaret. Clarence will be King only if Prince Edward begets no heirs—whether on Anne Neville or some other woman. I would not be at all surprised if George Plantagenet should meet an unfortunate accident while in his cups to get him out of the way. Your cousin Margaret Beaufort certainly hopes so.!"

I glanced at him sharply. "Margaret? Why so?" I had heard that Henry Tudor was back in the care of his Uncle Jasper, which would please her, but unaware she had a problem with George of Clarence—at least not more than most people did.

"He has been allowed to keep the lordship of Richmond—for life."

Ah…that should have been Henry's birthright. His father Edmund had borne the title Earl of Richmond. A hard blow for the lad and his proud mother.

"Anyway," Richard continued, quite jolly, "I expect it will all come to a head soon, likely before the middle of the year. That is what the spies say. Charles of Burgundy has been wavering back and forth in his allegiances…but it looks like he may well support Edward."

"Well, that is *not* good news." I frowned, crossing my arms.

"No…but I doubt the men-at-arms he offers will amount to much as he needs most of his soldiers for his own endless wars. Anything he musters will be puny before the might of Warwick and the Queen's combined forces. But we shall see."

We shall see…

"King Edward had landed at Ravenspur!" A courier from Hungerford, galloping on a sweat-soaked bay, delivered the news to Littlecote before riding on in a mad flurry across the shire.

"So it begins," said Richard with a grim smile, gazing from the gate into the early evening sky, tinted a pale orange-red, the clouds ripping asunder like war-torn banners.

"You seem undismayed." I stood at his side, blinking into the last of the light. From the hall behind us drifted a plaintive song; a minstrel was playing a haunting air on a little bone pipe. I could hear Pearl laughing, her little clear voice like bells, and I knew she was dancing. She loved to dance. Lucie acted almost like an older sister, lifting her off her feet and twirling her around when music was played.

"I am not a fighting man, as you know," Richard said. "I am a man of law, of quills and parchments and judgments…not a soldier. I'll get by, no matter who is on the throne—I've said it before."

"Red sky." The orange sunset had faded to sullen scarlet; a cloud flamed, streaked out on the horizon then turned a purplish hue. "The colour of blood."

"None of those fancies now, wife," Richard said sternly. "It's not good for you."

I was toying with my rosary beads, running them incessantly through my fingers. The smooth, cool feel was comforting. "Queen Margaret's army has not yet reached England. It would be better if she was here with the full might of the Lancastrian supporters."

He shrugged. "She's on her way, I heard…but I am sure Warwick can stop Edward on his own. Even without Margaret, his army is larger by far, and he has a score to settle with his former protégé."

"The reverse is also true. Edward will want revenge on his old mentor."

"Aye, but Warwick is older and more experienced, and beyond that, he has the Earl of Oxford and his levies with him. Oxford is a great fighter and tactician and bears the House of York great enmity. His father and brother were beheaded at Edward's command. He had not forgotten. Already he drove Edward's force away from the Norfolk shore, forcing him to sail north and ensuring his army's march will be a long one."

"But Edward of March had never been beaten in battle. Have you forgotten Towton? And Warwick was defeated at the second Battle of St Alban's, and at the first…" my voice grew hard, "he crept through gardens like a common sneak which is how he got close enough to kill my father! Hardly the actions of a great warrior, are they? More like a cutpurse and pirate who got lucky!"

"Edward got lucky too, with the snow flying into his enemy's faces at Towton," said Richard. "Who knows how it would have gone otherwise? I still think that Warwick will prevail. Edward's Sun in Splendour has set." He laughed at his own joke.

A moth fluttered around the lantern hanging over the guard hut by the gate, manned by a dispirited-looking sentry. The sun was extinguished between the trees; mist exhaled from the damp ground.

"Come on," Richard said, shivering and pulling his Great Coat close. "It's dark out. I doubt more news will come tonight. I could use some wine, Meg. Mayhap you could use some too."

Edward Plantagenet was victorious.

At Barnet, the armies of the rivals had clashed at dawn, the bloody conflict taking place in a sea of thick grey fog.

It was the vagaries of the English weather that swung the day for the young King, just as they had at Towton where the snow blinded his foes and sent their arrows spinning. On Barnet Field, the mist made men unable to tell friend from foe, and Oxford's banner, bearing his Star and Streamers, was mistaken in the murk for the Sunne in Splendour. Allies unwittingly fought allies while their foes hewed them down from all sides.

The Earl of Warwick met his end that day, his bravado forever ended. He was cornered in a little wood and stabbed through the eye as he tried to mount a horse and flee the field. Montagu was slain too, and the brothers' bodies taken to St Paul's for display.

"I truly thought Edward would not prevail against Warwick," said Richard, after telling me of the slaughter. Earlier he had been in Marlborough where the royal castle had swift, trustworthy couriers bringing news of the outcome. "But I admit, when I heard old King Henry had been abandoned by his own councillors at the Bishop's Palace in London…"

"What?" I sputtered. "They left him alone, unguarded?"

"So it would seem, Meg. When Henry's so-called companions heard of the approach of the victorious Yorkist host, they feared they could not defend the city against forcible entry. Henry is too feeble to make swift journeys…so they abandoned him. The Yorkists found him wandering about in his soiled robes, spluttering and wailing. He is now in the Tower."

"Jesu," I murmured, crossing myself. "The poor King, to lie prisoner in his own fortress, where he sat on his seat of estate only days before! What of Queen Margaret? Will she turn her ships back toward France, do you think?"

"No...she has landed at Weymouth...Some counselled her to retreat, but I have heard that your brother, Edmond, urged her onwards, saying she would be better off without a man as dishonourable as Warwick. She listened and is marching to Cerne Abbas to spend the night in the guesthouse of the abbey there. Her son, the Prince of Wales, and his little Neville wife are with her. I dare say it will not be a very pleasant stay for the girl, having found out about her father's miserable death."

"No," I said. Despite the fact I despised Anne Neville's father, I could not wish ill on a young girl who would feel the same tearing sorrow as I did when my sire died. I bore Warwick no love, but no doubt, Anne did.

"And of course, who knows what will happen to her now?" Richard continued "If it's true the marriage to the Prince was not consummated, she could easily end up being put side..."

I remembered that fear too. Sadly, I smiled to myself, staring down at my folded hands.

"What was that smile for?" Richard leaned forward across the table that separated us, puzzled.

"Oh...just that one way or another, soon these wars will end. And with time, I grow much like you—I am no longer bothered who reigns as long as I am left alone. The young Margaret of my past wanted Lancaster, the Margaret who has two living children merely wants peace."

"But you looked sorrowful as you smiled." I had never thought my husband in anywise perceptive before now.

"Yes, because even if peace *is* found at last—from each side, a mother will bury her son, a wife her husband...a family their hopes of the future. This battle at Barnet has been fierce, but it's not over...but there will be one more."

The pedlar came to Littlecote; an old man with pots and knives and medals and other trinkets, driving a rickety cart pulled by a swaybacked donkey.

Lucie rushed into the solar to inform me of the unexpected arrival. "There's a strange old greybeard outside selling gewgaws and pots and other such. The steward told him we had no need of his wares and bid him go on his way, but he is insisting that he sees you. He says you've done business with him in the past and that he brings something he is sure you will desire."

"A pedlar, say you? How strange. I do not remember any commerce with pedlars—at least not recently." I began to rise from my seat, laying my embroidery aside—a silk panel for a dress for Pearl, decorated with blue Forget Me Nots, which the Beauforts had used as an emblem since the time of King Henry IV.

"I would not go down if I were you," said Lucie, shaking her head. "He was very intense and demanding for a mere pedlar, but he was so insistent the steward asked me to inform you."

Uneasy, I reached for my dark blue mantle. "I will go and see what he wants. While I am dealing with this man, I want you to go rouse the stable lads. Anyone large and brawny. Just in case there is trouble."

I swept from the room and Lucie bounded after me. We parted ways as we exited the house into the rain-washed courtyard, Lucie hiking her skirts and raced towards the stable in a spray of muddy water while I walked on, alone.

The pedlar and his cart stood over by the wall, the steward pacing nearby, arms folded in a slightly threatening manner, his brow lowered in a scowl. I beckoned him to move a few feet further away so that I could have some privacy with the stranger. Grudgingly he moved back, but his fingers were hovering about the hilt of the knife at his belt.

The pedlar was, as Lucie had described, elderly, with a thick grey beard, dull homespun garments and a battered hat, His eyes, however, were keen and blue beneath his low-hanging white eyebrows. My gaze fell to his hands, holding the reins of his donkey. They were surprisingly clean and unlined, the nails reasonably pared; not the hands one expected of a rough traveller.

"My maid has informed me you wanted to see me," I said. "She tells me you claim I had business dealings with you in the past. I regret that I do not remember your face, goodman. So state your business now or I would ask you to depart."

"Do you not, my lady? Oh, how that grieves me. I was at your family's manor in Milton Fauconbridge many years ago. I gave you a blue ribbon for your hair, without fee, for it was your birthday. You had two younger brothers, Edmund and John…"

A jolt ran through me. I knew beyond the shadow of a doubt that I had never met this man before, yet he was aware of my childhood home, and mentioned only my two younger brothers, the ones who were in exile. Even more telling, *John* had gifted me a blue ribbon one year.

"Maybe I do remember…something?" I leaned closer to the man, though not so near he could easily lay hands on me if that was his intent. "Should I recall that particular ribbon…what of it? What is your purpose here, pedlar? I doubt it is for old reminiscences, as we are far from Milton both in leagues and in time."

He cleared his throat, lowering his voice. "I come to give you certain tokens, my Lady; the memory of the ribbon was to let you know from whence I am sent." His hand shot out, caught mine. I gasped at the audacity and made to withdraw, but then he pressed a cold metal object into my palm. A ring. I stared at it. A worn gold ring with my sire's seal. I had seen it on his finger and, once, on Hal's after Father's death. This could have only come from a member of my family. By rights, it should be Edmond's now.

I stared up into the intense blue eyes of the pedlar, searching. "Take care, Lady," he said. "Even here there may be those watching you."

"Yes, yes…" Quickly I tucked the ring into the purse at my belt.

"This is yours too," the greybeard murmured and he slipped a folded slip of parchment into my hanging sleeve. I fastened my fingers around it, crushing it against my sweating palm.

The pedlar moved back, clearing his throat again and raising his voice. "Well, thank you, my Lady," he boomed, "for the purchase of my pot. I knew you'd recognise the fine craftsmanship, even after so many years." He nodded at some ugly earthenware lying in a crate on the back of the cart. "If you could remove your piece, I'll be on my way—I am travelling on to Swindon so have a good deal of ground to cover."

I snatched a round black cooking pot from the crate and the pedlar cracked the reins over his donkey's back. The cart juddered off towards the road beyond the haze of trees.

The steward was staring at me as if he did not believe what he had seen. His mistress doing business with one near enough a beggar-man and then standing, whey-faced, clutching a sooty, poorly-crafted bowl in one hand as if it was the Holy Grail itself. "Is everything all right, my Lady?"

"Absolutely fine. Now go see to your other duties and I shall see to mine." Grasping the bowl in my free hand and the other, more important acquisition in the folds of my sleeve, I hastened for the house.

Summoned by Lucie, the stable lads, great youthful bruisers with more muscle than sense who were spoiling for a brawl with an unwelcome visitor, stared after me in disappointment.

In the quiet of my bedchamber, I opened the folded note crushed into my palm and held it near the candlelight. The writing was cramped but legible. *Most Wholly Beloved, Sister, I send this missive and Father's ring as a token that what you read is genuine. We have returned from long days endured in exile, and have offered the strength of our sword arms to the Queen. Soon battle will take place and I fear we will either prevail, this time, or our noble line be extinguished, as there are no legitimate sons of our bodies. Edmund and I would see you before the fray commences and God makes his final judgement on our House. We shall visit the deer park of the Bishop's Palace that lies near Ramsbury in three nights, approaching from the west, God willing; Bishop Beachamp, our distant kinsman, is aware and we come with his blessing, so do not fear on that account. If you cannot come, no rancour will we feel because a woman's business is not so free as a man's, since she is her husband's to command.*

Seek the blighted oak after Nones; you will hear a nightbird cry in day. Your loving brother, J.

Hurriedly I crumpled the letter and tossed it on the fire. The Bishop's Palace stood on the edge of Ramsbury, an ancient seat of the Bishop of Sarum. I could easily find an excuse to go there, as the Bishop was a distant kinsman and on reasonably good terms with Richard...but it was Richard himself I worried about. He must not know of my meeting. It was too dangerous for everyone. If he insisted on accompanying me, he would be tainted by association if Edward were to re-take the throne and the meeting became public knowledge. Whereas if I went alone and was discovered, I could beg forgiveness as a sister who merely wished to see her brothers, for love and not for treasonous reasons.

I paced the room, frantically trying to work out Richard's schedule. Five days...I was sure it was around that time he said he would return home. Of course, he was often late in returning when business dictated—but on occasion, he came back early, footsore and sometimes drunk.

Well, there was no helping it. What would be, would be. At the worst, I would have to insist Richard not attend the meeting with my brothers even if he raged and demanded. Perhaps if I told him his head might lie on the block beside theirs if the upcoming battle was lost, he might think better of any involvement at all, and blame the entire thing on his mad, imbecilic wife...

When the third day came, Richard was still not home. I gave thanks to God in the chapel, suppressing my small frissons of guilt over what I was about to do behind Richard's back. I had donned a dowdy workaday gown, nothing that proclaimed wealth or invited stares, and a subdued wimple in a more matronly style than I was accustomed to, with linen bands below my chin and a loose veil that I could modestly pull across my face. It was impossible to travel alone, of course, which would have set tongues wagging, so I summoned Lucie and a couple of manservants who were dour fellows and not likely to wag their tongues or ask any questions. It was market day in Ramsbury, so plenty of diversions for them while I did what I must.

My little party reached the town mid-way through the morning; although the market was not as large as the fairs in Marlborough or Hungerford, the streets were brimming with visitors and traders—potters, fullers, coopers, weavers all gathered on one side of the street, while on the other were bakers, pie-sellers, butchers and fishmongers.

We left out horses stabled at one of the town's inns, browsed the stalls for a while, and then I leaned over to touch Lucie's shoulder. "I forgot to tell you…I must see the bishop on business," I said. "It is a private matter, but you may stay in the town with the servants. I will come meet you when I am done." I took out some coin and pressed it into her hand. "For your silence, Lucie. Distract the others, if you will."

"How may I do that?" she frowned, staring at the coins on her palm.

"Tell the others I have gone to seek the Bishop's blessing…on a particularly important personal matter. It is not altogether untrue."

She glanced up at me, a new light in her face. "My Lady, are you…are you…"

I knew she had this mad hope that Richard and I would produce another child, despite the fact our congress was fleetingly rare and our marriage bleak. However, if she thought I was asking the bishop for prayers or blessings for conception or a safe birth, so much the better. The male servants would have little interest in such matters; indeed, might even feel uncomfortable discussing them. This, too, was good.

"Who knows what may occur in the future, Lucie," I lied. "With God's help, anything is possible."

I left her with the servants near the market cross and then hurried across town towards the Bishop's Palace. Soon the gate appeared within the crenellated wall licensed by the King in the last century. The large iron-studded doors were closed, since the palace was not open to all-comers, unlike many abbeys and friaries, and I was forced to grasp a thick brass ring and pound.

The noise echoed in the stone passage behind, and moments later a man-sized exit door opened in the larger door. A servant wearing the bishop's colours peered around the wooden edging and eyed me with nervous suspicion. I doubted he had ever seen an unaccompanied woman there before.

"I am Lady Margaret from Littlecote," I said. "I am expected by Bishop Beauchamp, my *kinsman*." I emphasised the last, in case the man was impertinent and asked too many questions.

"Yes, milady, it is as you say." He gave a little half-bow and stepped aside to let me pass. I stepped over the threshold, holding in a sigh of relief.

Inside the palace walls, a long lawn stretched over to a handsome house of warm yellow stone which had two large wings and a multitude of windows. The customary garden surrounded it, filled with flowers and fruit trees, while beyond were fishponds gleaming silver in the wan sunlight and then another wall with an open door that led into the vast deer park.

The park where my brothers, God willing, would await me.

The bishop's man re-barred the gate and led me over the lawns to the cloister attached to the house. We walked through the cool corridor, the flagstones smooth underfoot, the smell of mint and rosemary hanging in the air, and from thence to the little chapel of the Virgin built into the far wall. "The Bishop is within, my Lady," said the servant. "Now I must take my leave and return to my post." He bowed again and left.

I entered the chapel, a place of light and beauty with many windows of gold-hued glass and paintings on the wall. Under the paintings were written paeans to light amidst darkness, as described in the gospels—*'When the Holy Ghost descended upon the apostles, there appeared unto them cloven tongues of fire'* and *'At the conversion of St Paul there shined round him a great light from heaven'*

Bishop Beauchamp was kneeling before the altar, head bowed. The flickering votive candles at the feet of a statue of the Virgin cast a warm glow onto the side of his face.

Hearing my soft footsteps, he rose effortlessly—a well-built man of middle years whose hair was only slightly greyed around the temples, his bearing more that of a soldier than a churchman. "Lady Margaret…kinswoman"

I genuflected before him, kissing the purple stone of his ring; then he raised me and kissed me on either cheek in chaste greeting. "It is good you have come in these unfortunate times, although I have no doubt that your mind is filled with doubt and worry."

"It is true, your Grace," I said. "I fear what may happen if the true reason I fared hither is revealed, should certain…unwelcome misfortunes…happen in the days to come. Yet is not loyalty to one's family as important as it is to a king? A king is anointed with Holy Chrism, yes, but what if he is an unrightful King? My loyalty lies with the King of Kings, and the laws he spoke…and with my beloved kin."

"Hush, hush, not so loud child," chided the bishop. "Even here, there may be listeners. My thoughts are with you, but I must be seen to have no open allegiances, which is why you must meet your brothers in the park rather than the palace. I pray you understand."

I nodded. "I do."

"Look for them near the lighting blasted oak. I believe they have instructed you thus? You will see it as you approach the deer path that runs near the wall. The tree was a giant of the forest once, now sadly blighted, but a landmark of the forest where the hunt often gathers."

I turned to leave, my desire to see Edmond and John overwhelming, but Bishop Beauchamp caught my sleeve. "One moment, Lady Margaret. Let us pray together for a short time. If there are watchers, let them believe that you are only here on Godly business."

"And so I am…at least in my heart," I said stoutly. "And family business."

He grinned, an unusual expression on one in such an exalted position. "Yes…and I am also family of sorts, am I not?"

We went to the altar and knelt together and prayed in silence awhile, and when we were done the bishop quoted from Isaiah, his voice reverberating around the tiny chapel—*Have not I commanded thee? Be strong and of good courage; be not afraid, neither be thou dismayed: for the Lord thy God is with thee whithersoever thou go.*

And my courage rallied and I knew that whatever might befall, it was right to seek my brothers, no matter the outcome of the forthcoming battle. They were blood, and that tie was deeper than loyalty to a husband who I loved not and who did not love me, and also trumped allegiance to any King, be it old Henry or King Edward.

"Thank you, your Grace." I looked gratefully at the bishop.

"Go now," he said, "and do not linger, for as I said, one does not know whose eyes are upon them. But remember—*The wicked flee when no man pursues: but the righteous are bold as a lion.*"

I departed the chapel then, hurrying through the cloister and out onto the lawns. Outside, I felt oddly exposed as I darted through the colourful gardens to the door that led out into the park. The sun beat down, bright and unseasonably hot, between puffed dark heads of rumpled clouds. I headed for the park's retaining wall, old and lichenous, patched up here and there by newer stones. I walked along its length, occasionally reaching out to touch it for support, whilst avoiding clawing brambles and the serrated leaves of stinging nettles.

Soon the first row of oak and alder closed around me, cutting off the brilliant sunlight and cooling my sweaty face. Birds darted through branches, their twitters the only sound save for the scuffle of my soft doeskin boots. Umbellifers shot up, making lacy dens and between the boles and roots ran carpets of buckrams, their garlicky scent heavy on the air.

Somewhere off to my left leaves began to shiver and there was a rustle. I sprang back in alarm, then relaxed as I saw a large black and white badger amble through the greenery towards its sett. I took a few more strides, the greenish light wavering as the boughs parted—and there it was, the lightning-blasted oak. Its head reared above all other trees in the park, split by nature's wrath into two fierce prongs which gave it the semblance of some kind of fantastical sorcerer's tower. The central split was charred black, while the wood that curved outward from the crevice was bleached almost silver-pale, shining in the sunlight.

I rushed headlong towards it, breath rattling as I heard the sweet but out-of-place song of a nightjar, and behind me, from the chapel in the Bishop's Palace, the boom of the Nones bell as it tolled the ninth hour.

In my eagerness, I was not careful, and suddenly the toe of my boot caught in a root hidden by the umbellifers. With a strangled cry, I pitched forward...straight into the arms of my brother, John.

I threw my arms around my neck, clinging to him as if I feared he would vanish in a puff of smoke. "John, oh John, I thought I might never see you again after you left England."

John half-carried me through the long grasses and wildflowers to the bole of the oak. The dead tree was wide as well as tall, its base hollowed out and rimed with great plates of yellowish fungus. Edmond stood within, while his horse and John's were tethered to one of the leafless, low-hanging branches.

"Meg," said Edmond, his normally solemn visage breaking into a smile. John released me and I ran to Edmond, embraced him and wept upon his shoulder. "I can scarce believe this! I...I have the ring, Father's ring. I must return it to you..." I fumbled at my belt.

"No, not yet," he said, shaking his head. "At the moment my enemies called me 'Edmond, styling himself the Duke of Somerset' as if I were a mere pretender to my sire's title. Well, I will prove with my body that I am not...and when all is settled and I am fully recognised as Duke, then I may ask for the ring back. Keep it safe till then, sister."

I gazed at my two brothers. Both had aged since last I saw them. Deep lines from nose to mouth on Edmond's face, made him look unduly sullen; lines fanned out from the corners of John's eyes, giving him a wearier appearance than I remembered. I wondered if they thought the same of me; I eschewed mirrors as much as possible since Pearl's birth. Time, illness and sorrow are hard upon the faces of mortal kind.

John clasped my hand. "We heard things, sister…about your life here. It made me outraged, having met your husband and seen his boorish manners first-hand. Are you still…?"

"It is fine, John. We have come to an understanding. My life at Littlecote is quiet enough these days, and I delight in the company of my little daughter, Pearl. I am sure the tales you have to tell are far more exciting. To see you both gladdens my heart, although the hour is still dark—and the days ahead uncertain. I am surprised, you found time to come here, though. Why are you not with Queen Margaret? I believed that you journeyed with her from France."

Edmond shook his head. "We have been in England since February, Meg, although lying low. We visited Mother's tomb, and Nell and some of the others if we thought it safe to do so."

"You've been here all along? But you did not fight for King Henry and the Queen at Barnet! At least…no one spoke of it…"

Edmond snorted, folding his arms. "We would never fight beside the Earl of Warwick, under any circumstance. A blackguard till the end. It is just as well we were not on the field that day, since God struck him and Montagu down. So he paid the final price for his hubris. He is out of the way—forever. Now true loyalists shall rise to take down the usurper Edward for once and for all!"

"We rode to Weymouth when her Grace arrived," interjected John. "Edmond persuaded her that the cause was not lost; that, with Warwick slain, she would find *more* Lancastrians offering their swords, for they trusted her and the King, but not the Earl."

"We will meet up with her forces soon," said Edmond. "We have raised many levies in the west in her name—and that of the young Prince, who is eager to partake of his first battle and blood his sword. The Queen has appointed me her foremost commander."

"I am so proud of you, Edmond," I said, the old fears worried at me as a dog worries a bone. In my mind's eye I saw two bloody heads on pikes, one Father, the other Hal…and a third and fourth stood empty, waiting. "Now, tell me—what of your exile in Burgundy? How did you fare so far from home? No letters came—not that I would expect them to in the circumstances."

"For a long time, we dwelt at the court of Charles the Bold. He had been Hal's dear friend and mourned his passing. He clothed us, fed us and gave us pensions to live on...then everything changed." An angry expression flitted over his features. "He married the York bitch, did he not? We had to abandon Bruges, but stayed in contact with Duke Charles as much as was possible, for despite the marriage, he still leaned towards the House of Lancaster over York. However, when Edward arrived with the younger brother, the pup with sharp teeth, Gloucester, the brothers and their interfering sister worked on Charles, convincing him to back their cause. I tried my best to convince him he was wrong, that it was ungodly and unnatural to set up one such as Edward on the throne, when he had no right and had deposed and deprived his own kinsman. But my pleas fell on deaf ears; King Louis is threatening to invade Burgundy, so that is foremost in Charles' mind, and Edward promised full support against the French if the Duke should aid him to reclaim the throne."

"I have heard King Henry is back in the Tower. As a prisoner."

Edmond suddenly stared at the ground, desolate, shame-faced. "So...you have heard of that. What else do you know, Meg?"

"Only that his friends abandoned him to his fate."

Edmond shuffled in discomfort, then struck out with his fist, striking the bole of the blasted oak. His knuckles came away bloody as I stared in confused horror. "I will not lie," he said, between gritted teeth, "it was my fault. I made the decision to leave the King in London. I asked him to flee with us, but he gibbered and flapped his hands and went and hid in his closet. What could I do, Meg? Fling the old man over my shoulder and drag him hence, kicking and wailing? No...if we should win the forthcoming battle, the future is not with Henry, but with the young Prince Edward."

I was shocked to find out Edmond was the one who had left the King. *People will hold you accountable, my brother...* Yet I understood why he had left him too. He was no longer a figure that men could rally around; he had become a millstone about the neck of the supporters of Lancaster.

Edmond was nursing his bruised and bloodied knuckles. "I feel guilt for what I did, Meg. I have prayed for forgiveness on bended knee. I have sworn that I will see Edward of Lancaster on the throne—or die in the attempt to set him there."

"Edmund, I beg you…do not speak of death." I pressed my hand to my brow. One of my megrims was beginning, lightning shivering at the edges of my vision. Far, far away, dream-like, the sound of bombards and men screaming filled my mind…It was Rouen again and Mother was shrieking as the cannonball smote the ground in front of my tiny satin slippers like a missile hurled from Hell…

"Meg, you look unwell." John reached out to steady me with a hand.

"Forgive me," I gasped. "I will be frank, as you are kin; you may already have heard the rumours—I am prone to fits of melancholy where I am not myself. It's more serious than just the *megrims*, I fear. This disgraces our family, I know…"

"You have brought no shame," said John fiercely. "If anyone speaks ill of you in my presence, I will call him to the duel."

I wiped tears from the corner of my eyes, imagining John throwing down the gauntlet to Elizabeth Calston, who had cruelly called me 'imbecile' on so many occasions.

Edmund was glancing up at the sky. "We must not stay too long," he warned. "We have a long road ahead, John. We must soon rendezvous with the Queen and Prince Edward."

"Such a short time together…" I whispered.

"So it must be." Edmund took hold of me and drew me close in a short, hard embrace. It made me weep again—the reunion so sweet and yet so devastatingly brief. John then embraced me too, his cheek pressed against mine, and I wept all the harder, for he was my favourite out of all my living siblings.

"Don't cry, Meg," he said, his own voice thick with emotion. "We will return, and if by ill-chance we do not...Well, at least you know that we did it for the honour of our House. For the Beauforts."

"For the Beauforts," I murmured, smiling through my tears as I let him go.

Quickly my two bright, valorous younger brothers untied their mounts and swung into their saddles. I stared up at them, shading my eyes against the sun flickering through the trees and they looked golden, handsome young men as proud and noble as those in the court of King Arthur.

Then they were gone, galloping out of the Park towards the front gate of the Bishop's Palace. I ran after them, stopping on the edge of the trees to raise a hand in farewell.

Above, a wild falcon shrieked, wheeling against the sky before diving down, down, to find its hapless prey.

It was a beautiful May morning, not long after sunrise. Pearl and I had attended early Mass before faring into the gardens to gather flowers and herbs. Pearl was delighted as the heavens lightened, and the flowers, curled up safe for the dark hours, began to unfurl their petals in a haze of blue, purple, pink, red and gold.

"They say washing your face in May dew will make a girl pretty," I told her, and she began catching dewdrops on her fingers and rubbing them into her rosy cheeks.

Deftly I made her a little crown of the Daisies—the Day's Eye. Daisy was another nickname for Margaret, too. "Now you are Queen of the May," I told her, though May Day had passed over a sennight before, a celebration of bonfires at night, of Moorish dances on the village green, of mummers in verdant ribbons.

The morning was so peaceful that it was easy to believe Littlecote was in a world of its own, cut off from the troubles that plagued the rest of England. I tried to keep it so, and not dwell on the last meeting with my brothers. Richard had returned from his travels the day after our meeting, and must have heard something, perhaps from one of the more talkative servants, for he had sniffed suspiciously around, asking many questions until he grew too bored and weary, to pursue the matter further, and retreated, grumbling about my obstinacy, to his bedchamber.

He still lay abed now, having missed Mass with the excuse of a sore head, which had come from too much drink the night before. When I poked my head into his chamber in the dimness before dawn, he had snarled at me like one of his dogs. "Leave me be! I am sick to my stomach, woman. Sick of you, sick of no sons, sick of the wars that rend this Godforsaken country. Christ, the combatants have probably met by now, and Christ knows whether we'll be favoured by the winner or made paupers…"

He had not spoken so harshly to me for some years, and I cringed at his hostility and slammed the door, heart hammering. *I have more to lose than you in this game, you whining dolt…*

I refused to think of him anymore today; only Pearl mattered, the overwhelming brightness in my life. And Harry, of course, but he wrote seldom and even then, his letters were mostly complaints. He still felt his position was not respected; he was hoping his marriage to the Woodville girl might be annulled if King Edward was slain, but no one would speak of it—could I help?

I could not, nor would I interfere, not knowing how the battle for power might play out. I was glad of one thing, though—he was still too young to fight, not sixteen till September. Another year or two…I shuddered, remembering the fate of the second son of York on Wakefield Bridge, cut down by Clifford. Also, there was our illustrious Lancastrian Prince, Edward, off to his first ever battle at but seventeen years.

"Mama! Look!" I broke from my reverie and faced my little daughter. She was pointing over the lawns to where a young boy ran madly towards us, arms flapping. I recognised him at once…the cook's son James.

Alarmed, I strode towards him. "James! What is it?"

"Soldiers, my Lady. In the town. Lots of talk of a big battle up country…somewhere."

My blood turned to ice. "What badge did they wear, James? Did they say who won?"

"They wear the Sun—my lady. The Sun in Splendour. King Edward is victorious. They say there was a great slaughter in a place called Bloody Meadow…and that the Prince of Wales is slain and old Queen Margaret a captive!"

A cloud, seemingly blown up from nowhere, stretched over the bright morning sun. Pearl glanced at me, lip wobbling, eyes filled with fear. I made to gather her in my arm but my legs sagged at the knees, and then I fell, down into the flowers, crushing them, destroying them. I smelt earth, like the grave, and saw the wriggling pink ends of earthworms near my face, and then the shadows claimed me.

Edmond was dead. John too. Edward of York and his brothers had won a decisive victory at Tewkesbury, crushing the final flowering of Lancaster beneath an armoured fist.

Matthew, an old retainer of the family had ridden in to tell the tale. He had served Edmond at the battle and seen what had occurred. "Forgive me, Lady, but I thought you would wish to know the truth of their lordships' last hours," he said. "I am riding to tell all the children of the old Duke, least they hear evil tales that are false."

I sat before him in the Great Hall, pale-cheeked but upright in my seat. Richard prowled outside the door, hungry for news like a hound, waiting to see if there could be any benefit in my family's misfortune…or doom.

"Speak, Matthew," I said. My voice was hoarse, an old woman's croak. I had screamed and shrieked for hours after I had woken from my faint in the gardens.

The old man's bristly mouth worked; he clutched his cap in his hand. "The Duke…your brother Edmond, I will always see him as Duke, no matter what others say…he joined the Queen's forces in the west. She sent him to meet with Jasper Tudor in Wales, but he never got there. Edward of York marched as if the devil was behind him and forced a battle at Tewkesbury, in the meadows surrounding the abbey there. At first, Lord Edmond's position was good; he held the higher ground while the Yorkists milled below. There were also ditches and lanes and bushes where soldiers could stage an ambush. However, there were two watercourses, a stream that runs nigh the abbey, and the damn, great dark river that can only be crossed by ferry. If you found yourself pushed towards either one..." He shook his head.

"If my brother's position was so good, Matthew, how did it all go so terribly wrong? Surely the Queen had the larger force even if Jasper Tudor's Welsh contingent was not there?"

Matthew licked his lips; his eyes darted to and fro nervously. There was something he did not want to tell me.

"Matthew?" I leaned forward, coaxing him to speak, although I feared to hear his bitter words of sorrow.

"I don't know what possessed my Lord Edmond, who was leading the van, but without warning, he descended with fury onto the right flank of King Edward's troops. He found himself engaged with both Edward and his brother Gloucester—and they were joined by spearmen Edward had concealed in the nearby wood. It was during this fighting that Lord John fell, God assoil him." He closed his eyes, face haggard and pain-wracked as he crossed himself. I did likewise, holding back a sob of grief.

"How...how did it happen? Did you see?" I managed to choke.

Matthew swallowed, his Adam's apple bobbing in his thin neck. "Struck by a spear, Lady Margaret. He went fast, likely knew nought. But at that very moment, seeing his brother fall, madness descended upon Duke Edmond. He spurred his mount into the centre of the battle, where Sir John Wenlock was fighting alongside the Prince of Wales. He accused Wenlock of holding back, of absconding his duties...and he smote him on the helm with a battle axe, cleaving his head in twain!"

"Oh, Jesu." Bile flooded my mouth. Well I knew how one's emotions could run riot...but Edmond! He had been a trained soldier.

"He did this right before the gaze of the young Prince, my Lady." Water was leaking from the corners of Matthew's faded grey eyes. "And he did not even halt to see the Prince to safety, but drove his steed straight back into the fray, slashing at all around him. At Wenlock's death, our forces began to mill in confusion, not sure what had happened, the centre battle leaderless save for Prince Edward, who knew not what to do next. The Yorkists continued to pelt us with arrows and spears and drive into our flanks, and eventually our centre broke and a rout began, terrible and bloody…"

He clutched his cap tighter, fingers kneading the cloth, the knuckles white. "The Prince…he was overwhelmed…He had no experience, my Lady. Hacked to death in the place that's now called Bloody Meadow. Men fell into the Swilgate by the Abbey; they trampled each other to death as they attempted flight and the water ran red. Some gained the riverbank, but the spearmen assailed them, and those that got into the water—they drowned. The opposite bank was too far and their armour too heavy. They are still dredging out bodies, I hear."

"Edmond…what happened to my brother in all this carnage?" Was he too cut down in the rout?" I clung to the arms of my chair. I had known the news would be dreadful, but it was unbearable to think that Edmond's unpredictable temper, his brief loss of control in his grief, had lost him the battle…and his own life.

"No, my Lady." The old man's fingers twisted the cloth cap as if he would rend it in twain. "He reached the abbey and sought sanctuary inside—but it is not a designated sanctuary. Desperate he hid behind a tomb…mere seconds before King Edward and his supporters stormed in, their swords still dripping from the slaughter. The abbot told Edward to stay his hand in the House of God and so he did, on one condition—that the captains surrendered. If this was done, he said, all the common foot soldiers would be allowed to go free, keeping their lives. Edmond surrendered, along with Hugh Courtenay of Devon and Sir John Langstrother of the Knights of St John. The next day, in Tewkesbury's Market Place, they were tried before Gloucester and Norfolk, and were beheaded."

My breath emerged, a shuddering sob.

"I am sorry, my Lady; I could not make their fate sound kinder. At least, though, the King did not have them quartered. Your brothers lie in honour within Tewkesbury Abbey, and the Prince of Wales too, before the altar."

I shut my eyes, fighting to stop the reeling of the world around me. "Thank you, Matthew. Your words were hard...but I needed to hear them. What has happened to the Queen?"

"Captured, along with Anne Neville, the Princess of Wales. She has been taken back to London to join her husband in the Tower. Paraded before the throng, I'd imagine, as added humiliation. I heard young Anne was turned over to the care of her sister Isabel and George of Clarence."

"So, it is all over...the Beaufort line, through male heirs, is extinguished."

"Aye, my Lady...but there are still boys carrying the blood. Your own son, the Duke of Buckingham, and Henry Tudor, although Tudor is gone..."

"Gone!" I shot upright, startled. "Where has he gone? What do you mean?"

"Jasper Tudor received tidings of the defeat at Tewkesbury and fled from Tenby to Brittany, my Lady, taking young Henry with him for safety."

"Jesu, how will my Cousin Margaret deal with such sorrow?" I breathed. "Her only child...an exile."

"Henry's loss is not her only sadness, my Lady," murmured Matthew. "She is a widow once more. Lord Stafford also fell at Tewkesbury...but he fought for Edward against his wife's wishes and his own family's long-term allegiances."

Another shock. My Humphrey's brother, that kindly man who bore his disfiguring illness with such dignity...gone, and in such awful circumstances. How these wars had ripped families apart, turning them to fight one against the other!

I wondered what Margaret would do now. Marry again, I suspected—and work on getting her son a safe passage home.

Giving Matthew some coin for his news, I left the hall, stumbling like an arthritic old woman.

In the dark corridor, I met up with my husband, who I knew had listened to every word spoken. He wore a strange unsavoury smile; I could smell the drink on him, old, stale ale. "Well, so it's all over at last..." he said. "We know what's what. I will make sure the King is well aware of the loyalty of his servant, Richard Dayrell. As I said once before and now say again—God Save King Edward!"

I glared at him and he stumbled away through the corridor.

"God Save King Edward!" His shouts echoed in my ears, loud as thunder.

EPILOGUE: 1473

I wait in the rosery beneath the trellises bearing roses white and red, their vines entwined, their thorns still bristling to catch hold of the unwary. I have already caught my finger on one, just in passing—two drops of crimson drop down to mar a snowy petal.

My *megrim* of yestereve has passed, leaving me as washed out as the sky after last night's heavy rain. I fear my deep blue gown will drain my complexion further, but Lucie has painted my face as best she could. I fear I still look a hag, an aged crone. I am so nervous. Harry, my son, is coming to visit me at Littlecote. He will come here and in the heavens the sun is shining.

He said he would arrive after the Sext bell has rung in Ramsbury church; he already warned me in his letters that he would not be early, for he likes to stay abed when no pressing duties call.

He is nearly eighteen years now, a man, not the boy I once knew. I cannot chastise him for being a slugabed or for anything else I might disapprove of, although I am his mother.

The years since Tewkesbury have been eventful for others, although quiet for me, here in peaceful Littlecote. Richard managed to entrench himself with the new Yorkist regime, and to his delight was given the position of sub-Treasurer of England, just like his father, William, before him. Soon after he was elected Sheriff of the Shire. His grand appointments mean he spends even less time at the manor, which is often a blessing. Pearl is growing into an attractive and well-tempered girl, quick in her lessons and an excellent dancer. Richard speaks of making a match for her with the son of John Tuchet, Lord Audley. If an agreement is reached, the wedding will not take place for many years, though—no daughter of mine will ever make a marriage in extreme youth like my Cousin Margaret. As for Margaret herself, as predicted, she wed again, to Lord Thomas Stanley, the Steward of the King's household, notable for his vast estates in Lancashire—and for his proclivity in changing sides during conflicts. It is a marriage of convenience, by all reports—a way for Margaret to re-enter court life once more and mediate for the return of her son.

As for *my* son…I hear the last distant peal of the Sext bell, then cries at the gates of the estate and the clatter of hooves in the courtyard. He is here, not early but not late. The time of waiting is over. I take a deep breath and turn toward him, remembering my dignity, fighting back the urge to run and clasp him in my arms.

He enters the garden, striding swiftly, purposefully. He is dressed in a doublet of sky-blue velvet shot through with blond silk and decorated with golden thread. His silken hose is particoloured, green and black, and his shoes long, tipped with gold. He wears a bonnet that matches the blue of his doublet; peacock feathers shimmer from its brim as does a brooch in the shape of a Stafford Knot.

He is, in look and bearing, a Duke, and a Duke well aware of his royal ancestry. As he draws closer, the light glimmers on his long curls, dusty dark gold. His face is so like his father's now, I want to weep.

"Lady Mother." He reaches my side, clasps my shaking hand and brings it to his lips. I cannot speak.

Then he drops my hand, glances around. "So. this is where you live." He sounds vaguely scandalised, as if I lived in a peasant's hovel.

"It's a fine house," I said, "though it needs some repairs."

"I should say so," said Harry, "but it's not just that it's a great old barn…It's so *green*…" He lifted his arm up, gesturing to the gardens and the long lawns and oak trees beyond. Then he must have realised what he sounded like and flushed. "I have spent much of my time in London or Greenwich, you understand, Mother. Although soon I will receive all my lands…and I'll be sent off to wild Wales, to Brecknock Castle. I've heard it's a mouldering old place too, in the middle of nowhere."

I force a little smile, remembering my own early thoughts about Brecknock. Now, those bygone days seem like a mythical paradise. "You will grow accustomed in time…as will your Lady Wife. I am sorry she has not accompanied you."

"Katherine..." His nose wrinkles slightly. "She is hard to drag away from her sisters—and the Queen. I could not persuade her to leave Westminster for a jaunt in some remote area of the country."

"Do you like her any better now, Harry?" I say hopefully.

"I've accepted my fate," he returns with a sneering little laugh. His teeth are straight and white; he is handsome yet I am forced to admit there is a vague sense of something ugly behind the beauty.

Silence falls between us. I had not expected these sudden new feelings. Harry glances around, almost seeking for something to say. "You tell me I have a sister of the half-blood? Where is she?"

I glance over my shoulder. Pearl is by the fishpond, trailing leaves through the water and teasing the fish. She is so intent on her game that she has not noticed the arrival of her brother. "Pearl!" I call. "Come here to meet his Grace, the Duke of Buckingham."

"Pearl? Why do you call her that?" Harry asks with a frown.

"Margaret means 'Pearl'—and there are so many Margarets in the family already."

Harry continues to frown. "It is a silly-sounding name, Mother. Meg or Marjorie is surely a more dignified nickname."

"There is a famous poem called 'Pearl'," I say. "A man who has lost his little daughter to the grave sees her in a dream-world, a spirit in white, her robes draped with pearls. She tells him not to grieve for her, for though her early form is no more, in Heaven she lives forever."

Harry stares at me, uncomprehending. "I do not read such things as that," he says dismissively.

I make no answer. Pearl has seen us and is running light-footed over the grass. Reaching the path, she becomes shy, blushing as she slows down. She stands at my side and curtseys low to her brother in the manner I have taught her. "Welcome to Littlecote, your G-grace," she stammers, casting down her gaze.

"Greetings, Margaret," he says, deliberately using her full given name."

"Mam never calls me that…"

"But I will, as it is proper," he says pompously. His eyes rake over her. "Charming…but why is she wearing such clothes, and why was she out dabbling in a reeking old pond? She's not a servant, Mother. If you want her to make a decent marriage, you must not let her look a complete hoyden."

Beside me, Pearl looks crestfallen. Again, my tongue is still. My son is a Duke; I cannot chastise him for his opinions, no matter that I find them cruel and unfair.

Harry waves a lazy hand, dismissing Pearl. She hurries away; I see the relief on her face and the faint glitter of tears on her long lashes.

She has escaped and I cannot comfort her. I think instead how long it's been since I saw Harry last, how I must make the most of this brief visit. I will ignore his hurtful words…*he is a Duke*…He is probably just weary, hot, hungry—I make all kinds of excuses.

I guide him to a bench and he announces he is ravenous. I summon a servant and small pies are brought out—magpie pigeon flavoured with currants and pepper. They were made especially for his arrival. He eats them almost piggishly, crumbs on his chin—did the Queen not teach manners at court? Of course, I had heard King Edward himself was a glutton, eating to the point where he would spew in the privy before setting into his meal again.

After the plate is picked clean, he releases a litany of complaints about almost everyone he knows—the King and Queen, his Woodville wife, the Duke of Clarence, his grandmother Anne Neville. He is particularly put out that the King has not spoken of any future grand positions in his court.

"You are young yet, Harry." I try to soothe him.

"He made his brothers royal Dukes when they were just boys and gave them many lands. His younger brother Gloucester is Constable of England and he is not yet one and twenty. I do not think Edward likes me, maybe does not trust me…"

"You must earn his trust, Harry."

"Must I?" His chin tilts up, arrogant. "Oh, I suppose you are correct, Mother." He lets out a long, irritated sigh and folds his arms.

The day is getting warm, last night's storm a distant memory. Bees and flies buzz on the warm air currents. Sunlight bounces off lawns and walls. I talk of Harry's father and the old Duke of Buckingham; I talk of my brothers, lost to me, lying beneath cold stone in Hexham and in Tewkesbury. For the first time, he seems moved. He stares into the distance. "I wonder how things would be for me if they still lived and old Harry were still on the throne…"

"You must not think of such things, my son," I say nervously. "Those days are gone. Honour your relatives who fought bravely for what they believed in, but do not emulate their deeds, lest you meet their fate."

"They say Edward ordered old mad Harry killed in the Tower. That he was bashed over the head till his brains came out. Edward had the gall to say he died of 'pure melancholy and displeasure.' Everyone guessed the truth, though, that he did what he must to hold the throne—cut down the last roots of the House of Lancaster. But there are still those with such blood, in other branches that yet thrive. I wonder if one day…"

"No, Harry, stop!" Now there is an edge sharpening my voice. "I want no treason spoken here. The country is at peace. May it stay that way forever."

My son looks uncomfortable and then he yawns and stretches like a great lazy cat. "The heat of the day affects my head and I speak foolishly. I must head on my way, Mother, back to London."

"You will not stay the night?" I fight to keep the disappointment from my voice.

"No." He rises, takes my hand, kisses it once more. His lips are dry, feather-light. "Duty calls in London, I fear…"

He walks away, swift, without glancing back. I watch him walk into a patch of sunlight, sky-blue and molten gold, blazing with the arrogance and strength of youth.

He *would* turn out to be a great man one day, I know this. Harry Stafford will take on the mantle of his slain kinsmen.

I only pray, above all, he will not share their fate.

AUTHOR'S NOTES

I've always had an interest in Henry Stafford, Duke of Buckingham, so decided to have a look at his ancestry.

I knew his mother was another Margaret Beaufort, and it turned out there was weird parallel between her and her more famous cousin, also named Margaret Beaufort, who was the mother of Henry Tudor. Soon it became clear a story was waiting to be written!

Both women were Beauforts, and the daughters of two Dukes of Somerset, John and his younger brother, Edmund. Both had a mother who was a Beauchamp. Both were married more than once, lost a husband to illness when their child was small, and both married a member of the Stafford family—two sons of Humphrey, Duke of Buckingham. Both had a son called Henry, with only a few years between the two.

However, whereas Henry Tudor's mother wed as her third husband, the infamous side-swapper, Thomas Stanley, the other Margaret married a little-known knight and retired to (probably) Wiltshire, where she had a daughter, Margaret, who eventually married James Tuchet, Baron Audley, in about 1483. Not many people realised Henry Duke of Buckingham had a half-sister.

Although Margaret was a Duke's daughter, little is known about her. Her approx. date of birth, and approx. date of death (1474-76), her marriages and her children are pretty much it.

The reason I decided to write about her was that there was a suggestion that she may have been suffering some kind of mental illness. She was definitely in the care of her husband's mother for some time, although this may have been due to her pregnancy. Still, the suggestion of illness is there, in documents from the 17thC, so I decided to run with that possibility. What was also odd is that her second husband Richard Dayrell, Dayrell, or Darell (varying medieval spellings) apparently did not pay his mother the promised money for looking after Margaret. This must have caused some family friction, as he does not appear to be named in his mother's will.

A lot of information seems to tie Margaret and her second husband to Littlecote Manor, but the house there with its Roman mosaic was actually owned by Richard Dayrell's brother George. They could have of course still resided there, renting it from the elder brother. As Richard was sheriff of Wiltshire, presumably he lived in the county. The older family seat was in Buckinghamshire but the Wiltshire Dayrells got their properties in Wiltshire through their mother, Elizabeth Calston/Calstone. The church at Ramsbury, near Littlecote Manor, contains a chantry chapel for the Dayrell family, and this may be Margaret's resting place, although this was never recorded.

I have no idea if Margaret's second marriage was happy or not and hence I hereby apologise to Richard Dayrell in the afterlife if I've sorely maligned him! However, there was a member of the Dayrell family called 'Wild William Dayrell', who was notoriously cruel. I took a little liberty and mentioned his legend in my book—but in reality, he lived in the century after Margaret and Richard, not before. I based Richard's character on this relative.

As Margaret's life is so obscure, I had to place her in many events where, in reality, she may not have been at the time. However, all listed major events did occur, and her Beaufort father and three brothers all perished in the battles of St Alban's, Hexham or Tewkesbury, either slain in combat or executed immediately after. I have compressed the timeline slightly for flow, but only slightly.

The Beaufort family is an interesting one and rather neglected in non-fiction, with the exception of Henry Tudor's mother who had loads written on her. I would heartily recommend Nathen Amin's non-fiction book on the Beauforts for more information about the rest of the family.

As usual, all poems/songs in the text are my own modernised versions of authentic medieval ones.

OTHER WORKS BY J.P. REEDMAN

RICHARD III and THE WARS OF THE ROSES:

I, RICHARD PLANTAGENET I: TANTE LE DESIREE. Richard in his own first-person perspective, as Duke of Gloucester

I, RICHARD PLANTAGENET II: LOYAULTE ME LIE. Second part of Richard's story, told in 1st person. The mystery of the Princes, the tragedy of Bosworth

A MAN WHO WOULD BE KING. First person account of Henry Stafford, Duke of Buckingham suspect in the murder of the Princes.

THE ROAD FROM FOTHERINGHAY—Richard III's childhood to his time in Warwick's household.

A VOUS ME LIE—Richard's youth in the household of Warwick the Kingmaker and beyond.

SACRED KING—Historical fantasy in which Richard III enters a fantastical afterlife and is 'returned to the world' in a Leicester carpark

WHITE ROSES, GOLDEN SUNNES. Collection of short stories about Richard III and his family.

SECRET MARRIAGES. Edward IV's romantic entanglements with Eleanor Talbot and Elizabeth Woodville

BLOOD OF ROSES. Edward IV defeats the Lancastrians at Mortimer's Cross and Towton.

RING OF WHITE ROSES. Two short stories featuring Richard III, including a time-travel tale about a lost traveller in the town of Bridport.

THE MISTLETOE BRIDE OF MINSTER LOVELL. Retelling of the folkloric tale featuring Francis Lovell, his wife and his friend the Duke of Gloucester.

IN A SILVER SEA: REIMAGINED BRITISH LEGENDS

ENDELIENTA: Kinswoman of King Arthur. Endelienta seeks a mystic's life, living solely on the milk of mystical white cows.

MELOR OF THE SILVER HAND. A young lad has his hand and foot cut off by the uncle who would steal his throne—but with the aid of an ancient god with a hand of silver, Melor takes his revenge.

THE CROOKED ASH. The Derbyshire legend of Crooker. In the Middle Ages, a young man is called out to his sick mother. On the dark paths he meets three strange green-clad women—and the guardian of the ash tree.

THE BARROW WOMAN'S BONES—short ghost story set around a real archaeological find.

STONEHENGE and prehistory:

THE STONEHENGE SAGA. Huge epic of the Bronze Age. Ritual, war, love and death. A prehistoric GAME OF STONES roughly based on the Arthurian legends but set in the British Bronze Age.

THE SWORD OF TULKAR-Collection of prehistoric-based short stories

THE GODS OF STONEHENGE-Short booklet about myths and legends associated with Stonehenge and about other possible mythological meanings.

MEDIEVAL BABES SERIES:

MY FAIR LADY: ELEANOR OF PROVENCE, HENRY III'S LOST QUEEN

MISTRESS OF THE MAZE: Rosamund Clifford, Mistress of Henry II

THE CAPTIVE PRINCESS: Eleanor of Brittany, sister of the murdered Arthur, a prisoner of King John.

THE WHITE ROSE RENT: The short life of Katherine, illegitimate daughter of Richard III

THE PRINCESS NUN. Mary of Woodstock, Daughter of Edward I, the nun who liked fun!

MY FATHER, MY ENEMY. Juliane, illegitimate daughter of Henry I, seeks to kill her father with a crossbow.

LONGSWORD'S LADY- Ela of Salisbury, married to William Longespee, half-brother to Richard I and King John. Found of Salisbury cathedral, female sheriff and powerful abbess.

POISONED CHALICE. The tale of Mabel de Belleme, Normandy's wicked lady, who poisoned her way to infamy.

THE OTHER MARGARET BEAUFORT. Margaret, Countess of Stafford, mother of Harry, Stafford Duke of Buckingham, suspect in the disappearance of the Princes in the Tower.

ROBIN HOOD

THE HOOD GAME: Rise of the Green Wood King, Shadow of the Brazen Head, and Blood of the Divine King.

Three-part historical fantasy series about the famous outlaw in a Sherwood Forest filled with spirits, old gods and magic. When young Robyn of Locksley wins 'the Hood' in an ancient winter rite, his life is changed forever.

Also many short story collections and novellas of fantasy or historical fantasy.

Printed in Great Britain
by Amazon